LOST
IN
TIME

By A.G. Riddle

The Atlantis Trilogy
The Atlantis Gene
The Atlantis Plague
The Atlantis World

The Extinction Files
Pandemic
Genome

The Long Winter Trilogy
Winter World
The Solar War
The Lost Colony

Standalone
The Extinction Trials
Lost in Time

A.G. RIDDLE

LOST IN TIME

An Ad Astra Book

First published in the UK in 2022 by Head of Zeus Ltd,
part of Bloomsbury Publishing Plc

9 7 5 3 1 2 4 6 8

A catalogue record for this book is available from the British Library.

ISBN (HB): 9781804541760
ISBN (XTPB): 9781804541777
ISBN (E): 9781804541753

Printed and bound in Great Britain by
CPI Group (UK) Ltd, Croydon CR0 4YY

Head of Zeus Ltd
First Floor East
5–8 Hardwick Street
London EC1R 4RG

WWW.HEADOFZEUS.COM

To the many readers who have invested their precious
time in my novels—past, present, and future.

PART I

A DISCOVERY ABOUT TIME

ONE

On the anniversary of his wife's death, Sam Anderson visited her grave.

It was a crisp spring morning in Nevada, with dew on the grass and fog rolling through the cemetery. In one hand, Sam carried a bouquet of flowers. In the other, he gripped his son's hand. Ryan was eleven years old and strong-willed and introverted, like his mother. After her death, he had withdrawn, spending even more time alone, playing with LEGOs, reading, and generally avoiding life.

Counseling had yielded little help for Ryan. At home, Sam had searched for a way to get through to his only son, but he had to admit: he wasn't half the parent his wife had been. Most days, he felt like he was simply reacting to his children, making it up as he went, working on a mystery without any clues.

He hoped the visit to Sarah's grave this morning would be the start of turning that around.

Sam's daughter, Adeline, gripped Ryan's other hand. She was nineteen years old, and to all outward appearances seemed to have coped better with her mother's passing. But Sam wondered if Adeline was just a better actor than Ryan or himself. He worried about that too, about her bottling it all up and carrying the burden of unaddressed grief.

Last night, he had seen a glimpse of her hidden rage. Adeline was still furious with him over the evening's argument. So angry she wouldn't even hold his hand or look at him. Hence, Ryan walking between them.

But she had agreed to be there that morning, and Sam was thankful for that.

They walked in silence through the cemetery much like they had floated through life since Sarah's death: hand-in-hand, trying to find their way through it all.

Fog drifted in front of the headstones like a curtain being drawn and opened. Across the cemetery, sprinkler heads rose and began deploying water. The cemetery likely cost a fortune to irrigate out in the Nevada desert, but of all the problems Absolom City had, money wasn't one.

At the edge of the grass, Sam thought he saw a figure watching them. He turned his head, and yes, there was a man there. He wore a dark uniform, though Sam couldn't make it out from this distance. Fog floated in front of the man, and when Sam looked again, he was gone.

Ryan must have felt his father slow down.

"What is it, Dad?"

"Nothing," he muttered, resuming their pace, tugging on his son's hand.

Near Sarah's grave, Sam spotted a man and a woman standing on the other side of the cemetery. They were also wearing dark uniforms. Sam's first instinct was that they were here for a burial service. But they didn't move deeper into the maze of graves. They stood there, staring at Sam and his family.

He set the flowers at the base of Sarah's headstone and tried to put the figures out of his mind.

Mentally, he had rehearsed the lines he wanted to say a hundred times. And as he spoke the first words into that foggy April morning, they sounded just like that to him: rehearsed and passionless.

"I'd like to say something."

Adeline's gaze shifted away from him. Ryan stared at his shoes.

Sam decided right then to drop the speech and say the first thing that came to his mind. That thing was a memory.

"I want to tell you what your mom said to me one of the last times I saw her."

Adeline's head turned quickly. Ryan looked up.

"She told me that it would make her very sad if she was what kept me from being happy after she was gone. I think she meant that for all of us. She was selfless like that—in life and even after."

Adeline closed her eyes and raised her fingers to her eyelids. A warm wind blew across the three of them. A tear leaked from the edge of Adeline's right eye and lingered there, soaking itself in mascara, and slowly began painting its way down her cheek as if an invisible hand was drawing warpaint on her face.

It was the first tear Sam had seen her shed in years.

"The second thing she told me is something I think about a lot: time heals all wounds. But it won't work if you don't give time a chance. That was her point: we just have to accept that sometimes things are going to be hard for a while. If we're strong enough—if we hold on long enough—things will get better. Every year, this hurt we feel is going to get a little better. I promise you."

He reached out and pulled Ryan into a hug, and Adeline closed the distance between them and wrapped her arms around Sam, and buried her face in his shoulder. He felt the warmth of her tears soaking through his shirt.

A buzzing overhead caught his attention. It was a drone. Not one, but three of them.

A computerized voice called through the fog.

"Dr. Samuel Anderson, please step away from the others."

Sam glanced around the cemetery. What was happening here?

"Dr. Samuel Anderson, this is your second warning. Step away and put your hands on your head."

"What?" Sam called out.

Adeline looked up. "Dad, what's going on?"

The three drones were hovering above them now. The computerized voice called again.

"Adeline Anderson, step away and put your hands on your head."

Sam realized the suited figures he had seen earlier were surrounding them now. There were seven in all, wearing Absolom City Police uniforms, standing with their hands on their belts within easy reach of the handcuffs and stun batons hanging there.

The drone called again.

"Dr. Samuel Anderson, this is your final warning. You have five seconds to separate yourself from the others and place your hands on your head."

"Dad..." Adeline's voice was ragged and panicked.

"It's okay," he whispered as he turned and scanned the police officers, searching for the person in charge to address.

"I'd like to talk to—"

The sharp pain in his neck was like a bee sting. He reached up and felt a circular piece of metal the size of a coin dug into his skin. He was trying to pry it loose when his vision blurred. His legs went weak, and he fell headfirst into the soft grass.

The last thing Sam saw before the darkness swallowed him was the engraved letters on his wife's headstone.

TWO

When he came to, Sam was lying in a hospital bed. His arms and legs were strapped down. A machine to his left showed his vitals, the charts and numbers updating in real time.

Sensors were adhered to his chest and forehead. He felt a slight pinch on his right hand. He looked down and found an IV snaking away, a clear tube with a piece of tape over it.

Beside him, a nurse sat on a metal chair, dressed in blue scrubs, reading a digital paper. He looked up and tapped a button on his chest.

"Timestamp. Subject is awake and appears alert."

Sam felt like his mouth was full of sawdust. He fought through it, forcing the words out. "Where am I?"

"Post-arrest medical observation at Absolom City Police, Central Station."

"Why?"

Before the nurse could answer, the door opened, and a man and a woman walked in, both dressed in suits, gold and silver police badges clipped at their waists.

"Dr. Anderson," the woman said. "I'm Detective Billings. This is my partner, Detective Holloway. How do you feel?"

"Very confused. Not very happy."

Billings made no reaction. "You were issued three requests to comply, which you refused. You were subsequently restrained in accordance with the standardized arrest protocol, which

7

protects law enforcement personnel and ensures all subjects of arrests are treated uniformly, regardless of—"

"Why am I here?"

"Dr. Anderson, you're under arrest for the murder of Dr. Nora Thomas."

Out of his peripheral vision, Sam saw his pulse number on the machine skyrocket. He opened his mouth to speak, but no words came.

Billings held up her arm and tapped a smartwatch. A woman's voice spoke loudly.

"You have the right to remain silent. Anything you say can and will be used against you in a court of law. You have the right to an attorney. If you cannot afford an attorney, one will be provided for you. Do you understand the rights that have just been read to you?"

Sam lay there, still in shock.

"Dr. Anderson?" Billings asked.

Nora was dead.

That was Sam's first thought.

How? was his second thought.

She had been murdered.

It was impossible. Who would murder Nora? Someone protesting Absolom? If so, were the other Absolom scientists in danger? Company personnel? His family?

"Dr. Anderson?"

His gaze drifted back to the woman.

"Do you understand the rights that have been read to you?"

"Yes," he muttered.

"With these rights in mind, do you wish to speak to me?"

"You better believe I want to speak with you. I want some answers."

"So do we, doctor. We're just here to find the truth."

"How..." Sam began, but his mind spun, unable to form

a question. A million of them fought a war in his brain, none emerging on top.

Billings reached inside her jacket and took out an e-ink tablet slightly bigger than her hand.

"Dr. Nora Thomas was found dead at her residence this morning at 7:13 a.m. after a friend she was scheduled to exercise with reported seeing blood and a motionless body inside her home."

Sam shook his head, still in disbelief.

Billings pressed on. "Dr. Anderson, when was the last time you saw Dr. Thomas?"

Sam tried to force the words out, but it was as if his mind wouldn't connect to his mouth.

Billings cut her eyes to her partner. The gray-haired man spoke slowly, his voice deep and calm, a sharp contrast to the tension in the room.

"We know you visited Dr. Thomas last night."

Sam stared at the man. He felt his heart hammering in his chest.

Detective Holloway shrugged. "We have the city surveillance camera recordings."

He paused, waiting, but Sam said nothing.

"We know you and your daughter, Adeline, arrived at Dr. Thomas's home at 9:06 p.m. and left at approximately 9:43 p.m. We're pretty sure Dr. Thomas was killed toward the end of that window."

"Impossible…" Sam whispered.

Billings cleared her throat. "Dr. Anderson, were you engaged in a romantic relationship with Dr. Thomas?"

Sam's heart beat even faster. This was wrong. A setup.

The nurse stared at the medical monitor, watching the numbers ticking up like a countdown to an explosion.

The two detectives glanced in Sam's direction, but not

directly at him, as if he had three heads and they were looking at the ones beside him.

Sam swallowed and forced the word out. "Yes."

"Is there anything you'd like to tell us about that?" Holloway asked.

Sam shook his head. The sedation drugs were wearing off. His head was finally starting to clear.

In the cemetery, the drones hadn't just called out his name. They called out for Adeline as well.

"Where's my daughter?"

Holloway held his hands up. "She's in a post-arrest interview room. Don't worry. She's fine."

"Why'd you arrest her?"

"The same reason we arrested you," Billings said.

Sam sat up and tried to raise his arms, but the restraints caught. An alarm on the machine next to him blared.

Billings took a step closer. "Relax, Dr. Anderson."

Before he could respond, the door flew open and Sam's long-time friend and colleague, Elliott Lucas, barged in.

Close behind him was Tom Morris, the chief counsel for the company they co-founded, Absolom Sciences. Tom spoke over the sound of the alarm. "Don't say another word, Sam."

Elliott eyed the detectives. "Why is he strapped down?"

"Protocol."

Tom pointed at Sam. "I want my client released from police custody right now."

Billings shook her head. "That's not possible."

"Why?" Tom asked.

Billings didn't flinch. "Dr. Anderson is being held on a murder charge—which is subject to Absolom. As I'm sure you know, pretrial bail is not allowed for Absolom-eligible crimes. The risk of flight and risk to the community is too great."

A silence stretched out in the room.

Billings glanced at Elliott and Tom. "Gentlemen, I'm going to have to ask you to leave the room."

Tom's eyes bulged. "On the contrary, detective. I'm going to have to ask you to leave. I'm this man's attorney, and he doesn't have to speak to you. I want Dr. Anderson moved to a comfortable room where we can talk in private."

Billings nodded to the nurse, who stepped closer to Sam and eyed him. "Dr. Anderson, do you feel you're a danger to yourself or others?"

"No."

The nurse pointed to the band around Sam's right wrist. "You're required to wear this medical monitor and locator device at all times. Tampering with it or trying to remove it is a felony. Do you understand?"

"Yes. I understand."

The nurse tapped the button on his shirt. "Timestamp. Subject is cleared to be held outside of medical observation."

THREE

Afrer the drone shot her father, Adeline had screamed. The drones had made her step away from her brother. The police moved in then and took her away, to Absolom City's central police station, to a holding room where she now sat in an uncomfortable chair, at a table with nothing on it.

She felt confused. And scared.

The door opened and a man and a woman walked in. They were dressed in plain clothes, their police badges clipped to their belts.

Without asking, they sat at the two chairs across the table.

The woman spoke first. "Miss Anderson, I'm Detective Billings. This is my partner, Detective Holloway."

"Where's my father?"

"He's here. We just spoke to him."

"I want to see him."

"Before we get to that, I need to apprise you of your rights." The woman tapped her smartwatch and a recording played, reciting the Miranda warning. Adeline had seen it hundreds of times in movies and TV shows. She never thought she'd hear it in person. This was so bizarre. It had to be some kind of mistake. That was the only plausible explanation.

"Do you understand the rights that have been read to you?" Billings asked.

"Yes," Adeline said quietly.

"We'd like to ask you some questions, Miss Anderson. With these rights in mind, are you willing to speak to me?"

Adeline stared at the two detectives. This was all wrong. Being arrested. Her father being arrested. It had to be a mistake. Talking to them could clear it up. After all, the cops existed to protect people like her father and her. Innocent people. Refusing to answer would look suspicious. Might even land her in trouble.

"What do you want to know?"

"Last night you visited Dr. Nora Thomas."

"Yes."

"Why?"

"She... wanted to give me some things."

"What sort of things?"

"Items my mother had given her. She thought I might want them."

"Was that the only reason she wanted you and your father to come over?"

"No."

"What was the other reason?"

With her thumb, Adeline began picking at the skin next to the nail on her middle finger. In her mind, she couldn't help replaying the fight that had taken place inside Nora's home.

"Last night," Billings said carefully, "you got upset, didn't you, Miss Anderson?"

"Yes."

FOUR

Two uniformed police officers led Sam from the hospital-like room to another holding area.

To him, the new cell felt more like a one-bedroom apartment. There was a sitting area with a couch, coffee table, and two club chairs, a long table with six chairs, and a separate bedroom and bathroom.

It certainly wasn't an average police holding cell. And for good reason: Absolom City wasn't a typical small town. Absolom Sciences Inc. had built the city to house its corporate headquarters and research facilities. It was located in Western Nevada, near the California border, in the middle of a vast expanse of desert. Around the town, a massive solar field spread out in every direction, collecting the immense amount of energy the Absolom machine needed to operate.

Most of the town's sixteen thousand residents worked at Absolom Sciences, and the houses had been designed and built specifically for their needs. So had the police station. With the sheer amount of surveillance cameras in the city (and Absolom as a penalty for the worst offenses), crime was nearly nonexistent in Absolom City. But like human nature, crime couldn't be completely eradicated. There was always the occasional drunk and disorderly. A domestic dispute. A teenager sowing wild oats—or crying for help.

These cells in the police station had been designed for those occasions. They were like hotel suites where wayward—but valued—citizens could sleep off the excess alcohol or reflect on what had landed them here.

As Sam sat on the couch, he wondered if he would ever leave this place a free man. He was certainly the first murder suspect to be arrested in Absolom City.

He did have one thing going for him: he could have visitors. In this day and age, everyone was well aware of the fifth amendment—and their right to an attorney. If a suspect under arrest wanted to avoid talking to the police and communicate with the outside world, it was simply a matter of asking for a lawyer and passing messages from that person to anyone outside the police station. As such, the police were more liberal with allowing people to visit suspects under arrest. In many cases, talking with loved ones even encouraged suspects to confess. And confession was the typical conclusion to crimes in Absolom City, thanks to the ubiquitous cameras recording all public spaces and a well-trained police force.

Tom sat in the club chair opposite Sam. Elliott plopped down in the other one.

"They can't record in this room," Tom said. "Can't even question you here."

Sam nodded absently. "They arrested Adeline as well. I want her released. This has to be some mistake."

Tom took his phone out and tapped out a text message.

Sam leaned forward. "Please, Tom. Do it right now. They could be questioning her for all we know."

Tom nodded, rose, and left the room.

To Elliott, Sam said, "How did you know I was here?"

"Dani called me."

"How did she know?"

"She said the cops came to her house to get access to city and company records. She must have used the cameras and seen you being arrested."

They were silent until the door opened and Tom strode back inside. "They were questioning her."

"What did they ask?" Sam asked.

"I don't know. They won't tell me. And they won't release her."

"This is insane. What's going on here?"

Tom crossed his arms. "I don't know, but it's outside my expertise. I've been in touch with Victor Levy's office. He's flying in from LA right now."

"Who?"

Tom furrowed his brow. "The celebrity attorney. Don't you know—"

"I don't need an attorney," Sam muttered. "I haven't done anything wrong."

Tom took a sharp breath and exhaled. "Sam, you know I respect you greatly. Your intellect. What you've accomplished. Your character. But what you're dealing with here is dangerous." He pointed toward the door. "They don't know you. They are going to follow the evidence. And if it says you're guilty, they will take that over your word, no matter what."

"Well, frankly, I don't see how the evidence can say I'm guilty if I'm not."

"Back up," Elliott said. "Tell us what happened last night."

"We should wait for Levy to get here," Tom said.

"No," Elliott shot back, "we shouldn't. I know and trust everyone in this room. Some celebrity attorney—forget it. For all we know, he'll leak everything to the press just to get his own name out there."

Sam took Tom's silence as some indication that he agreed with Elliott.

"Last night," Sam began, "I came home after the meeting."

"The meeting in the lab, with the six of us," Elliott said.

"Right. I was supposed to have dinner at Nora's house. Adeline and I were both going to go over. But it was too late for dinner when I got home. Adeline and Ryan had already ordered take-out."

Elliott nodded. "Then what happened?"

"We went over to Nora's anyway."

Elliott looked confused. But Tom nodded. "Because you had to."

"Yes," Sam whispered. "Because we had to."

Elliott's gaze shifted between Sam and Tom.

The attorney, still looking at Sam, said, "Because of the pictures."

"Yes."

Elliott stood. "What pictures?"

"Nora and I had been seeing each other."

Elliott's jaw dropped. "What? How long? Why didn't you tell me?"

"For a while. We just... we wanted to keep it private until we knew where it was going."

"But you couldn't hide it anymore," Tom said.

Elliott turned and stared at Tom. "You knew about this?"

"Of course. He informed Absolom legal when he got the blackmail message."

"Blackmail?"

"We slipped up," Sam said. "Last week at the conference in Davos, Nora and I had dinner, and we were walking back to the hotel, and it was freezing cold, and I leaned over and kissed her and..." Sam shook his head, the memory of that night overtaking him—the way Nora's soft lips had felt on his, the white steam of her hot breath in the frigid night, his arms around her, lifting her gently off the cobblestones.

It was more than the memory that gripped him. It was how

it felt in his mind, how he had felt that night on the narrow street under the yellow glow of the lanterns, leaning in to kiss her, feeling like himself again for the first time in years. He had realized something then: a part of him that he thought he had buried with his wife was still very much alive. And clawing its way to the surface.

Tom, perhaps assuming Sam couldn't, supplied the rest. "A photographer snapped some pictures of them. He emailed Sam. The subject was: *Love in Absolom*. Said it was a touching story the world deserved to hear. He was going to sell it to the tabloids unless Sam wanted the pictures for himself." Tom shook his head. "Legally, there was nothing we could do. We could buy the pictures, but that's still no guarantee, and a story like that is always going to get out eventually."

Sam swallowed. "I told Adeline that Nora wanted to give her some things. Just trinkets and reminders of Sarah. But the real purpose of going over there last night was to tell Adeline that Nora and I had been seeing each other. We wanted her to hear it from us before she saw it online."

"Okay," Elliott said slowly. "So what happened?"

"We got there around nine. Everything went fine at first. Adeline was thankful for the reminders of her mom. And then—" Sam glanced up at the ceiling.

"And then you told her," Tom said.

"Yes."

"How did she react?" Tom asked.

Sam closed his eyes and slowly shook his head, remembering the scene. "She just... lost it."

"Lost it how?" Elliott asked.

"We were in the living room, sitting on couches and chairs just like we are here, and she jumped up and started pacing and yelling at us, telling us we had been sneaking around behind her back—which *is* technically true. She said that we were a disgrace to her mother's memory, that she was never going to talk to either of us after she went back to college, and that she was leaving the city immediately."

Sam took a deep breath.

"I think it's just the fact that she had kept it all bottled up for so long. She just wasn't ready—not ready for anything to change. She screamed at Nora, told her she wasn't half the woman her mother had been and that we should both be ashamed of ourselves. She punched the living-room wall hard enough to make two of the framed photos fall off. She grabbed one of the other pictures—one with the Absolom Six—and slammed it on the floor."

"What did you and Nora do?" Elliott asked.

"We just sat there, letting Adeline get it all out. But Nora jumped up when she realized Adeline was bleeding."

"From the glass in the picture frames?" Tom asked.

"No. From hitting the wall. Her knuckles were bleeding. Nora went to the master bathroom and got some things and tried to clean the wound, but Adeline was still in a rage. She pushed her away." Sam rubbed his forehead. "Nora stumbled and slipped on the broken glass on the floor. It all happened so fast. Seeing Nora fall sort of snapped Adeline out of it. She immediately tried to help her up."

Elliott stared at Sam. "Did... she get up?"

"Of course she got up. She landed on her hand, on some glass. She had a cut, but she was fine. We both helped her up and washed the blood off. Once Adeline saw that Nora was okay, she just wanted to leave. She stormed out, and Nora assured me she was fine, so I ran after Adeline. I didn't see her when I got home, and she was still angry the next morning— too angry to even hold my hand as we walked to Sarah's grave."

Sam closed his eyes and rubbed his eyebrows. "It was a disaster. The whole night."

Elliott put his hands on the seat back and braced himself. "This is bad, Sam. We need to know what the police know. And we need to keep this out of the press."

"That's going to be impossible," Tom said. "Absolutely impossible. One of the scientists whose invention almost eradicated crime is arrested for murdering another scientist who also helped eradicate crime? It's the story of the century. The world loves a mystery. Especially one with love involved. And rich people. And irony."

"Forget the press." Sam focused on Elliott. "We need to bring Hiro, Connie, and Dani here."

"Why?"

"Several reasons. First, if someone is killing Absolom scientists, they might be in danger. Second, Nora's death might be related to Absolom Two. If so, we need to talk about precautions. And finally, one of us might know something that could help us find Nora's killer."

"We're scientists, Sam, not some crack team of detectives."

Sam leaned back in the chair. "Well, technically, we're frauds, so I'd say that makes us equally qualified for detective work."

Tom's head snapped back and forth between Elliott and Sam, finally settling on Elliott. "What does that mean?"

"Ignore it, Tom. Sam is under a lot of stress. He doesn't know what he's saying."

"Oh yes I do. Get them here, Elliott. And Tom, go get the detectives. It's time we found out what happened at Nora's house after Adeline and I left last night."

FIVE

The police offered Sam lunch, but he was too nervous to eat. Apparently, so were Elliott and Tom. They sat in the small living area, rehashing what they knew, until the door's deadbolt slammed open with a loud crack that made Sam jump.

A uniformed officer leaned in. She looked to be in her twenties, and peered at Sam with a grave look, like someone who knew the bad news he was yet to receive.

"They're ready, sir," she said quietly.

As he exited the room, Sam noticed an Absolom Sciences security guard standing by the door to his room.

Tom shrugged. "I want to make sure no one gets in your room, Sam. We can't be too careful about listening devices. The police agreed to let our security do that."

Sam followed the officer down the hall and past the offices and cubicles. With each step, he felt eyes watching him, some subtly looking up from their computers, others standing and openly gawking. In small towns—and small offices—news traveled fast. Secrets were impossible to keep. Sam wondered what they thought they were looking at. A murderer? A dead man walking?

The young officer left Sam, Elliott, and Tom in an interview room with no windows and minimal furniture: only six chairs and a long metal table. The walls were covered in fabric. Sam assumed it was for noise deadening.

Detectives Billings and Holloway arrived soon after.

Billings set down a tablet. "You're making the right decision to talk with us, Dr. Anderson."

Tom held his hands up. "I want to state first, for the record, that my client, Doctor Samuel Anderson, is innocent of murder."

Holloway cut his eyes to Billings. She nodded once at him.

"Based on the evidence analyzed this morning," Holloway said slowly, "at this juncture, we're inclined to agree."

Sam exhaled a breath he felt like he had been holding for a thousand years.

"Good," Tom said, nodding.

"We believe," Holloway continued, "that Dr. Anderson is actually an accessory to a murder in the second degree."

Sam's body went numb.

"A murder," Holloway said, "committed by Adeline Anderson, in a moment of rage."

Before he walked into that room, Sam thought that being convicted of murder was the worst thing he had to fear. But now he saw a fate far worse: Adeline being convicted, losing her freedom, and on the other side of Absolom, her life.

He had lost his wife.

He couldn't lose his daughter.

The room seemed to explode then. Tom and Elliott began talking at the same time, both men growing louder as each tried to talk over the other.

Sam held his hands up. "Stop. Both of you."

To Billings, he said, "Please tell me why you think Adeline is guilty."

"We'll show you why," Billings said. "If you're willing to meet us halfway."

Tom began to speak, but Sam extended his hand in front of the man. "Please begin."

Billings slid the tablet toward Sam and tapped it once.

A video began, showing the outside of Nora's home. It was night, and Sam and Adeline were walking up to the front door, their faces clearly visible as he reached out and rang the doorbell. The video stopped with a still image of Nora, smiling as she swung the door wide to let them in.

Billings and Holloway both studied Sam's face, but he simply stared at the tablet, revealing nothing. He was genuinely curious to see what was on the next video.

Nora was dead. He wanted to know what had happened. At the same time, he dreaded what he might see.

Billings touched the tablet again, and the second video played.

The timestamp was thirty-seven minutes later than the first. Once again, the front door to Nora's home opened, and this time Adeline ran out into the street, tapping on her phone as she went. At the closest intersection, she got into an autocar and slipped away into the night.

On the video, Sam exited Nora's home, looked both ways on the street, glimpsed the car driving away, and began the short walk back to his house.

Billings pulled the tablet back to her side of the table and tapped on it as she spoke.

"The next person to visit Dr. Thomas's residence was a friend who was coming to join her for a morning jog. She peered in through the glass in the front door and noticed a body lying motionless and blood on the floor."

"Is there a question?" Tom asked. "Where's the actual evidence that Dr. Anderson or his daughter were involved in her death? This confirms they visited her and left—no more."

Sam was lost in thought. His mind felt like it was trapped in a torture chamber of grief for Nora and confusion about what was happening—about what they were trying to do to Adeline.

"Mr. Morris," Billings said, "we wouldn't be here if we didn't have evidence. Evidence we know is strong enough to convict."

"Do you have video of my house?" Sam asked. "Of Adeline arriving?"

"Yes," Billings said.

Sam braced for the answer to his question—a question he had to ask. He had to know. "Did she leave in the night?"

Holloway cocked his head. Billings studied Sam for a long moment. "No. She didn't. After you and Miss Anderson returned to your residence, no one left until the two of you— along with your son—departed that morning for the cemetery."

Tom was saying something. But Sam was in another place. He was only vaguely aware of the interrogation room. What he had learned, at that moment, was that Adeline was innocent. She hadn't returned to Nora's house. Not that he could ever imagine her doing that. But the world was strange sometimes.

Adeline had gotten her feelings hurt that night. But she hadn't done something that couldn't be undone. The truth would free her. And him. He clung to that thought like a rope hanging over a cliff. Absolom was below, and the facts would pull them free.

Sam had given the eulogy at his wife's funeral service. It had been the hardest thing he'd ever done. The words he said next were a close second.

"How did she die?"

Holloway turned in his chair to Billings, who seemed troubled by Sam's question.

"We think you know."

"Just show me. Please."

Elliott and Tom shared a glance, and so did Holloway and Billings. The detective slid the tablet forward.

The picture Sam saw there nearly made him vomit.

Nora lay on the floor of her kitchen, a wide gash in her neck. A pool of blood spread out around her on the tile floor.

Sam inhaled.

And exhaled.

He felt like he had woken from a nightmare only to learn that it wasn't a dream. This was reality.

It couldn't be.

It was wrong.

Nora Thomas was the kindest, gentlest woman he knew.

The picture of Nora lying dead, her blood spilled out like the liquid contents of a shattered wine bottle, gutted Sam.

If he stared at it much longer, the picture would break him. He had to focus. He had to protect Adeline. That was his life now. He knew it then. And nothing else mattered.

"Why," Sam said, "do you think Adeline killed Nora? She clearly went home. And you admitted she didn't leave that night. Until the morning."

"The murder weapon," Billings said.

"What about it?" Sam asked.

Billings tapped the tablet again, and a picture appeared of a knife laid out on a white plastic background.

"We found it in the tank of the toilet in the half bathroom off the foyer," Billings said. "They have Miss Anderson's prints on the handle. We detected significant amounts of Dr. Thomas's blood on the blade. The water didn't wash it away completely— or the prints, as Miss Anderson hoped they would."

Billings watched Sam, but he couldn't bring himself to speak.

She pressed on. "CSI detected a significant amount of both females' blood in the living area and kitchen. Your prints are everywhere. We detected both women's blood on your skin—we collected the sample while you were unconscious this morning. We also found trace amounts of Dr. Thomas's blood on your daughter's skin. Lastly, audio from surveillance cameras outside the home confirms the verbal altercation between the victim and Miss Anderson. It overlaps with the deceased's projected time of death. It's easily enough to convict both of you. You were there. Her prints are on the murder weapon. Both of you have blood on your hands."

"We're done here," Sam said. "I want to see my daughter. Right now."

SIX

In the plush holding cell, the door opened, and Adeline marched in, eyes wide.

Sam rose from the club chair and held out his arms.

She ran to him and wrapped her arms around him and buried her face in his chest and sobbed, a long, ragged cry filled with hurt. It was a single word: "Dad."

"It's going to be okay," he whispered. "Did they tell you?" he asked.

"Yeah." Adeline sobbed again. "I was so mean to her, Dad. *So mean.*"

"You were upset. You had every right to be. It's understandable. She understood. I promise you."

Her sobs receded, and Adeline broke the hug and looked up at her father. "What happened?"

Sam sensed that now was a time for truth. And he told her the truth: "I don't know."

"She was alive when we left."

"Yes. She was."

"And somebody killed her."

"They did."

"Why?"

"I don't know that either."

"What happens now?"

"Frankly, I'm not sure. Whoever killed Nora is one step ahead of us—and you're obviously their other target."

"They're trying to frame me."

"It would seem so."

"Why?"

"I have no idea."

Adeline studied her father's face and seemed to decide something. "I don't believe you, Dad."

When Sam didn't say anything, Adeline scoffed. "I thought we were done with secrets. Please tell me what you know. That's all I'm asking."

Sam scratched the side of his head. "My best theory is that this is somehow related to my work."

"As in…"

"Absolom."

"What about it?"

"We've made a discovery. Elliott and Hiro did. A breakthrough. A… new version of Absolom. Nora was opposed to it. My best guess is that maybe that's why she was killed."

SEVEN

Shortly after Adeline left, the door to the holding cell opened again and Elliott walked in. Two of the other founders and inventors of Absolom were with him: Hiroshi Sato and Daniele Danneros.

Daniele marched to Sam and hugged him tightly. "My God, Sam," she said, shaking her head.

When she released him, Hiro nodded solemnly. Sam couldn't help but notice the deep bags under his eyes. The man looked like he had been up all night.

Elliott held up a take-out bag from a sushi restaurant. "Dani brought food. If you're ready to eat."

"I am."

They moved to the dining table and began laying out the trays.

"Connie is on her way," Elliott said. "It turns out she spent the night at a medical clinic in San Francisco. She left for there on a private plane right after our meeting yesterday."

Daniele furrowed her brows. "Is she all right?"

"I think so," Elliott said. "I think it was a scheduled treatment."

Hiro set his chopsticks down. "Then let us state the obvious: if she was not present in the city, she could not have committed the murder."

Hiro had always been the most blunt of the group. Some

29

mistook his directness for aggression, but Sam had always appreciated his approach—both in the lab and now here.

"And even if she was," Sam said, "I don't think she's physically capable of overpowering Nora."

"I will go first," Hiro said, taking a deep breath. "After our meeting last night, I stayed in the lab to work on Absolom Two."

"What time did you get home?" Sam asked.

"I didn't. I spent the night there. I showered in my office, and I came directly here when Elliott informed me of what had happened. The video surveillance cameras on campus will confirm my movements."

Daniele screwed the top back on her water bottle and set it down. "I went directly home after our meeting last night. I ate leftovers, ran a bath, and read." She glanced at the others. "My home video surveillance will also verify that."

No one looked at Elliott, but he shifted in his chair. "I went home after the meeting. Had a few drinks and went to sleep. But I did call Nora last night."

The room was silent and still.

"Before or after Adeline and I visited?" Sam asked.

"Before."

"Why?" Hiro asked.

"The obvious," Elliott replied. "I wanted to finish Absolom Two. She didn't. She wanted to destroy it."

"What was said?" Sam asked.

"I asked if I could come over to talk. Nora said no." Elliott glanced at Sam. "She said she was having guests."

Sam stared at the table. "How did it go? The discussion about Absolom Two?"

"How do you think it went, Sam?"

When no one said anything, Elliott added, "She was

absolutely adamant that we destroy the prototype and cease any further research. It didn't matter what I said."

A knock at the door drew the group's attention. Sam stood and opened it and found Constance standing there, a scarf wrapped around her head, brown eyes peering up at him, already filled with tears. She reached out and hugged him. In his arms, she felt small and fragile, and Sam didn't dare hug her tight.

Her voice sounded as fragile as her body felt. "I'm so sorry, Sam. How are you holding up?"

"All right," he lied.

She broke the hug and stared at him. "We're going to figure this out."

They joined the others at the table, but Constance didn't eat. She briefly confirmed Elliott's account of what she had done after the meeting, and when the group fell silent, Hiro stood from the table.

"We must start with motive. I believe the most likely explanation is that Nora was killed because she opposed Absolom Two."

Elliott stood. "I take that as a veiled accusation against me."

"Your perception is incorrect."

Daniele held her hands up. "Let's back up a second."

Elliott strode to the door. "You can back up without me."

"Elliott, where are you going?" Daniele asked.

"This will hit the press soon. We need to make a statement. If we don't, the narrative will get away from us."

Hiro cocked his head. "And what precisely is our narrative?"

"The truth: a wonderful human being was tragically and senselessly taken from us. And Sam Anderson and his daughter had nothing to do with it."

Without another word, Elliott marched out.

"He's right about the press," Constance said. "If the public perception is that you're guilty, it'll be hard to change that—even after the facts come out. And kids can be cruel. We need to get ahead of this for Ryan's sake."

"True," Sam muttered.

"Back to motive," Daniele said. "I'm not sure the Absolom connection is right."

"How so?" Hiro asked.

"I think Absolom—and the next generation of it—is on our minds, and that's the first thing we see. But we should look at the more obvious motives. The two classic reasons for murder."

"Which are?" Sam asked.

"Love and money."

Sam shrugged. "Not sure that helps. If love is the motive, that would seem to lead back to me."

"But framing you doesn't," Daniele said. "Think about it—what if the person who killed Nora was in love with her? The killer finds out you've been seeing her. They know it's getting serious. And they can't handle it."

"Then why would they frame Adeline?" Constance asked.

Daniele focused on Sam. "I believe you can answer that."

"Maximum pain."

Daniele nodded. "The only thing worse than losing your future is seeing your kids lose theirs. Whoever killed Nora might have seen an opportunity to strike back at both of the people responsible for their unreturned affection: Nora and Sam."

"That leaves money," Hiro said.

"And Nora would have left a lot of it," Daniele said. "Her shares in Absolom Sciences are worth billions."

Hiro nodded. "But she doesn't have any children. And she's a widow. Who would it go to?"

"I think we should find that out. And I think we should make a list of everyone who knew the contents of her will."

"I agree," Sam said. "But if it's for the money, why frame me?"

"Convenience," Daniele said. "In homicide investigations, the police almost always start with lovers and former lovers. You were there. There was an altercation. It works out well."

"Next steps?" Constance asked.

"I'll call Tom Morris," Daniele said. "Nora may have filed her will with the company."

"I'll start trying to track down any former romantic acquaintances," Hiro said.

Sam turned to Daniele. "I hate to ask, but Ryan's still here at the station. And..."

"You want me to keep him? Of course. I'm happy to, Sam."

When they left, Sam began clearing the take-out containers from the dining table. A small slip of paper was lying under one of the sushi trays. At first, Sam thought it was the message from a fortune cookie, but there weren't any of those with the meal.

He picked it up and read the short message:

LOOK UNDER THE TABLE

He felt his pulse quicken.

Still holding the slip of paper, he moved to the door, locked it, and set the short note back on the table. They would need to get fingerprints off of it, though he figured that was likely a long shot.

He looked under the dining table, but there was nothing

there. He got down on his hands and knees and crawled under and peered up.

Taped to the underside of the table was a small cream-colored envelope.

EIGHT

For a while, Sam simply stared at the envelope attached to the bottom side of the dining table.

He knew he should call the police and have it fingerprinted and analyzed.

But what if it incriminated him somehow?

Whoever had taped it there was clearly a step ahead of him. And there were only four people who could have put it there— the only four people who had sat at the table: Elliott, Hiro, Daniele, and Constance.

His closest friends and colleagues.

Could he add Tom Morris, the Absolom chief counsel, to the suspect list? Sam thought back. No. The entire time Tom had been in the room, he had sat in the lounge area, never at the dining table.

Could someone else have gotten in here? No. The room had been guarded by a staffer from Absolom Security while he was gone.

It had to have been left by one of the four.

Sam reached up, pulled the envelope free, and flipped it over. The entire outside was blank.

He opened it, slipped the folded page out, and read the typed message.

Sam,

You have a choice.

Confess to Nora's murder, and Adeline will go free. No harm will come to her.

If you refuse, I will send the police irrefutable evidence of Adeline's guilt.

You have until 5pm.

Choose wisely.

Absolom awaits.

The small page shook as Sam's hand began to tremble. His chest heaved as he sucked in breath after breath, but try as he might, he couldn't fill his lungs. It was like they were shrinking.

He was suffocating.

His legs felt weak. He staggered to the couch, closed his eyes, and tried to breathe.

He was losing the battle.

He was dying.

A knock at the door sounded a million miles away.

"Dr. Anderson!" The man's shout was muffled, as though Sam was underwater. "Dr. Anderson! Are you all right?"

Sam's vision spotted.

A wave of nausea overtook him.

His last thought before he passed out was of the note. He couldn't let them find it.

His arms were heavy and sluggish, but he forced them to move, to stuff the small page under one of the couch cushions as darkness swallowed him up and the door lock clicked open.

Sam was lying on the couch when he regained consciousness. The bright lights above hurt his eyes, so he squeezed them shut.

Elliott was practically screaming. "You've nearly killed him.

LOST IN TIME

I want Dr. Anderson released. Right now."

Billings replied: "That's not going to happen."

Elliott again: "So help me God, if this man dies here, I will bury this police station in lawsuits. The paperwork alone will kill every last one of you."

Another man spoke then. Sam thought it was the nurse from the post-arrest room. "We could move him to the hospital for continuous observation."

"I'm okay," Sam croaked as he tried to sit up.

The nurse gripped Sam's shoulders and helped him up.

"How do you feel?" he asked.

"I'm fine."

"You're not fine," Elliott said. "You had a panic attack, Sam. The next one could kill you."

"Can you tell us what happened?" the nurse asked.

Sam's eyes drifted to the couch cushion where he had hidden the note.

"Dr. Anderson?" the nurse said, leaning forward.

Sam made a decision then, one he sensed was about to determine the rest of his life. And Adeline's life.

"Nothing. Nothing happened. I just started feeling a little overwhelmed."

The nurse nodded. "That's very common. If you'd like, we can transfer you to the hospital where we can run some diagnostic tests and monitor you more closely."

"I don't want any tests. Or to be monitored."

"Well," Billings said, "to be on the safe side, we're going to halt any further meetings with Dr. Anderson for twenty-four hours."

The nurse pointed to the medical armband on Sam's wrist. "We'll continue to monitor your vitals, but please notify us if you experience any changes—mental or physical. Okay, Dr. Anderson?"

37

"Sure thing."

Elliott muttered and paced as Billings and the medical team left the room. When the door closed, he plopped down in one of the club chairs.

"What really happened?"

Sam glanced at the couch cushion again. Elliott was one of his oldest friends. And probably his closest friend at work. Except for Nora.

But for some reason, Sam couldn't bring himself to show him the note. At least, not yet. Maybe it was because Nora was opposed to Elliott's Absolom breakthrough. That was as close to a murder motive as Sam could see right now. The other problem was that, deep down, he sensed that if he showed Elliott the note, he might take it to the police. Or even the press—to prove Sam's innocence. There were too many unknowns.

Sam had to decide who to trust. For some reason, Elliott wasn't one of those people.

"It all just sort of caught up with me. I'm fine."

"We're going to figure this out. Victor Levy should be here within the hour."

When Elliott was gone, Sam glanced at the clock on the wall.

It was 1:43 p.m.

He had a decision to make. And soon.

NINE

When the door to the suite opened again, Elliott walked through, followed by Tom and a well-dressed man with coiffed hair. He looked like he had just sauntered off the set of a Hollywood movie.

"Sam," Tom said. "This is Victor Levy."

"I'm sorry we had to meet under these circumstances, Dr. Anderson, but I assure you, I'm going to do all I can for you and your daughter. We're going to handle this situation."

Against his will, a flicker of hope rose inside of Sam.

The group moved to the couch and chairs, sat, and Levy opened his briefcase.

"Dr. Anderson, I'm going to start by telling you how we're going to win this case."

"Call me Sam."

"Sam, do you know what mutually assured destruction is?"

"Sure."

"That's how we win, Sam. We attack the system itself." Levy held up his hands. "But let me back up a second. I couldn't be here sooner because I wanted to review the evidence against you and learn about you and the other individuals involved." He paused a moment. "Do you know the best thing about the American criminal justice system?"

Sam shook his head. The question sounded rhetorical to him.

"Do-overs." Levy said. "If at first you don't succeed, you try again."

"Appeals," Tom said.

"That's right, Tom." Levy put a hand on the other attorney's shoulder. "But Absolom changed that. You can't get an appeal for a client who no longer exists in this universe. So we're going to have to start right there."

Levy waited, Sam thought for dramatic effect, then proceeded.

"The first thing we're going to do is scare the world to death. We're going to pose a simple question: could sentencing Sam and Adeline Anderson to Absolom end the entire world? This is going to be a different kind of trial, Sam, one that will have the public enraptured. Why? Because everyone watching is going to think their lives are on the line too. It's going to make the O. J. trial look like a box office bomb."

"What exactly are you saying?" Tom asked.

Levy pointed to Sam. "We have one advantage here, gentlemen. Our defendant is unique in one very important way: he is one of the inventors of Absolom."

Elliott shrugged. "Why does that matter?"

"It might not," Levy said. "But the question is: what if it does? What if, by the act of creating Absolom, Sam is somehow tethered to it in ways we don't understand, by some connection of quantum entanglement or a space-time mechanism we don't fully understand? And what if, by sending him through Absolom, we somehow break the causality bridge that created our entire present existence? What if, by sentencing Sam to Absolom, we're sentencing our entire present reality to nonexistence? Is that a chance the world can take? To punish one man and his daughter for a crime of passion—a crime we intend to sow doubt about as well?"

Elliott rolled his eyes. "That's not even scientifically accurate."

"Does it have to be?"

"Yes," Elliott said, "it has to be."

"This is a court of law, Dr. Lucas, not a laboratory. The laws of quantum physics are a bit player in the great experiment of justice. Do you know what the prevailing force is in a courtroom?"

Sam sensed that this was another rhetorical question. They were getting a real preview of Levy's courtroom performance skills. Elliott, however, took the bait, instantly answering: "Truth."

"Fear," Levy shot back.

Elliott's eyebrows bunched together. "Fear?"

"*Fear*, Dr. Lucas. Everyone in that courtroom is scared of something. The defendant is afraid of being convicted. Myself, I'm scared of losing—because losing trial attorneys become former trial attorneys. The DA is scared of losing, too. Because superstar DAs become attorney generals and, if they're lucky, senators, governors, and occasionally presidents. They're thinking about their book deal, too—and who will play them in the miniseries. The judge is thinking about their next appointment. Or election. The jury is thinking about their own reputation. In the paper and on TV, they'll be anonymous— juror number three and juror number nine—but let's face it: their identities will leak. Online discussion boards will be obsessed with every aspect of this trial, including the jurors. There will be a daily—even a real-time—dissection of every witness who takes the stand and every potential tell from those twelve men and women in the jury box. Their backgrounds will be exposed. Their potential biases analyzed."

Elliott held his hands up. "I still don't get it."

"You're looking at it like a scientist," Levy said.

"I fail to see the flaw in that," Elliott shot back.

Levy let the silence draw out. Sam thought it was to let Elliott's momentum fade, which worked.

When Levy spoke again, his tone was almost reflective. "Gentlemen, let's back up for a moment. Let's look at this from the public's point of view. Because ultimately, that's the true court in which our first trial will be adjudicated."

Levy spread his hands. "First, consider what the public knows about Absolom. It's a machine that sends the world's worst convicted criminals back in time. Serial killers. Terrorists. Genocidal dictators. War criminals. They go into the Absolom chamber, and in a flash, they are gone from this world, sent back in time, hundreds of millions of years in the past, to the age of the dinosaurs. They'll be alone for the rest of their life. They'll die a terrible death. And do you know what the worst part of it is?"

This time, Levy didn't pause for dramatic effect. He pressed on. "The unknown. That's Absolom's true power. That's why every person on Earth knows the phrase, 'A fate worse than Absolom.' Because no one knows for sure what exactly happens to those sentenced to Absolom. We just know they disappear from our world, and never come back. And that's terrifying, even to the world's worst criminals."

Elliott rolled his eyes. "We know what happens to them."

"How do you know?" Levy asked, his voice reflective.

"Entanglement proves—"

Levy quickly pointed at Elliott. "Exactly. *Exactly*, Dr. Elliott. Your entanglement data shows that Absolom payloads arrive in the past. And the reason the entire system works is that they don't arrive in our past. Absolom activation branches our timeline. It makes a copy and it sends the criminal back to an alternate universe. A copy of our universe, where nothing they do can impact our reality. That's why it's safe, isn't it? Because they're utterly and truly *gone* from this universe. That's why the public accepts it."

"I wouldn't say everyone accepts it," Sam said.

"True," Levy replied. "Every Absolom departure sparks protests. Since its introduction, the efforts to shut it down haven't stopped. Because a lot of people think it's too cruel and unusual. And even more people are, to some degree, afraid of this mysterious box. They like what it has done for society. They like getting rid of the world's worst criminals. But they also fear it. And that fear is what we will use.

"Again, our question to the world will be: what if, in the case of Dr. Samuel Anderson, because he is one of the six inventors of Absolom, he's entangled with it in a unique way? What if, by trying to tear him from this universe, it rips the very fabric of our reality? Can the world take that chance? Would you risk ending everything to punish one man?"

The room was quiet until Levy continued. "*Fear*, gentlemen. We're going to give that courtroom a new fear. A greater fear. One that will light the world on fire. One that will apply pressure—from inside the courtroom and from outside, from every corner of the world. Mutually assured destruction. That's what we're talking about here."

"Forgive me," Tom said, "I'm not trying to throw cold water on this, but the evidence is still pretty bad."

Levy stood, looming over the other three men. "Tom's right. The evidence is bad: Dr. Thomas's blood is on your hands, Sam. *Actually* on your hands. Adeline's, too. They have the house on camera. You two were the only ones who entered the home before she died. You're the only ones who could have committed the crime. I'm not going to lie to you, Sam, or give you false hope. Based on the evidence, you and your daughter will be convicted of this crime. What I'm proposing isn't trying for an acquittal. At least, not in the first trial."

"Then what's the plan?" Elliott asked.

"We use the fear that an Absolom sentence could end the world to get a life imprisonment sentence. Maybe the DA will crack under the pressure and do a deal. Maybe we convince the judge at sentencing. Or perhaps we get the jury to convict of a lesser crime—one not eligible for Absolom." Levy held his arms out. "And that's when the real work begins, Sam."

"Do-overs," Tom said.

Levy drew a deep breath. "That's right. Appeals. The world will be enraptured by Sam and Adeline's first trial. But the sequel won't get as much attention. And the one after that will get even less press time. Every time we appeal the case, the world will be less interested. There will be less pressure on future judges and juries. Like a ball of string, we'll pull at the threads, and we'll keep pulling—as long as we have to—until it all unravels and the world has virtually forgotten about Sam and his daughter. And then, one day, they'll walk free. It'll take years. Probably decades. But, one day, we'll beat it."

Sam tried to imagine what a trial like that would do to Adeline. What would years, maybe decades, in prison do to her? That only made him more sure about what he had to do.

"There's not going to be a trial," Sam said. "Or any appeals."

Levy paused, studying Sam, then broke into a smile. "A man after my own heart. I like the way you think, Sam. If we can get the charges dismissed, we skip it all. But it's a long shot. We'll have to dig into how they collected the evidence. They're very careful about that these days. They use robots mostly, so we can't pick apart any biases the officers may have had."

"Mr. Levy," Sam said, "you're paid to get the results the client desires, correct? Not necessarily to win."

Levy nodded slowly. "That's right. I work for you and your daughter, Sam. To get you the outcome you want. We take a holistic approach at the Levy Group. That includes PR and post-trial services. We can get you transferred to any prison you want—if it ends up that way."

"What I want," Sam said, "is to confess."

Elliott's head snapped around to stare at Sam.

Levy's face was a mask of concentration.

"I'm going to tell the police that there was an altercation. During that incident, I killed Nora. Adeline tried to stop it— that's why her prints are on the weapon. She's innocent. I'll take Absolom, and she goes free. That's what I want. And I want to minimize the PR around it. I want it to be handled as quietly as possible."

For a few seconds, no one said anything. And then Elliott exploded. "Sam, you've lost your mind!" He spun and spoke to Levy. "Our client is insane. We need to plead insanity. He had a nervous breakdown an hour ago."

Sam focused on Levy. "Do I seem insane to you?"

"I'll bite, Sam. Why do you want to confess?"

"I have my reasons."

Levy studied him. "In my entire career, I've never asked a client this. But I'd like to know: did you do it, Sam?"

"I'm going to confess. With or without your help. Can you live with that as an answer?"

"I can live with that. In my work, ambiguity is the rule, not the exception."

"How do we go about this?"

Elliott stood and gripped Sam's shoulders. "Sam, what are you doing?"

Sam pushed Elliott away. "Stop, Elliott. I have to."

"You can't."

Sam stared at his old friend. "I have to, okay? I have to."

TEN

Adeline couldn't stop thinking about Nora and her father and last night. She had replayed the scene in her mind a hundred times, but that only made her feel worse. She regretted what she had done. It was all her fault. If she hadn't lost it—if she hadn't lashed out, maybe Nora would still be alive; maybe she and her father would still be free—

The door to her suite opened, and two of her father's friends—Elliott and Tom—strode in. Behind them was a man she didn't know. The stranger introduced himself as Victor Levy, an attorney Adeline's father had hired to represent them.

He set a recorder on the coffee table and asked what Adeline had said to the police.

When she had told him, he said something Adeline had been hoping to hear since this morning: "We're going to get you out of here, Miss Anderson. Soon, I hope."

Sam checked the time.

2:54 p.m.

That meant it was almost eleven in the evening in London, but Sarah's sister, Amanda, was a night owl. She was Sarah's only sibling and had never married, unless one counted her marriage to her job as a stage actress.

Sam picked up the phone and talked with the police operator.

They didn't seem to have any issues placing the call. After all, Sam was allowed a phone call, and technically, he hadn't used it.

Amanda answered on the third ring, sounding confused. "Hello?"

"Hi. It's Sam."

"Sam," she breathed out. "I thought I might hear from you today. I haven't stopped thinking about her. I could barely get through rehearsal."

"Yeah. It's a tough day. But that's not why I'm calling. Listen, I know this is unexpected, but I'm wondering if Adeline and Ryan could come and stay with you."

"Um, well, it's not a good time, Sam. We're set to go out on tour on Monday. They could come around the end of June."

"No, I'm not saying for a visit. I mean permanently."

"I don't understand. What are you playing at?"

"I'm going away, Amanda."

"To where? Why? What's happened?"

"I can't tell you. At least, not yet. I just need to know if you can take them."

"Well, frankly, no, I can't. My life simply isn't set up to have children at home. And to be quite honest, I'm not sure I am either. And I'd like to know what this is all about. I think I'm owed that much."

"You sure are. I'll call you back, Amanda, when I can, and when I can tell you."

When they had hung up, Sam paced the room, mentally debating who would be the best guardian for his children. Adeline was technically already over the age of majority in the State of Nevada. But she couldn't reasonably adopt Ryan, or raise him. Sam couldn't ask her to do that. And she was still enrolled in college.

His first thought was Elliott, but the more he thought about it, the less he liked that idea.

A knock at the door brought him out of the mental debate, and Sam found Levy and Tom waiting outside.

When they were seated, Levy said, "We have an agreement with the DA—in principle. Our offered account agrees with their evidence, and I think, between you and me, they also would rather avoid a trial."

"So what happens now?"

"They want to see the exact text of the confession before they'll formally make an offer. Then you'll sign it."

Levy took out his laptop, and the three of them worked on the language until they were satisfied.

When they were done, Sam made one last request. "I need to see Dani."

"I'll tell her," Tom said.

As the two attorneys were leaving, Levy paused. "With my clientele, I see some pretty strange cases. But once I get the whole picture and study it long enough, it makes sense, even the crazy things people do. But I've been trying to get my head around this one, Sam, and I can't."

"Maybe it will one day. If you give it enough time."

ELEVEN

Daniele sat across from Sam, a somber look on her face. He inhaled and said the words he dreaded saying.

"I've confessed to Nora's murder."

In his mind, Sam had imagined a number of reactions from Daniele. Shock. Rage. Confusion.

He saw the last thing he expected: nothing. Daniele didn't react at all.

"Who told you?" Sam asked.

"Elliott called me. He was drunk. And enraged. He wants me to talk you out of it."

"It's already done."

Daniele nodded.

"Are you going to ask me if I actually did it?"

"I don't need to. I already know the answer."

Sam had wondered how she would take his confession. Her, and his other friends and colleagues. It was one thing to be accused of a crime. It was another to confess.

Her reaction was a relief, knowing that even if he was convicted, it wouldn't change her mind about him.

"Do you know why I asked you here?"

Daniele nodded. "I do. But tell me anyway."

"When I'm gone..." Sam swallowed. "I need someone to take care of Adeline and Ryan, to provide a home, and watch out for them, and serve as a legal guardian for Ryan."

49

Daniele waited, and Sam continued, "We don't have any family—none that can take them. I thought about asking Elliott, but he drinks too much. He works too much. And I think..." Sam clenched his teeth.

"You think he might have done it," Daniele said, sparing him from having to say it—which Sam was thankful for.

"What about Constance?" Daniele asked.

"She's too sick. And Hiro, well, I think he's still struggling with his... problem."

"My answer is yes, Sam. I promise you, I'll do my very best to care for them the same way you and Sarah would have."

"I know you will. You know you were always very special to Sarah. Almost like a daughter to her."

After a pause, he said, "Can I ask you a question?"

"Anything."

"Why didn't you ever get married?"

Daniele shrugged. "Work mostly. There was never enough room for what I knew I had to do and someone else."

Sam rose, assuming the meeting was over, but Daniele held up a hand. "Sam."

He raised his eyebrows.

"We're wasting time."

"Wasting time?"

"We need to be working on the only thing that matters now."

"Which is?"

"Figuring out how to get you back after Absolom sends you to the past."

"That's impossible."

"Today it is. But not one day. I'm going to make sure that day comes. That you see your family again, Sam. But I need one thing from you."

"What's that?"

"Your help."

Sam made another important decision then. He reached under the couch cushion and handed Daniele the note.

"I found it taped to the bottom of the dining table."

She scanned the page quickly and looked up. "You were going to keep this from me, weren't you?"

"Yes."

"Why?"

"Because I think whoever is doing this is way ahead of me and unbeatable."

"I don't ever want to hear you say that again. Or think it, Sam. That's a dangerous thought."

She set the note between them. "Do you ever wonder what happens to them—the people we send through Absolom?"

"A lot, actually."

"They're alone, in the distant past, millions of years ago. It's a survival situation. Do you know what the most important thing is in a survival situation?"

"Shelter? Food? Water?"

"Those sustain life, but the most important thing is your will to live. You lose that, you die." Daniele fixed Sam with an intense gaze. "Promise me you won't lose that will. That you won't give up. Because I won't give up on you. Promise me, Sam."

He exhaled. "I promise."

Daniele held up the note. "Who do you think wrote it?"

"It has to be either Elliott, Hiro, or Constance. They are the only ones that sat at that table—besides you and me."

"And you're assuming it's not me?"

"I'm betting my life—and my family's future—that it isn't."

"Of the three, who do you think did it?"

Sam tilted his head back. "Elliott is the most likely. He's got a motive for Nora's murder—she opposed Absolom Two. So did I. That gives him a motive to get rid of me as well. And to scare the others into helping finish his work." Sam shook his head. "But I refuse to believe it. He's one of my oldest friends. And... I just don't think it's him."

"Connie?"

"I can't see it. For the same reason I know she can't take Adeline and Ryan: she's too sick. And she wasn't even in town that night."

"She could have hired someone."

"True. But I doubt it."

"Hiro?"

"Wouldn't hurt a fly," Sam said. "I don't think it's him."

"Then who?"

"That's the question. I simply have no idea who could have done it. That's one of the reasons I confessed. But that's not my greatest concern."

"What is?"

"I fear that Nora was just the start. That they got rid of her for a reason we can't see. And that the same thing is going to happen to others. Maybe you. Or Elliott. Or Adeline. When I'm gone, the killer will still be here."

TWELVE

The door opened and Adeline looked up to see Daniele Danneros, one of her father's friends and colleagues.

Adeline had known the woman for a long time (she had been close with Adeline's mother), but she hadn't seen her that much in recent years.

Daniele hugged Adeline and explained that she would be coming home with her.

"I want to see my father."

"We're working on that."

"What's happening? Why are they releasing me and not him?"

"I'll explain when we get home."

Daniele's home was quite similar to the one Adeline shared with her father and Ryan. Almost eerily so.

In fact, the bedroom Daniele led her to was a near mirror image of Adeline's own bedroom. The size was the same and the bed was in the same location. Even the furniture was a similar style.

Daniele seemed to read Adeline's unease.

"It's the same builder and floor plan—with some slight modifications. Same interior designer too."

"I want answers."

"You should sit down, Adeline."

"I don't want to sit down."

Daniele placed a hand—gently—on Adeline's shoulder, guided her to the bed, and sat beside her.

"What I'm about to say is going to be hard to hear."

"What is?"

"It's going to hurt, but I promise you, it's going to get better. You just have to give it some time."

Adeline's eyes filled with tears. Somehow, in that moment she knew what Daniele was going to tell her. One feeling rose above the others: rage.

"Everyone keeps telling me everything is going to get better. But things just keep getting worse."

"They always do," Daniele said. "Before they get better."

A short time after he signed the confession, they came to transport Sam.

The guards shackled his feet, but they didn't handcuff him. They put him in a straitjacket.

One of them, a young man who looked to be in his early twenties, shrugged as he held the garment up. "I'm sorry, sir, but it's protocol."

Sam understood. People sentenced to Absolom were desperate individuals. They had no future. Nothing to lose. No hope.

People with nothing to lose were the most dangerous thing in the world.

The transport van was windowless. Two guards sat across from Sam, stun batons in their hands, at the ready.

Although the Absolom technology had been licensed to every government on Earth, there was only one operating Absolom machine in the world, and it was here, in Absolom

City, in the middle of the Nevada desert. The reason was simple: safety.

Victor Levy had been right about one thing: the world was still a little afraid of Absolom, in the same way they had feared the atomic bomb and the Large Hadron Collider when it had first started up. It was a new technology, one that seemed almost surreal at first, a leap forward some still weren't comfortable with. If there was an accident with Absolom, people didn't want it to occur near a populated area.

The other reason Absolom Sciences kept the only functioning Absolom machine under their control was practical: they didn't want anyone studying the technology and reverse engineering it. At the moment, they had a monopoly on exiling criminals from this universe.

Sam felt the van angle downward. They were on a descending ramp now, which meant they had reached the Absolom departure facility in the heart of the city.

The cell they led Sam to wasn't nearly as plush as the holding room at the police station. It also had a few strange modifications. The walls were padded. There was no metal at all. No bathroom. No mirror. Only a soft floor, a ceiling that couldn't have been over eight feet tall, and a squishy foam mattress.

He understood why. There was no way for an Absolom prisoner to hurt themselves in here.

The guards removed the straitjacket and left Sam alone in the room for a long time—how long, he didn't know. There was no clock and no view of the sun.

A woman's voice came over the speaker and asked him a series of questions—ones Sam had anticipated.

What would he like his last meal to be?

Who would he like to be present for his Absolom departure?

Would he like to update his will?

Who would he like to visit with before his departure?

When Sam had finished answering, the woman told him that he had received several requests for visitation and that it was up to him if they were allowed to visit. The list was one he could have guessed: Elliott, Constance, Hiro, Daniele, and Adeline.

Sam said yes to all of them.

He needed to say goodbye.

THIRTEEN

In the padded cell, one of the wall panels lifted slightly, revealing a Styrofoam tray with dinner.

Sam took it, but he couldn't bring himself to eat.

The woman's voice over the speaker asked if he wanted to watch a movie or TV or read a book or listen to an audiobook.

Sam didn't.

He wanted to think. It was the only thing that might save his life. And his family.

The lights dimmed soon, and Sam lay there on the mattress, staring up at the padded ceiling, trying to wrap his mind around what was happening.

Sleep wouldn't come. But at some point in the night, bad thoughts did. Thoughts of blaming himself. And others. And even worse than that: what-ifs.

With his last bit of strength, he forced those thoughts from his mind and tried to hold his mind still, to think about nothing at all. Somewhere in that void, sleep found him.

He didn't know how long he had slept, but Sam sensed that it hadn't been much time. When he opened his eyes, the lights were bright, and the woman's gentle voice over the speaker was calling to him again.

"Dr. Anderson, can you hear me?"

"Yes," he croaked.

One of the wall panels opened, like a door swinging in, revealing a shower stall, a toilet, and a sink. There was a change of clothes waiting atop a foam cube next to the sink.

Sam tried to force himself to eat breakfast, but he didn't get very far.

"You should eat," the gentle voice said over the speaker. "Food may be harder to find on the other side."

The other side. So that's what they called the world waiting beyond Absolom. It sounded so benign when you put it that way.

Regardless of the syntax, the reminder motivated Sam to finish the tray.

When it was gone, another padded wall panel swung in, revealing a small desk and a soft stool built into the floor. The wall ahead was glass, and there was an empty visiting room on the other side.

"Are you ready for your first visitor?" the voice asked.

Sam thought, *no*, but said, "Yes."

Elliott was the first to arrive. His eyes were bloodshot. He hadn't shaved, and he fidgeted in the chair.

He asked the question Sam expected: "Why?" And Sam gave him the only answer he had: "Because I had to."

They argued after that, and when it was clear Sam wasn't going to recant his confession, Elliott screamed at him, a string of curses and accusations that cut deep into Sam and lingered long after his old friend had stormed out of the visiting room, slamming the door behind him.

Sam hoped those wouldn't be the last words Elliott said to him—for Elliott's sake. He knew the man would feel guilty about it. At some point.

Constance was next. She looked even more fragile than she had the day before—in body and mind. Her bottom lip quivered, and her eyes gushed tears. Her voice shook so much Sam could barely make out the words.

"Why, Sam? Help me understand why you're doing this. Please."

"I can't. I'm sorry."

Hiro arrived shortly after Constance had left. His face was a mask and his words were to the point.

"How can I help?"

"There's nothing to be done now."

"It would be a shame if Absolom experienced a technical difficulty. It's a very complex device. A routine check could reveal potential malfunctions. Our clients require our technical sign-off before operating it."

"Don't do that."

"It would buy us time."

"Not enough time, Hiro."

After lunch, Daniele arrived. Her face was pale, and dark bags loomed under her eyes.

"You've been up all night," Sam said.

"Look who's talking."

"Why?"

Daniele took out a printed page with a timeline and percentage numbers next to the date ranges.

"You've plotted my destination date."

"*Probable* destination date," Daniele said. "You of all people know that we're uncertain of the exact date Absolom convicts arrive at, but we can make a good guess based on your mass and volume."

"How does that help me?"

"Get your head in the game, Sam. This is a survival exercise now. Don't just blindly march through this. You need to be studying survival techniques while you're waiting for departure—and those strategies will vary based on the destination environment."

"Okay. Where do you think I'll end up?"

Daniele placed the page against the glass. "My best guess is that you'll arrive in the Late Triassic period, about 202 million years ago." She took the page away from the glass. "Which is sort of bad news."

Sam frowned. "Why is that bad news?"

"Well, where to start... I guess with the dinosaurs."

"Are we talking fast dinosaurs or slow dinosaurs?"

"Both—and probably a lot of other animals that are just as dangerous."

"Wonderful."

"At the end of the Triassic period, all the continents were still part of a single landmass."

"Pangea."

"That's right."

"Interesting," Sam said, glancing away. The fatigue was catching up with him. So was the stress. And the realization that he was about to be ripped away from this reality, his family, and everything he had ever known. How long would he last—

"Focus, Sam." Daniele leaned in. "We're running out of time."

"Okay. Okay." Sam rubbed his face. "You know, you're as insistent as Adeline."

"I know. Now can we continue?"

"Sure."

"The Triassic period lasted about fifty million years. This is the period when dinosaurs first evolved. Because there was only a single landmass on Earth, scientists think the variation in plant and animal life was low—relative to other periods."

Daniele flipped the page and scanned her notes. "The climate was hot and dry. We think most of Pangea was covered with large deserts. There were no polar ice caps back then. But what concerns me are the major events at the end of the Triassic."

"Such as?"

"Researchers believe that the Triassic ended in a series of massive earthquakes and volcanic eruptions and the separation of Pangea, which formed the North Atlantic Ocean."

Sam had assumed hunger and predators would be his biggest threats.

"If you arrive during that period, Sam, I think your chances of survival are extremely low. We know there was a mass extinction at the end of the Triassic, though the cause isn't clear. It could have been the ecological disruption or maybe a pathogen of some sort. Scientists estimate that the end-Triassic extinction event—or the Triassic–Jurassic extinction, as it's sometimes called—saw the permanent end of over seventy-five percent of all species on Earth. One in five taxonomic families ended in the Triassic. Of the five major extinction events in history, only the one at the end of the Permian was worse. The massive change is what allowed the dinosaurs to become the dominant species on Earth."

"This just keeps getting better."

"It would be ideal if you arrive before the transition from the Triassic to the Jurassic period. Or later in the Jurassic period. The years between the two saw Pangea split into Laurasia in the north and Gondwana in the south. Based on fossil records, we know there were land bridges between the two. And we know the global temperature fell, though it was still far warmer in the Jurassic than it is today—there was more carbon dioxide in the atmosphere back then. The deserts turned to jungles, and rainfall increased because of the seas between the landmasses."

Sam shook his head. In a way, it was a fitting end for him. He felt as though his world before being arrested was like Pangea: one solid mass, not perfect, but holding together. The events of the past few days had shaken him like the earthquakes and volcanoes and mass extinctions of the past. And like Pangea, he felt his life was separating forever. He would soon be separated from his family and the only world he had ever known.

"Seriously, Dani. How long do you think I'll last out there?"

"You're going to last as long as you have to, Sam. You're going to do it because you have to. Because you have two children who are going to be waiting for you to return."

Sam laughed, a frustrated, hopeless laugh that made him feel even worse. "Return how?"

"You let me work on that." Daniele held up another piece of paper with a list of three things. "This is what you need to focus on."

"What is it?" Sam asked.

"Your homework. A book on basic survival, one on desert survival, and one on jungle survival—just in case you arrive in the Jurassic instead of the Triassic. And about that: you need to keep your weight up. If you lose more weight, it will decrease your time distance—you'll arrive sooner, likely in the Jurassic. More dinosaurs, more rain, probably more disease, and more likelihood of landing in that mass extinction event during the transition between periods. There's never been a better reason to clean your plate, Sam."

That night, Adeline hugged her brother and found herself telling him that everything was going to be okay, though she wasn't sure she believed it herself. She wondered if that act was a small glimpse of what being a parent was like.

She knew Daniele was at the Absolom departure facility, visiting her father. The woman had insisted that she see him before Adeline, that she had information to share that her father needed to prepare him for the past.

Adeline had raged at Daniele, screaming at her, but she had barely reacted. She stood there listening, saying nothing, like a massive redwood tree weathering a windstorm. Then, without another word, Daniele had marched out. Which made Adeline even more angry.

After talking with Ryan, Adeline sat at the desk in her bedroom, took out a notebook, and wrote a single line at the top:

Who killed Nora?

Then she crossed out the question mark and added two words.

Who killed Nora and Dad?

Because that's exactly what they had done. Whoever had framed her father had killed him. Effectively. Soon, he would be put into a box, and he would never come back. That's what Absolom was. A death chamber. One that simply absolved society from the guilt of executing the people it didn't want around. Absolom was less messy. More ambiguous.

Adeline decided then that she hated it. She wished her father and his friends had never invented it.

Which brought her to the next order of business: suspects. There was no doubt in her mind who they were. She wrote their names in neat block letters.

ELLIOTT LUCAS

HIROSHI SATO

CONSTANCE NIVEN

Holding the pen above the page, she hesitated a moment, then pressed it in harder than before and wrote the final name.

DANIELE DANNEROS

She paused and stared at the name, a strange sensation coming over her. Daniele had told her about the note her father had found under the dining table in his holding cell. Adeline wondered if she had done that to deflect attention from herself—to make it look like she was helping her, like she was someone Adeline could trust.

Daniele's voice behind her made Adeline nearly leap out of the seat. She slammed the notebook shut and spun.

"Don't you knock?"

"I did knock."

"But apparently you didn't wait to barge in here."

Daniele nodded to the notebook. "Working on something?"

"It's none of your business."

"On the contrary. What you're working on is my only business now."

Adeline swallowed, suddenly nervous as Daniele took a step closer and spoke again, her voice steady and calm.

"You're making a list of the people who might have killed Nora and framed your father."

"You can't stop me."

"True. Nor do I want to. I'm going to help you, Adeline. We're going to figure it out. Together. And we're going to get him back."

Daniele turned and strode out, pausing at the doorway. "But right now, we're going to have dinner. And we're going to be civil."

FOURTEEN

Sam did indeed force himself to eat that night.

After dinner, he read the survival books Daniele had recommended.

He had to admit: reading calmed his racing, panicked mind. And the words he read gave him confidence about what he would soon face.

The knowledge bolstered his hope that he could actually survive, that he would be reunited with his family. He realized then what a truly powerful thing hope was.

He slept deeply that night. Either because he was weary to his bones or because he had a purpose now. And hope. Maybe because of both.

That morning, Sam showered, forced himself to eat every scrap of breakfast, and waited for the wall panel to slide in and reveal the visiting booth. When it did, he sat on the padded stool and waited. Butterflies filled his stomach. His palms began to sweat, and they didn't stop, no matter how many times he wiped them on his pants.

Trying to look confident for her was only making Sam more nervous.

The door opened, and Adeline charged in and stopped abruptly, face confused as she studied the glass partition. Sam sensed that she had expected to be able to hug him. But the glass wall was more than that. It was a stark reminder that they were separated forever now. Because of Sam's confession, they would never touch each other again. Never share a meal. Never stand outside in the sun together.

Adeline closed her eyes, and tears gushed out, and her voice was ragged and hurt as she said the word "Dad."

Sam rose and put his hand on the glass. "I'm here…"

Sam heard his voice trailing off as his own emotions overtook him. He had mentally rehearsed all the things he wanted to say to her, but in that raw moment, it all crumbled like a sandcastle on the beach being hit by a crashing wave.

It was Adeline who composed herself first. She walked to the glass and placed her hand on the opposite side of Sam's. The tears were still coming but her voice was steadier when she spoke.

"Are they treating you well?"

"Yeah."

That seemed to steel Adeline. She wiped the tears away with one hand as the other fell away from the glass. She sat at the desk, opened a notebook, and fixed Sam with a serious look.

"They're only giving me an hour. We should use it wisely."

"Wisely for what?"

"Work."

Sam laughed. "Work on what?"

"Figuring out who actually killed Nora."

The smile faded from Sam's face. "Adeline, I've thought a lot about that."

"Good," she mumbled, drawing lines on the page, ready to take notes. "What are you thinking?"

"I'm thinking that it would be better for you to let this go."

She glanced up. Her pen was still on the notebook.

"Since I saw you last, there have been some developments. What's happening here is complicated. I think it's better if—"

"I'm not going to let this go, Dad."

"You have to, Adeline."

"I can't."

"If you don't, it will eat you up. That's what scares me the most. It scares me more than Absolom. My fear is that when I'm gone, you'll obsess over what happened. That you won't move on with your life. I don't want this to take your life too."

"Scares you enough to confess?"

Sam clenched his jaw.

"I'm not dumb, Dad. I know that I'm the only reason you would do it. Me and Ryan. How do you think that makes me feel?"

Sam exhaled. "I'm begging you, Adeline. Move on. It'll destroy you if you don't."

"No, Dad. It will give me strength."

"Maybe at first. But when you stop making progress, that fire will turn to frustration and then bitterness and then it will rot you from the inside out. You'll be a shell of who you were meant to be—all because of hate and resentment about what happened. If you don't get free from it, it will take everything from you."

"Well, good news: I don't have anything left to take. Not after they beam you to the dinosaur age. We lost Mom. Now you."

"Wrong. You have Ryan. And you have to let it go for his sake. *You* are all *he* has left. Don't desert him, not for some quest of vengeance for me."

Sam waited, hoping Adeline would see reason. When she said nothing, he pressed on. "This is my fate, Adeline. You have to accept it."

"I don't accept it. I never will."

"These are the last hours we have together. I don't want to spend them arguing with you. I want to spend them doing what I should have done more of: listening. I want you to tell me all your plans for the future."

"I don't have *plans*, Dad. I have *a plan*. One plan. Do you want to hear it?"

Sam exhaled, knowing where this was going.

"I'm going to figure out who killed Nora. I'm going to get them convicted. Then I'm going to get you back, Dad. You can either help me or desert me, but it won't change anything. I'm going to finish this, if it takes the rest of my life."

"Can we make a deal?"

Adeline squinted at him, then nodded once.

"Two years."

She cocked her head. "For what?"

"I'll tell you what I know on one condition."

"Which is?"

"Starting today, you can spend two years of your life trying to right this wrong. Not a second or a minute or an hour more."

Adeline fixed his gaze. "Sure."

"I know that look. I'm serious, Adeline. Two years. No more."

"I don't like this deal."

"It's the only one you're going to get. Because I made a deal too—a promise to your mother that I would do my very best to take care of you."

"After you go through the machine, you can't stop me from spending fifty years on this."

"True. But you'll have to live with knowing you broke the last promise you made to me." Sam stared at her. "Promise me. Like I promised her."

"Dad—"

"Two years. No more."

The silence seemed to bend time more than Absolom. Finally, Adeline breathed a single-word response. "Fine."

"Good."

"Do you know who killed Nora?"

"Only a general idea at this point."

"Who?"

"There's something you should know first, Adeline."

"Okay."

"I'm going to tell you a secret. Two, actually. They are very big secrets, things only six people in the entire world know." Sam caught himself. "Only five people now. I think these secrets are the key to figuring out who killed Nora. And to clearing my name."

Sam looked at his daughter and mentally prepared himself to tell her the secret he had harbored for so many years. Unexpectedly, he felt a strange sense of relief at knowing it was about to happen, like a long-awaited release was finally at hand, a confession to one of the two people he cared about most.

"We're frauds."

Adeline cocked her head. "Who?"

"The Absolom Six. We're frauds."

"Dad, I don't understand."

"We never meant for Absolom to be crime deterrent."

"That's your secret?"

"No. The real secret is stranger than that. The truth is, we never even intended to create a time machine at all."

FIFTEEN

Adeline stared at her father for a long moment, then opened her mouth to speak, closed it again, and finally spoke slowly, carefully.

"You're telling me that Absolom—"

"Was an accident. One we never imagined. In fact, the entire experiment, from the very beginning, is something we never thought would work in the first place. Never in a million years did we dream Absolom would work. The truth is, we're double frauds."

Adeline held her hands up. "If you didn't think it would work, why even create it?"

"Money."

"Money?"

"We needed money."

"Who?"

"All of us. Everyone in the original group: me, Elliott, Constance, Nora, and Hiro. For different reasons."

"What exactly are you telling me?"

"I'm telling you that the most celebrated scientists in the world began as nothing more than a group of desperate people who were basically trying to scam a venture capital fund."

"Back up, Dad. To the beginning."

Sam exhaled. "Did you know Elliott and I have been friends since college? We were roommates our second year and after."

"No. I thought you were friends because they lived next to us in Palo Alto."

"Just the opposite. Elliott was one of the reasons we bought the house next door—it was in pre-foreclosure, and he found out about it before it hit the market. Elliott and Claire had their first child the year after we graduated college, so you probably thought they were older since Charlie was about eight years older than you." Sam took a breath. "Anyway, the point is, we've been close for a long time. Back before Absolom, Elliott was doing research on quantum entanglement. His work was really amazing. He was studying how the Higgs interacted with gravitational waves and dilated time—"

"Dad. English, please."

"Right. Suffice it to say, Elliott was doing groundbreaking research. With a lot of potential. But he had problems at home."

"Charlie."

"That's right. I don't know how much you remember about those years, but Charlie was in and out of substance abuse programs and rehab facilities. Elliott and Claire had spent virtually every last dollar they had, and Charlie was still in terrible shape. Elliott was desperate."

Adeline nodded. "And so were you back then."

"I was."

"Because of Mom."

"That's right. Every day, I watched her get sicker. She put a brave face on, but we were facing some tough decisions too. The only treatment options left for her were complete long shots. Nothing that was covered by insurance. Nothing we could afford on my university salary."

"And the others? Hiro, Constance, and Nora?"

"We were at a conference in London, the five of us, at dinner, just commiserating about our various money problems. Just colleagues complaining about their lot in life to others going through the same thing."

Sam interlaced his fingers. "Nora's parents were aging and in poor health. Their financial advisor had swindled them. Took every last dollar they had saved their entire lives. Nora wanted to keep them in an assisted living facility, but she couldn't afford it. She had already drained her savings. They were going to be evicted, and she had no idea what she was going to do."

"And Hiro?" Adeline asked.

"He was deep in debt and at risk of losing his house. But Connie had it worst. She was sick."

"Even back then?"

"She's been sick a long time. She needed money for a new therapy."

"What's her diagnosis?"

"I can't say."

"You don't know?"

"I know. I just won't betray her confidence. That secret is hers alone to tell."

"Is that why she never married and never had kids?"

"Yes," Sam said. "It is."

"What about Daniele?"

"She wasn't at the dinner where we hatched our plan. At that point, none of us had ever met her in person."

"She wasn't one of the original group?"

"No."

"So she wasn't in financial trouble?"

"No. Just the opposite, actually. She was what got us *out* of financial trouble."

"She's not a fraud, then?"

Sam laughed. "As it turns out, she *is* a fraud—or became one—but not for the same reason the rest of us are."

"What do you mean?"

"In a way, Dani started it all. She had contacted Elliott a few months before the conference."

"About what?"

"His research. Back then, Dani was a partner at a venture capital firm—San Andreas Capital. She still has the fund, but I don't think she invests much anymore since Absolom took off. The point is, at the time, she was looking for a big opportunity to invest in, a technology that could revolutionize an entire industry—or ideally, multiple industries. Her words to Elliott were: 'I think you've stumbled upon something bigger than the internet.'"

"Pretty grandiose."

"Very grandiose. And for good reason: billions of dollars in capital require big ideas to realize decent returns. Dani thought she had found one. She had read some of Elliott's published research and wanted to know if it could be applied to a new technology that San Andreas was interested in."

"Which was?"

"The other secret the six—now five—of us have kept from the world all this time." Sam took a deep breath. "As I said before, Absolom's original intention had nothing to do with time travel. Or prisons. Or reducing crime."

"What was it?"

"Shipping."

Adeline squinted at him. "Shipping?"

"Parcel shipping. Think about it—shipping is at the heart of the entire global economy. E-commerce. Healthcare. Construction. You name it. At its core, the internet changed one thing: the speed at which information could *easily and instantly* be transmitted anywhere. Look how profound the effect has been. With Absolom, Dani wanted to do for physical matter what the internet had done for data. She wanted to invent a machine that would take any item and instantly transport it anywhere in the world."

Adeline sat back in her chair. "Wow. That's incredible."

"It was. Truly incredible. And something none of us—the original five scientists at dinner that night—thought was possible. In fact, it's still not. But the original business plan, which cited research by Elliott, Constance, Nora, Hiro, and myself, made it seem inevitable. That original business plan for Absolom Sciences—which has since been deleted, purged, and shredded—was to revolutionize shipping. And to make an unimaginable fortune for San Andreas Capital."

"So what happened?"

"Elliott set up a meeting with Dani. I admit, I felt guilty about it, but he did most of the talking. He told her we were somewhat skeptical that Absolom transportation could become a reality, but the five of us were willing to work on it full-time—assuming we were paid well. We insisted that since we were giving up cushy salaried jobs—and for some of us, tenured teaching positions—we needed massive signing bonuses, generous pay packages, and stock. Some of the stock would vest at signing and some over time. Dani also agreed to let the science founders sell stock at every funding round—and with board permission, in between rounds, assuming the shares had vested."

"I'm assuming that solved your money problems."

"It did. For all of us."

"And then what happened?"

"And then," Sam said slowly, "the strangest thing in the world happened. We all went to work at the newly formed Absolom Sciences, we built the machine that none of us thought would work, we hired some of the brightest minds, and we sort of assumed the ruse would soon run its course. The crazy part is that along the way, we made breakthroughs we never imagined.

Bringing that many geniuses together has a way of making the impossible a reality."

Sam stared at his daughter. "I'll tell you, some days back then, it was like magic—we'd be at lunch talking about big ideas in physics and how they might impact our work and a week later, we were putting them into practice in the lab. And one day, we made a discovery that changed everything. It was a discovery about time."

Sam held his hands out. "Time and gravity are linked. For example, if the gravity pulling against my right hand was twice as strong as the gravity acting upon my left, do you know what would happen?"

"Your right hand would be pulled to the ground."

"That's technically true, but assume I can exert a counterforce sufficient to keep my hand where it is. Think about it in the context of time."

Adeline shrugged.

"Strong gravity slows time," Sam explained. "In fact, for my right hand, time would pass at half the rate of my left. If you had a time-lapse camera and watched these hands for years, you would see my left begin to wrinkle and discolor while my right barely aged. That is gravity's effect on time. But our breakthrough was about the third piece of the puzzle: energy."

Sam let his hands drop. "Did you know that according to general relativity, any form of energy is a source of gravity?"

"Of course I didn't know that, Dad."

Sam laughed. "Relativity proved that gravity and energy are essentially manifestations of the same thing. In particular, both distort the curvature of space-time. Our breakthrough is that we could use increasingly large amounts of energy to modify gravity and distort space-time, essentially causing a specific object to be displaced in space and time."

"You're losing me, Dad."

"The point is that we, much to our surprise, were indeed able to create a machine that could transport items from one location to another, just as Dani had theorized."

"So Absolom did work?"

"Yes and no."

"What does that mean?"

"It means that the payloads Absolom transported did arrive at their destination—we used quantum entanglement as a form of tracking. The problem was that the packages weren't actually there, despite the quantum tracking confirmation."

"They were in the past," Adeline said.

"That's right—that was our second discovery about time. If we used energy and gravity to displace an object in space, it was also displaced in time. It was sent into the past. But the worst part was the final realization: that the act of transporting something with Absolom essentially branched our universe—it created an alternate timeline where the payload was deposited. This is consistent with the many-worlds interpretation of quantum mechanics, which is the idea that we are constantly creating copies of our universe, even as we speak."

Sam laughed. "Frankly, I thought we were finished. We'd spent billions to build a machine that was no use for anything I could imagine—I mean, what good is sending items to the past in an alternate universe?"

Sam paused. "But Dani saw what none of the rest of us could: she saw the potential to use Absolom for prisons, to exile the worst of humanity and make the world a better place. That day, she destroyed the original business plan, and all documents related to shipping. Everyone at the company was under an NDA, and it was a very secretive place to work. Actually, very few even knew what we were working on in the first place—at least, what it was supposed to be used for. I think half the staff probably thought it was a new form of energy generation, a replacement to nuclear power. Some thought it was a new weapon."

"So Dani sold it to the world?"

"She did. It all happened so fast. Absolom Sciences transformed from a secretive start-up to this purpose-built city in the desert that changed the world."

Sam stared at his hands. "And along the way, we lost your mother anyway. In a strange twist of fate, we had accomplished the very thing none of us believed in—using Absolom to better the world and make a fortune—and all of us from the original five had lost the reason we were doing it. For me, your mother. For Elliott, his son. For Constance, her health. For Nora, her parents—they never really recovered from their financial advisor and friend's betrayal. Nora moved them to the nicest facility in the area, but their health declined. She thought it was maybe them feeling like they had lost the last bit of control and independence they had in the world. Losing your life savings has a way of doing that to you."

"And Hiro?"

"He's still fighting his demon. And he's always in financial trouble."

"One thing I don't get, Dad. How is all that related to Nora's death?"

"Because I think it's all happening again."

"What's happening again?"

"The night Nora was killed, Elliott gathered us in the lab and showed us a new prototype he'd been working on, Absolom Two. He'd made another breakthrough."

"What kind of breakthrough?"

"I can't tell you."

Adeline squinted at her father. "Why?"

"You're smart enough to know why."

"Because you think if I knew, I'd be in danger."

"Exactly."

"You think that's why someone killed Nora."

"I think that's half the reason she was killed. That night in the lab, after Elliott showed us his experiment, Nora insisted he destroy the machine. She felt it was too big of a risk."

"What did everyone else say?" Adeline asked.

"I agreed with Nora. Hiro had been working with Elliott on the Absolom Two. He was for it. Constance agreed with Nora and me. She was against it."

"And Daniele?"

"Dani was as insistent as Nora. Except she wanted the opposite. She wanted to continue Elliott's work, and to finish it, regardless of the risks."

SIXTEEN

That night, when Adeline returned to Daniele's home, the older woman was sitting at the kitchen island waiting for her.

"How was the visit?"

"Informative."

Daniele cocked her head. "Do you know the biggest mistake people make?"

"Asking rhetorical questions?"

Daniele smiled. "Making up their minds before they have all the facts. I hope you won't make that mistake, Adeline."

In the padded cell, Sam ate, exercised, slept, and read. Perhaps it was the absence of the sun or the brutal repetition of his life, but time seemed to slow down.

In that strange room out of time, visitors came daily, and they made confessions of their own, stories they knew they would never get another chance to tell.

Hiro confided in Sam that his father had been an alcoholic, and for that reason he had never taken a single drink in his life. He knew he had an addictive personality, and that it would ruin him sooner or later, and that alcohol would only hasten his fate.

Constance confessed that she had spent the years after

college as a nomad, crashing on couches after raves and parties and hiking through Europe and generally living a hedonistic lifestyle that brought her immense ecstasy at the time but that she now deeply regretted.

One line of hers stuck in Sam's mind long after she left: "I would do a lot of things differently... if that sort of thing were possible."

Elliott apologized for his previous outburst, for the rage he had shown. He begged Sam to reconsider, to come to his senses. And then he cried for the coming loss of his friend.

Adeline and Ryan came in the mornings and the afternoons, and in the small room with the glass divider, the three of them clung to the last fleeting shreds of time they had left together.

They cried. They laughed. They talked. And they played games they could through the glass.

Daniele's visits were a crash course in survival. She was constantly drilling Sam on the books she had found and planning for contingencies. The closer Sam's departure date got, the more nervous he became. He felt like a man who was inching toward the gallows, the dread of his fate growing as his remaining time dwindled.

Finally, that day arrived.

Sam wasn't sure what to expect. The protocol for an Absolom departure wasn't public knowledge.

Sam willed himself to sleep that night, but he couldn't. He tossed and turned and stared at the ceiling, his mind clinging to every waking second in this world where his children existed. He second-guessed himself. He blamed himself. And the world.

The wall opened with a pop, and Sam sat up and found a breakfast tray waiting in the alcove. He wasn't hungry. But he knew he couldn't afford to lose more weight.

He wolfed the meal down and stared at the place in the

padded wall where the outer door was, expecting it to open and for the guards to come for him.

But the door didn't open. It blurred. Everything was blurring. Moving slowly. His limbs felt heavy, mind groggy.

As darkness closed in, his last thought was, *that was a smart way to do it.*

When he woke, Sam was lying on the cold metal floor of the Absolom chamber. He could tell they had washed his body and his hair because there was absolutely no smell anymore—gone was the slightly minty fragrance of the shampoo he had used in the cell. That was a kindness, Sam thought. Less scent for predators to track. He wondered how long that might extend his life. Hours? Days?

They had changed him too—into warm clothes, with several layers. Another kindness. If it was indeed warm where he arrived—as Daniele thought it would be—he could always remove layers and use them for other things (a blanket, part of a shelter, or even tinder for a fire).

Sam lifted his head from the floor. Through the glass door of the Absolom machine, he saw a viewing box directly across from him. It was slightly elevated from the room's floor, with a wide glass window that revealed two rows of seats. Adeline, Ryan, and Daniele sat in the front row, staring at him, eyes bloodshot and full of tears. As Sam watched, Adeline stood and ran to the glass and slammed the side of her fist into it, pounding as her mouth moved.

But the sound didn't reach Sam.

Daniele rose, placed her hands on Adeline's shoulders, and guided her back to the seat.

In the row behind them, Elliott, Constance, and Hiro sat watching.

Sam stood—because he wanted to look brave for Adeline and Ryan. He didn't want the last thing they saw to be him lying down, looking confused and scared. He tried to smile, but his lips were shaking too much.

He glanced around at the inside of the machine he had helped build, at the smooth white walls and ceiling and floor. Of all the surprises life had dealt him, this was the biggest: to lose his life to his creation, which had made the world a safer place.

He swallowed, and on the second try, he was able to form that smile.

The last thing he saw was Adeline reaching an arm around her brother.

The machine vibrated. A hum rose all around him, and the world snapped out of existence.

When Sam Anderson opened his eyes, he was in the past.

PART II

A MYSTERY OF PAST, PRESENT, AND FUTURE

SEVENTEEN

In the days before his Absolom departure, Sam had imagined what arriving in the Late Triassic epoch would be like.

He had expected to see a vast desert. Perhaps dinosaurs. Or volcanoes erupting. Possibly earthquakes shaking the ground.

When he arrived, he saw none of those things.

Only darkness.

Rain splattered him and pounded in the night like a million horses galloping around him.

And he was falling, no ground under his feet.

He reached out, panicking, head spinning, looking for any sign—

He hit the water hard, his mouth open, and it filled with a salty mix that made him gag as he sank into the blackness.

He writhed, waving his arms, kicking his legs. When his face reached the surface, he coughed and hacked just before a wave crashed into him and rolled him over, forcing the burning water down his throat again.

Sam fought, and the waves fought back, slamming into him, relentless, never tiring. He felt like he was at war with the sea, and he knew the sea would win and that he would be buried here.

The rain fell in sheets, and the waves came like a battering ram until Sam simply stopped fighting. He was too tired. He rolled onto his back and left his mouth open to collect rainwater. His body flowed with the waves, not struggling against them.

He realized then that the thick departure outfit served as a life preserver as well. It was probably saving his life.

The moon was a sliver, but even in that small crescent, it was brighter than Sam had ever seen. It seemed a bit larger too. That made sense. The moon was closer to the Earth back then.

In the rocking of the waves and pitter-patter of the storm, Sam realized the big mistake he had made in thinking that he would arrive on land. In the Late Triassic, Pangea contained all of Earth's landmass—and the supercontinent only covered a quarter of Earth's surface. There were no ice caps, which meant the rest of the planet was covered in water. The odds of him arriving on solid land had always been one in four.

Had Daniele known? Surely she had. She would have realized it.

Why hadn't she told him?

The obvious answer was that there was not much he could do about it. It was simply bad luck. For all Sam knew, he was a thousand miles from Pangea, from the coast and salvation.

In a way, it was a fitting end. This was what Absolom was—leaving a person adrift, in a sea of time, with no hope of spotting land and no future, only the endless expanse of time and open sea around them.

As he stared at the unfamiliar stars in the sky, blinking the rain out of his eyes, he wondered if dawn would bring the sight of land. He hoped so. If not, he was finished out here. Hunger, dehydration, or a predator would claim him soon, and he would belong to the sea forever.

EIGHTEEN

The day Adeline's father was exiled via Absolom, she dressed in black and promised herself she wouldn't cry. Not in front of the others in that viewing box. One of those people, sitting right beside her, was Nora's killer. That person was responsible for ripping her father out of her life.

But she couldn't. As she sat there watching her father wake up and struggle to stand, her world was shattered. After her mother's death, her father had been her anchor in the world. Now he was being torn away, and she had never felt more adrift. Or angry.

She stood and ran to the glass and pounded on it and lost control.

After her father's departure, Adeline went home to Daniele's and locked herself in her room and buried her head in a pillow and thought the darkest thoughts of her life. The worst among them was that if she killed Constance, Hiro, Elliott, and Daniele, she would have revenge for her father. The real killer would be dead. But three innocent people would also die. Well, assuming one or more of them weren't in it together.

She probably would have kept spiraling if there hadn't been a knock at the door.

She barely lifted her head enough to shout, "Go away!"

The knocking stopped. Ryan's soft voice cracked as he called through the door, "Addy. It's me."

She pushed up and let him in, and he wrapped his arms around her. She squeezed him and kicked the door shut.

He looked up through tear-filled eyes. "I want to go home."

"We can't."

"You can adopt me—"

"It's not that." Adeline dropped her voice and moved away from the door. "We have to stay here."

"Why?"

"We're going to get Dad back."

"What? How? I thought that was impossible."

"It is. Today. But maybe not someday."

"What are you talking about?"

"Daniele knows more about what's going on than she's saying."

"You think..."

"I think she's a big part of whatever is going on."

"Okay, fine, but why can't you figure it out from our house?"

"We need to stay here so I can watch her and find out what she knows."

Ryan closed his eyes and rubbed his eyelids. "Can you at least adopt me? I don't want her to be my only parent."

"She is *not* your parent. And never will be."

"So you will?"

"I don't think the court would approve it."

"Why? You're old enough, aren't you?"

"Technically, yes. But let's face it: I was just accused of murder. Until our dad confessed to that murder. A court is not going to love that home setting. Plus, Dad wrote a letter endorsing Daniele's adoption application."

Ryan shook his head and stared out the window. A hopeless,

blank expression settled over his face. His eyes were almost glassy, as if the fight had just gone out of him.

A strange thing happened to Adeline then. In her younger brother, she saw a mirror of the despair she felt. There was no one to pull her out of the abyss. But she could help Ryan. And that filled her with purpose.

"Look at me."

Ryan cut his eyes to her.

"One day—I don't know when—it could be a month from now. Or a year. Or more. But one day, I'm going to come to you and say, 'It's over and we're going home and Dad is waiting there for us.'"

Ryan blinked and inhaled a deep breath.

Adeline stared at him. "Do you believe me?"

"Yes."

"I don't know exactly how it's going to work out. But I know it will. I also know that it's going to be tough for a while. We'll face it together. Me and you. Because we're the only ones we can trust. We're all we have left, Ryan."

Adeline spent the afternoon answering emails and messages from friends. There was an outpouring from people who had seen the media coverage of her father's sentence—and still believed he was innocent.

She found some comfort in that. People who truly knew you didn't believe what they read online—or saw in the news.

Dinner was a somber affair. As soon as Ryan's plate was clean, he asked to be excused, and Daniele said, "Yes, but homework first, then a max of two hours of video games."

The eleven-year-old boy nodded and trudged upstairs.

Adeline set her fork down. "I think he should be allowed to play video games as long as he wants. He just lost his father. He needs distraction."

"He needs a firm hand in his life."

"You're a parenting expert now?"

Daniele ignored the taunt. "His two-hour deadline isn't the one that should concern you."

"Which deadline should concern me?"

"Two years."

"He told you."

"He did. Your father was adamant that you spend no more than two years of your life on getting him back. He didn't want this tragedy to consume you too."

"I'm finished. Can I be excused?"

"We're not finished."

"What do you want from me?"

Daniele leaned forward. "I want the same thing you do."

"Which is?"

"I told you before. We're going to get him back. To do that, you're going to have to start cooperating with me. You're going to have to trust me."

Adeline clenched her jaw. "That night Nora was murdered, at the lab, you wanted to continue building Absolom Two, didn't you?"

"I did."

"So did Elliott."

"That's right."

"And Dad and Nora opposed it. Now they're both gone. One dead. One... may have already died two hundred million years ago, and there's nothing we can do."

"First off, there is something we can do. Second, I backed Absolom Two because I had to."

"Why?"

"Because it's futile to fight the future."

Those words gave Adeline pause. "What do you mean by that?"

"You'll see. In time. For now, we need to talk about how we get your father back."

"I'm all ears."

"When are you going back to college?"

"I'm not. I already emailed my advisor and told her I couldn't make up the classes I've missed. Or take final exams. They expect me in the fall, but I'm not going."

Daniele nodded.

"Are you going to talk me out of it?"

"No. You being here will make our work easier."

That surprised Adeline.

"What work?"

"There are places you can go that I can't. Questions you can ask that I can't. And now is the time."

"Time to do what?"

"First, I'm going to get you an internship at Absolom Sciences. But it's the other part of the plan that's more important now."

When Daniele had detailed what she wanted Adeline to do, the younger woman sat there, stunned. It was brilliant. And it might work.

"One last thing," Daniele said.

Adeline raised an eyebrow.

"Your father trusted me. I'm asking you to trust me. If you don't, our chances of getting him back are zero. I know how lonely you feel right now. How betrayed you feel, like the world isn't fair. You feel helpless and angry and determined all at the same time. If you give me time, I'll show you a way to set all this right."

* * *

Upstairs, in her bedroom, Adeline considered what Daniele had said. She wanted to trust the woman. She needed someone to trust, to talk with, to be there in case she was caught doing what she was about to do.

But deep down, Adeline sensed that there was something off about Daniele. Try as she might, Adeline couldn't put her finger on it.

She had to admit, however, that Daniele's plan was good. It might actually work.

She took out her laptop and composed an email.

Dear Constance,

I'm doing therapy to help me deal with my father's departure.

I don't know if you'd be open to it, but my therapist suggested I spend time with the people who knew him best, to talk about him and get to know the side of him I never saw. She thinks it will help.

I understand if you don't want to participate, but I know you were important to him.

- Adeline

The next morning, a response was waiting in Adeline's inbox.

My dear girl, of course. Anything you need is yours.
Where and when?

~ Connie

Adeline typed out a quick response:

Thank you!

Today if possible. If not, I can make any time work.

I really want to get out of Daniele's house. I can't go back to mine for... reasons.

Can we meet at your place?

Adeline chewed a nail as she hit send.

At breakfast, she told Daniele the news.

"Good."

"What if she doesn't want to meet at her place?" Adeline asked.

"She will. Trust me."

Daniele led Adeline to the basement, into a room with a hard rubber floor and a stack of free weights gathering dust in the corner. It had been designed as a home gym, but it seemed Daniele had never filled it with equipment. Or used it much.

It was, however, full of boxes. Daniele opened the closest one and drew out several bubble-wrapped items: picture frames, soap dishes, a small decorative plate, and a painted porcelain figurine of Adeline's father. Seeing the physical likeness of him sent a sharp stab of sadness through Adeline, as if she had been walking around the basement in the dark and stepped on a nail with her bare feet.

Daniele drew a laptop out of a carrying case, booted it, and opened the surveillance software. One by one, she activated the frames and figurine and soap dishes and tested them to make sure the audio and video came through clearly.

"When did you order all this?" Adeline asked.

"The day he told me he was going to confess."

Adeline picked up the items and studied them, looking for the tiny cameras and microphones. It took her a while to find them, but she did. She wondered if Constance would realize she had made the swap.

"So we're really doing this?" Adeline said, still studying the surveillance items.

"We really are. The frames match the ones in Connie's house exactly, but you'll have to switch the pictures out. You'll have to do it quickly."

Adeline swallowed. "Okay."

"If you think about it too much, it'll only make you nervous. Put it out of your mind until the time comes."

Adeline nodded, but she didn't feel any less nervous. She wasn't a secret agent. She wondered if she could really do this.

Daniele gripped her shoulders. "Relax. You *can* do this. And if there isn't an opportunity to deploy the devices this time, we'll figure out another way."

"You said the timing was important."

"It is. But so is your safety."

"If she catches me—if she is the killer—"

"I'll be listening," Daniele said. "If something happens, I'll come. I promise you."

She reached into the box and unwrapped a handheld electroshock weapon.

"And just in case, I want you to carry this."

Adeline took the weapon, held it up, and depressed the button on the handle. An electric arc crackled between the two electrodes, causing Adeline to jump.

"This is crazy."

"It is. But we have no choice."

Daniele took the weapon and placed it in a backpack. "We can't be too careful. We can't take anything for granted,

Adeline. What we're working on here is extremely complex. It's a mystery of past, present, and future. And you and I are going to solve it. No matter what it takes."

NINETEEN

Through the night, the storm raged, and Sam floated on the sea and waited, hoping morning would bring salvation.

On his back, he rode the waves, staring at the moon, his mind wandering through the past.

The first memory that the night and the sea dredged up was from college. In it, he was standing in his dorm room shaking his head.

"It's not mine," Sam said.

Their sophomore year, he and Elliott lived with two suitemates on a substance-free hall. The floor's resident advisor was nosy, annoying, and fanatical about the rules. He never missed an opportunity to exercise his authority, and at that moment he was holding up a half-gallon of Jack Daniels whiskey he had found under Sam's bed.

"I don't make the rules, Anderson. But I have to enforce them."

Sam wondered how many times he had recited that line.

The door opened, and Elliott strode in and glanced between Sam and the bottle the RA was holding in the air.

Sam opened his mouth to speak, but Elliott beat him to it. "Give it back."

He reached for the bottle, but the RA dodged him, taking a step toward the door. "It's yours?"

"Of course it's mine."

The RA pointed at Sam. "I found it under his bed."

"Of course you did."

The RA squinted, confused.

"I figured hiding it under the honor roll kid's bed would be safer than mine. Congrats. You found it. Now what do you want?"

"I'm turning it in, and I'm writing *both of you* up."

And he had. When Sam asked Elliott why he had falsely confessed, his friend smiled. "It was the obvious solution. My grandfather went broke a few years ago, but for decades before that, he gave millions to this school. I figure those deposits will square this. Mom and Dad will come down, and we'll meet with the school, and it will be tense, but it'll be fine. I'll catch hell at home and probably have to go to some alcohol abuse awareness class—and we will probably have to change dorms, but it will all be fine. But you wouldn't be, Sam. Not by yourself. You'd lose your scholarship at the very least."

It was probably the kindest, most self-sacrificing thing anyone had ever done for him.

"We're not just friends," Elliott had said. "We're brothers."

It was a good thing he had. A week later, after finals, Sam was standing in the kitchen at a house party, holding a red cup full of warm beer, staring out past the bar into the family room at a girl from his calculus class. She wore a striped sweater, a shy smile, and shoulder-length blonde hair. Her name was Sarah Reynolds, and that night Sam walked over to her and said, "Hi," and after that, and until her death, she was the center of his life.

A tall wave flowed over Sam, sloshing saltwater into his mouth. He flailed and coughed and fought with his arms and legs as another wave slammed into him.

When he finally caught his breath, the rain had slowed. He was thankful for that. But a thought occurred to him—the rain was his only source of fresh water. If it stopped, he'd die of thirst before he starved to death. That was all from Daniele's crash course in survival: generally, a person could survive for three minutes without oxygen, three days without water, and three weeks without food. Every person's body was different, but those were a good rough estimate.

His survival books had made it clear that he couldn't survive on seawater alone. The salt was the problem. To clear excess salt from the body, the body combines the salt with water and excretes it as urine. The trouble was that saltwater was too salty. It didn't contain enough water for the body to clear the salt. So, with each gulp of seawater, the body would use more of its store of water to clear the salt it took in. As Sam drank more seawater, he would become more dehydrated. Eventually, without fresh water to replenish what his body had lost clearing the salt, his kidneys and other organs would fail completely.

As such, when the rain stopped, he kept his mouth shut and hoped he saw land soon.

Floating on the sea, it was easy for Sam to imagine giving up. Simply taking off the outfit and letting the ocean take him. That was easier than fighting. But he had something to fight for. A reason to survive.

He imagined himself stepping out of the Absolom machine, holding his arms wide, reaching out and bracing himself as Adeline and Ryan ran to him. That mental image—of reuniting with his children—was his anchor in this harsh wilderness. They were his hull against the waves. He hung on for them, for a future that might not happen, but one he could never give up on.

Slowly, the night sky faded, and the stars dissolved as the sun rose.

In the light of day, Sam rolled off his back and worked his arms in the water and spun and gazed in every direction.

But all he saw was water and waves. And not a single sign of Pangea's coast.

TWENTY

That afternoon, Adeline visited Constance.

As she walked up the brick-paved path to the red front door, her heart hammered in her chest. Her palms oozed sweat. Adeline hadn't even done anything wrong, but just knowing she was going to made her nervous.

She wasn't cut out for this. What was she thinking? As she knocked on the door, holding the backpack, she considered calling the whole thing off—just sitting with Constance and talking and never deploying the listening devices.

But she couldn't do that. Her father was counting on her.

Constance's small home was styled like an English cottage. Inside, it was cozy, filled with art and personal pictures and large, plush furniture. Every wall was painted a warm color. The ceilings were all detailed, with painted shiplap and distressed brick.

Constance led her to a living room at the back of the home, where a natural gas fire burned in the fireplace and the accordion door was open to the patio outside. A cool breeze blew through. Adeline found it refreshing, a nice complement to the fire.

On the horizon, a thunderstorm was gathering, just starting to lay rain on the vast solar field known as the sea of glass. It moved toward the city as they began to talk.

Constance wore a teal wrap around her body and a knit hat. In her hands was a cup of chamomile tea, and on the pushcart nearby was a pot and cup for Adeline, which she had declined.

An older woman with gray hair pulled back into a bun and wearing a light blue uniform stopped at the edge of the living room.

"Do you need anything, ma'am?"

"No thank you, Gretta."

When her footsteps had receded, Constance smiled at Adeline. "First, I want to tell you something about your father that I've never told anyone."

Adeline swallowed as she nodded, suddenly nervous again.

"People who have never been sick think that the worst thing about losing your health is what it takes from you. Not being able to do what you want. To live the life you desire—to have the enjoyment taken from you. That's not the worst of it. The worst part is seeing how the people around you change. Some leave you behind. The best lean in. And they treat you the same. They know you've changed, but they see the old you, and that's what they remind you of. They treat you like the person you were before. They are your tether to your true self."

Constance took a sip of tea. "The thing about your father is that as I got sicker, he never changed. He never treated me any differently. Not like I was sick. Or fragile. He treated me like a person—like the person he had known, a person who was simply trapped in a sick body. He was like the Rock of Gibraltar to me. He was my link to my old life."

A strong wind gusted through the living room, whipping against the fire, making it hiss like a provoked snake in the desert.

Constance set the teacup down. "I think he learned that from your mother, from seeing what she went through. Watching someone you love lose their health has an effect on a person. It teaches you lessons no human should ever have to learn. And could never forget."

Adeline stood on weak legs, fighting tears she knew were coming. "I need to use the restroom."

She didn't wait for Constance to respond. She staggered out of the cozy sitting room, down the hall, and slipped into the powder room. She placed her hands on the counter of the vanity and let the tears come.

She felt like she was in a sea in the middle of a storm, adrift in the dark, with no hope of sighting shore.

She felt lost.

Alone.

Confused.

She stared at herself in the mirror, at her bloodshot eyes and trembling lips. And she wondered if she was strong enough to do what she knew she had to.

TWENTY-ONE

On the open sea, Sam swam with the current. It was his only option. In a world where your strength is insignificant against the forces around you, swimming against the current hurts only one person: you.

He swam with the wind at his back, cresting the waves and flowing into the troughs, up and down, over and over again.

When he was too tired to swim, he rolled onto his back and caught his breath.

By the time the sun was midway in the sky—at noon—he was exhausted. He would have given a year of his life for a drink of cold water.

Around him was only hot water, filled with salt, which would only drag him closer to death with every gulp, no matter how good it made him feel.

He floated.

And he swam.

He repeated the exercise, chasing the sun, never seeing land.

On one of his breaks, staring up at the burning star that he felt charring his face, a memory gripped him, of the last time his face had been so red.

He sat in a conference room. Hiro was across from him. Constance beside him. Nora diagonal across the way. Elliott stood at the head of the table, a projector shining on half his face and onto the wall, his slide deck progressing as he spoke.

Daniele sat at the other end of the table, and when Elliott's presentation was done, she sat back in her chair and listened as a partner at her venture capital firm peppered the scientists with questions. He wanted to hear from all the scientists—he wanted to know that they were committed to this new venture.

One by one, they declared their confidence in the proposed technology that would be called Absolom. When it came to Sam, he glanced at Elliott. In that moment, he saw himself in his old friend, the version of himself that had been busted in that dorm room. He saw a friend who needed help—help to save his son. And Sam did what Elliott had done for him: he lied.

"Yes. There's a lot of work to do. But what we're talking about here is possible. With the right funding." He stared at Elliott. "And enough time."

Because that's what all of them needed: time and money to save their families and themselves.

Sam had felt his face turn red. He wondered if it was a giveaway—if the venture capitalists in the room knew it was a sham, if they had a sixth sense about lying scientists desperate for funding.

They didn't seem to.

The meeting ended soon after, and when the others had filed out of the room, Sam lingered behind. Daniele had sat there, at the head of the table, as if she were waiting for him.

His voice was thick and scratchy when he spoke. "Thank you for making time for us."

"It was time well spent."

Sam swallowed. "I just wanted to say..." His mind grasped for the right words—the words that would make him feel better, more like the person he knew he was. Less like what he was becoming.

"I wanted to say that while this..."—he motioned to the

projector mounted on the ceiling—"idea is promising, it's still risky."

"I'm aware of that."

"It may not work."

"It will. In time."

"I just wanted you to be aware of the risk."

"Managing risk is our business, Dr. Anderson. We're not afraid to be far from the shore without a paddle."

Under the Triassic sun, Sam could feel his face and his hands starting to blister. His mouth felt like it was filled with sawdust.

The rule of thumb was that death would come after three days without water. Sam wondered if that accounted for the perspiration from his physical exertion and the heat. Surely that would reduce his survival time. How long did he have out here in these conditions? Another day? Less? Would tonight be his last?

One thing was certain: sunburn could be deadly too. If his skin peeled and blistered, and he began bleeding in the water, it would bring predators. He'd be like floating chum in the ocean.

He reached under the thick sweater and ripped his undershirt into strips that he draped over his face. That would provide some protection from the sun, and he could still breathe through the thin white material and see the distorted glow of the sun. Under the shroud, the waves were like a carnival ride, up and down, a rhythmic rocking that finally coaxed him to sleep.

Sam awoke to the burn of saltwater in his mouth, pushing down his throat like a snake slithering inside of him.

He coughed, but the wet strips of cloth covering his face repelled the water back into his mouth.

He ripped the shirt pieces from his face and spun and pumped his arms and legs, coughing as another wave slammed into him.

He closed his eyes and mouth and waited while the wave crested and passed.

When he had emptied his mouth and caught his breath, Sam opened his eyes and realized the sea was no longer an expanse of glass with gentle ridges. It was choppy and dimpled, the falling rain punching a pattern of holes all around him.

Rain.

He threw his head back and opened his mouth, his tongue reaching out, lapping up every drop. His arms and legs and the buoyant garments kept him out of the water as he closed his eyes again and drank from the sky.

The drops of rain collected in his mouth like grains of sand through an hourglass, slow at first, then stacking atop each other until Sam took a gulp, and in it, he tasted hope. What happened next brought even more.

He opened his eyes again and caught sight of the sun. It was low in the sky, threatening to escape beyond the horizon. At that line between light and dark, he saw salvation: a tiny glimpse of land, small and looming.

Pangea.

Waiting for him.

TWENTY-TWO

In the bathroom at Constance's home, Adeline stared at herself in the mirror until the tears stopped and she had convinced herself that she could do what she had come there to do.

Constance rose when Adeline returned.

"I didn't mean to upset you."

Adeline shook her head. "It's not you. This is why I came here. I need to work through my feelings."

They sat, and this time Constance seemed resigned to listen rather than talk. She asked Adeline a series of questions, and finally she said, "Dani tells me you're taking a semester off."

"I am."

"And interning at Absolom."

"Yes."

"I admit, when Dani emailed us, I was opposed to it."

That surprised Adeline. "Why?"

"I don't think Absolom—or college, for that matter—is where you should be right now."

"I don't understand."

"You should get away from here, Adeline. I don't know exactly what's happening, but it seems to me that someone used you to get to your father." The older woman held up a bony, spotted hand. "I hope you don't mind me saying that."

"Not at all. I agree with you."

"Staying here, in my view, is dangerous. And not just for your physical safety. You risk your mental health, which, frankly, is any person's last resource, a citadel you can rebuild from. When I envision you walking through the doors of Absolom Sciences, I can only imagine the hurt you'll feel, seeing his picture on the wall in that lobby, knowing you're walking the halls he did. The looks you'll get. It'll only remind you of him and what you've lost. That's the last thing you need right now."

"What's the alternative?"

"Get away, Adeline. Go to Europe. Or Asia. Or just take a long cruise around the world and don't look back. And don't come back until you can see a picture of your father or hear his name without crying inside—or outside. That's how you'll know you're healed."

Adeline had to admit: it was tempting. She imagined herself standing on the deck of a ship, looking out at the open sea, hearing the clink of champagne glasses behind her, waves crashing on the bow below, a warm wind blowing through her hair. But mentally, as she put herself in that place, she knew the truth, and she spoke it next.

"I don't think I could ever travel far enough to outrun the hurt I feel. But I might work my way through it."

Constance smiled—a sad, somber smile that seemed to wrap Adeline in its arms. "I know exactly how you feel."

Constance turned, and Adeline realized that Gretta was standing on the patio. She pointed to her watch. "Sorry, ma'am. It's time."

Constance thanked her and rose. "When you get to my age—when your health starts failing you—there's a lot of maintenance. If you'll excuse me."

Constance exited the room and ascended the staircase in slow, labored steps.

Adeline watched as Gretta strode off the patio, past the pool, and back to the guesthouse just beyond, which must have been where she lived or at least stayed while she was on duty.

Adeline sensed that this was her moment. It wouldn't last, but it would be the best chance she had. Now or never. Commit or give up.

She made her decision.

She grabbed her bag, drew out the first picture frame, and swapped it with its match in the living room. In the kitchen, she replaced the soap dish.

She glanced out the window at the backyard, to the guesthouse. The door was still closed.

Her heart was racing. She listened, but the house was quiet. How much time did she have?

She dashed to the foyer and set the small plate down and shoved the original in the backpack.

Now came the risky part.

She ascended the stairs, eyes wide, watching, listening, ready to retreat.

At the landing, Adeline heard a noise at the end of the hall. Beyond the closed door of the master bedroom. Constance was in the bathroom.

One of the matching picture frames sat on a console table a few feet away. Adeline pulled the surveillance frame from the backpack and slipped the picture inside it and stowed the original in the bag.

She crept across the hardwood floor to the closest door, which she expected to lead to a guest bedroom. When she opened it, Adeline stopped cold. There was no bed in the room. Only a small desk and rolling chair. The walls were covered in cork. Pinned to it were dozens of pictures. And sheets of paper with names. And dates. All in the last twenty years. There was also a massive map of Europe, America, and Asia. Some of the pictures were tacked to places on the map with a note and the date of death.

It was like something out of the movies. A serial killer's den. A shrine to deaths across the globe.

Adeline wanted to run. Every fiber of her being told her to. But she stepped deeper inside the room and gently closed the door. There was too much information here for her to write down. Or memorize. She took out her phone and clicked the video option and began holding it up to everything she saw. She walked around the room, taking it all in.

Beyond the door, she heard footsteps on the landing.

Adeline was near the end of the room. The steps drew closer. Her hand shook.

She reached her other hand up to steady the phone, her eyes on the door, expecting the knob to turn. The electroshock weapon was in the bag. Overpowering Constance wasn't the problem. But what if Constance had help here in the house? What if the caretaker, Gretta, was more than that? What if she was an accomplice?

Outside the bedroom, Adeline heard footsteps on the stairs, labored, slow steps going down.

Constance.

Carefully, Adeline opened the door and peered out. The stairway was clear.

She heard footfalls on the rug in the foyer.

Now or never.

She raced across the upper landing on her tiptoes, hoping the sound didn't echo below. In the master bedroom, she set down one of the frames and picked up the original, fingers fumbling for the tabs that held the glass and picture in place.

"Adeline?" Constance called from below.

Adeline froze. She focused on the frame, but her fingers wouldn't work. It was as if they had turned to soft rubber.

"Adeline?" Constance called again from downstairs.

She was caught.

Adeline made for the door but stopped. One last chance.

In the master bathroom, she replaced the soap dish and pulled the medicine cabinet open. Bottles of prescription medications spread out in rows, filling each shelf.

"Adeline?" Constance's voice was closer now. Was she on the stairs?

Adeline drew her phone out, snapped a picture, and dashed out of the room, out into the hallway.

Constance arrived on the landing a second after, panting, gripping the rail, head down. She looked up and saw Adeline.

"What are you doing here?"

The question struck fear into Adeline. She was caught.

It was over.

Adeline did the only thing she could. She lied. And she was surprised at how easily it came.

"I thought you might need help. You were gone so long."

Constance squinted at her.

"And then I needed to use the bathroom."

"You went earlier."

"I didn't... I only cried. I had to actually go this time."

Constance studied Adeline's face for a long moment. Her gaze shifted to the strap across her shoulder that led to the backpack filled with the pictures and items Adeline had just stolen from Constance's home. It was as if the older woman could see right through the bag—and Adeline herself. She had never felt so exposed in all her life. How had she ever thought she could do this? That she could walk into Constance's home and ever get away with it?

Had Daniele set her up?

Constance exhaled, as if disappointed. As if she was dreading whatever she had just decided. She turned and descended the stairs. She didn't ask Adeline to follow, but the younger woman fell in behind her.

In the living room, Constance didn't sit. She stood, the fire crackling behind her, staring at Adeline as she entered the room.

"Dani said you had something you wanted to give me."

Adeline hesitated. The porcelain figurine of her father had a glass eye with a camera in it. Inside it contained the router that would transmit all the signals from the surveillance items she had placed throughout the house to a satellite. But if Constance broke the small statue open, she would instantly see what it really was. All she had to do was release it, and let it drop to the stone patio floor, and it would all be over.

"Do you have it?" Constance asked.

Adeline set down the backpack and took out the figurine and handed it to the older woman, who gripped it with both hands and studied it.

"Interesting," she murmured. Adeline had the distinct impression that she was staring at the camera in the statue's eye.

TWENTY-THREE

The sun set, and Sam swam for the shore.

He crested the waves and pumped his arms, making his way toward the small sliver of land on the horizon that was his only chance of survival.

Soon, the darkness began to swallow the coast. Using the stars above, Sam committed the location to memory. Getting off course could be deadly. This was his second night in the Triassic. It might well be his last. Swimming in the wrong direction might be the last mistake he ever made. Assuming he could even reach the shore.

With night came another storm that roiled the sea.

Sam swam on, stopping only to float on his back to rest and gather rainwater in his mouth. The rain and the buoyant outfit were his salvation on the open sea. Would they be enough to see him ashore?

Sam wasn't so sure.

He was weak. A day without food would do that. And Sam had exercised more that day than he had in a long time.

He felt as though the sea was testing him, and there was no pass or fail. Only live or die.

The crescent moon glowing above him hung silently like a proctor watching, waiting to see if he had what it took to survive here.

In his mind, he returned to that source of strength: the vision of him stepping out of Absolom, reaching out and hugging his children, of the world set right again. He didn't know how he could do it, only that the prospect of seeing them again was worth giving everything he had.

Sam rolled over and began cutting through the water as the rain pelted harder and the sky grumbled. The storm was growing stronger. He wondered if that was the pattern of this corner of the Pangea coast: late afternoon showers and night storms.

When the muscles in his arms and legs were burning, he once again flipped onto his back and rested, letting the rain gather in his mouth. He was weary to his bones. And hungry. Exhausted in a way he had never known—or even knew was possible.

He wondered if he were only swimming for himself—if he didn't have anyone to come back to—if he would have given it up.

It wasn't just seeing his family again. He needed to get back to protect them. Whoever had framed him might be watching them right now—plotting something else.

He had a promise to keep. And he would, no matter how far he had to swim. He would make it to that shore or die trying. Those were the only two possibilities for him now.

He realized then what a powerful source of strength a child in danger could be. Nothing gave a parent superpowers like knowing their child needed them and that no one else could help them.

Sam had never experienced that until now. But he had seen it.

As he floated, staring at the stars, gathering his strength to battle the sea again, a memory came of lying on a narrow child's bed, staring up at a smattering of plastic glow-in-the-dark stars that had been puttied to the ceiling. He was holding a book, *The Lion, the Witch and the Wardrobe* by C. S. Lewis.

Adeline lay beside him, her eyes drooping, her small left hand gently resting on his chest. Sleep would come soon for her, but she always fought it with the last shred of strength she had. During her childhood, Sam had likely asked her a million times, "Are you tired?"

In those years, he had only ever heard one reply: "No."

That included the instances when her eyelids were nearly closed and when she fell asleep within sixty seconds of declaring her lack of fatigue. This was one of those times.

As Sam turned the page, he glanced over at her, checking to see if Adeline had drifted off.

She saw him and instantly raised her eyelids, fighting to stay awake. He was caught. She wasn't going to let him get away that easy tonight.

He continued reading. Across the hall, Ryan was crying. Sarah exited the master bedroom, cradling him in her arms, lightly rocking, her sing-song voice starting a tune to soothe him. This was the anthem of their nights now: a reading dad, a singing, marching mother, and a crying baby.

On his hip, Sam felt a gentle vibration.

He drew the phone out and read the caller.

Elliott.

Adeline's eyes were closed again, probably for good for the night.

Sam gently peeled her hand from his chest, rose, and crept out of the room, swiping to answer the call as he closed the door.

Elliott was shouting in the background—and someone was screaming back at him.

Sam jogged down the hallway, his bare feet patting against the creaking hardwood floor.

"Elliott?"

In the living room, Sarah was sitting with Ryan in her arms, a finger pressed to the pacifier in his mouth. She looked up at him with bulging eyes that said, *I just got him to sleep! Be quiet!*

Sam couldn't make out the voice shouting back at Elliott. In the background, there was a crash.

"Elliott!" Sam called. His heart beat faster. His eyes darted back and forth, thinking.

Sarah's expression turned from annoyance to concern.

"Sam?"

Sam was about to yell into the phone when Elliott spoke, voice ragged. "Sam, I need help."

"Where are you? Are you hurt?"

"I'm at home."

The moment Elliott spoke the word *home*, Sam bolted from the living room, through the tiny foyer, and out the front door, not bothering to put his shoes on. Sarah called to him, but the thundering in Sam's ears swallowed the words.

His feet pounded the pavement of the sidewalk between his house and Elliott's.

Sam raced across the front yard, grimacing as sticks dug into his feet. But he never slowed. He heard the screams through the closed front door.

He turned the handle just as another crash came, glass hitting the wall, shattering, the shards spraying the backside of the door. Sam stopped and waited for the barrage to pass, then stepped out, first surveying the floor for glass. It was one thing to charge across an unkempt lawn. Walking across broken glass was another. It seemed the shards weren't the only dangerous thing in the room.

At the edge of the living room, under a cased opening that led to the kitchen, Elliott's only son, Charlie, was screaming at his parents, the words slurred, indecipherable to Sam. Dark black bags hung under his wild eyes. His black hair was stringy and greasy, partially covering his eyes like a predator staring through blades of tall grass.

His mother, Claire, stood in the dining room to the left, clutching a phone in her hand. "I'm calling the police."

Elliott held out a hand. "Don't. He'll resist, and they'll arrest him—"

The boy bolted then, through the kitchen, throwing the door open and slamming it into the wall.

Elliott gave chase, and Sam, eying the broken glass, stepped through the room, falling in behind his friend. When he reached the deck, Charlie had already crossed the backyard and was bounding over the wooden fence into a neighbor's yard.

Elliott bent down, placing his hands on his knees, gasping for breath. "I need you…" he whispered.

Sam wasn't sure if Elliott was addressing him or calling for strength from a higher power.

Elliott reached into his pocket, drew out a car key, and handed it to Sam. "I need you to drive. I'll get out and run him down when we find him."

Sam didn't mention his bare feet. He merely followed Elliott to the garage, got behind the wheel, and drove the streets and blocks of the neighborhood, stopping at Charlie's friends' homes as Elliott worked the phone, calling other parents to see if his son had shown up there.

As the night wore on, the stress of not finding the boy seemed to weigh on Elliott. At 3 a.m., they stopped at an all-night coffee shop and bought large cups of the steaming, caffeine-laden liquid that would see them through the night. Thankfully, Elliott had gone in, sparing Sam the awkwardness of padding through the café in his bare feet.

They sat at a red light, sipping coffee.

Elliott's eyes were glassy, staring straight ahead. "We're losing him, Sam."

"We'll keep looking—"

"No. Us. Me and Claire. I can feel Charlie slipping away. The drugs are changing him."

"He'll straighten up."

Elliott took a long pull of coffee. "I wish I could find that person who gave him that first pill. They killed him, Sam. They took his life when they did that. They threw him in the sea, and I feel like he's drowning, and I can't get to him. I'm just watching from the shore as the tide carries him out. I'm scared he's already too far gone."

Sam didn't know what to say. The light changed, and he drove into the night.

Those hours spent prowling the empty streets were like the sea Sam swam across now. Dark and scary and hopeless and, most of all, unavoidable. It was a road he had to travel—for the sake of his family.

TWENTY-FOUR

When the car dropped Adeline off at Daniele's home, she was on the verge of hyperventilating. Just inside the front door, Daniele stood waiting for her.

"She knew," Adeline said between breaths. "She practically caught me."

Daniele placed her hands on Adeline's shoulders. "Breathe. You're probably imagining it."

Adeline closed her eyes and shook her head. "I'm not. She. Caught me."

"Did you see—"

Adeline held her phone up. "I got it. She's the killer. She has a whole bedroom set up like a murder board. She's tracking people. Dates. Pictures. Crazy stuff."

Daniele took the phone and moved to the study off the foyer that she used as a private office. She plugged Adeline's phone into her laptop, downloaded the photos and video, and then deleted them from the phone.

"Hey, I wanted to keep those."

"You can't. Not on your phone."

"Why?"

"You know why."

Adeline realized why: because if Constance was the killer, her next move would be to try to find out what Adeline had discovered. She might hire someone to hack her phone remotely.

"What happens now?"

"They're coming over. At six p.m."

"Who? Constance?"

"Yes. And Hiro and Elliott. We're going to meet in the basement."

"About?"

"I can't tell you."

"Absolom Two."

Daniele exhaled. "No comment. The point is, this is an opportunity for us."

"How?"

"When the three arrive, they're going to leave their phones on the kitchen island."

"To make sure no one is listening."

"That's right."

Daniele held up a small white item. "When we're in the basement, plug this into Hiro's phone and wait for the LED to turn from red to green."

"What is it? Spyware?"

"Nothing that intrusive. It just tracks his movements."

"Should I use it on the other phones—Elliott's and Constance's?"

"No," Daniele said quickly. "Constance, as you said, might be suspicious now. And I know Elliott is."

"How do you know?"

"He's hired a private investigator to follow me."

"Are you in danger? Are we?"

"Maybe," Daniele said quietly. "I've hired a private security firm to watch the house."

★ ★ ★

In her bedroom upstairs, Adeline watched from the window as Elliott, Constance, and Hiro arrived.

One question nagged at her: why would Elliott hire someone to watch Daniele? There was only one good answer: he thought she had killed Nora. If that was the case, it meant he hadn't killed Nora.

Could it be true?

If it was, it would mean Constance was innocent. Which was hard for Adeline to believe given what she had just seen at her home.

But something was still bothering Adeline: how fragile Constance was. And how kind. On the outside, she seemed like anything but a killer. That mystery would have to wait.

She had work to do.

Adeline exited her bedroom onto the landing and listened. It was quiet downstairs.

She crept down the hardwood steps, into the stair hall. In the foyer, she eyed the closed door that led to the basement.

Basement homes were rare in this part of Nevada. They were hard to dig because of the caliche, a sedimentary rock-like material that was prevalent in the area. But all it took to break the rock was money, and Daniele Danneros had that kind of money. And thus, a full basement.

Adeline wondered what was being said down there.

She walked away from the basement door, down the hall to the kitchen, where the four phones sat on the island. She tapped each one to awaken the lock-screen image, and quickly found Hiro's (it had a picture of his niece and nephew hugging at Disneyland).

Adeline plugged the small device into the port at the bottom of the phone and watched the stair hall for any movement, occasionally glancing down at the red light.

When the light on the device turned green, she disconnected

it from Hiro's phone and crept softly through the stair hall, still careful to avoid making footfalls that would be heard in the basement.

In the foyer, she stared at the closed door to the basement.

She should go back upstairs.

But she couldn't.

Adeline padded forward on her bare feet, slowly, and held her ear to the door.

It was quiet.

She turned the door handle, pulled it open, and waited.

She couldn't hear a thing.

She stepped out onto the first stair and listened, but the voices below were too faint to hear.

Holding her breath, she descended the stairs more slowly until she reached the landing, where it switched back. She couldn't see the four Absolom scientists, but she could just make out their conversation.

Hiro was talking, his voice muffled. "Technically, it's possible, but impractical."

"Why?" Elliott asked.

"There's no way to transport that much matter back without someone knowing—the power required would give us away."

Elliott again: "But you can miniaturize it."

"Yes, but not enough."

"Then we're stuck," Elliott said. He sounded impatient now.

"I can break it into pieces," Hiro said. "That's the only real solution."

Constance spoke next, voice soft. Adeline had to lean forward to hear her.

"If the pieces are small, Sam might not even find them."

"We have to assume he will," Elliott said.

"I still wish we had told him," Constance said. "He doesn't

even know what to look for—or that he's supposed to be looking for something."

Elliott sounded frustrated. Or annoyed. "We've been over this. If they knew, we'd be shut down. He's gone. It's done."

"Yes, but the point remains," Constance said, her voice rising, quivering now. "How long will it take him to find the pieces? Months? Years? He may not last a week in the Triassic."

"There's nothing we can do about that," Hiro said.

"But that's my point," Constance said. "We have to help him find it. Because if he doesn't find it, we may as well write him off."

The silence that followed felt awkward, even to Adeline, who couldn't see their faces from the stairwell.

Daniele spoke next. She sounded closer than the others.

"Let's go back to the experiments. They're clearly the key to getting Sam back safely."

"All right," Constance said, some of the strength back in her voice. "How do we begin? Should we start digging in Death Valley to see if the items are there?"

Daniele spoke again, sounding even closer. She was moving. "We've been over this. It doesn't work that way."

"Why?" Constance asked.

Adeline wondered if her sickness somehow affected her memory.

"The order is wrong," Elliott said. "Remember? We need to plan the experiments first—because of causality."

"I have an idea," Daniele said. "About how we can send something to Sam in a way that he could find it."

She was dangerously close now.

Adeline froze as Daniele stepped into view at the bottom of the stairwell. The older woman looked up at her and stared. Slowly, she tilted her head, silently telling her *get out of here.*

Adeline's heart thundered in her chest. She wondered if the others had caught on to the signal.

Footsteps echoed on the basement's concrete floor.

Someone was coming over to Daniele.

Elliott spoke next. He was closer now. Moving. "What do you mean, Dani?"

Adeline turned on the landing and ascended the stairs, terrified that one of the wooden risers would creak, announcing her presence. But they didn't. They were well made, and she thought that just might have saved her life.

She closed the door and let out the breath she had been holding. A few seconds later, she was back in her bedroom, exhaling heavily.

From her bedroom window, Adeline watched the three scientists depart. Her door opened a moment later, and Daniele stared at her.

"That was dangerous. And foolish."

"What are you looking for in Death Valley?"

"Did you update Hiro's phone?"

"I asked you a question."

"Did you?"

"Yes," Adeline muttered. "Now tell me—"

Daniele turned and gripped the door handle and pulled it open.

Adeline rose, rushed to it, and slammed the door shut. "Hey. I asked you a question."

Daniele smiled. That surprised Adeline.

"Good for you. You need that for what's coming."

"Need what?"

"Nerve. Now give me your phone."

Adeline handed it to her.

Daniele searched for an app, tapped install, and handed the phone back to Adeline for facial recognition to authorize the update. When it had finished loading, Adeline studied the new app. It was called BuddyLoc, and it showed a single glowing dot four blocks away in Absolom City.

"That's Hiro," Adeline whispered.

"Yes."

"Why are you giving me access?"

"Guess."

"Because you might not be able to follow him. If... something happens to you."

"That's right."

"But you won't let me see the photos and video from Constance's house?"

"Not yet."

"What's buried in Death Valley?"

"The past. And the future."

TWENTY-FIVE

The storm gathered strength as Sam lost his. The rain pelted him, and he drank from it, knowing it could stop at any moment.

Each time he rolled off of his back to resume swimming, it was a little harder. He was a little weaker, his limbs heavier.

Somewhere in the night, the rain stopped, and the storm clouds rolled away. Their departure calmed the sea. The silence that followed was serene. The rocking of the waves and sheer exhaustion conspired to lull Sam to sleep, but he fought to stay awake. He had to swim while he could. His belly was full of water now, and tomorrow the sun would sap his strength and burn his skin even more, until the blisters popped and blood flowed, and the predators came and ripped him to pieces, the sea swallowing him forever.

He refused to let that be his fate. He had to swim.

He had to reach the shore.

There would be a high tide tonight. Sam sensed that it was his best chance of making landfall. He was about to turn over when he heard a splash. He stopped, lay still, and watched a giant beast punch through the surface of the sea. It was bony and textured, with large plates that were almost like metal scales. Its head never cleared the water line to breathe, and there was no blowhole.

It wasn't a mammal. It hadn't surfaced to breathe. Had it come for him?

Another scaly spine broke through the water. It was smaller. A child, perhaps.

Sam swallowed and watched, not daring to move his arms or legs. He floated, watching the creatures, wondering if they could smell him or sense him. The sea was their arena. He was virtually powerless here.

To his relief, the dark creatures sank back into the water. Sam waited for his heart to stop hammering, and when it did, he began to swim again, with even more urgency now. He rode the waves and raced the sun and hoped the blisters on his hands and face wouldn't pop before his fingers dug into the sand. With every last bit of strength he had, Sam swam for the shore.

But as the night wore on and his body slowly gave out, it became clear that his last bit of strength wasn't enough to carry him to land.

His limbs went slack and he floated on the water, on his back, staring at the judgmental moon that he could almost feel laughing at him. In his mind, he cursed it. He was so angry he would have pulled it down from the sky and crashed it into the Earth as it once had billions of years ago, just to see it all burn. He was that mad at the world.

Not just this one, but the one he had left. And at whoever had framed him and that his wife had died and fate and everything else that had wrecked his life. It wasn't fair. He was a good man doing the best he could.

He realized another truth then: one of the things extreme exhaustion took from you was emotional control. His mind was like the evening storm: raging and unpredictable.

Anger wasn't the only thing he felt.

Helpless. That was the other feeling.

Between the two, Sam preferred rage. That was something he could use.

Mentally, he wanted to roll over and swim. But his body wouldn't respond. His mind was telling his arms and legs to work—to fight, to swim—but they refused to comply. His body had quit. His brain still worked, leaving him feeling locked in, as if he was silently shouting orders that his limbs wouldn't obey.

He refused to feel sorry for himself. Refused to close his eyes. If this was his fate—to die stranded in time and lost at sea—he would do it with his eyes open, teeth clenched.

But sleep tugged at him, a force as strong as the long waves of the tide moving across the ocean, propelled by gravity, directed by the pull of the moon and the sun.

Sam tried to fight the darkness and sleep, but soon, it came for him, and it was complete.

Light woke him. A hot, burning light on his face.

Sound washed over him next. Crash after crash.

A soothing, cool hand rubbing his legs. Reaching up and drawing away.

Sam cracked his eyelids and slammed them shut when the bright sun lanced through his eyes, bringing pain with it.

The gentle, cool hand came again, but it wasn't a hand. It was a wave. Washing over him.

Sam's fingers ached, but he forced them to move, to curl and dig—into the sand.

The beach.

He was lying on the beach.

His head rolled to the side, and he saw the sand. Tears flowed down his face.

He hadn't swum to shore. He had gone as far as he could

and given every last bit he had. The tide had carried him in. That was the way of the world, he thought: you give it your all; sometimes it's enough, sometimes it's not, and sometimes, the tide carries you in.

But the tide can't help you if you don't get close enough.

A strong wave washed over him, across his sunburned face, the saltwater stinging the blisters. The pain shocked his body into movement. He pushed up and scampered up the beach, getting his first clear look at Pangea.

A thick forest lay beyond the beach. At the edge were rows of broad-leaved shrubs. Behind them, trees reached to the sky. The forest looked so dense he wondered if he could even pass it, as if it was a wall of green, blue, and purple plants preventing anything from the beach from getting inside.

But what stopped Sam cold wasn't the trees or the shrubs. It was the thing hanging from the lowest limb on the closest tree. Blowing in the sea breeze was a thick white sweater. There were no words on it. But even in his exhausted, nearly delirious state, Sam recognized the garment. It was the same type of sweater he was wearing. The type worn by an Absolom prisoner.

He knew instantly what it meant. And that scared him more than the sea he had just escaped.

TWENTY-SIX

The next morning, Daniele took Adeline and Ryan to work with her. Ryan received a visitor badge.

Adeline's badge was similar, but it was actually an employee key card with the word INTERN printed across the top.

The older woman held the card out to Adeline. "Keep this with you at all times. You never know when you might need it."

She slipped the card into a plastic sleeve that dangled from a lanyard around Adeline's neck.

The three of them walked the halls of the Absolom research building, Daniele dictating the tour. There were team rooms that looked to Adeline almost like classrooms as well as clean labs where suited figures were working on mechanical prototypes.

Standing at a wide glass window, Adeline motioned to a figure holding a soldering gun. "What're they building?"

Daniele smiled. "Pieces for an experiment."

They had lunch at Daniele's house, and after, Ryan went to visit some friends a few blocks away. Daniele announced to Adeline that she needed to talk to her about something.

They met in Daniele's home library, where Adeline was expecting them to discuss the plan to find Nora's killer. Or how to get her father back. Or both.

The meeting was about neither of those things.

Daniele set a stack of books on a long table. "I want to discuss a subject of great importance to me. I would appreciate it if you would pay attention and learn from these books." She paused. "Can you do that?"

"What's the subject?"

"Finance."

"Are you serious?"

"I am."

"Why? Dad was rich, right? And he got a check every three months from the company. Interest or like a—"

"A dividend."

"A dividend, right. It's probably millions of dollars."

"The most recent quarterly dividend paid on your father's stake in Absolom Sciences was 1.17 billion dollars."

It took Adeline a few seconds to process that. She had known her father's stake in Absolom had made him wealthy, but she had no idea how rich.

"Your father was also a good investor," Daniele said. "A little on the conservative side, but that's better than being too aggressive."

"Look, can we do this after we get him back? I promise: I'll learn all about finance after that."

"No. We can't. This is important, Adeline."

"Why?"

"Because I made a promise to your father that I would do everything in my power to take care of you."

Adeline laughed. "There's a killer on the loose, and you're protecting me by teaching me about stocks and bonds? I think you've lost it."

"I haven't."

"Let's face it, money is maybe the *only* thing I'm not worried about."

"Because you have money."

"Exactly."

"You're making an assumption—the same mistake Nora's parents made."

Adeline narrowed her eyes, and Daniele continued.

"You're assuming your circumstances will never change. They could. They do for a lot of people—in the blink of an eye. One minute your family is rich. The next, you're carrying every dollar to your name in your pocket, you have no home, and you don't know where you're going to sleep that night. Right now, you don't care about money because you have it. You've never had to wonder how you'll afford your next meal."

"That happened to you?"

"It did."

"When?"

Daniele studied Adeline a moment. "When I was about your age. A little older."

"What happened?"

"We're not going to talk about that. My point is, knowing how to manage your money is an important life skill. Even if someone else is investing it, you should be able to read the statements and understand what they're doing. Your father is gone. Preparing you for what's ahead is now my responsibility. Finance is something I know a lot about. And I'm going to teach you about it—because someone was kind enough to teach me a long time ago, and frankly, that's the only reason I'm here talking to you now."

"I thought you went to Stanford."

"I did. For a while. But I had to drop out."

"Why?"

"My family needed me. And then… things changed. But this isn't about me. Will you at least listen?"

"All right."

"First things first. There are two rules that will greatly simplify investing for you."

"I like simplicity."

"The number one thing to know is that investing is, at its core, an exercise in predicting the future."

Adeline was surprised by that. "I don't get it."

"Think about it. When you buy a stock, bond, or other security, you're making an educated guess about what's going to happen, not just with the company or interest rates, but about what the future is going to look like. And you're also making a guess about the market—whether it's too optimistic about the future or too pessimistic. That is where fortunes are made and lost: in excess. In knowing when there's exuberance or despair. But that's only half of the key. The other half is the human factor. Both yourself and others."

Daniele stood. "Remember this: people matter. The history of capitalism is fundamentally about people. Great companies are built by great people. That's the key to making market-beating returns—spotting those people."

She slid one of the books across the table. "But let's go back to times of exuberance and despair. We're going to start by studying the global financial crisis that began in 2008."

That night, Adeline lay in her bed, mentally examining the pieces of the puzzle that was the mystery of Nora's death and her father's banishment.

In Daniele's basement, the four scientists had sounded sincere in wanting to get her father back from the past. And clearly, they had some method of doing it. That had to be Absolom Two. But there seemed to be a problem with it.

Was killing Nora and getting rid of her father just a means

to an end—to ensure Absolom Two was built? That made sense to Adeline.

That was a motive for the murder and for framing him. But what was the larger purpose of completing Absolom Two?

The answer seemed obvious to Adeline: to bring someone from the past to the present, as they were talking about doing with her father. If that was the case, it reinforced her theory that Constance was the killer—she was clearly obsessed with the past, with tracking people and finding their whereabouts in the past.

Her mind went around and around with those thoughts, debating how she could get to the bottom of what was happening.

Finally, she took out her phone and checked her email and social media feeds. Condolences for her father and messages from friends were still trickling in. They had helped a great deal in the days and weeks after her father's arrest. Now, Adeline found that they just made her sad. They reminded her of what had happened. She didn't want to remember. She wanted to work on the problem. She wanted to solve it.

She was about to set the phone down when she remembered the tracking app for Hiro's phone: BuddyLoc.

She clicked the icon and studied the map that appeared. It showed a residential neighborhood in Las Vegas, easily within an afternoon's drive from Absolom City. She pulled up the history and found that Hiro had worked at the Absolom Sciences research labs until about 5 p.m., then driven straight home. He had been there since.

Like all the Absolom founders, Hiro had a home in Absolom City.

What was he doing in Vegas? Visiting a friend?

While possible, it didn't really fit with what she knew about Hiro. He was easily the least social of the Absolom Six.

Adeline got out of bed, opened her laptop, and went to the Clark County tax records website and looked up the address. The property Hiro was visiting was owned by Molosba LLC.

Adeline stared at the word Molosba.

It was simply Absolom spelled backward. Adeline sensed that she was staring at a clue to something, but she couldn't figure out what it was.

She did know that she had to get inside that house to see what Hiro was doing there.

TWENTY-SEVEN

In the Triassic, Sam stood on the beach, staring at the Absolom sweater hanging from the tree.

He looked down at his own sweater, searching for any differences. He didn't see any. Which opened another possibility: the sweater in the tree might be his sweater, left here in the past.

There was one way to test that.

Sam had needed the sweater to float better on the sea. But it was far too warm to wear it on shore.

He pulled the garment off and stretched it tight with his hands. He stared at the sweater in the tree as he ripped his own.

The one hanging above didn't change.

It wasn't his.

Which meant there was another prisoner here. Why?

The people sent back via Absolom were the worst of human society. Murderers. Terrorists. Serial killers.

Well, with the exception of Sam himself.

Why would someone send a killer here? There was only one good answer Sam could see: to kill him.

The scientist in him couldn't help but wonder how the other prisoner had gotten here. Absolom should have sent him to an alternate timeline—and it should have sent other prisoners to their own timeline. No two Absolom prisoners should ever meet. Unless they had somehow used Absolom Two to send the other person—and sweater—here.

Sam realized then that he had more to do here than survive. He had a mystery to solve. A secret to unravel.

If he was going to do that, he needed to recuperate. The sea and a few days without food had left him weak. He needed to get his strength back. Then he would sort out who else was here. And why. And how they had gotten here. He sensed that in that answer was the key to learning who had killed Nora and perhaps a way to get home.

He tied his sweater around his waist and waded into the forest, stopping near the tree where the other sweater hung.

There wasn't any sort of trap that he could see. It seemed the white garment was some sort of sign, a signal perhaps to any other prisoners who might see it. But why? Was it a lure of some kind?

The mystery would have to wait. Sam was hungry. And thirsty.

Past the shrubs, the forest was dark where the thick tree canopy blotted out the sun. Sam felt as though night had fallen in just a few steps. Behind him, the light-drenched beach was disappearing.

The trees around him reminded Sam of redwoods. The bark was thick with deep grooves, and the wide trunks seemed to extend all the way to the clouds. He felt as though he had been shrunk and dropped in a land where everything was oversized— which was technically the case.

The forest floor was covered in moss. Large ferns clumped together where there were holes in the tree canopy, positioning themselves to get hit by the sunlight.

Sam reached out and touched one of the fern leaves. It was thick and soft, almost like velvet. On the underside were spongy red spores. In the valley of the blades, small puddles of water remained from the storm. Sam tipped the closest one and drank the cool water. It coated his throat like aloe on a sunburn.

He exhaled and breathed a few times, savoring the relief.

He moved to the next fern frond and tipped the leaf to his mouth and drank. He repeated the action until his belly was full and his chin and undershirt were soaked. Sam was so consumed with quenching his thirst that he didn't hear the rustling beside him. When he looked up, the creature was ten feet away, staring up at him, its scaly head cocked, as if curious.

The dinosaur was a small theropod, shaped like a T. rex, with large hind legs and small forelimbs. But this creature was smaller and more slender, about six feet long, with a head that came up to Sam's waist.

But it was big enough to do Sam some serious damage. Or kill him. Even a deep wound would be deadly out here. The smell of blood would draw larger predators.

Slowly, the dinosaur opened its mouth, revealing jagged teeth that were razor sharp. This was a carnivore. No question about it. And it was hungry. Its tongue slithered in its mouth, bouncing left and right.

Sam didn't move.

The forest was quiet as the carnivore took a step toward him, the three sharp claws on its hind legs digging into the green moss. Its forelimbs rose. Anticipating.

Sam's breath came out of his nose with the force of a wind tunnel, the sound like a foghorn to him. Could the dinosaur sense his fear? Smell it?

A thud landed somewhere nearby, followed by a screech, another screech, and the cracking of limbs and twigs underfoot.

The dinosaur advancing on Sam whipped its head around, eyes darting back and forth, and launched into the forest, feet pounding the ground as it gave chase to the other creatures.

Sam fell to his knees and exhaled.

He had to get his head in the game. He was reminded of his

sessions with Daniele, of her verbally shaking him, trying to convince him to focus and learn.

He had to get it together. Or he wouldn't last the night.

What was the priority now?

A weapon. That was number one.

He glanced around, found a piece of fallen wood, but it was too soggy. Moss had already begun to grow over it, breaking it down.

In fact, everything in this forest seemed to be rain-soaked and dissolving, as if the darkness and dampness were turning everything to mush.

He tried two more sticks before finding one he liked. It must have recently fallen from a tree during a windstorm. It was about the length of his arm and strong, but light enough for him to easily carry and swing.

What he really needed was a fire. If he had had a burning torch, that dinosaur would never have approached him.

The problem was that a fire would draw the other Absolom prisoner—if they were still out here.

He was going to have to make some hard choices. In a world where everything can kill you, one must choose which battles to fight.

The next challenge was what to eat. He was too weak to hunt or fish. He also didn't have a fire to cook the meat. Not yet.

That meant foraging. For plants. Or insects.

He tried to remember the survival food pyramid from Daniele's book, but his mind was like molasses flowing through a fine cheese grater.

Insects. They were usually safe. But not other bugs. Not spiders. Or ticks or scorpions. They were arachnids—with eight legs. Eight legs: bad. Six legs: good. Or, probably not death. Insects had six legs. And what else? Sam rubbed his temples.

Insects had... an exoskeleton. A three-part body. Six legs. And something else. But he couldn't remember. He did know this: if he saw one, he would shove it in his mouth.

He was that hungry.

A week ago, he wouldn't have dreamed of it.

Now, he was hungry in a way he had never known.

Mentally, he went over the rules he could remember. If the bug was hairy or had a stinger, it was best to avoid it. Same for anything brightly colored.

At the moment, Sam just wanted to get something in his system. Food was the lubricant he needed to make the gears of his mind work. And his mind was the only thing that could truly keep him alive out here.

He reached out and rubbed the fern leaf between his fingers. Probably not edible. The survival food pyramid recommended wild greens, berries, fruits, tubers, roots, shoots, and flowers.

Except berries and fruits were likely out. The books and articles Sam had read indicated that flowering plants that produced edible fruit and berries were nonexistent in the Late Triassic.

He figured his best bet was to find a plant that showed signs of having been fed on. If his new Triassic neighbors could eat it, that increased the odds that Sam could.

He began stepping through the forest, slowly, careful to place his footfalls in the moss or soft ground. Noise could be deadly.

As he walked, he took stock of the plants he saw, as well as the nuts and seeds on the forest floor. He thought it better to wait on trying those. A plant's reproductive material naturally evolves to harm any predators that might snack on them.

Sam stopped and eyed a group of mushrooms, his mouth starting to water. They might be okay. But he wasn't ready to take that risk. Not yet.

The ground soon began to incline. The moss grew thinner, and the ferns were smaller with each step. Rocks covered more of the ground.

Up ahead, the tree line broke. Sunlight poured in like dawn through a stained-glass window. There was a clearing ahead, calling to Sam like an oasis in the desert.

When the trees began to thin, he slowed to allow his eyes to adjust to the light.

The clearing was a rocky expanse about half the size of a football field. From where Sam stood to the trees across the way, the ground rose perhaps twelve feet. Sam figured this was a large stony outcropping on the side of a hill.

He glanced up and sighted the sun. It was halfway past the point of midday. It would set in perhaps three or four hours.

A few feet away, rising up from the white rock, was a small, wiry shrub. It had green fruit-like pods that looked like faded olives.

Sam ran to it and jerked one of the oval pods off and split it open. There was a hard, textured seed inside. Sam discarded the seed and lifted the plant to his nose and inhaled. There was no odor except for an earthy scent.

He stretched out his left arm and placed the split pod against the inside of his elbow, where blood might be drawn, letting the plant flesh touch his skin. He held it there, waiting for any reaction—skin irritation, itching, burning, or numbness.

A breeze barreled through the clearing, bringing with it a cloud of spores like dust in an Old West town. Insects followed the cloud, zooming in and out.

Sam inspected his skin where the plant had been. It was fine.

It would be best to boil the green pod, but there was no time for that. He held it to his lips and waited again for any reaction. He really needed a watch. Without it, in his hungry, exhausted state, it was hard for him to judge the passage of time.

Finally, when his lips made no reaction, he stuffed the fruit in his mouth and held it there, using his last bit of self-control to keep from swallowing it whole. It had a slightly bitter taste, but it didn't seem rotten. There was no irritation in his mouth, but it soon filled with saliva.

His mind screamed for him to eat, and finally, Sam swallowed the fruit down. He told himself to wait before eating any more, to see if his body rejected the potential sustenance. But he couldn't.

He snapped the green pods off the shrub, threw the seeds on the ground, and chewed and swallowed like a robotic farm drone as he moved around the rocky expanse. With each gulp, life flowed back into him.

His mind unfroze. As he munched on the green balls of life-giving food, the name came to him: a ginkgo. That was what he was eating—a ginkgo, a type of nonflowering seed plant common in the Late Triassic.

The name of the dinosaur he had seen occurred to him too. It was a Coelophysis. Daniele had pronounced the C like an S, the first part of the name pronounced like "seel," the middle like "oh." He was amazed that his mind worked like that— he could remember the tiniest details that fascinated him (like dinosaurs), but most days he could barely remember what he did the day before.

He decided to call the dinosaur a "seelo." If he ever saw one again.

He hoped he didn't.

Sam moved to the next ginkgo bush and began picking the fruits and stuffing his mouth. They needed a name too. Green pods. That worked. It wasn't exactly inspired, but it would do.

That's how his mind worked: he liked to name things and order them. That may have been what made him a successful physicist.

Almost against his will, Sam laughed at that. Successful. Yeah right. What a career he'd had: faking enthusiasm for a time travel machine he thought was baloney (in order to make money to save his dying wife), then accidentally helping to create that supposedly fake time travel machine, and finally being banished from his own universe with the machine he had faked enthusiasm for in the first place. There were disasters, and then there was his life.

The question was: what was the next step to turning it all around? Surviving the night. That was the answer. And to do that, he needed shelter. A better way to protect himself would also help. The small stick wouldn't be much protection against a major predator. A fire would do. It might draw the other prisoner, but Sam felt that was a risk he'd have to take.

He moved across the rock outcropping, picking the green pods and filling his pockets and his mouth. One thing struck him: there were no bite marks on the plants. The dinosaurs hadn't been feeding on them. Why? Were they not ripe yet?

By the time he had circled the perimeter of the rocky area, his pockets were full and so was his stomach. Fatigue was catching up with him, and all of a sudden the sun seemed achingly bright. It was sinking faster now, diving in the sky like a roller coaster racing down its finale.

Shelter.

And fire.

Those were the priorities now.

Sam moved toward the interior of the rocky area, leaning on the stick. With each step, it was harder to keep his eyes open. The exertion from the day, mainly the journey from the beach, seemed to have caught up with him all at once.

Or was it something else?

He hadn't been stung by an insect. He didn't think. Couldn't remember it. How long had he lain on that beach?

Near the middle of the rocky expanse, a large stone rose into the air. At the base was a hole about waist high.

Sam planted his feet and extended the stick into the mouth of the small cave and pushed into the darkness, half expecting a creature to burst out and maul him.

But it wasn't a beast emerging from the depths of the cave that assaulted him. The attack came from inside. His stomach seemed to seize up like a fist closing, tightening, pain punching out through his abdomen.

Green mush flowed up through his throat and out of his mouth, a soupy goo that sprayed across the white-gray rock.

Sam's vision blurred. Legs went weak. He sank to the ground, still clutching the stick, watching the dark hole for any sign of a predator. He saw only darkness.

Another wave of semi-digested fruit sprayed out. Then another. It was like an invisible attacker was reaching down through his throat and yanking out his insides. It kept pulling until his heaves were dry. His abs ached. Throat burned. Eyes bulged. He felt like his body was self-destructing, trying to explode.

The sun slipped behind the treetops, as if it couldn't bear to watch.

Sam lowered himself from his hands and knees onto his side. The rock was cold on his face.

The rain started then, a soft pattering on the stones at first, then drumming, and finally pounding all around, like a symphony signaling his end.

In a fitting touch, the light from the sun faded behind the trees. A curtain being drawn on Pangea.

And maybe his life.

Was this his final act? Would it end in this rocky expanse in the distant past?

If not, what would darkness on land bring? A predator to

finish him? The green pods had felled him. The kill was all that remained.

Get up, his mind said. *Get up or you never will again.*

He planted his hand on the rock, but it slipped on the wet surface, slamming him back down. He tried to push up again, but his body didn't move.

He just needed to rest.

Just a little longer, he told himself. But there wasn't any longer. It was now or never. He had to get up.

In his mind, he imagined himself stepping out of Absolom, hugging Adeline and Ryan, back in the world he knew, in his life, vindicated.

He had to fight.

He rolled onto his belly, set his forearms on the rock, and pushed. He got his knees under him. He reached out, grabbed the stick, and shoved it into the small cave. It hit rock at the back.

He army-crawled closer. There were no animal droppings near the mouth. Or inside.

He pulled himself deeper inside. It wasn't really a cave, just a deep indentation in the rock, barely large enough for him to hide, with an opening small enough for him to defend.

He held the stick out, ready to stab anything that might approach.

He waited, eyes growing heavy. He retched twice more before night fell completely. In that time, he drifted somewhere between sleep and waking, and in the darkness, in one of those moments, under the soft glow of the moonlight, he heard rustling in the forest, near the tree line.

Slowly, tentatively, the creature stepped out of the shadows, into the clearing, and began moving toward him.

TWENTY-EIGHT

On Saturday afternoon, Adeline attended a memorial service for her father. It was held at Elliott's home, and on the whole, it was an awkward affair, for a few reasons.

First, Elliott had insisted on the event being a dual remembrance of life for Nora and for Adeline's father—who was, according to the court (and his own confession), guilty of her murder.

Many of those in attendance were employees at Absolom Sciences. They saw both Nora and Sam as victims.

Others, like Nora's former university colleagues, looked at Adeline with a barely concealed accusation in their eyes. When their glares cut into Adeline, she didn't back away. Just the opposite. She stared back, not hiding her own contempt, silently declaring, *My father is innocent, and you should be ashamed, not me.*

Adeline was discovering a whole new side of herself. There was a fighter inside of her, a person she never knew existed and wouldn't have if not for Nora's death and her father's exile. She marveled then that one never knew what they were made of until their back was against the wall.

Ryan seemed less equipped to endure the stares from the adults. In those interactions, Adeline realized she wasn't the only fighter on the prowl at the service. Daniele stuck close to Ryan, and when she caught someone whispering, pointing, or scrutinizing him, she fired back. Her gaze was like a nuclear explosion hitting the gawkers. They fell silent, eyes wide as they melted away. Once, she even crossed the living room and said, "Is there something you want to say?"

As it turned out, the person didn't have anything they wanted to say.

Adeline soon learned that while she could stand the judgmental stares of strangers, that of friends was much harder.

She turned the corner to the dining room and found Constance standing there, alone, holding a small plate heavy with hors d'oeuvres, a bottle of water in her other hand. Her head was wrapped in a decorative scarf that was blue with white and yellow flowers. The vivid colors were a sharp contrast to her ashy skin and hollowed-out eyes. She stared at Adeline with a mix of sympathy and hurt. Whether it was hurt from Nora's death and her father's departure or Adeline's betrayal, the younger woman wasn't sure, but she did know that Constance's stare fell on her like a sledgehammer. The silence that accompanied it merely drove the blow deeper into her.

"Adeline," a voice said from behind her. It was Lauren, one of Adeline's friends from high school who had made the trip from college in California. Many of Adeline's friends who were off at school on the east coast couldn't make it home for the service, but quite a few were there, and in that moment, Adeline was incredibly grateful.

She turned to her friend, who was standing in the kitchen, and bolted from the dining room, away from Constance.

In the great room, Elliott stood by the fire, a glass of champagne in his hand, a fork held at the ready. Adeline knew what was coming next.

Constance ventured out of the dining room, eyes still on Adeline.

Elliott tapped the glass. The *ding-ding-ding* echoed through the room, extinguishing conversations like a bucket of water on a campfire.

Hiro stood next to Elliott, looking exhausted, eyes bloodshot as if he had been up the entire night before.

By the accordion door that led to the lanai, Daniele stood beside Ryan, gazing wearily at Elliott. As he began to speak, she slipped her arm around Ryan's shoulders, as if bracing him for a windstorm about to come.

"In the tradition of the greatest Starfleet Medical Officer in history, Dr. Leonard McCoy, I'll just say this for myself: 'I'm a scientist for God's sake, not a speechmaker.'"

The lame *Star Trek* joke sent a ripple of laughter through the room, but the tension was still there. Apparently, it wasn't lost on Elliott.

"Let's start with the elephant in the room, shall we? We're used to that in science: dealing with facts, even if they make us uncomfortable. And the fact of the matter is that you've come here today for a memorial service for a murder victim and for the person convicted of that murder. I applaud you for that. I thank you for being here, and I hope that you will take what I'm about to say to heart. I hope you'll look at the facts too."

Elliott swallowed and took a deep breath.

"Sam Anderson was my best friend. He was one of my oldest friends. If, right now, something happened in my life, and I was in trouble or needed help or just needed someone to talk to, he is the first person I would call. That's how fresh the wound of his departure is. Like a limb that's been chopped off, and I still can't get used to the fact that it's not there. Because he was always there for me. He was more than a friend. He was family. And I simply can't get used to the fact that he's gone. I don't think I ever will."

Elliott stared at Adeline.

"And I won't accept it. As long as I live."

Elliott took a deep swig from the champagne glass.

"Nora is someone I knew professionally for a long time but had never gotten to know personally until we worked together on Absolom. She's someone whose intellect I have always admired. She was a sharp mind, but there are a lot of those in our field. What I can say about her—that I can't say about many—is that she never got too invested in her own ideas. She wasn't blinded by her own discoveries. She wasn't in it for personal gain. Or fame. Her interest was always the truth and helping people, and I think that's what made her such a great scientist. It's that same quality that made her such a great person. I found that out when our Charlie died."

The champagne glass in Elliott's right hand began to shake.

"It's a sad truth that the people who understand tragedy the best are the ones who have gone through it. Sam was my rock. But when Charlie..."

Elliott clenched his teeth and swallowed, the words coming out slower now.

"When Charlie was taken from us, I was adrift and what I needed was to get back to shore. I was going through life like a lucid dream. Hopeless. Aimless. And Nora was there for me. More than anyone I ever met, she had this almost supernatural ability to listen and make you feel at ease. It was a selfless kind of gift that drew people in like a vortex. I don't know what you call it. Animal magnetism or charisma or what, but she had it. For her, that gift wasn't a loud, ostentatious sort of charisma. She was like the sun in the sky, burning and warm and unwavering and pulling you in with gravity you couldn't escape." Elliott paused. "That's what she was to me back then. My world was frozen, and she was the sun that helped thaw it out. I don't know how she did it. Maybe it's because she had lost her husband in a car accident a few years after they were married. One minute he was there. The next, he was gone. Just like our Charlie. And now, just like Nora herself. And Sam."

Adeline felt as though the walls were closing in on her, as if Elliott's words were shrinking the house, suffocating her.

She set her glass on the marble countertop of the kitchen island and staggered through the people around her, through the dining room, and into the foyer. A stair hall led to a large study at the front of the home. She had intended to retreat there and wait for the assault of the words to be over, but another thought occurred to her then.

An opportunity.

The U-shaped stairway before her led to the bedrooms and rec room upstairs. A door beneath the landing opened to the stairs to the basement. Like Daniele, Elliott had the resources to dig a full basement. Adeline had been down there a few times, mostly at Christmas parties when the kids were relegated to the lower level where there was a game room with a pool table, arcade games, and a full home theater.

She gripped the door handle and it turned and she quickly slipped inside and descended the stairs. She was reminded of spying on the four scientists at Daniele's home. But this time, she didn't stop on the landing.

She kept going, out into the open game room. The door to the half bath stood open. So did the double doors to the theater. It was empty.

The far wall was almost entirely glass, and beyond was a cavernous wine cellar. There were only two other rooms in the basement. One was a mechanical space that Adeline had seen once. To her, it looked like the belly of a giant boat: there were air handlers and mechanical pumps, and through another glass wall, on a raised platform, a giant server room that ran the home automation system, window shades, security, whole-house audio, and probably stuff Adeline didn't even know about.

The other door led to a home gym. Adeline had seen it once. Mirrors hung on the walls, and thick rubber covered the concrete floor. There were no windows.

And something had been added to the wall beside the door to the gym since her last visit here: a touchscreen panel.

Adeline tapped it. A menu came up for the home automation system. The door handle had no keyhole, but it was locked.

She navigated the system until she came to the screen for a room named *workout*. It had a keyless entry option that showed a full keyboard. The code to open the door was a series of letters.

Adeline listened for a moment, trying to determine if Elliott's speech was over. If someone found her down here, she could always say she had felt overwhelmed and needed to get away. In this case, it was true.

But this was also an opportunity. One she likely wouldn't soon see again.

What could the door code be?

Charlie was her first thought. But that was too obvious. What was a word no one would think of?

Adeline raised her finger to the panel and typed:

M

O

L

O

S

B

A

The door lock whined, gears grinding as the bolt receded. Adeline tried the handle. It turned. She swung the heavy wooden slab in and gasped at what she saw.

The mirrors on the wall were gone. In their place was a dark gray soundproof foam from floor to ceiling.

The rubber still spread out at her feet. The opposite wall was covered in photos of Charlie. In them, he was about Adeline's age now—late teens or early twenties. He was strung out in most. Loitering outside nightclubs or on the deck at house parties, a drink in his hand and a cigarette dangling from his lips. Some photos had been taken from a distance, through closed windows, showing him in the living room or bathroom of a home or apartment, often consuming drugs or simply slouched in a chair or couch, listening or laughing.

Based on Charlie's age in the photos—and the fact that he was wearing the same clothes—they appeared to have all been taken around the same time, in the days leading up to his death, which had hit Elliott hard.

The last time Adeline had seen Charlie had been at his family's Christmas party that year. He hadn't been himself then. There was an edge to him, an anger underneath everything that even crept into his infectious laugh. He had been mad at the world.

As she turned that memory over in her mind, Adeline had to admit that she felt herself standing on that precipice. She wondered if she would descend into the abyss of blame and bitterness too. Probably. If she didn't get answers—and justice—soon.

On the left-hand wall was a bank of computer screens playing videos. Most were from home security cameras. They displayed the street or the alley beside the home or the backyard. In each video, Charlie was walking back to his apartment.

Other videos were from mobile phones, the scenes showing a house party that raged into the night, one Charlie had attended.

In one of the videos playing in a rectangle near the bottom of the screen, Adeline saw something that made her jaw drop: Daniele. She was walking down the same street Charlie was trudging across in the other videos. The timestamp said she was only an hour behind him.

Adeline caught a glimpse of her in another video. She was entering Charlie's apartment building, proceeding up the stairs. The night he died.

The voice behind her made Adeline jump.

"Thought I'd find you here."

Adeline took a step back.

Elliott followed her deeper into the room, his hand gripping the handle to the thick wooden door.

"I was looking for the—"

Adeline was going to say bathroom, but Elliott laughed and cut her off. "I know what you were looking for."

He swung the door closed with a thud. And locked it.

Adeline opened her mouth.

Elliott held up a hand. "Don't scream. It won't matter. No one can hear you down here."

TWENTY-NINE

From the shallow cave, under the glow of moonlight, Sam watched the seelo emerge from the tree line. The carnivorous dinosaur, which reminded him of a miniature T. rex, ventured onto the rocky expanse, its sharp claws clacking as it went, rain pouring down around it.

The deadly creature looked directly at Sam. Over the rain, the *clack-clack-clack* of more claws called out in the night. Sam heard the other seelo before he saw it, but soon, it emerged from the forest and came to stand beside the first. They stared at Sam, a Triassic jury of two deciding his fate.

The first took a step forward, as if a decision had been made.

Sam figured he looked weak to them. Half dead. Easy prey.

Maybe he was. But that didn't mean he wasn't going to fight.

He dropped the stick and crawled forward, out of the small cave.

The seelos advanced.

Rain poured down, drops bouncing on the white stone like balls of hail.

Shock and awe. That was his only chance. He was weak. That was the truth. But he had one advantage they didn't: his mind.

Sam gripped a loose rock by the cave entrance and hurled it at the two seelos. Both their heads snapped around.

He picked up another stone and launched it, this time

connecting with the closest dinosaur's head. It reeled back, screeching, and wheeled around, racing into the dark forest, the other chasing after it.

Sam exhaled and dropped to the ground like a balloon deflating.

He gathered a few stones and stacked them by the cave entrance. He smiled at his little stockpile of missiles, ready to fight the Pangean war he had started.

He kept the stick in his hand, but he couldn't watch the woods any longer. The pattering of the rain soon lulled him to sleep.

The morning light poured into the cave like an invading army.

Sam covered his eyes with his arm and tried to go back to sleep.

The hunger finally made him move. It was a hunger like he had never known, an ache deep down inside that felt more like sickness, as though his own body was eating itself.

He crawled to the mouth of the cave and stopped at the stack of stones. In the indentions in the dirt where they had been, small worms were writhing in the baking sun, snaking their way under nearby rocks to escape.

Sam's stomach rumbled.

His mouth watered.

So this is what it's come to, eh?

He turned over one of the rocks, revealing three larger earthworms. They were brown and gray and as he watched them, wondering if he was actually capable of eating them, they began inching way.

Sam picked one up, brushed off the dirt caked on it and dropped it in his mouth. He was that hungry.

The worm was slimy and earthy. His first instinct was to

gag. He certainly couldn't chew it. He swallowed it down and winced and forced himself to pick up the next one, and the next.

There, under the morning sun, near the mouth of the cave, he broke his fast on a Triassic earthworm buffet. It was probably the grossest thing Sam had ever done. It was also, strangely, the most fulfilling meal of his entire life.

The worms brought strength. And he was going to use it.

He needed water. And fire.

In the forest, he drank rainwater from the fern leaves until he had washed the earthy taste out of his mouth and filled his belly. With each step, he watched for the seelos, careful not to make any noise as he gathered sticks for his fire.

Soon, he had a pile of kindling and fuel near the small cave. In his mind's eye, he saw a blazing inferno. Around it, he imagined a stack of stones and a flat, thin rock on top, a fish lying on it, grilling in the heat of the crackling fire. The thought made his mouth water even more. He had seen two other types of seed ferns in the forest that morning— one with large fleshy pods hanging down. But the memory of yesterday's food poisoning made his stomach turn at the thought of trying other plants.

He wanted meat.

But first, he needed a fire. For protection.

He ventured deeper into the forest, the stick held at the ready. Up ahead, he found what he had been looking for. The white bones of a rib cage rose through the ferns like ivory swords buried at the hilt.

He pushed the green fern fronds back and caught sight of the skeleton's skull. Sam looked around and spotted the end of the tail. The beast had been at least thirty-five feet long and maybe twice as tall as him.

At the skull, he brushed away the dirt and inspected the

teeth. Unfortunately, they were blunted. This was an omnivore. Probably a Melanorosaurus, based on the books Daniele had drilled into him.

Sam was about to turn away when a thought occurred to him. He examined the skull a little closer. The top was flat and about as wide as his chest, with enclosed sides. He smiled. Nature tests you. And nature provides.

Sam lifted the skull away and stopped when he saw the earthworms writhing where it had been. His Triassic seafood grill wouldn't be a reality for a while. And he was hungry from scavenging in the woods.

He squatted and ate his fill, marveling at how the slimy worms no longer triggered his gag reflex.

At his camp (which is how he now thought of the small cave and soon-to-be fire), he set the upper part of the skull on top of a pile of rocks. He lined the inside with layers of thick fern leaves, covering the openings and using clean rocks to make sure the leaves were firmly joined together.

When he was done, Sam sat back and smiled at it. A dinosaur skull rain barrel. By nightfall—if it rained again in the afternoon—the small reservoir would be full of water, and Sam could drink from it, staying by his camp instead of venturing back into the woods to drink from the velvety fern leaves. That might save his life.

On his next trip to the woods, he found what he had been searching for the first time: the skeleton of a carnivore. He snapped off a sharp tooth and brought it back to camp. He grabbed a stick of wood and ran the tooth up and down it, sawing away. Tiny slivers of wood peeled off, some as thin as human hairs. They would do. He placed them atop the twigs and dry leaves in the pile of tinder.

He then used the tooth to sharpen his self-defense stick. When he was done, he inspected the small spear. It would do. He carried it into the woods and found another stick and sharpened it (for a backup).

Finally, he turned his focus to the fire. He carved a deep groove in a piece of flat softwood, then sharpened another stick and began plowing up and down the groove, creating friction and shearing off thin layers of wood.

The friction and heat ignited the hairs of wood above and soon, smoke rose from the tinder pile. Sam leaned forward, eager to see flames sprout up. He blew gently, but the smoke drifted away and the fire died.

He had been too eager.

Total rookie move.

He sat back on his haunches and exhaled. At the end of the piece of flat wood, he repacked the tinder, careful to ensure the fine wood fibers were at the end of the groove.

Then he began plowing again.

As he rowed back and forth, he thought: *that's life*. You push and pull and sometimes things catch fire and sometimes they don't. You keep going: that's the key.

Soon, smoke rose again.

But still he plowed. He wanted to be sure this time. The flames needed to be strong before he gave them oxygen. When he smelled the fire and saw the first flames rising, he leaned down and blew and fueled it. The fire licked the twigs and ignited them and burned into the sticks steepled above it.

He had made a fire.

He sat back, watching the growing flames. It was a representation of so many things he had taken for granted in his old life. Before, fire was always a click away. Here, it was a struggle. And probably the key to his survival.

To survive, he needed to take the fire with him. That was easier said than done.

He needed a torch. The ideal torch would have a slow-burning fuel. Tree sap, pitch, oil, or animal fat were best. All were problematic. Specifically, they were hard to come by.

The best fuel options available to him at the moment were moss, wood, and leaves. They wouldn't burn long. And if the torch itself was wooden, it would burn down to his hand.

A thought occurred to him. A prehistoric innovation.

He returned to the Melanorosaurus skeleton, gripped one of the long rib bones, and leaned back until it cracked and broke free. As he suspected, it was hollow inside. It was also just the right size to be stuffed with a piece of hardwood wrapped in moss. And that's what he did.

He held the torch over the fire, lit it, and hoisted it up.

In one hand, he held a spear. In the other, a dinosaur bone torch. He hadn't mastered this land, but he felt safer than he had since the night Nora had died. The thought of her brought a sharp pain to his soul. He wasn't ready to think about her. But his mind wanted to, like it was trying to lick a wound that was still raw.

Would that cut ever heal? Probably not.

That hurt reminded him of his wife. She had also been taken from him. Sam had watched her wither away. In a way, it had broken him. Irreparably.

Nora had a similar hurt, from the loss of her husband. She and Sam had that in common. Wounds that wouldn't heal. And they shared the bond of the secret of Absolom. And, as they had discovered, an attraction to each other. In a way, she had brought Sam back to life, awakened something inside of him. Just when he thought they were ready to take the next step, she was gone, torn out of his life.

If he dwelled on the things that had happened to him, if he kept feeling sorry for himself, he knew it would drown him, just as the sea had wanted to. As in the water, here on land, he needed to swim, to propel himself forward, toward the shore, toward the future. The past pulled at him like the depths of the ocean, the abyss, but he resisted. He was going to fight. For Adeline. For Ryan. For his friends. And lastly, for himself.

With the torch in one hand, he reached into his pockets and emptied them. He threw the sickening green pods across the white rocks and put small pebbles in their place. If he lost the torch and spear, they would be his last line of defense. The small rocks wouldn't hurt the large reptiles here. But, as he had learned last night, they would scare them. They had never seen prey (or a predator) who could hurl rocks at them. Something new represented danger. Something to flee. Thanks to evolution, they were programmed to avoid uncertainty.

He glanced up at the sun. It was low in the sky. Sam figured it was probably two in the afternoon. Plenty of day left. And much to do.

He knew he needed food. Something hardier than Triassic earthworms. He wouldn't find it in the forest behind him— unless he was ready to fell a seelo. He wasn't.

Ahead lay unexplored territory, and within it, the prospect of easier prey. Perhaps a mammal he could eat. Or fish in a pond or a stream.

He had the fire now, and that gave him the option to cook larger animals.

Yet the prospect scared him. Ahead was new, unknown territory. That was the way of the world: even slowly starving, we cling to the lands we know instead of striking out into the unknown. But he had to now.

With his pockets full of stones, a spear in one hand, a torch in the other, Sam marched across the rocky expanse to the far tree line and stepped into the unexplored forest.

Under the canopy, the world turned dark. Around him, he heard animals scurrying. This thicket was alive, and the animals here were on the move. Why?

Sam realized the answer then. It was the smoke. That was rare in the Triassic. It probably heralded the beginning of a forest fire. Animals in this time had evolved to recognize the smell, to fear it, to run from it. That was going to be a problem for his hunting expedition. But it was also keeping him safe.

The terrain rose for a while, then turned downward before inclining again. Soon, the ground grew rockier, and finally the forest gave way to a ridge, where the trees were gone and stone covered the ground. At the top of a tall rock outcropping, Sam got his first glimpse of the world around him.

Ahead lay hills covered in dense forest, like what lay behind him. They cascaded down into a desert that stretched out as far as Sam could see. Turning back, he realized that the forest he had been hiking through was but a small strip between a massive sea of water on one side and a sea of sand on the other.

The desert ahead was barren except for narrow shadows that looked like stripes. Sam didn't understand where they came from, but there were hundreds of them. He wasn't about to trek down there to find out what they were.

To the right of the desert lay a swamp that flowed to the horizon, probably to the ocean. The low-lying land was likely a mix of saltwater from the sea and freshwater from the rain that pooled in the desert and washed away toward the coast.

Sam turned and surveyed the ridgeline. Another peak rose to his right. It didn't have a pointed top. It was blunted, like a mountain that had been sawed off. In the center, there was an indentation. It was a volcano.

Sam eyed the volcano like a dragon he had caught by the tail. A dangerous thing that could go off at any moment and burn him and the entire world to a crisp. But for now, it was asleep.

In the volcano's shadow, Sam spotted a small pond (or what looked like a small pond from where he stood). A stream flowed away from it, into the forest. He imagined that it eventually snaked its way to the sea. Another branch from the pond flowed toward the desert.

Sam glanced at the sun, mentally estimating the time and distance to the pond. He could make it there and back before nightfall. At least, he thought he could. If he couldn't, the torch would be his salvation in the dark forest. But it was burning down. He needed to resupply it.

Using the torch, he lit a small fire on the ground. Carefully, he extinguished the torch, emptied the bone, and packed it again. He lit the reconstituted torch, extinguished the fire on the ground, and set off toward the stream.

When he reached it, he built another fire on the bank and waded into the water, holding the spear up. There were indeed fish here. They were long and fast and looked absolutely delicious.

Sam stabbed down with the spear. Time after time, he missed. They were too fast.

He even bent and put his hands in the water and waited and tried to grab one. He was hungry enough to rip its head off. He imaged himself skewering it with a stick, holding it over the fire, and ripping strips of meat off and feasting on it.

The thought made his mouth water.

The sun set on that dream.

When it disappeared over the tree line, he stormed out of the creek, picked up the torch, and began hiking back to his camp.

When he reached it, he found the fire nearly dead, only a rubble of embers smoldering.

He covered the dying fire with twigs and branches from the forest and feasted from the stream that he knew: earthworms from beneath the stones near his camp. He would run out of those at some point, but tomorrow was another day. Today, he had made a lot of progress. He had woken at death's door and would lay his head down with food in his belly and a fire burning before him. That was progress, such as it was in the Triassic.

Soon, it became clear that the fire wouldn't survive the night. The rain extinguished it, the sheets smothering it like a blanket.

That sucked. Sam should have thought of that. But what could he do? The light monsoon was a late afternoon tradition on this part of Pangea.

He made a note to gather some dry wood in the cave to start again tomorrow. That was the key to survival—doing better tomorrow than you did today. Getting up every day and improving.

When the smoke of the fire was gone, and the moonlight bathed the rock expanse, night was complete, and with it came the thoughts of what he had left behind. The first memory was of hugging Adeline in that incarceration room. He wondered where she was now. Had she given up on him yet? It didn't matter. He would either die here or make it home. Losing his ability to see her and Ryan made him realize how much he missed them. For a moment, he was back in that Absolom chamber, staring through the glass, seeing them peering out at him.

In that moment, his world had been ripped apart in more ways than one.

But now, here in the past, a different set of eyes stared at Sam. They belonged to an old man. He stood at the tree line, in the rain, his long hair stringy and gray, his beard thick and matted. A wide scar ran down the left side of his face. He smiled, revealing crooked, broken teeth. He wore the same tank top as Sam—the kind issued by the Absolom departure facility.

The other prisoner had finally found him.

Sam's heart beat faster. He gripped the stick.

The man stepped forward, into the clearing. His ratty tank top was stained with blood. He had killed before. Sam studied the man, the gleam in his eyes, the smile on his lips, and knew, with almost certainty, that he was here to kill again.

THIRTY

Adeline stared into Elliott's eyes as her hand moved down to the small pocket in her dress. Her fingers were wrapping around the mobile phone when Elliott smiled. "There's no service down here." He studied her. "Which is good. We need to talk, and we don't want anyone who can hack a mobile phone to be listening."

He waited.

"Do you know anyone like that?"

Adeline swallowed. "I want to leave."

Elliott smiled, a silent denial of her request.

A single thought ran through her mind: if she could keep him talking, that would buy her time, maybe enough time for Daniele to come looking for her.

Elliott's tone was almost casual when he spoke. "You're making a habit of this, aren't you, my dear?"

"Habit of what?"

"Sneaking around people's houses. Looking for their secrets."

Adeline felt herself begin to shake.

"Constance called me. She's worried about you."

"She's..."

"Not the killer."

"She has a room. With pictures. From the past."

"Yes."

"You knew?"

"I've seen it."

"Who are they?"

"People from Connie's past. People she's trying to track down."

"Why?"

"It's private. And it's not what you think it is."

Elliott motioned to the screen, to the video where Daniele was walking down the street. At the end of the loop, it paused on a frame where she was looking up at the camera.

"It's not Connie's secret that should concern you. It's Daniele's."

"What secret is that?"

"That's the question. She's hiding things, Adeline. Her life doesn't add up."

Elliott pointed at the still image from the video. "She was there the night Charlie died." He raised a finger. "And not once in my life has she told me that. Now ask yourself why? Why would she do that? She didn't even know him. Sure, she knew he was having... issues, but in person, she had never even met him. Why was she there?"

Elliott waited. When Adeline said nothing, he stepped toward her. "She's using you, Adeline."

"She's not."

"She knows Connie's secret."

A chill ran through Adeline. "She does?"

"Of course. All of us do. Go ahead—when you get home, ask her. See if she denies it. See if she tells you. She won't. For one reason."

"Which is?"

"The same reason she sent you to Connie's house."

Adeline waited, staring at Elliott, knowing what came next.

"I told you. She's using you, Adeline. She wants you to think it's Connie because if you do, you won't investigate her. But you're the only person who really can. You're living in her house. You have access none of us do. Why do you think that is? Why do you think you're in that house?" Elliott paused, a smile forming on his lips. "Your father. He chose for you to live with Daniele for a very good reason, and it's not the one you think. Do you know what it is?"

"Let's assume I don't."

"I think you do. I think you want to find your father's killer, Adeline, more than anything. So do I. Daniele doesn't want that killer to be found—for one reason, and you're smart enough to know what that reason is."

In the car on the way home from the service, Adeline sat in the front seat, staring out the passenger window, struggling with whether to believe Elliott.

From the back seat, Daniele called to Adeline, "You disappeared for a while."

"I needed to be alone."

"You went to the basement?"

"Yes."

"See anything interesting?"

To Adeline, the question was a fork in the road. One with consequences.

Tell the truth and trust Daniele. Or lie.

Adeline tried to make her voice even. "No."

Daniele said nothing.

When Adeline turned to look back, the older woman was staring at her.

"Did you ever meet Elliott's son, Charlie?" Adeline asked.

Daniele didn't flinch. "No."

Adeline learned something then. Daniele was a good liar.

* * *

That night, Adeline tossed and turned and tried to grab hold of sleep, but it was like a fish in a stream slipping through her fingers.

Her mind wandered. She thought about what she had found in the basement of Elliott's house and in the spare bedroom in Constance's home. They had secrets. Daniele did too. Everyone around her seemed to have secrets. Were those secrets the key to saving her father? Or were they simply part of the transition to adulthood—realizing that the world wasn't what it seemed before, that everyone was hiding something, that every adult, on some level, wasn't who they wanted children to think they were?

She pulled the blanket aside, got on top of it and stared at it. Her mother had created this quilt. In fact, it had been one of her last acts before her death. It was a photomosaic that included pictures of Adeline's mother, father, her, and her brother. Together, the pictures joined to form a family photo taken at the beach years ago, when Ryan was barely walking. Every time Adeline looked at the quilt, it reminded her of what she had lost. And it steeled her to get her father back.

It also reminded Adeline of her mother—and her strength. It reminded Adeline that even at the end, when she was so sick, she kept working on something to leave behind. That something wasn't a grand monument, but a soft, sentimental gift, a blanket that would comfort her children on a cold night. It was fitting. Because that was what her mother had been to Adeline: inspiring, comforting, always there for her—until she wasn't, until she couldn't be. She lived on in that blanket.

Her mother was never coming back. But Adeline refused to believe that her father's fate would be the same.

She pulled out her phone and opened the BuddyLoc app.

Hiro was once again at the home in Las Vegas. On the screen, his red dot glowed on the map, inside the house, not moving. What was he doing there every night?

She resolved to find out. And soon.

It could be the key to unraveling what was really happening.

On Monday morning, Ryan went to school, and Daniele left for work. She had invited Adeline to come to work to start her internship, but Adeline had shrugged and lied, telling her that she wanted to study the investment books.

Daniele had smiled at that. "In that case, you have a lot of work to do."

Adeline waited until Daniele had been gone thirty minutes. Then she searched the entire house. Under every bed. In every drawer. Inside every cushion. Beneath all the rugs.

She examined every corner of the attic and the basement.

Nothing.

She found nothing.

No clue that indicated that Daniele was the killer—and no clue about anything else.

As Adeline sat in the living room, drenched in sweat and covered in dust, she had a single thought: if you searched someone's entire home and didn't learn a thing about them, that was probably someone who was hiding something.

It was probably someone who was very good at hiding things.

The thought of someone hiding things reminded her of Hiro. Adeline took out her phone and opened BuddyLoc. She stood up immediately when she saw the dot on the map. Hiro was in Death Valley. He was stopped somewhere just across the Nevada border.

Death Valley. The Absolom scientists had mentioned it

in Daniele's basement. They were doing experiments there. Experiments that they thought would get her father back.

At the kitchen island, Adeline wrote down the Death Valley GPS coordinates on a slip of paper and tore it off. She set her phone on the counter. She didn't want to be tracked.

THIRTY-ONE

In the rocky clearing, rain poured down. At the tree line, the Absolom prisoner drew a bone from his pocket. The ivory object practically glowed in the pale moonlight as rainwater coated it, glistening. Two sharp dinosaur teeth were attached to the end. It was a makeshift knife. A Triassic weapon.

At the first sight of the man, Sam had thought he was killer. It was the look in his eyes. The blood on his clothes. The jawbone and attached teeth confirmed it.

The old prisoner's grin widened, his eyes bulged, and his tongue snaked out and licked his bottom lip.

Sam's breath came fast through his nose, and his mind churned.

The old man began to run across the rocky ground, dodging the green ginkgo plants, his double-toothed knife held at the ready, eyes never leaving Sam.

"Hey!" Sam called out, desperately hoping the sound of a human voice might bring the man back to reason, might snap him out of his murderous attack.

The man raised the knife and charged faster.

Sam crawled out of the cave. He had no choice. The crazy fool was twenty feet away.

"Stop!" Sam yelled.

The prisoner leaped. Sam shifted as the man reached him, swiping with the knife, ripping a gash in the sweater.

"Stop!" Sam pleaded, holding his hands up.

The man seemed even more incensed at the sound of Sam's voice. He slashed with the knife, mouth open, as if he could taste the coming kill.

Sam stumbled backward, and his feet slipped on the wet rock. He landed on his back, near the extinguished fire.

The man shifted the bone knife in his hand and leaped again, bringing it down like a stake. Sam rolled, heard the knife hit the rock where he had been, and felt it come across his upper back, cutting into him. He cried out, rolled again, and caught hold of the sharpened stick he had tried to fish with.

The man charged again, and Sam reached out and caught his knife hand with his left hand, still holding his spear with his right, and they both went down, Sam on his back, the stick planted in the rocky ground. It caught in an indention in the stone and locked in place there. The spear pierced the man's abdomen just above his belly button and didn't stop until the whittled wooden end emerged from his back.

The man's knife hand went slack, and the makeshift blade dropped to the rock below.

The man smiled. "Got me."

Sam shook his head. "I didn't mean to."

The fool threw his head back and laughed.

"Quiet," Sam hissed.

The man smiled, showing blood-coated teeth. "Killed two before you. Got sloppy."

"Why?"

"Watched you, boy. Thought you... Thought you was soft."

The man coughed blood, and Sam spun, throwing him over, trying to dodge the thick paste that he knew would bring predators.

Time was slipping away. Sam needed answers from the man.

"How did you get here?"

The prisoner stared up at the moon, and his eyes went glassy.

A wind blew through the trees. Or maybe it was something else—a predator moving.

Sam stared at the dead man. He had killed two others. Why? The man was clearly crazy. He had probably been a killer before he got here—and certainly was after. Maybe the time alone had driven him insane, or maybe he had been out of his mind before he arrived. If Sam didn't get home, was that his fate? Or worse?

He was sure of one thing: the dead body would soon be a homing beacon for hungry animals. He couldn't leave it on his doorstep.

He considered removing the man's clothes, but they were soaked in blood. Too dangerous to keep.

And looting his corpse felt wrong. The man had tried to kill him, but he was still a human being. He should be buried. Or at least burned so vultures couldn't pick him clean.

But propriety was a luxury. Survival wasn't.

Sam gripped the man beneath his armpits and lifted him, the strain bringing pain to the cut on his upper back. The blood oozing there was another problem. It would attract hungry carnivores too, but he couldn't exactly get rid of his own body.

Breathing heavily, Sam dragged the dead man away from the cave, into the woods, and dropped him with a thud. It was indecent. Shameful. And necessary.

He ran back to the cave, watching for predators. But he didn't see any. In fact, the forest was eerily quiet.

Sam knew he should build the fire back. But the wood at the rock outcropping was still wet from the rain. Scavenging for dry wood in the forest felt like a bad idea—especially at night, with a cut on his back and a dead body nearby.

He took the sweater from his waist and tied it around the wound, hoping it would help stop the bleeding.

At the cave, he stacked the firewood vertically across the

mouth, put a pile of sticks inside, and crawled in. Once settled, he erected the remaining logs until the mouth of the cave was completely covered up. He could see through the narrow gaps, but he hoped it would be enough to hide him from predators passing by. Assuming they didn't smell his blood.

Sam thought sleep would be elusive.

But it wasn't. He was dead tired.

He woke to the sound of thunder. Or what he thought was thunder. One by one, the sticks in front of the cave entrance toppled like dominoes falling over.

The ground shook, punching up at him.

An earthquake.

It was an earthquake.

Sam scrambled to his feet and cleared the cave just as the rock above him came loose.

THIRTY-TWO

A deline didn't take an autocar to Death Valley.

She walked the three blocks to her home and stood outside for a long time. The last time she had been inside, her father had been alive. Or at least, he had been alive in this universe.

Staffers from Absolom Sciences had packed up her things and Ryan's things and brought them to Daniele's house. They had been thorough. There had been no need for her to return home. Until now.

At the side door to the garage, she keyed in the code and turned the handle. Inside, she mounted her electric bike, donned her helmet, and rode out into the street.

At Walmart, she bought a few Visa gift cards, then went back into the store and used them to buy what she really needed: a burner phone. She selected a model with a good camera. That would be important.

She downloaded the BuddyLoc app to the burner and keyed in the code to check Hiro's location. He was still in Death Valley.

She reached his location that afternoon, and by then he had moved into the California section of Death Valley, where most of the national park spread out along the Nevada border.

She turned off the state road and rode the bike across the dusty, rocky terrain. There was no defined trail here, but she could see the wide tire tracks left by a convoy that had come through. Mountains loomed in the distance, the sun shining behind them, casting the peaks in dark shadows like sharp, rotten teeth, the mouth of a world about to take a bite out of the sky.

Adeline stopped the bike at the next ridge. She was about to take the phone out to check Hiro's location but realized she didn't need to. She could see him from where she stood.

In the valley below, two white tents had been set up. The wind blew across them, whipping sand across the sides as the sun baked their tops.

Hiro stood near one of the tents. In his hand was a large remote with a silver antenna extended like a fencing sword.

About a hundred feet away, a box truck was parked, and beyond it a mini excavator was digging into the rock at the base of a mountain. Hiro seemed to be directing the excavator.

A tent flap opened, and a figure marched out carrying a duffel bag. Adeline recognized Daniele at once. Elliott strode out after her.

Adeline backed her bike down the ridge, out of sight, and moved behind a rock.

Using her phone, she began recording a movie and zoomed in on the scene.

Where the excavator had been digging, Daniele took a shovel from the bag, unfolded it, and began moving sand and rock away. Elliott got another shovel out and fell in opposite her, helping to dig.

Soon, Daniele was on her hands and knees, using a small brush like a painter—or archaeologist—might use.

That thought brought a dark possibility to Adeline's mind. What if they were looking for her father's remains? Were they digging for his bones out here?

Was this the part of Pangea where he had arrived? What would his bones tell them? His exact date of death?

No. That couldn't be right. Adeline reminded herself that Absolom had sent him to an alternate universe, not this one. They were digging for something else. But what?

She heard Daniele call something out, but she couldn't discern the words.

The tent flaps parted again, and another figure waded out into the late afternoon sun, lumbering with effort, head covered in a white scarf.

Constance.

They were all here. Each with their secrets. Digging up another secret, buried for how long?

Adeline was starving by the time she left Death Valley. She ate alone at a small roadside diner. After, she returned to the Walmart. There was one other thing she needed: a laptop. If she assumed Daniele had hacked her phone, her computer was likely also compromised.

At her home, she stowed her bike, the burner phone, and the new laptop in the garage. It was dark by the time she walked back to Daniele's house.

Inside, she found the first floor empty. Her first instinct was that Daniele and Ryan had gone out.

In the kitchen, she picked up her phone and read the missed text messages and social media communications. There were the routine check-ins from a few friends and a question from Daniele wondering if she would be home for dinner—and if so, what she might want.

Upstairs, she heard the sound of laughter. Ryan's laughter.

Adeline ascended the stairs, following the sound. The two sets of glass pocket doors that led to the library were closed. Through the closest one, Adeline saw Daniele and Ryan sitting on a banquette, a wall of books behind them, a color e-ink tablet sitting on the long table. Ryan was writing with a stylus, eyes down, concentrating. Daniele was leaning over, watching. She said something. He smiled. She continued, and he laughed, and she put her arm around him in a quick hug.

Adeline's cheeks flushed with rage.

Daniele looked up and spotted her through the glass pocket door. Adeline turned and stalked down the hall to her room, where she closed the door with a little too much force and plopped down at her desk.

She was still stewing when the door opened. Daniele stood at the threshold, studying her for a moment. "Where were you?"

Adeline didn't look up. "I went for a walk."

"See anything interesting?"

Adeline's heart beat faster—from either the fear or anger rising up inside of her. Or maybe both. Her next words came from a place of hurt. And the strength of her voice surprised even her.

"You're not his mother."

Daniele gently closed the door, but she lingered close by, keeping her distance.

"Is that the best you can do?"

Daniele's response caught Adeline off guard. "What?"

"You lost your mother. Then your father. It wasn't fair. Neither of those things. In the case of your father, it was a wrong very few ever come close to in a lifetime. You feel betrayed, Adeline. You feel alone. Ryan is all you have left. Now, you're scared to death of losing him."

"You don't know how I feel. You can't even imagine."

"I can."

"What do you want from me?"

"When I was young, someone helped me. In the darkest chapter of my life, she was there for me. I wouldn't have made it without her. I want to be that for you. So give me all the hurt

you're bottling up. Blame me. Shout at me. If it helps you, give
me the hate you feel for this unfair world."

"Get out."

That night, Adeline lay in bed, checking her messages. She
opened the BuddyLoc app and once again found Hiro at the
home in Las Vegas.

What was he doing there?

Through the closed bedroom door, Adeline heard the faint
sound of talking. Daniele talking.

Adeline checked the time. It was after 10 p.m.

At the window, she drew the curtain and scanned the street.
There were no cars parked outside. No one had come to visit.
Daniele was talking on the phone.

Adeline exited her room and padded quietly across the
landing to the rail that looked over the staircase. She could
hear Daniele clearly now. Her voice was raised.

"You'll simply have to be late for dinner, senator."

A pause. Daniele seemed even more frustrated when she
resumed speaking.

"No. You listen to me. If we can't perform these surgeries
on the Absolom convicts, we'll have to pause the program.
What do you think will happen then? To crime? To law and
order? Who will they blame, senator? It won't be us. Because
Absolom Sciences is going to issue a statement saying that
above all else, we must ensure the safety of the program, and
to do that, we need to tag these inmates before departure to
ensure they don't arrive in our universe. Because if they do, it
could end everything. And when they ask why we can't tag the
prisoners, we'll simply tell them that the Senate subcommittee
with oversight never acted on our request."

Another pause. Daniele laughed.

"I don't make threats. I'm telling you what's going to happen. You have forty-eight hours to amend the Absolom operating resolution. I want it passed by both houses and on the President's desk by the time that inmate is prepped for surgery. If not, there will be no surgery and no departures until we can do so."

Adeline heard a cabinet open, a bowl being placed on the marble countertop, and the freezer door open and close with a swoosh. Soon, the clink of a spoon on the glass bowl echoed up the stairwell. Daniele was eating ice cream, if Adeline had to guess.

As quietly as possible, Adeline returned to her room and lay in bed, staring up at the ceiling. Why did Daniele want to operate on the Absolom convicts? What would that accomplish? Was she trying to send them to her father's timeline? If so, why? The people sentenced to Absolom—besides her father—were dangerous individuals. Killers. Mass murderers. Psychopaths. If one came into contact with her father—even if they were the last two people on Earth—what would happen?

The larger question was why Daniele would even want to send them there? There was only one rational explanation: to kill Adeline's father.

THIRTY-THREE

Outside the cave, Sam crouched, a spear in his hand, waiting as the ground shook.

The earthquake came in waves. Every time Sam thought it was over, the ground rumbled again.

By morning, the world was quiet again, as though the disturbance had simply been night terrors. But the damage was real.

In the forest, the canopy was broken. Trees were felled as though a giant bowling ball had rolled through. Sam's small cave was also wrecked, the entrance nearly covered in crumbled rock.

The world around him popped and creaked as fallen trees and branches surrendered to gravity.

Sam set about gathering his morning meal of earthworms, but in the forest he found the fern fronds dry, the rainwater from yesterday's storm shaken to the ground. The dinosaur skull rain barrel had also capsized in the night.

One thing was abundant: wood. In short order, Sam had a fire going. Using a tooth from a seelo skeleton, he sharpened another spear, replacing the one that had impaled the crazy man (and was still buried inside him). Sam hadn't mustered the courage to check on his body. He had bigger fish to fry. And frying fish was exactly the thing on his mind. The thought of it made his mouth water.

The man's attack—and the Earthquake—had taught him how dangerous being trapped here was.

He needed to make a new camp, one by the stream, where he had access to fresh water at all times, and food, assuming he could learn to fish.

He needed to move. The thought of moving brought back a memory, of moving from San Francisco to Absolom City, of taking a risk, of moving on with his life.

In the memory, he stood in Nora's office, staring at the posters on the wall: one of Einstein, his hair standing on end, the other with a UFO hanging in the air and the words *I WANT TO BELIEVE* printed in white across the trees under it.

"I hate moving," Nora said.

"Same," Sam replied.

Nora began chewing the end of a pen. "It's Dave's stuff. Even after all these years, I can't bring myself to get rid of it."

"I know what you mean. Sarah's things are still in boxes. I tried to give some to her sister, but she didn't want them. Sarah would want me to donate them to Goodwill or a women's shelter, but I can't bring myself to do it."

"It feels like you're getting rid of them, the memories too."

Sam nodded. "Yes. It feels wrong. I keep telling myself Adeline will want those clothes—because her mother made some of them—but deep down..."

"You're hanging on to her."

"I am."

"Me too. I can't throw Dave's things away. Or sell them. I donated his guitar and video games, but I regretted it that night. I was sick over it. But I also can't take them to the new house in A-City. It's like bringing his ghost with me or something. And I can't imagine packing his stuff up. Going through it again."

"Let's make a deal."

Nora looked up at him. "I warn you: I'm a weak negotiator."

"Luckily, so am I. Tell you what: we'll do it together. I'll come over and help you pack. We'll take everything to A-City. But not to our houses. We'll rent a storage unit. Two of them. So that they'll be with us, there when we're ready to sort it out."

"I like that plan."

That night, they packed Nora's deceased husband's things into boxes. They made two groups—those bound for the storage unit and those Nora couldn't bear to part with, even if they were locked up a few blocks away. The box that would go to her new home was filled with pictures and notebooks with songs Dave had written, a cheap pair of plastic sunglasses he had once bought on vacation, scanned boarding passes from their honeymoon, and a hundred other things that, taken together, wouldn't bring a nickel at a pawn shop. But as she packed the items in the small box, they brought a slow release of tears from her.

Sam thought that separating the things that represented Dave from the items he had merely owned was cathartic for Nora. She was getting rid of her husband's things, but she was keeping him in her heart, holding on to things that were so uniquely him.

They ordered Chinese and drank wine from a box, and despite working for hours, Sam thought they had probably said only a dozen words that night. It wasn't awkward, though sorting through the boxes was a difficult, emotional task. It was simply that it was that easy for the two of them to be together. They were good at working together. Sam knew that. Absolom had proved that. But as the night wore on, he realized they were good at simply being together, when the work was simply their lives—and their lives shared a common thread, a painful, rare one, that few would understand. They were linked. That night, for the first time, Sam felt that link. He wondered if she did too.

In the living room, they sat on pillows on the floor at the coffee table, the plastic cartons of Chinese food and half-filled wine glasses between them. Music from Pandora filled the room, a station seeded with Natalie Merchant. "Fade into You" by Mazzy Star was just starting up.

Nora took a sip of wine. "For months after Dave passed, I was in denial about what happened. It was so sudden. It wasn't real. Not for a long time. And then it was and life hasn't really been the same since. Not really. People talk about their greatest fears being public speaking or heights or snakes. For me, it's none of those things. It's something like Dave's death happening again." She tipped the wine glass up again and swallowed hard. "He would be irate if he knew that."

Sam reached over and took her hand. He had done it to comfort her, but when she turned and looked at him, he knew she was feeling what he had felt earlier. Half of him wanted to hang on to that because he hadn't felt it in a long time. The other half of him felt guilty. Because of Sarah. Because, like Nora, he was still holding on. It was the guilty half that let go of Nora's hand. And he knew Sarah, like Dave, would have been irate about that.

Sam knew he was still a wreck. He couldn't bring Nora into that. At least, that's what he had told himself that night. That's how he had rationalized his pulling away.

Back then, he was a lot like the Triassic looked now: battered but still alive, ready for another day.

With the spear in one hand and a burning torch in the other, Sam set out from the ruined camp. At the tree line, he stopped and decided to take one last look at the prisoner who had tried to kill him, just in case he saw something in the light of day that had been shrouded in the darkness of night. The crazy man's presence here was still a mystery to Sam.

He walked across the rocky ground, weaving through the green pod bushes to where he had left the other prisoner. His body hadn't been picked clean, but something—perhaps several somethings—had taken bites out of him. Bugs were already making camp around the corpse, digging in.

Sam was about to turn away when a glint of metal caught his eye. He leaned in, the torch held out, sending the bugs scurrying away. Attached to the prisoner's femur were three small pieces of metal, like toothpicks. Sam didn't think they were pins that might have supported his weight. They were too small.

Using the spear, Sam pried the metal pins loose. Tiny letters were printed on each, starting with "ASI." As in Absolom Sciences Inc. Were they some sort of quantum tracking tag? To make sure the prisoner arrived in the right universe? If so, it had seemed to malfunction. Or, if the intention had been to send him here, it had worked perfectly.

Sam scanned the rest of the body but didn't see any other pins. He slipped the ones he had found in his pocket and trekked into the woods, toward the pond and stream he had seen before.

The going was slower today. The woods were a thick mess of fallen trees and limbs. He really needed a machete. Among other things.

At the stream, he set up a basic camp, with stones in a circle and a fire crackling in the midday sun, which he lit with the torch.

Under the blazing sun, Sam stood in the stream with the spear and jabbed and cursed and came up empty until he remembered a scene from one of his favorite novels, *Hatchet*. Like Sam, the young protagonist in the book is all alone, trying to survive in the wild. His first attempts at fishing are unsuccessful until he starts accounting for the refraction of light underwater. With that adjustment, the hero from *Hatchet*, Brian, is able to catch fish and feed himself.

Sam knew he should have accounted for that on the first visit to the stream. But he wasn't exactly in top shape then. Days of hunger and thirst have a way of dulling in the mind. Even for scientists.

Sam slipped the end of the spear into the water and waited. Soon, he jabbed the stick down and jerked it out of the water, a fish flopping on the end.

Finally, a real meal. With the protein from the fish, he could get back on his feet. Maybe even figure out what was going on here.

Whoever thought books didn't save lives was so very wrong.

On the riverbank, under the afternoon sun, Sam cleaned the fish and grilled it and ate every last morsel. It was the best meal he had eaten in ages.

The satisfaction brought by the earthworms had been a fullness of necessity, a sort of carnal relief that his life had been extended. The grilled wild-caught fish was absolutely luxurious, the taste and contentment lingering as he used a fishbone to pick the pieces out of his teeth and swallow them down.

Shelter was the next task, but that was as far as Sam got with the thought.

Across the pond, thunder rose, a slow rumbling. But the sky was clear.

Sam took the bone torch from the fire and walked to the stream edge. The treetops swayed. But there was no wind.

What's happening here?

The river filled with fish. They were swimming to the sea.

The forest burst then, dinosaurs and large reptiles charging forth, a Triassic stampede barreling toward him.

Not toward him—away from something. Whatever it was,

Sam couldn't see it. And he didn't want to. If they were running from it, that thing could hurt him too.

Sam didn't bother to pick up his spear. Or extinguish the fire. He turned and ran.

THIRTY-FOUR

For a few weeks, life fell into a routine for Adeline. She rode with Ryan to school—until he told her he was fine ("really, I'm fine, seriously, quit hovering over me like I'm a hurt animal or something").

Each morning, she went to work at Absolom Sciences and soaked it all in. She was fascinated by the Absolom machine.

She sat in on the seminars for the new scientists joining the company. There were a lot new terms, which she had to look up. And concepts that online definitions couldn't convey in a few seconds. She didn't understand it all, but like a mountain she was climbing, each step she took got her closer to seeing the whole picture.

Every day, the ground she had covered before built on itself, and the task ahead seemed smaller. Eventually, she developed a basic understanding of how Absolom operated and the history of how it had come into being. Unlike the others in the auditorium, she knew the behind-the-scenes details her father had shared with her, the history only the Absolom Six knew.

But Absolom wasn't what she really wanted to learn about. It was the next version of the machine that would change the world. Absolom Two. On that subject, information was nonexistent. She searched the company intranet. It was never mentioned by anyone working at the company, and she never asked. She sensed that would be a mistake.

Absolom Two wasn't the only mystery haunting her. Each day, she checked the BuddyLoc app and watched Hiro's movements. Every morning, he drove out to Death Valley and stayed until early afternoon. Daniele was with him, or so Adeline assumed. She wasn't at work. And the two times Adeline had ventured out to the desert to spy on him, she had seen Daniele there. It seemed that it was the four of them—the remaining Absolom founders—digging in the desert and refilling the holes.

But what were they looking for?

Almost every night, Hiro left the dig site and drove directly to the modest home in Las Vegas. Was he taking what they had found there? That seemed a reasonable assumption to Adeline.

And then there was the room in Constance's home, with the photos from the past, of people and their locations, spread across the wall like a murder board.

Elliott's home had a similar room, in the basement, where videos of the night of Charlie's death played on repeat and photos of that evening hung on the wall.

Were the two connected?

What did it all mean?

Adeline sensed that there was a piece that would tie it all together. Her gut told her that Absolom Two was that piece. And that Daniele was the only person who would give her answers. Getting those answers would be tricky.

She was sitting in the library of Daniele's home, contemplating what move to make, when the older woman stuck her head in. "I'm home."

Adeline beckoned for her to enter.

Daniele eyed the finance books on the table. "You're making progress."

"I am."

"Riveting, isn't it?"

"Mind-numbingly boring."

"True. And that's why I appreciate you sticking with it."

Adeline eyed the dirt and sand on Daniele's clothes. She sensed this was her opening, the right time to ask the questions burning inside of her. She made a decision then: to lead with the truth.

"I saw you in Death Valley. Digging. I used the app to find Hiro, and I saw him there operating the excavator. I saw all of you there."

"I know."

"At first, I thought you might be looking for Dad's bones."

"He's not even in our universe."

"I remembered that shortly after I thought it. My guess is you're working on Absolom Two."

Daniele smiled. "No comment."

"Can I ask you a question?"

"You can ask."

"Can we use Absolom Two and prevent Nora's murder? Can we prevent Dad from ever being sent back?"

Daniele reached behind her and slid the pocket door closed. Her voice was hard and serious when she spoke. "No. The past cannot be changed. It *must not* be changed. For all of our sakes."

"Why?"

"The past is the causal sequence of events that created our present."

"Okay. Can you be more vague? What does that actually mean? Why can't we just go back, stop Nora's killer, and be done with it?"

"There are several problems with that."

"Which are?"

"First of all, what you're talking about is not possible with the current technology."

"With Absolom One?"

"Correct."

"But it is with Absolom Two."

"No comment."

"I'll take that as a yes."

"Take it however you like. What you should be focused on are the other problems."

"What sort of problems?"

"The second problem is what I mentioned before: the present moment that you and I are experiencing now is the eventuality of a series of causal events. Those events, those thin slices of time, all stack on top of each other like building blocks with no end and no beginning. And if you modify one of the blocks we're standing on right now, do you know what happens?"

"We all fall down?"

"In a sense. Our best guess is that breaking the causality of our reality will make it cease to exist at the moment causality is ruptured. It's like a black hole. We know that once matter crosses the event horizon, it cannot escape the pull of the singularity's gravity. For a long time, scientists have theorized about what happens to that matter, but we don't know exactly. What we do know is that nothing that crosses an event horizon will ever come back."

Daniele paused. "What you're talking about—modifying the past—is like crossing a temporal event horizon. What lies beyond is a temporal black hole from which nothing will return. Or ever exist. *You. Cannot. Change the past.* Do you understand?"

Adeline didn't respond. The words were like a sledgehammer smashing her hopes.

"In fact," Daniele said, "it's possible that breaking causality may be the reason we're alone in the universe."

"I don't understand."

"Think about it. If another sufficiently advanced species had evolved before us, they would have eventually developed an Absolom machine. And eventually, they would have developed a second version and used it on their past, disrupting the causality in their universe, hence ending that universe. Ergo, why it hasn't yet happened in this universe and why we are alone—and the likely explanation for how our universe will end."

Adeline's head was spinning. Was Daniele just trying to overload her with technobabble so she would stop asking questions? It was sort of working. She inhaled, trying to focus.

"Do the others share this view? That the past can't be changed?"

"It remains a subject of some debate among the four."

"Who wants to change the past?"

"No comment."

"Elliott? He wants to save Charlie, doesn't he?"

"You know he does."

"And Constance. She wants to change the past. What happened to her?"

"It's her secret. It's not what you think it is."

"What's Hiro's secret? What's in that house in Vegas?"

"Not what you think either."

"You know what's there?"

"I do."

"Please," Adeline said. "Tell me."

"His secret is not mine to share."

"Elliott wants Absolom Two to save his son. Constance is clearly obsessed with the past. And changing it. What's Hiro hiding?"

"What's happening here is complex, Adeline. Leave it to me. You've done enough. And you've endured a tragedy. The loss of a parent is an injury that takes time to heal. You've lost both of yours too soon."

The last line set Adeline off. "I haven't lost my father. Not yet. The fact that you would say that, frankly, infuriates me. It's like you've written him off. Like you want him gone—for whatever plans you're making."

Adeline sucked in a breath and stared at Daniele. The woman was a statue. As if the barrage of insults hadn't even registered.

So Adeline doubled down. "I thought he left Ryan and me to your custody so we could get him back together. Instead, you've buried me in finance books and cryptic non-answers." Adeline cocked her head. "I think that's what you would do if you really wanted him gone."

Daniele smiled.

That enraged Adeline even more.

"You want answers?" Daniele asked, her voice quiet and firm.

"I think I deserve answers."

"Here's one. See if you can figure out what it means: if you can't change the past without destroying the present, what does that tell you?"

Adeline, almost against her will, instantly saw what it meant. "That in order for our present reality to exist, the past must have happened as it did."

The edges of Daniele's lips curved up, the hint of a smile forming. "That's correct."

"So Nora has to die? And my dad has to be sentenced to Absolom?"

"Yes."

"Then it's hopeless. I'll never get Dad back. He's two hundred million years in the past. And whatever happened back then has already happened. He was probably eaten by a dinosaur."

"Don't say that."

"Why not?"

"Because it's not in your nature."

"What's not?"

"Defeatism. People like you never give up, Adeline. They find a way. People like you made the world we live in. Now think hard. You've made one *very* important oversight."

"Which is?"

"Think."

Adeline saw it then: the one fact her rage had blinded her to. "Dad isn't in our timeline."

"Correct."

"We can change the timeline he's in all we want, and nothing will happen to us."

"Correct."

"That's what you were talking about, wasn't it? With Elliott, Constance, and Hiro? Sending something back to him."

Daniele moved to the pocket door and slid it open. "I need to shower."

"Hey, I'm talking to you."

"No. You're not. This conversation is over. Remember what I said: leave this to me, Adeline. It's dangerous. And complicated. There are factors here you don't appreciate."

That night, Adeline was too tired to sleep. She tossed and turned in bed, and rage burned inside of her. She hated Daniele. And the world. And the Absolom founders, for not doing more to save her father.

Daniele had been right about one thing: Adeline wasn't about to give up. Not in a million years.

She was going to fight.

She wanted answers.

She was going to get them. Even if it killed her.

Adeline opened the BuddyLoc app on her phone and searched for Hiro's location, but it didn't show up. He had disappeared.

That was a first. What did it mean? Had he discovered the spyware? Or was his phone off or simply outside of cell reception?

One thing was certain: he wasn't at the home in Las Vegas. That presented an opportunity, one Adeline wasn't going to miss.

She threw off the photomosaic quilt of her family, rose from the bed, and got dressed. In her black V-neck T-shirt and faded blue jeans, she slipped out of her room and down the stairs. In the kitchen, she stood at the touch panel for the home automation system. The security system was armed. She typed the code to disable it and carefully left out the back door. She would be back before dawn and would arm it again, ensuring Daniele was none the wiser.

In the darkness of the night, she walked the few blocks to her home and retrieved her bike from the garage. She had left her phone in her bedroom at Daniele's, but she retrieved her backpack with the burner phone and once again checked the BuddyLoc app. Hiro's location still wasn't registering.

On the bike, Adeline proceeded at slow speed through the streets of Absolom City, which were mostly deserted. On the highway to Las Vegas, she opened the bike up. It had a governor, but it still hummed in the night, the wind the only noise, hissing by her as she carved into the darkness.

She realized then that the feeling of movement was its own kind of progress. Moving from one place to another felt like an accomplishment. Was that hardwired into the human brain? A learned trait from thousands of years of tribes trekking across unknown land to find fields and forests with less competition?

Probably so.

On the horizon, the bright lights of Las Vegas loomed, an oasis in the night calling: we have answers, come to us, don't let off the accelerator.

And she didn't. Not until she reached the quiet neighborhood with the two- and three-car garages and stucco exteriors and red clay-tiled roofs.

Adeline parked the bike three doors down from Hiro's house and hung her helmet on the handlebar. She checked the BuddyLoc app and still didn't see Hiro's phone on the map. She casually strode down the sidewalk, the streetlamps buzzing above her, glancing at Hiro's house. It was dark inside, and the curtains were drawn. There was no car in the driveway.

In front of the home, Adeline bent over, studying the façade as she took a thin ziplock plastic bag from her pocket and reached down, into the grass, as if picking up dog poop her pet had dropped earlier during a walk. It was the best cover she could come up with on short notice (the bags had been in Daniele's pantry).

There was no movement inside the home.

Adeline walked around to the side, looking, listening. It was utterly still.

In the home next door, someone was either playing a video game or watching a movie. The window flashed like a strobe light through the thin curtain. The lot lines were tight but wide enough for her to make her way to the back, where a pool lay in the middle of beige stone decking.

Adeline moved quickly to the door that led to the living room.

Locked.

The door to the breakfast nook overlooking the backyard was locked too.

At the closest window, she put her palms on the glass and pushed up. It didn't budge.

She tried the next one. It was locked as well.

Adeline's heart rattled in her chest. She was heaving now, the nerves and exertion overtaking her. She planted her feet and pushed up on the window again. Her palms slid across the glass, screeching. She dried them on her pants and pushed again. This time, she heard a pop, like plastic snapping. The window shot up, jamming her fingers into the small crack where the double-hung sashes met.

She was in.

She let the window down and quickly examined her fingers. The nail under her middle finger was already filling with blood, turning purple, almost black. It throbbed with pain, all the way into her hand. The other fingers hurt, but they were only red.

She lifted the window again and high-stepped into the home, her foot landing on marble tile.

What she saw shocked her.

Nothing.

The home was completely empty. No furniture. No paintings or pictures. The floor and walls and counters were bare. Like a house waiting to be sold.

Or a trap.

Adeline's every instinct told her to turn and run.

But she if she did, she would be right back where she began that night: with no answers.

She listened a moment. There was no sound anywhere.

The kitchen off the breakfast nook opened onto a living room with no fireplace, only two receptacles on the wall: one for data, one for power.

Adeline walked down the hall, past an empty bedroom on the right. The front door loomed ahead. To her surprise, she saw a straight-run staircase descending on the left. From the street view, this looked like a typical ranch home. But it had a basement. The open rail staircase down to it was ominous, like the mouth of a monster waiting for her.

Another secret room. It was fitting. Each of the remaining Absolom Four seemed to have one.

She had seen Constance's secret room. Spied in Daniele's basement. Then broken into Elliott's lair where he hid the pictures of his dead son. What was Hiro hiding down there?

Adeline considered going right out the front door.

That was the smart move. The safe move.

Yes.

This was stupid. Dangerous.

She walked toward the front door and gripped the handle. But she didn't turn it.

Because Daniele was right about one thing: Adeline wasn't the quitting type.

She spun and crept back down the hall and swerved into the stairway and descended the wooden steps, conscious not to make too much noise.

The basement was pitch black except for the dim light from above, the glow of the moon and the streetlights shining into the foyer and stair hall.

This space was empty too. The walls and floor were concrete. The floor joists hung above like the ribs of a beast that had swallowed her.

With each passing second, Adeline's eyes adjusted. As she adapted to the darkness, she realized there was one source of light down here: a panel on the right-hand wall. Beside it was a locked door. A metal door. The kind you might see in a prison.

Adeline moved to the panel. It was similar to the one in Elliott's home, except this one had no place for a key code for the lock. Only a fingerprint and retinal scanner.

But it was the blinking message that sent a chill through Adeline:

SECURITY ALERT: PERIMETER BREACH, NOOK, WINDOW 3.

Adeline turned to run.

The door beside the panel opened.

Against her will, she whipped her head around to look.

Hiro stepped out, eyes wide, mouth open.

Adeline leaped forward, ready to run.

Hiro was faster. He lunged and wrapped his arms around her, dragging both of them down to the concrete floor.

THIRTY-FIVE

Sam reached the tree line a few seconds before the herd of charging dinosaurs and large reptiles reached him. There was no question what he had to do: climb a tree.

It was his only chance of surviving.

He jumped up on a fallen tree and walked up it, arms held out to balance, the torch still in one hand, flame dancing as he went. At the trunk it was leaning against, Sam put the bone torch in his mouth and climbed, wincing when the wind carried the fire close to his face. He considered dropping the torch, but it was too valuable. If he had to return to the ground, it was his only defense against the herd.

Below, the animals pounded the forest floor, shaking the tree and the limbs. The screeching was earsplitting. Around him, other trees wobbled. The skinnier ones fell.

Smaller animals were trampled by larger beasts as the herd passed below like a prehistoric cattle drive, the strong grinding the weak into the ground. The carnage was breathtaking. The smell gagged him, but Sam held tight to the grilled fish he had eaten at lunch. He had worked hard for that meal, and he didn't want to give it up.

Based on what he saw, if he lived through this, food wouldn't be a problem for a few days. There would be plenty to scavenge.

When the herd had passed, the forest fell silent. Sam was about to climb down when the ground began shaking. At first, he thought it was another herd. But this vibration was different, deeper, the force enough to move the tree trunk up and down.

Another earthquake.

Is that what the animals were running from?

Sam began shimmying down the tree. He got about halfway before the shockwave hit.

The trunk slammed Sam in the face. The last thing he saw was the torch wink out like a bedside lamp being turned off.

Sam woke in a bed of twigs and flesh. His nose was filled with the smell of sulfur. The forest was full of smoke.

He had no doubt about what had happened. And what he had to do: run.

He had to run for his life. As far as he could.

There was one problem. His body.

It was bruised and sore and refused to move.

He tried to sit up, but his back cried out in pain, pinning him down. It wasn't just the impact. Whatever he had landed on had reopened the cut on his back from the fight with the prisoner. He could feel his blood seeping out through the makeshift bandage.

He promised himself he would lie there for three breaths. Then get up.

In. Out.

In. Out.

Mentally, he formed an image of himself stepping out of the Absolom machine, holding his arms wide and Adeline and Ryan rushing to him, hugging him, his daughter whispering "Welcome home, Dad."

The imagined reunion was like a ghost taking root in Sam's body, powering him.

He rolled onto his side, face-to-face with the open eyes of a felled dinosaur, its mouth open, backward curving white teeth just inches from his nose.

He pushed up and stumbled away. Nearby, he found his spear and used the blunt end as a walking stick.

The forest was easier to move through now. The herds had carved paths through the underbrush like a flood across a mountain range.

At the ridge, Sam stopped to catch his breath. What he saw confirmed his theory: a cloud of ash rose from the volcano. Lava seeped over the crater wall in waves. Halfway up the rise, magma was pushing through a secondary vent, dribbling down the side, joining the main lava flow.

The scientist in Sam wondered if this was the opening salvo in the Triassic–Jurassic extinction event. The survivor in him said it didn't matter. The eruption was enough to cause his extinction, and that was all that mattered at the moment.

At the volcano's base, a fire was consuming the forest, lit either from the lava or the volcanic bombs thrown during the eruption.

Below, in the desert, he spotted the herd of dinosaurs and reptiles moving away over a high dune.

He had hoped to avoid the desert. But the fire made his choice for him.

Sam began hiking down the ridge. His body ached, but he pushed through. With each step, the smoke from the forest fire grew thicker, joining the volcanic cloud of ash spreading out, slowly blotting out the sun.

By the time the forest gave way to the desert, the shadow from above was already spreading across the sand.

Nearby, Sam spotted a massive bony rib cage sticking up. As he studied the skeleton, a sense of dread settled over him. He recognized the creature—it had been one of the exhibits in Daniele's Triassic creature picture book. One near the end.

The remains before him were from the apex predator of the era: the Prestosuchus. It was a large reptile shaped like a crocodile, except it could walk on its hind legs and had small arms similar to a T. rex. Upon seeing the picture in Daniele's book, that's what Sam had thought: it was like a love child of a T. rex and a crocodile. Mentally, he decided to simply call it a giant croc, because, well, Prestosuchus was a mouthful, even to think.

Archaeologists had found giant croc skeletons up to twenty-five feet long. This one was the same shape, but it was larger. At least forty feet, if Sam had to guess. There was no doubt that this was the biggest carnivore he had seen since arriving in the Triassic.

The giant crocs would be hard to deal with. If they were still around. His gaze moved over to the swamp, where the trees were swaying.

Sam realized then that the bones sticking up were what had made the black shadows in the desert that he had previously seen from the ridge.

There were more of them across the sand. A lot more.

Beyond the skeleton, he spotted another oddity: the twinkle of metal. The last rays of sunlight peeking through the cloud of smoke and ash danced across the small object, reflecting as though it was a diamond half-buried.

Sam trudged across the sand, feet sinking as he went. As he approached, he realized the metal was attached to another human skeleton, to the femur, just like the man who had attacked him. The object was the same, too: three pins with an Absolom Sciences serial number.

These bones were pitted and older, though he had no idea how much older. Hundreds of years? Thousands?

He was so caught up in his thoughts that he barely noticed the dinosaur rushing past him. Another skipped past, throwing sand in its wake.

They paid him no mind. Their only thought was getting away from the volcanic catastrophe taking place.

Sam collected the three pins and shoved them in his pocket.

On the ridge, the wildfire was burning fast now, carried by the wind. From the desert, looking up, it was a stunning scene. The forest was alight with flames, belching smoke into the sky where the cloud of ash grew, spreading across the world like a dark, thick blanket.

Another dinosaur charged past, propelling itself on its hind legs, forelimbs dancing back and forth. A quadruped barreled by next.

At the base of the hill, where the desert began, the forest seemed to expel every animal it had left, the fast-moving fire driving them. They were large and small and flowed like waves from the ocean toward Sam.

Behind him, he heard what sounded like gunfire.

He turned and immediately realized what it was: branches and fallen logs breaking under the massive feet of giant crocs emerging from the swamp. They trampled the wide bushes and dug into the sand, rushing forward in leaps and bounds, their long jaws open, teeth gleaming as they barreled toward Sam.

THIRTY-SIX

In the basement of Hiro's home in Las Vegas, Adeline writhed on the floor, trying to break free of his grasp.

"Stop!" he shouted, his breath hot on her ear. "Please. I just want to show you."

That gave Adeline pause. Hiro relaxed his grip.

She took that opening. She planted the base of her hand on the floor, pushed with her feet, and broke free. She scrambled toward the stairwell. Her fingers were almost at the baluster when Hiro caught her again.

He wrapped an arm around her waist and dragged her backward.

Adeline balled up her fists and pummeled the man. Hiro hung his head, trying to keep the blows from hitting his face, and charged forward.

At the metal door in the basement, he drew something from his pocket and tapped on it, and said, "She's here. I've got her. Come help."

Adeline beat harder on him, but that didn't seem to faze him. He was like a robot on a mission.

"Yes. At the house in Vegas. Hurry."

He dropped the phone, the glass and plastic clattering on the hard floor, and charged through the doorway, dragging Adeline with him. He slammed the metal door and held his thumb on the panel on the other side, locking it.

He released Adeline then, and she gripped the door handle and tried to turn it, but it wouldn't budge.

Hiro put his hands on his knees and gasped for breath.

Adeline spun on him and raised her fists.

Hiro staggered away from her, down what Adeline now realized was a narrow concrete passage with beady LED lights hanging above.

"Let me out!" she yelled.

Hiro didn't turn back. Or answer her. He kept trudging through the tunnel, as if he was running from her now. That surprised Adeline. She gave chase, and Hiro began to jog.

"Hey. Where are you going?"

When she caught up to him, she grabbed his shirt and pinned him to the wall.

"What're you doing?"

"You want to see it, right?"

Adeline squinted. "What?"

"My secret."

"What secret?"

"What I'm hiding here. That's why you came."

Slowly, she released her grip on his shirt.

"Follow me," Hiro said, turning and marching deeper into the tunnel.

They walked in silence. Adeline took out the burner phone, but there was no reception in the tunnel, which explained why Hiro had disappeared from the BuddyLoc app. As they walked, Adeline wished she had left a note for Daniele. Or sent an email to herself, revealing where she was. No one knew she was here. What if this was some sort of dungeon where Hiro was going to imprison her?

But his body language told her that he wasn't a threat. It was almost like he was afraid of her now. Or maybe he was scared of whatever was waiting at the end of the tunnel.

Up ahead, Adeline spotted a metal door, much like the one in the basement of the home where they had entered the tunnel. There was a panel too, the same type as at the other end.

Hiro pressed his thumb to the glass and the door lock clicked. Hiro opened it, revealing an oval room with three metal doors like the one they had come through.

In the center, on the far wall, was a wide wooden door. Sitting in front of it was a muscle-clad man perched on a small stool. He was looking down at a hardcover novel encased in plastic, the type a library might wrap around a book. He closed the tome and slid off the stool with a creak.

"Dr. Sato," he said. "Forget something?"

"No. Let us in."

The burly man eyed Adeline. "She's a bit young."

Hiro's silent stare was like the sun. The muscle man—a bouncer, Adeline assumed—was like a stick of butter. With every second, he melted.

Finally, he reached back and opened the door and held out his hand.

Adeline stood rooted on the spot, taking in the scene.

Tables spread out, wall-to-wall, filled with people sitting at them, studying the cards in their hands, stacks of chips arrayed around them like walls of a fortress, some tall, others crumbling. Dozens of conversations mingled in the air, which was tinged with the clouds from vaping pens.

Adeline stepped forward, through the door, and joined Hiro at the edge of the room.

An attendant in a white shirt and black vest raised a radio to his mouth and whispered something, then pressed a finger to his earpiece, listening.

He turned to Hiro. "We have a spot for you, Dr. Sato."

Hiro turned to Adeline. "Seen enough?"

"Yes," she said quietly.

In the tunnel, on the way back, they walked in silence for a while. Finally, Hiro said, "It's a sickness."

"Gambling?"

"I wish I could go back and never place that first bet. Never experience the rush from that first win."

Adeline wasn't sure what to say to that.

Hiro looked back at her. "Daniele didn't tell you?"

"About the gambling? No. She knows?"

"Of course. She helped me. She holds my shares in Absolom in a trust. Ninety percent of the dividends go to charity. I gamble with the rest. That feeds the hunger."

He said it like a fact, but Adeline could hear the shame in his voice.

"As I said. It's a sickness."

"That's why you needed to work on Absolom. For gambling debts back then."

"Yes."

At the door, Hiro pressed his thumb to the panel. When the metal slab swung open, another figure was standing in the dark basement.

Elliott.

So that's who Hiro had called.

His face was grim, but as he stared at Adeline, a small smile began to form. "It was unwise to come here. And very brave. You're a lot like your father: courageous to a fault. That's *one* of the reasons I loved him so much."

"I want answers."

"You deserve answers."

Hiro closed the door, shutting out the light from the tunnel. The three of them stood in near darkness, only the glow from the panel beside the door and the moonlight shining down the stairwell lighting the space. Adeline spoke first.

"Who killed Nora?"

Elliott answered: "I don't know."

"Who do you think killed her?"

"Daniele."

"Why?"

"She's in love with your father."

"What?"

"It's the only thing that makes sense. She killed Nora because she knew Sam and Nora were in love with each other."

"But why would she frame my father?"

"To have him all for herself. To control him completely and hide him away from the world."

"I don't understand."

"Think about it, Adeline. You know we're trying to get him back, right?"

"Yes."

"If we're successful, what do you think will happen?"

"We try to prove his innocence—"

Elliott shook his head. "My dear, that ship has sailed."

Adeline swallowed, the words like a final judgment on the dream she had held onto. "Okay," she said slowly. "What happens *when* we get him back?"

"Did you know Daniele bought an island in the Pacific?"

"No."

"She's working on treaties with governments around the world to make it a sovereign nation. She's even begun seasteading to expand it. She's richer than any of us—and she has wealth beyond Absolom Sciences, money from before, from the other start-ups she funded and public market investments. Things don't add up about Daniele. What we know is that she's building something. A sort of paradise hidden away from the world."

"I don't understand."

"We think she wants to get Sam back, take him there, and

build a new society." Elliott cut his eyes to Hiro. "We don't know what her plans are for us. But she needs us for now."

"Why?"

"Absolom Two. After we created the first version, innovation on the technology essentially stopped. But I never did. I kept researching, experimenting."

"Because you want to save Charlie."

"That's right."

"Daniele told me you can't change the past."

"That's one opinion. What do you think?"

Adeline laughed. "I don't know. I'm not a scientist."

"As it turns out," Elliott said, "we don't think Daniele is either. And that's just one of the things she's lying about."

THIRTY-SEVEN

In the desert, there was no tree for Sam to climb to safety. Wave after wave of animals flowed from the forest onto the sand, fleeing the fire.

The herd was easy pickings for the giant crocs pouring out of the swamp. The carnage was breathtaking, like seeing an army of Godzillas feasting on baby T. rexes and assorted reptiles and dinosaurs.

Sam knew he couldn't outrun the dinosaurs. Or the crocs. He certainly couldn't fight either.

Luckily, there was one place to hide. He rushed toward the croc skeleton. The ribs sticking out of the sand weren't as wide as Sam, but if he turned, they almost entirely hid him. He hoped it would be enough.

As the herd flowed past, he waited, trying to control his breathing. Moving could be deadly.

He felt like he was in a human roulette wheel. If a massive animal crashed into the rib he was hiding behind, it would be his end. If not, he would live. Sometimes one's life came down to simple chance. This was one of those times.

Several seelos bounded in the air, their claws catching the bones, and propelled themselves forward, landing in the sand and sinking as if it was mud, their hind legs disappearing almost to their torsos.

A few feet away, a small dinosaur slammed into the croc

skeleton. Its head stuck through the ribs, and it screeched before drawing back and charging again, this time breaking through before it scurried out the end.

Sam stood as still as he could, his body aching from the first volcano blast. He waited, watching the herd move past.

Above, the thick dome of dark clouds kept pushing down. The smell of sulfur filled the air, and the sound of the carnage was its symphony.

Soon, it was as dark as night, and the heat from the fire warmed the air.

Another boom swept across the desert, throwing Sam into the ribs across the way, the spear flying from his grip.

The shockwave hit the herd like an invisible hand sweeping across the sand, rolling the animals over. It stirred a dust cloud in its wake, the sand in the air seeming to fight a war with the smoke above.

Sam squeezed his eyes shut and crouched down low.

All around him, he heard a spitting sound. Curiosity got the better of him, and he cracked his eyes enough to see the desert rippling where super-hot rocks were landing. They were volcano bombs, and where they touched the sand, green rings of glass spread out.

They would have been beautiful if they weren't so deadly. If one hit Sam, he was finished. The super-hot rock would go through him like an oversized bullet.

He lay still, listening, waiting, feeling like a man in a deadly dunking booth, hoping one of the bombs wouldn't land on his back.

Behind him, he heard a screech and something stirred in the sand. He turned. Just beyond the skeleton he was hiding in, a seelo was struggling to get to its feet. It had been trampled by the herd but only maimed. A deep gash ran down its left hind leg.

It took a step forward on shaky legs, then another, more steadily.

It stopped and shook its head as if trying to clear it. Slowly, it turned until its eyes fixed on Sam. He exhaled as the beast opened its mouth and charged at him.

THIRTY-EIGHT

In the basement of Hiro's home in Las Vegas, Adeline said to Elliott, "I want to hear what Daniele is lying about, but first, I want you to tell me what you're doing in Death Valley—what you're digging up out there."

For a long moment, both Elliott and Hiro were silent.

Finally, Elliott said, "What has Daniele told you about Absolom Two?"

"Vague generalities that only create more questions. I believe you know that routine."

"Here's a straight answer, Adeline: Absolom Two allows us to transport matter back to any timeline we want. Including our own. But there's a problem."

"Which is?"

"We're still not able to send things to exact times. Or locations. My breakthrough was figuring out how to target Absolom to specific universes—but they have to be universes created from our own."

"Why?"

"Entanglement. It's the only bridge between the universes, otherwise they're completely separate. We'd have no way to even know they existed. In my experiments, I used entanglement like a tracking beacon, as a string pulled between the separate timelines, a string we could use to guide something else to that universe. All I needed was matter that was already entangled with the target universe to tag the payload. That breakthrough is what I showed the other Absolom scientists the night Nora was killed."

Elliott inhaled sharply. Adeline sensed regret on his part.

"Of course, they instantly knew what it meant—that Absolom was now capable of changing our past. Nora and Sam thought it was the most dangerous thing ever created, that it would be the end of our reality. Nora even thought it was the answer to the Fermi Paradox—that Absolom Two was how all sufficiently developed universes ended, in causality failures."

"But you wanted to use it, didn't you, Elliott?"

"Of course."

"For Charlie."

"Yes, for Charlie," he said, turning away from her. "But Daniele was also in favor of using it."

"Why?"

Elliott turned back to her. "We have a theory now. We believe Daniele knows that Absolom Two has already been used."

"How? When?"

"We don't know yet. In fact, you now know as much as we do."

"No, I don't," Adeline said. "Tell me how it works. Absolom Two."

"No," Elliott replied, studying her. "You tell me. This is a good exercise for you. Go ahead. You've been working at Absolom Sciences, studying how the machine works. You know we're working on the time and location delivery for Absolom Two. You know we're testing it in Death Valley. How do you think we're conducting those tests?"

Adeline thought for a moment. "You take an object—it would have to be a small mass, because the amount of power required to send something via Absolom is exponentially proportional to the mass of the object."

"Good so far."

"You'd want an object that contained some isotope that decayed over time so that you could measure how far back it went via radiometric dating—that would be your accuracy check. You target a time, then you find it and determine how old it is."

"Very good."

"But finding it would be difficult. Because, again, it's small, and the world is large. But I guess you guys have figured that out, to a certain degree. You map the movements of the continents over time, and you know if you deposit something in a certain area in the past where it would be today."

"That's right."

"But that could be anywhere in an area of, say, a few hundred miles or even a thousand-mile radius. You'd need a specific way to locate it. Like a radio isotope. Something harmless but strong enough for you to detect, even if it was buried below the surface."

Elliott smiled and nodded. "Very good."

"So you fashion one of these... test strips—"

"We call them tuning bars," Elliott said.

"Tuning bars, which can be dated, and which give off a locating isotope, and you send it back, and then you go out to Death Valley, and you dig it up and see how close the location and time was to your predicted arrival?"

"Almost right."

Adeline cocked her head. "Almost right?"

"Almost."

"No. It is right. What I described is what you're doing."

"True. But the order is wrong."

"It can't be. You send it back, and then you go look for it."

"It doesn't work like that." Elliott stepped closer to her. "Think about it in terms of causality."

Adeline's eyes went wide. "No way."

"Do you see it?"

Adeline spoke carefully, her mind still trying to grasp what she was saying. "First, you make a plan."

Elliott nodded. "Correct. We discuss the experiment in the lab. We make a pact between ourselves—Daniele, Constance, Hiro, and myself—that we will carry out the experiment no matter what happens."

"And you acquire the tuning bar," Adeline said.

"Yes."

"But you don't send it back."

"No. We don't. We lock it in a box in the lab, one only the four of us can access."

Adeline nodded, still amazed. "Then you go out to Death Valley, and you try to find it."

"That's right."

"And if you do, you send it."

"Correct. Because if we don't find it, then we never sent it."

Adeline buried her face in her hands. "This is breaking my brain."

Elliott's voice was reflective. "What Hiro and I showed the group the night Nora died was one of our first successful experiments. We had been working on the updates to Absolom for quite some time and were finally sure we could target our universe consistently. So we planned the experiment. We went out to Death Valley and found the bar. We put it in a box. Then we procured the bar and put it in the machine and sent it back. I opened the box on the table and showed the group the aged version we had found. Proof positive that it was feasible to target our own universe. That set everything in motion. For that, I feel guilty."

"Well, there's one way to make it right," Adeline said. "We

get Dad back. Can we use Absolom Two to transport him to our timeline?"

"No. It doesn't work that way."

"Why?"

"Power. And machine mass. We can't effectively transmit what he needs to the past."

"But you're changing that."

"No. We can't. That's pretty much unsolvable."

"I see. But you can send something to Dad?"

"We can," Elliott said slowly. "Something smaller. But there are two issues."

"I don't like the sound of that."

"The first is power."

Adeline shook her head. "What are you talking about? You have a virtually limitless power source from the solar field in the sea of glass."

"Accessing the power isn't the problem. It's using it without anyone knowing."

Adeline shrugged. "Why?"

"Our agreement with the government is that we can perform experiments on Absolom, but we are strictly prohibited from using it on any objects with a mass over twenty-five grams. That's not massive enough to really help us."

"You said there were two issues?"

"The second problem is that your dad was sent to the past with an untuned prototype of Absolom Two."

Adeline shook her head. "No, he was sent with the main machine."

"We switched out the control module," Hiro said.

Adeline smiled. "Which enables you to target his timeline."

"That's right," Elliott said. "But the second problem is that the version of Absolom Two we used isn't completely done. It's not capable of targeting specific times and locations."

"Are you serious? You don't know exactly what year he's in? Or where?"

"Correct."

"Then he's effectively lost in time. And you're guessing when you send things back to him."

"Yes. We are."

THIRTY-NINE

The dinosaur lunged forward, its head easily slipping through the ribs of the skeleton where Sam was hiding. But thankfully its shoulders were too wide. It was stuck. That enraged the creature. It thrashed back and forth, jaws snapping a few feet from Sam's face, its tiny arms clawing at the skeleton's ribs. Sam felt like he was trapped in a bony cage, an angry, miniature T. rex outside desperate to get it. And it probably would, eventually. But the seelo wasn't his only problem.

The creature's screams were like fireworks in the serene desert. They would draw other predators. Maybe bigger ones.

Still facing the creature, Sam stepped away until his back hit the rib bone behind him. The cut there pulsed with pain when he made contact.

The seelo reversed out of the skeleton and swiveled its head left and right, up and down, its tiny Triassic brain trying to devise a way to get to the tasty human snack that was Sam.

Like a prowler searching for a break in the fence, the seelo shuffled right, eying the ribs jutting up from the sand.

It was just a matter of time before it found an opening and slipped through.

Sam turned and reached back through the rib bones, trying to grab the wooden spear. He didn't like his chances against the seelo. But he also didn't like being eaten alive. Or going down without a fight.

His fingers brushed the spear. He risked venturing outside the skeleton, grabbed the piece of sharpened wood, and returned to the safety of the rib cage (he liked his chances inside, against one hungry dinosaur, more than his odds outside, against the stragglers from the herd).

The seelo finally found a break in the rib cage and burst through, instantly turning to Sam, mouth open.

Instead of jabbing with the pointy end, Sam brought the stick down from overhead, holding it with both hands, swinging like a sledgehammer. The blow connected midway down the beast's long head, between the eyes and nose.

The creature reeled back and screeched. Sam swung the stick sideways, like a baseball bat, connecting again. He wasn't going to kill the beast this way, but it was buying him time. And maybe it would convince the dinosaur that he wasn't easy prey.

He was so consumed with the fight that he didn't hear the rhythmic pattering to his right—the sound of strong hind legs digging in the sand as another theropod galloped across the desert.

Sam looked up just in time to see the dinosaur. It had the same body type as the seelo attacking him, but it was over twice as large. When it reached the skeleton, it slowed, bent, mouth open, and reached down through the opening where the ribs ended and sank its teeth into the seelo's back. It lifted the smaller dinosaur in the air and thrashed left and right, its sharp teeth tearing into its victim.

Sam staggered back and fell to the ground, watching in horror as blood soaked the sand and the two creatures clawed and bit at each other.

The picture of the larger beast in Daniele's book hadn't been completely accurate. The head was different. But this was definitely a Chindesaurus, and it had just saved Sam's life. For now. But would he be next?

Yes. He would.

Sam got to his feet, grabbed the spear, and backed away, keeping his eyes on the fight—or bloodbath, more accurately.

He retreated to the end of the skeleton, where the ribs were shorter and deeper in the sand, the clearance so low he couldn't even stand. That was good. Standing up—and making noise—was deadly out here.

On his hands and knees, he sank his fingers into the sand and began to dig.

The seelo was dead now. The Chindesaurus was ripping long strips of meat off of it, eating in the dark desert under a cloud of ash, a monster enjoying a prehistoric afternoon picnic in the shadow of a volcanic eruption that might be the opening act in an extinction event.

Sam kept digging.

A dark cloud drifted past and behind it a giant croc emerged, as if conjured by magic, its footsteps silenced by the sand. The Chindesaurus barely had time to turn its head before it was ripped off by the massive jaws of the croc. The prey didn't even have time to scream.

The croc tossed the severed head aside, scooped the body up with its mouth, and slipped back into the black clouds.

Sam's heart skipped a beat. For a long moment, he didn't move. He simply stared at the place where the giant croc had disappeared.

In a world where giant creatures battled to the death, it was good to be small.

Sam resumed digging until the shallow pit was deep enough for him to lie down in. He reached back and covered his legs and lower body in the sand. The gash on his back hurt like crazy, but there was nothing he could do about it. He sensed that it was infected. It needed to be addressed soon. Like so many small problems in life, it would fester and become a real issue. Maybe he could find some sort of natural antiseptic, perhaps some sap from the large trees in the forest. He could certainly cauterize the wound. But that all assumed he didn't get eaten in the desert.

It was a big assumption.

For a long while, Sam lay in his sand pit, only his arms and head exposed, waiting, watching the desert.

With each passing minute, the cloud of smoke and ash pushed down to the ground, filling the air. Sam pulled his tank top up to cover his mouth, but his body still wanted to cough. He resisted. That small sound would paint a target on him, bringing predators across the haze.

In the dense smoke, he heard the volcano belching out more eruptions, far smaller than the first two.

In the seconds after each one, Sam heard the pattering of rocks landing in the sand.

Every eruption stirred a few of the dinosaurs and reptiles, inciting them to move across the sand, perhaps back to the forest or the swamp, where they thought they might find safety.

It made sense—if death was falling from the sky, getting to shelter was wise. But the motion was their downfall. Through the cloud of smoke, Sam heard screeches as the animals fought each other or were caught by the giant crocs. The brutal killings were hidden in the darkness, and Sam was thankful for that.

There was something about the smoke around him and being buried in the sand that made Sam reflect on his life. Or maybe it was facing death, but for whatever reason, he saw his life then as it truly was. To him, there were two clearly defined epochs. The time before: when he and Sarah were young and hopeful, with two kids and their life ahead of them. And the time after. After she passed. After Absolom was invented. In those long years, it had felt as though the universe tilted, and he couldn't get his footing. In those years, he felt buried by the events of his life, shrouded in smoke from the wreckage of the loss, waiting for the next eruption, for a burning hot rock to fall on him, or life's next monster to maul him out of earthly existence.

Lying there in the sand, in this prehistoric time, he finally did what he couldn't do in his own time: he faced the fact that he had been mentally stuck. In a way, even before Absolom sent him to this place, he had been lost in time. He knew that now. He had been trapped in the past, never moving forward with his life. That was the reason he could never really commit to Nora.

In the after epoch, he had sort of floated through life, reacting, trying not to get hurt again. Even before Absolom, he had been a prisoner of time.

He vowed that if he ever got home, he would start a third era of his existence. He would love again with his whole heart. He would engage with friends and family, knowing life was full of pain and that was simply the way it was.

He had heard of people going out into the wilderness to search for the meaning of life. Before that moment, he had thought that was nonsense. Now, he saw it. There was no single meaning of life—there was only the meaning of your life. For Sam, that meaning came from understanding the past and how it impacted his thinking—and mastering it. That was the key to his future.

And he sensed that, in a practical way, he held the key to getting back to that future in his pocket. The pins. They were made by Absolom Sciences. Sent here for some reason. It had to be related to him, to rescuing him.

He reached down, through the sand, and took out the six metal pins he had collected. In the darkness, he saw something he had missed in the light of day: a red LED that glowed at the end of each pin.

He turned the pins, and the red light turned to yellow,

then green. He spun it again, and the color changed. Slowly, he twisted them, watching the colors change. They were more than just quantum entanglement trackers. They were some kind of locator device, pointing him to something in the forest—or where the forest had been before the fire.

Sam looked around at the smoke, and a plan formed in his mind.

FORTY

Adeline paced in the dark basement, turning over what Elliott had told her.

Since the moment she had seen her father disappear inside the Absolom chamber, she had hoped that they would simply be able to return him home, to reach out and beam him back to this timeline.

But that wasn't going to be possible.

"Then what's the plan?" she asked Elliott.

"We have to send your father a device that allows Absolom to lock on and pull back. We call it a recall ring."

"At Daniele's house, when the four of you met in the basement, you were talking about miniaturizing it." She looked at Hiro. "That was your job."

He squinted at her. "You heard?"

"I was eavesdropping."

"Good for you," Elliott said quietly. "Yes, that is the plan. The recall ring essentially uses entanglement to remotely activate Absolom. The machine then uses the entanglement connection to pull the tagged mass across space and time back to Absolom. The problem, as mentioned before, is the mass of the recall ring. Our agreement with the government limits us to using twenty-five grams for testing purposes. Our second problem is time. We don't know *when* Sam is—so we can't send the ring directly to him. But we've solved the mass problem."

Another piece fell into place for Adeline. "Prisoners. I heard Daniele telling a senator you wanted to operate on them."

Elliott nodded, his face pained. "There was no other option. We've been implanting pieces in them and sending them to Sam's timeline."

That shocked Adeline. "That's—"

"Not ideal," Elliott said simply. "But necessary. Our working theory is that they will arrive long before your father. He simply needs to survive long enough to find the pieces and assemble them."

"So, piece of cake. Prehistoric Absolom Easter egg hunt on Pangea."

Elliott eyed her. "If you have a better plan to get him back, we're all ears."

Adeline exhaled. She was tired. And frustrated. She had finally gotten her answers. Some of them, anyway. She had hoped they held the key to her father's safe return. As it turned out, the master plan amounted to a quantum physics Hail Mary.

"What can I do?" Adeline asked.

Elliott studied her. "I thought you'd never ask."

"The problem," Hiro said, "is Daniele."

"How so?"

"She seems to be working with us to get Sam back. But we're not sure what she'll do when he returns. Our best guess is that she'll kill us, the way she did Nora. Or simply send us to another timeline via Absolom. She may have the same in mind for you."

"How sure are you that she's the killer?" Adeline asked.

Elliott spoke slowly. "If you eliminate all other possibilities, what remains must be the correct answer. We know Constance didn't kill Nora. And neither Hiro nor I killed her. We also know Daniele had a motive—her love for Sam. And finally, she had means and opportunity. Ergo, she killed Nora."

Adeline shook her head. "Her whereabouts were accounted for that night."

Elliott and Hiro were silent. Both avoided eye contact.

Adeline pressed her point. "That seems like a pretty big hole in your theory."

"We can explain that," Elliott said, not looking at Adeline.

"How?"

Elliott shook his head.

"Tell her," Hiro said. "She can handle it."

Elliott eyed the other man, then let his gaze drift to the ceiling, the floor joists hanging down. "Our working theory is that Daniele hasn't killed Nora—yet. But she will."

Adeline's mouth ran dry.

"With Absolom Two," Elliott said. "That's the other reason she wanted to build it. And the reason she knew it would be used—because she wanted Nora dead and that night she saw the experiment, she thought about doing it, just like we think about sending those tuning bars back to the past and then go find them."

Elliott put his hands on Adeline's shoulders. "As I told you before: I think there's a very good reason why your father wanted you to live with Daniele. You may be the only one who can stop her from using Absolom to kill Nora."

FORTY-ONE

Sam felt as though he was being slowly suffocated. The smoke from the fire and volcano grew thicker by the second. He couldn't breathe in now without feeling the acrid sulfuric air burn his nose and mouth.

Lying half-buried in the sand, he suppressed his coughs, terrified that they might draw the dinosaurs and crocs stalking across the dark desert.

He had to get out.

He glanced again at the metal pins he'd collected from the two dead humans. He turned them, watching the lights change from red to green.

What was waiting for him out there?

It was time to find out. And it was probably now or never.

As quietly as possible, he moved the sand off his lower body and stood. With the spear in his hand, he ventured to the end of the skeleton, to the opening where a living croc had ripped through the remains of a dead one.

Sam took out the metal pins, oriented himself toward his unknown prize, and trekked out into the desert.

He navigated by sound, keeping clear of any shifting sand or screeches or feet pounding the ground.

A gentle wind stirred the smoke, reminding Sam of the fog clouds in London, of walking across Tower Bridge one night, Nora beside him.

"I'm worried about Elliott," she had said.

"Me too. He's working too much."

"It's not just that. He's obsessing."

"Over Absolom."

"Absolom is what he's working on, but it's Charlie he's obsessed with. Do you know what he's doing in the lab?"

"Something with entanglement. I think working helps him. It's a distraction."

"It's a sand trap. It's sucking him in."

In the hotel room, after dinner, Nora sat on a couch, looking out at the River Thames. "You ever think about confessing?"

"Confessing?"

"Telling the world that we never thought Absolom would be a reality. That we were faking it in the beginning."

"No. Of the things I think about, that's not one."

"I do."

"Why?"

"Guilt. The way people look at me—like I'm some kind of god." Nora raised her eyebrows as if pained. "I just want to scream: 'It was all a fluke. A happy accident. We never even thought it would work. I'm a fraud, a big worthless fraud!'"

Sam laughed. "It's natural."

"What is?"

"Feeling that way. I imagine all celebrities feel like some of the adoration they receive is undeserved." Sam shrugged. "Well, the ones who aren't egomaniacs."

Nora stared at a boat on the river, its lights carving into the night as it motored along.

"We were at the right place at the right time."

"We were," Sam agreed. "And we had the right skills."

"Look at what it cost us."

Sam squinted at her. "What do you mean?"

"We did it for all the wrong reasons. For money."

"We did it for family."

Nora rose from the couch and sat on the coffee table in front of Sam's chair. "Yes. And look at what happened. You lost Sarah. I lost my parents. Elliott lost Charlie. Constance is still sick, and Hiro still gambles." Nora closed her eyes as if trying to conjure the right words. "It's like we made a deal with the devil. We told a lie and got what we wanted but we lost the things we loved— what we truly cared about in the world. In that deep hole, we got wealth and fame and adoration that we don't deserve."

Sam reached out and took her hands. "Hey, where's this coming from?"

"I don't know, Sam. I just feel like the world doesn't make any sense."

"Because you've lost someone—"

"It's not just Dave. Or my parents. It's like things don't add up. Life is surreal, like a dream I can't wake up from. I feel like it has to have some meaning that I can't see. What we're doing has to be part of something bigger."

"Like what?"

"I don't know... some grand plan."

"I don't know about any grand plan, but I do know Absolom brought us together." Sam reached up and ran his thumb across her cheek.

Nora froze, as if the touch had paralyzed her.

Sam thought she was going to reel back, but slowly, she turned her face into his hand. Her voice was soft and heavy with emotion when she spoke. "Sam, we shouldn't."

"Why not?"

"I'm not a whole person, Sam."

"Neither am I. Maybe our halves make a whole. Maybe that's the grand plan you can't see."

She smiled. "You have a career writing Valentine's Day cards if Absolom ever goes under."

231

"Is that a yes?"

"It's still a bad idea."

"Look how our last bad idea turned out. Crime almost eliminated. Billions in the bank."

Across the sand, a pattering started, pitting the brown expanse all around Sam's feet.

Rain.

The late afternoon storm had come like clockwork, and with it, the wind.

It took Sam a moment to realize how dangerous that was.

Like a curtain being jerked back, the thick cloud lifted from the desert and rolled deeper into the interior of Pangea. Within a few minutes, the smoke screen was gone, and Sam was standing in the open, as if he had been swimming naked and the tide had gone out. He hadn't been the only one swimming across the sea of sand to the shore of the forest. Dozens of bipedal dinosaurs and reptiles were scattered across the desert, looking around, waiting for someone to make the first move. There were even more small quadrupeds, clumped together like schools of fish.

Sam took off, running for the trees as a Chindesaurus lunged for a nearby seelo, jaws open, tearing into it.

The carnage had started again.

FORTY-TWO

Adeline rode the bike through the night, across the Nevada desert, back toward Daniele's house. She had a decision to make: trust Elliott and Hiro. Or Daniele.

She sensed that her father's life hung in the balance. Maybe much more. Maybe the fate of the past. And the future.

Soon Absolom City rose on the horizon. The solar panels of the sea of glass glittered in the moonlight like the event horizon of a black hole about to swallow her up.

By the time she reached her home and stowed the bike, Adeline had made her decision. She didn't know if it was the right one, but she sensed there would be no turning back.

She walked the streets to Daniele's home, slipped inside, and re-enabled the security system.

Adeline half expected Daniele to be sitting by the kitchen bar, a cup of coffee in her hands, a stern expression on her face as she whispered, "I know where you've been."

But the home was quiet.

In her bedroom, Adeline took out the burner phone and sent a text to Elliott.

It's Adeline. Count me in.

★ ★ ★

A text from Elliott was waiting for her that morning.

Good. Your dad would be proud.

Adeline typed a response.

What should I do?

Elliott replied a few seconds later.

Install this app.

Adeline clicked the link and installed an app called VoiceActivate. On the home screen, a collaboration request popped up from Elliott's number. Adeline approved it, and another message from Elliott appeared.

Leave the app running. Hide the phone in Dani's study. Make sure you plug it into the wall. Then get another phone and come to my office at work. We can talk here.

In the kitchen, Ryan was eating cereal. Daniele was sipping coffee as she read an e-ink paper. She didn't look up.

"You were out late."

"Seeing some friends."

Daniele smiled. "My parents always said, 'We don't mind you being out at night. As long as you're keeping the right company.'"

The words stopped Adeline cold. Daniele knew. She had to.

"Well," Daniele said, setting the e-ink sheet down. "I told myself I wouldn't lecture you. So I'll stop. You're an adult now. Capable of making your own decisions. And mistakes. Sometimes our mistakes are the best teachers."

Ryan looked up from the bowl, his spoon hanging in the air. The awkwardness was evident even to him.

Daniele breezed past Adeline without making eye contact and made her way upstairs, to shower, Adeline assumed.

For a long moment, she stood there debating whether to follow through with the plan. Hiding the burner phone in the study would be proof-positive that she had betrayed Daniele, a land mine buried, waiting to go off.

She felt as though she was standing on the precipice now, unsure whether to take the next step or retreat.

Ryan was staring at her as he chewed his cereal. "You all right?"

"I'm fine."

"You guys are acting weird."

"It's a weird time."

Ryan muttered something, but Adeline didn't hear it. She was already walking down the hall, off the precipice, toward the study, where she stowed the phone under a fabric-covered club chair. The bottom was open enough for sound to reach the device, but the phone was deep enough under there to avoid being seen, even if someone was looking. Reaching into the darkness was the only way to find it. And Adeline felt like that's what she was doing now: reaching into the darkness.

She connected the power cord to the wall socket behind the flowing curtain and exited the room, hoping she had made the right decision.

An hour later, she was walking the halls of Absolom Sciences' main research building, the Intern badge hanging around her neck, the new burner phone in her pocket.

In the reception area of Elliott's office suite, his long-time assistant rose to greet Adeline. "Hello, dear."

"Hi, Gloria. I'm here to meet with Elliott."

She glanced at the computer screen. "Well, I'm sorry, but you're not on the schedule, and this is a very busy—"

The office door opened, and Elliott leaned out. "It's okay, Gloria. Adeline is always on the schedule."

Inside the office, Hiro was sitting in a chair by the window. He rose and nodded to Adeline. His eyes were more kind than she was used to, as if they had a bond now. Adeline had wondered how him divulging his secret to her would change things between them. Would he feel shame at seeing her? It seemed the opposite was the case. The man before Adeline was more at ease, as though revealing his secret had lifted a burden, removed a barrier that had been between them.

Elliott took a chair opposite Hiro and motioned Adeline to another.

His phone lay on the coffee table, the VoiceActivate app opened. Daniele was speaking, but Adeline missed what she had said. To her surprise, Constance spoke next.

Hiro turned to the window as if looking for a way to escape what was being said. "This is private. We shouldn't be listening."

"It might be important," Elliott said, holding out a hand to silence everyone.

"They've found another one," Constance said. Her voice was faint, but the phone speaker was turned up enough to hear it.

"Where?" Daniele asked.

"In Germany. I'm leaving today to go meet with him."

"Are you nervous?"

"Very."

"You'll do fine. Your body is weak, but your mind is strong."

They made small talk then, but there was never any mention

of Absolom or Adeline or her father or anything that might be of interest.

Silence followed for about fifteen minutes. Elliott took the break to order sandwiches for them.

Thirty minutes later, Hiro wiped a glob of mayonnaise off the corner of his mouth and said, "We're supposed to meet in the valley in two hours. Maybe she's done at home for the day."

But as he said it, Daniele's voice called out through the speaker. It was far off. Adeline estimated that Daniele was in the foyer. Another voice joined hers—a woman's voice, but Adeline couldn't make out what they were saying.

The voice drew closer—very close—as if one of them was sitting in the chair where the phone was hidden. Adeline realized then that they were not speaking English.

Elliott pointed to Hiro, but the scientist shook his head. "They're speaking Korean, not Japanese."

He waited, listening, then drew out his phone.

"What?" Elliott said, moving to the chair to stare over his shoulder.

"They've mentioned a non-Korean word a few times. Syntran. It's a Korean company."

"It's one of Dani's investments," Elliott said. "One San Andreas funded. What do they do?"

"Synthetic organs. They grow them for transplant."

Elliott exhaled. "It's just some update from a portfolio company."

That afternoon, Adeline sat in a seminar entitled "Entanglement: The Quantum Tie that Binds."

Halfway through the lecture, the lights dimmed. The presenter smiled. "Don't be alarmed. That's just the machine transmitting. There are typically a few departures each week.

That power fluctuation is the sign of a very bad person leaving this Earth."

Not always, Adeline thought.

When she got home, Adeline found Daniele sitting on the back patio, an empty wine glass on the table, staring at the sun hovering over the mountains beyond the sea of glass.

"Tough day?" Adeline asked, motioning to the wine glass.

"No. I'm celebrating."

"Celebrating what?"

"A discovery. One that could change everything. A very unexpected discovery."

"In the desert?"

"No. I knew what we would find in the desert. This... this I didn't see coming."

Adeline asked a few probing questions, but it was clear Daniele was keeping whatever this discovery was to herself.

That night, Adeline texted Elliott.

Daniele was celebrating some discovery tonight.

What?

Don't know.

Interesting.

What was said in her second meeting—with the Korean speaker?

Unknown. We need a translator. Don't want to ask anyone around here. Hiro thinks he can find a dealer in Vegas who speaks Korean. Someone who can keep quiet. Should have it translated in a few days.

What about A-2?

Adeline wasn't sure if Elliott would catch on to her shorthand for Absolom Two, but he seemed to understand.

Almost done. Maybe days away. The tuning bars are pretty close to the predicted time and location now. Hiro and I are hiding some of the progress from Dani. Changing the data we show her.

Good.

For the next few days, Adeline's life settled into a pattern. She went to work at Absolom Sciences, learned what she could, and waited for Elliott to text. But he didn't. He and Hiro and Daniele spent nearly all their time in the lab or in the desert.

Finally, before bed one night, she sat at her desk and sent Elliott a text.

What's happening? Did you find a translator?

Yes.

And?

The visitor was the CEO of Syntran. She was just giving a business update and talking about some new product offering. But something else happened. Are you alone?

Yes.

Put your headphones on.

She pushed her earbuds in and typed a reply.

Ready.

Elliott's next message was a link to a video taken on a phone. It was shaky, as if the phone was in someone's shirt pocket and the person was walking around. They were in some kind of medical lab.

No. It was a morgue. Through a wide window, Adeline saw three metal tables. One had a dead body on it. And Daniele was standing over it.

The person walked to the window, giving the camera a better look at the body. It was Nora.

The video stopped, and Adeline stared at it for a long time. Then she typed the three-letter response running through her mind.

WTF?

Dani ordered Nora's body exhumed.

Why?

Isn't it obvious? So she could study how she died. To get the wounds in the right place when she uses Absolom Two to kill her.

The next morning, Adeline could barely look Daniele in the eye.

"Everything all right?" she asked, setting her coffee mug on the counter.

Adeline shrugged. "That's a bit like asking me how the weather is during a hurricane. My mom is dead. My dad is in the Triassic. It's not going great, Daniele."

"It will get better."

"How? When? What's your plan?"

"I told you before. I'm going to get your dad back."

"How?"

"As soon as Absolom Two is finished—when it's accurate enough—I'll use it. Before Elliott. That's important. The past can't be changed, Adeline. And he can't be reasoned with. Do you understand?"

Adeline swallowed and nodded.

"Is there anything you want to tell me?"

"No."

When Adeline got home, a delivery company was unloading a massive box into Daniele's garage.

"What's that?" Adeline asked.

"It's for a trip I'll be taking."

"Trip where?"

"It's none of your concern."

Adeline glanced away, to the street, where two black SUVs were parked. They were unmarked, with dark tinted windows.

Daniele spoke before Adeline could ask about them. "I've hired some additional security. For the house. And the office."

"Private security."

"Yes. I needed people who only answer to me."

★ ★ ★

Ryan was at a friend's house, and Adeline was sitting at the outdoor dining table with Daniele when she felt the burner phone buzz with a text message.

Before she could check it, Daniele reached into her purse, drew out a small box, and pushed it across the table. "I got you a small gift."

Adeline didn't want a small gift. She wanted to get up and leave and go check the text message.

Instead, she smiled and took the box and quickly began removing the wrapper.

"What's the occasion?"

Daniele smiled. "New beginnings. I feel like we got off on the wrong foot."

Adeline opened the box. It was a pair of diamond stud earrings. The stones were massive.

"They're beautiful," she said, wincing when she heard how hasty she sounded.

"Someone very special gave them to me. Someone who's no longer in my life."

She set the box down beside her plate. "Sorry, I need to—"

Daniele rose. "Please try them on."

Hastily, Adeline attached them to her ears and forced a smile.

Daniele leaned forward, fingers interlocked. "They're perfect."

Adeline didn't reply. She rose, marched directly to the hall bathroom, and took out her phone. The text message from Elliott read:

Are you with Daniele?

Yes.

Where?

Home.

Keep her there.

Why?

A-2 is almost done. We're going to use it. The power might fluctuate. She'll know it's us because there's no departure scheduled.

How do I keep her here?

Figure it out. Just do it.

Adeline waited, but no other messages appeared. The thought of physically restraining Daniele made her nervous. She could already feel her palms beginning to sweat.

She deleted the text message chain and tried to form a plan. The basement was the key. If she could get Daniele down there, without her phone, and lock her in a room, it wouldn't matter if she screamed.

But how?

She would have to lure her down there. She would tell her she had something she wanted to talk about—and was worried someone was listening. Then she would run out of the room and jam the door somehow—or tie it closed. That part of the plan needed work.

She would have to go to the garage and see what was there to work with.

Then she'd have to get past the security team outside. Maybe they wouldn't even stop her.

Adeline opened the bathroom door and stepped out into the hall. She barely saw the figure to her right before the person lunged and pressed a cold device to her neck. There was a pop and a pinch against her skin, as if a rubber band had been snapped.

Adeline whirled around, ready to fight, holding her fists out. But they felt heavy, as though she was holding weights that were growing larger by the second.

In the glow of the moonlight through the glass in the front door, Adeline saw Daniele staring at her. There was an injector in her right hand.

Adeline opened her mouth to ask why, but the words wouldn't come. She pitched forward. Her arms were too heavy to raise to break her fall. But Daniele caught her.

Adeline woke groggy and stiff and sore. She was lying on the floor of the machine that had ripped her life apart.

Absolom.

The inside of this version wasn't painted and polished like the production model. It was silver and raw, with an unpainted door that lay open.

This was Absolom Two, and it was still in the lab.

The room beyond the Absolom chamber seemed empty, but someone was shouting, banging on the door to the lab.

"Daniele! I'm calling the police," Elliott yelled.

Adeline tried to push up, but her arms failed her. She slammed into the porcelain floor like a bag of meat on a butcher counter.

Daniele appeared at the door. Her face was stricken, as if struggling with an emotion she couldn't voice.

Adeline opened her mouth but couldn't form words.

Daniele gripped the Absolom door. "Sorry."

She slammed it shut.

Adeline pushed up and peered out through the small window.

A large black bag lay on the floor of the lab. It looked like a body bag.

Around her, the machine began to vibrate and hum.

Adeline blinked, and her world disappeared.

FORTY-THREE

The desert was a battlefield. Dead animals lay in heaps. Blood stained the sand. Dark holes dotted the deadly landscape like gunshot wounds where the volcano bombs had punched through the sand, heating it, turning it to green glass as they sank and cooled.

It was breathtaking, but the thing taking Sam's breath even more was his sprint across the sand, away from the dinosaurs and large reptiles barreling out of the desert, away from the giant crocs that stalked across the open plain, mouths open, stooping to rip into their prey with their long jaws.

Ahead, the forest loomed. The rain was pelting the wildfire, which hissed and belched steam and smoke as the flames died.

The rain was producing steam and smoke from the volcano too, the plumes joining those from the fire, forming a massive cloud that was rolling down the hill to the desert.

It was Sam's salvation—cover—if he could reach it.

Behind him, he heard a screech and a beast fall to the sand, thrashing and screaming.

There was nothing like hearing another runner get mauled to give one that extra bit of motivation to push harder. Sam ran faster. His battered body ached. The cut in his upper back pulsed with pain. But he pushed through it.

He imagined the smell of his blood being a homing beacon for the carnivores on the desert plain.

He pumped his legs, knowing his life depended upon it, until he reached the tree line. The dark cloud there engulfed him like a fortress welcoming a refugee within its walls. In the smoke, he was nearly invisible. At the same time, he could barely see ten feet in front of him.

He moved slower through the shrubs and small trees, using the worn paths carved through the forest when the herds had fled to the desert. Tides are associated with the sea, but Sam realized then that they existed here on land too—the flow of life in response to the forces of nature.

The foothills felt like dunes after a strong tide, rutted and mangled, the foliage matted but still retaining the same general shape.

He walked until it was quiet around him. At the base of a massive tree, he sank down and let his body rest, careful to keep the cut on his back from making contact with the trunk. It was incredibly tender to the touch. Probably infected.

He'd deal with that if he didn't get eaten. And at that moment, he realized that he hadn't eaten in quite some time. With the adrenaline fading, his hunger was reasserting itself.

A handful of earthworms would hit the spot about now.

There's something Sam never thought he'd look forward to.

A grilled fish would be better, but he didn't see himself building a fire tonight—and the cloud of smoke reduced his visibility too much. The smell of that tasty meal would draw predators, especially if they couldn't see the fire. It was too much trouble.

Still sitting, Sam took the metal pins from his pocket. The light on the end was green and blinking. He was pointed in the right direction.

When he was rested, he rose and trekked into the woods, the pins like a compass guiding his way. He sensed that whatever was waiting for him might save him. Or end everything for good.

He was hoping it was better than being eaten by a dinosaur, because sooner or later, that was likely his fate here in the Triassic.

At the top of the ridge, he checked the pins again. The lights were blinking faster now. He was close.

Near the valley, the lights went solid green. He turned the pins slightly, and they began to fade from green to white.

He kept walking, head down, careful to avoid the charred, fallen trees and limbs. Finally, the small lights on the pins turned solid white. He kept walking, and when he did, the green tinge began to return. He backed up until the white was solid.

It was here.

Sam looked around. There was nothing on the ground except for two trampled ferns, the thick velvety fronds hanging in ripped, broken pieces, and soggy dirt and rocks at his feet.

Sam dug his foot in, making a mark in the ground, and stalked off into the forest, searching. He found what he needed a few minutes later. Based on the size, the skeleton was from a Chindesaurus, if he had to guess. He snapped off the top of the T. rex-like skull, careful to avoid the sharp teeth.

Back at the mark he had made, he got down on his hands and knees and began digging with the skull, throwing the dark, spongy dirt aside.

Somewhere along the way, the rain stopped, and Sam was thankful for that. Having dry hands made holding his dinosaur hand shovel easier.

Soon, he spotted a small speck of white protruding through the earth. Sam sank the Chindesaurus skull into the dirt, and this time it hit a rib bone, snapping off the end.

Sam dug with his hands then, uncovering the rib cage—a

human rib cage. These bones were old. Fragile and brittle and worn away.

Sam sat back on his haunches to catch his breath and consult the metal pins. The white light had turned to blue.

With the dark clouds flowing around him and the forest creaking with the aftermath of the volcano, fire, and storm, Sam moved the dirt away until he uncovered the femur and the large piece of metal waiting there.

With the Chindesaurus skull, he broke the metal device free. It seemed to be made from the same metal as the pins, but this piece was different—it was larger and round, reminding Sam of the face of watch. In the center of the device was a dial with a single switch. At the bottom was an O. At the top was an I—or a one.

Off and On.

At the top of the piece, there was what looked like a small port. Another port sat at the bottom. Sam plugged a pin in the top port. On the round metal piece, a blue light came on. Sam joined another pin to the first and repeated until the last pin connected to the bottom port. The blue light on the dial turned golden.

It was like a watch. The pins formed a sort of band. Was he supposed to wear it? To put it on his wrist?

Nearby, through the fog, he heard branches snapping under the foot of something very large. The snapping grew closer.

Sam disconnected the last pin, slipped the device around his left wrist, and fumbled to get the pin back into the port. It had been far easier to connect with two hands.

The cloud parted. A Chindesaurus stepped through the opening. Its head tilted to the left, as if confused by what it saw: Sam sitting in a shallow pit, a dinosaur skull beside him.

The deadly creature stepped forward, nostrils flared, sniffing the air.

Sam set his wrist on his knee, held the dial with his thumb, and shoved the pin home.

The light on the dial turned golden again.

The Chindesaurus opened its mouth and screamed.

Sam turned the dial, from off to on, and the Triassic disappeared.

PART III

ALL OUR FORGOTTEN
TOMORROWS

FORTY-FOUR

A deline didn't know what she would see on the other side of Absolom, but she expected to feel her feet on the ground. They weren't.

She emerged in the air, the earth rushing up toward her. She slammed into the green grass face-first.

Her head swam. Vision blurred.

She heard voices but couldn't make out what was being said. A set of hands gripped her shoulders and began turning her, but a woman's voice called out, "Don't move her! She might have a concussion."

A man said, "Did she wreck her bike?"

The woman again: "I don't know. I didn't see it."

The hands released her, and Adeline rolled onto her back. The sun was unimaginably bright. She squinted, letting her eyes adjust.

"I'm okay," she muttered.

She didn't feel okay, but she also didn't want to draw attention to herself. She didn't know where or when she was. If they took her to a hospital, it would likely cause issues for her—uncomfortable questions such as, *Hey, you seem to be from the future.* Or the past.

Her first order of business was figuring out exactly *when* she was.

When her vision came into focus, Adeline saw a woman

leaning over her. She looked to be in her early forties. Her hair was in a ponytail, and she wore a t-shirt with Barack Obama's face on it and the word HOPE written below.

Adeline turned, taking in the scene. Pedestrians were everywhere. So were bikes. Most of the crowd was about her age: late teens, early twenties. She recognized this place. In fact, she knew it well: it was the campus of Stanford University. Specifically, she was in one of the grass sections of Lomita Mall. The Stanford machine shop was to her left, the mathematics building on her right.

A young man Adeline's age offered her a hand. Behind him, another man was pacing, holding a Palm Treo smartphone, tapping it with the silver stylus, the call on speakerphone.

"I'm telling you, the J. P. Morgan offer is a lowball. It's highway robbery. Bear Stearns is worth at least ten dollars a share—probably far more. I'm buying it hand over fist, Greg."

Adeline got to her feet, chest heaving.

"You sure you're all right?" the woman asked.

Over her shoulder, someone was talking on the phone. "Look, they're basically tied, and Hilary has control of the party machinery. She's gonna win. Plus, the Jeremiah Wright stuff will sink him."

"I'm fine," Adeline mumbled.

She wandered out of the small crowd, ignoring the whispers behind her.

Up ahead was a wide pedestrian and bicycle mall that ran across the front of the Stanford Campus.

Adeline stared at the street sign for a long moment. It read *Serra Mall*.

In her time, it had been renamed Jane Stanford Way after a review of campus historical names.

Adeline walked down the mall and turned and stared at building 420, which housed the university's psychology department. In the middle of the tan stone façade were green letters that read *Jordan Hall*. Beside the sign was a white marble statue of Louis Agassiz, Jordan's mentor. He was perched on the second floor, looking down.

In Adeline's time, both the statue and the name on the building had been removed because of complaints about the two men's connection to the eugenics movement.

But this clearly wasn't Adeline's time.

She marched into the building, almost holding her breath as she wandered the corridors. Finally, she found the lecture hall for PSYCH 20N: How Beliefs Create Reality.

The door was open, and the rows were filling with undergraduate students.

Adeline stepped inside and stared, eyes wide.

At the front of the room, the instructor was stacking papers, which she handed to someone sitting in the front row. "Could you please pass those around?"

When the woman looked up at her, Adeline blinked rapidly, a deer in the headlights. She thought the professor was going to say something, but she merely nodded as she smiled.

Adeline staggered over to a desk and slipped behind it.

At the long table, the professor tapped the keyboard on her laptop, and a slide appeared on the screen behind her.

"We've been talking about how our beliefs and expectations shape our perception of reality. For the next few lectures, we're going to explore an equally powerful force: our stress levels and physical and mental health. As you'll see, how we feel has a huge impact on how we perceive the world around us."

For the next forty-five minutes, Adeline felt as though she was caught in a riptide. The professor's lecture was a rabbit hole of fascinating ideas, but it was her passion for the subject that drew the students in.

And like the students around her, it was the instructor who

had drawn Adeline into the lecture hall. For the first time in years, Adeline saw her mother again. And she saw the woman she barely remembered: a person vibrant and full of life.

Adeline caught herself glancing at the clock, willing the class not to end. She wanted to savor every second with her mother. Life, in two cruel lessons, had taught her that time with family isn't an unlimited thing. She knew precisely how much time Sarah Anderson had.

But in a strange twist of fate, Adeline now had more time with her mother, in a period when she was whole and young— all the things Adeline wanted her to be.

She was so lost in her thoughts that she didn't realize the class had ended. Most of the students had already left. At the long table at the front, her mother was leaning over to put her laptop in a messenger bag. The baby bump was already showing, the daughter growing inside of her that would be born in six months, a daughter they would name Adeline Grace.

Her mother looked up and eyed Adeline, the kind smile returning.

She slung the messenger bag over her shoulder and began climbing the steps of the rows of desks, making a beeline for Adeline, who found that she couldn't move.

"Hi," her mother said, breathing a little heavy from the climb.

Adeline swallowed. "Hi." She said the word carefully. This was dangerous. Causality and all that. But she stayed. Because this was also the one thing Adeline had wanted for so many years: another chance to talk to her mother.

"It's too late to add the class, I'm afraid."

Adeline nodded. Of course her mother wouldn't recognize her. She didn't know what the daughter she was carrying inside of her would look like nineteen years from now. The Adeline sitting before her simply looked like a Stanford undergrad—because Adeline was one (or would be).

"It's okay," Adeline said.

"I don't mind if you audit." Her mother shrugged. "I'm not supposed to, but I'll even grade your test. Just can't give you credit."

"I understand."

"Okay then."

Her mother moved to leave. Adeline stood. "Hey. I could help."

Her mother cocked her head. "Help with what?"

"Anything. You don't have a TA, right?"

She laughed. "Not this semester. Or the last few."

"I'd be happy to volunteer."

"What's your name?"

"Adeline."

Her mother considered that a moment and smiled. "That's a pretty name."

Adeline nodded. She swallowed, emotion overtaking her, not trusting her voice to speak.

"You don't hear it much."

"No," Adeline managed. "You don't."

"Well. The truth is, I'd love some help."

Adeline nodded again. She couldn't remember being this happy in a long time.

Her mother moved to the door and paused there and looked. "See you Wednesday, Adeline. I typically get to class about twenty minutes early."

"I'll be here."

FORTY-FIVE

When she left Jordan Hall, Adeline walked down Serra Mall to the bus stop and rode into Palo Alto.

At this point, she needed what every time traveler eventually needs: money. In the local currency.

Daniele, when she had knocked Adeline out and placed her in the Absolom machine, had seen fit to remove her electronic devices and credit cards—not that they would work here anyway. She had, however, left her something very valuable that she could trade, and those two items were hanging from Adeline's ears.

She contemplated that mystery and others as she stood in the jewelry store on University Avenue, waiting as the jeweler eyed the diamond earrings with a loupe.

Why had Daniele sent her here? To Stanford, her own university, a place she knew well? And why now, Monday, March 17, 2008?

It was St. Patrick's Day. That much was clear from the signs in the windows of the bars along the bus route. The upcoming weekend was Easter. That was clear from the signs in front of the churches.

The country was still nominating its candidates for a presidential election that would have the biggest turnout in forty years. It would be the first time in fifty-six years that a sitting president or vice president wasn't on the ticket.

In the background was an event very few realized the significance of: a brewing global financial crisis that would roil markets. Fortunes would be lost. And made.

"I'll give you eight thousand," the jeweler said, setting the earrings down.

"Twelve."

"Can I see your ID?"

Adeline stared at him. "You can't, actually."

"Why?"

Adeline opted for the truth—or a small part of it that fit the situation. "I don't have it on me."

The man squinted at her, then picked up the stone again. "May I ask why you're selling such a lovely piece?"

"Financial need. I recently lost my parents."

Adeline was surprised at how easily the half-truth came, how comfortable she was with deception.

The man shifted the stone. "There's something written here."

"What?"

"I think it's a series of numbers, but I can't read them. The letters are too small."

The man set the earrings down again and motioned to the corner, where a woman was working on a microscope. "It's broken."

Adeline wondered if this was some kind of trap—something Daniele had set up. Perhaps some way to land her in jail? Or worse, get her killed? Maybe the stones were from some dead mobster's wife who was robbed and killed and now the entire criminal organization was looking for the assassin to exact revenge.

Adeline closed her eyes and rubbed her eyelids. She really had to get control of her imagination. The engraving was probably a serial number of some kind.

"I'll give you ten," the man said. "But only with ID."

★★★

It turned out, all the reputable jewelers around Stanford University wanted to see a government ID before purchasing ten-thousand-dollar diamond earrings. Adeline knew that because she had been to all of them.

She was walking down Alma Street contemplating going to a non-reputable jeweler when the skies opened, and rain poured down. She was so lost in her thoughts she barely felt herself getting drenched.

Would the pawnshop or shady jeweler simply rob her? They'd certainly lowball her. And there weren't any pawn shops in walking distance—that she knew of in her time. Maybe not here in 2008 either. Assuming she found one, maybe they'd pay and have someone jump her outside, in an alley or at the bus stop, taking the money back.

She had to get her hands on an ID. That was the long and short of it. But how? In her mind's eye, she saw herself walking by the windows of bars, peering in until she found someone who looked like her. She would go inside and hop on the stool beside the girl, waiting for her to go to the bathroom, and then slip her hand inside a backpack or purse and snatch the ID and make a run for it.

That would never work. She'd probably get caught red-handed. The bartender would likely stop her. Or another patron. She was becoming a liar, but she wasn't a pickpocket yet. Hopefully, it wouldn't come to that.

And besides, how many people would be out drinking in the afternoon? And even if they were, the odds of finding someone who looked like her were remote. She had to play the odds now. Time was running out.

What did that leave?

The dorms.

She would stalk the dorms on campus. Somebody's room would be open. She'd slip inside and find an ID lying on a desk, waiting for her.

Or the library. Yes, that was an even better idea. Find someone who looked like her, sitting at a study carrel or long table and plop down beside them with a stack of magazines, wait until they went to the bathroom, and grab their ID.

Adeline was a little shocked at herself—that her mind could adapt to crime and deception so easily.

But this was survival. She was alone in a strange land with no one to call, no help, and no money. If she let herself think about it, it was terrifying. But she wasn't going to think about it. She was going to focus on the task in front of her and do it—

"Dear, are you okay?"

Adeline looked up to find an older woman with a large umbrella and a small white dog pulling at the end of a pink leash. With the hand holding the umbrella, she pointed to Adeline's chest.

"Are you... bleeding?"

Adeline looked down and saw black and red splotches spreading out on her white dress, just above her left breast. She reached a hand up and felt a plastic sleeve there, the one that held her intern badge from Absolom Sciences. It hung from the lanyard, which was Absolom blue but had no words on it. Adeline had planned to shred the plastic ID when she got the chance. She certainly couldn't take it out here. Absolom Sciences didn't exist yet.

Adeline shrugged. "I'm fine. Just a cheap ink pen."

The woman nodded slowly, taking in Adeline's drenched form and soaking hair. "Do you need some help?"

"I'm okay. Thanks."

Adeline marched away, turned onto Hamilton Avenue, and

sought refuge under a wide red umbrella outside a café. When she was sure no one was watching, she reached inside her dress, pulled out the plastic cardholder, and removed the Absolom ID.

For a moment, she wasn't sure what she was seeing. The letters were washing away. But Adeline's picture remained.

Where the card had said Absolom Sciences at the top, it now read *CALIFORNIA DRIVER LICENSE*.

At the bottom of the license, the sex, hair, eyes, height, and weight were an exact match for her.

But under the expiration date, her name was wrong. She expected to see:

Anderson

Adeline G.

Instead, she saw the same letters that were in her name. But they were arranged in a different order. When she read them, she began to shake.

Danneros

Daniele P.

FORTY-SIX

A deline stared at the driver's license.
Her license.

Daniele's license.

Her license.

It was the link between the two halves of her life: the half she'd already lived and the half she had yet to live. Both periods took place over the same stretch of nineteen years.

Because she was Daniele.

It was enough to break her mind.

Her stomach broke first.

She scrambled to the flower bed by the café's door, bent over, and emptied the meal Daniele had served her at home—the last meal she had served herself, the night she had given her the earrings, knowing she would need them, the night she had put her in Absolom and sent her back to do the things she knew had already happened.

Daniele's words echoed through her mind like a bowling ball through a china shop, shattering her:

The past cannot be changed. It must occur as it did.

If that was true, was she destined to kill Nora? Adeline decided then and there that she wouldn't do it. No matter what secrets were lurking here in the past, she wouldn't let it change her. She wouldn't become a killer. Not even if causality required it. The thin stacks of reality and events that needed to occur could break for all she cared. She wasn't going to become a monster for the sake of the universe. It could all end, because becoming a murderer would end her. If that was being selfish, then she was selfish.

The thought of killing Nora made her retch again.

The café door opened and a man in his mid-twenties leaned out, a disappointed look on his face. Adeline probably looked like a day-drinking college student, maybe one who had bombed a big test, or just been dumped, or just couldn't handle her liquor.

She wiped her mouth and shrugged. He simply shook his head and slipped back inside.

Adeline ventured back out into the rain, making her way to one of the jewelry shops. If she hadn't been there before, they probably wouldn't have allowed her soaking wet form inside, but they knew what she had to sell.

"I found my ID," she said as she slipped the earrings across the counter. "And I want to know what number is on the stones."

Three hours later, Adeline was dry and sitting in the small living area of her extended stay hotel room. On the coffee table was approximately seven thousand dollars in cash—the balance that remained after buying what she needed: clothes from Goodwill; a MetroPCS prepaid cell phone and a Compaq Presario laptop at Circuit City; and two nights' stay at the hotel.

There was also a small slip of paper on the table, with ten numbers written on it—the numbers that had been engraved on the earrings.

Adeline sensed that it was the other thing she needed. She punched the numbers into the phone, and a man answered on the second ring. His accent was Asian, and he spoke so fast Adeline could barely understand him.

"Shen Photo."

"Hello. Do you have something waiting for me?"

"Name?"

Adeline swallowed. "Danneros. Daniele."

"Spell it."

As she spelled it, she heard him typing on the keyboard. "No."

When she hung up, Adeline looked up the store online. There was no website and scarcely any information about it, only an address in East Palo Alto.

She turned on the TV and switched to CNBC.

Financials were hit again today, despite the Fed's move on Friday to inject two hundred billion dollars of liquidity into markets to help stem the credit collapse. Shares of MF Global plunged sixty percent on the day, and Lehman Brothers' stock dropped twenty percent on fears that either or both could be the next Bear Stearns. Government-supported housing lenders were also in the crosshairs of sellers as Fannie Mae and Freddie Mac rushed to the exit. Even financial execution stocks were punished, with E*Trade, TradeStation, and Interactive Brokers all dropping.

Adeline smiled and shook her head, remembering those lines Daniele had said in the library: *Right now, you don't care about money because you have it. You've never had to wonder how you'll afford your next meal.*

Adeline looked at the stack of cash on the table. It was all the money to her name.

Daniele's words echoed again. *You're assuming your circumstances will never change. They could. They do for a lot of people—in the blink of an eye. One minute your family is rich. The next, you're carrying every dollar to your name in your pocket, you have no home, and you don't know where you're going to sleep that night.*

At the rate she was expending cash—on the hotel room and food—she would be broke shortly. She glanced back to the muted television. The financial education Daniele had imparted had indeed been important.

She navigated to the E*Trade website and began opening an account. She got as far as the page that asked for her social security number. This wasn't going to work. She would probably run into the same issue if she tried to get a normal job—any background check would likely reveal that the ID was a fake.

Adeline's gaze drifted back to the ten numbers on the slip of paper on the coffee table.

The solution to her problem was right here.

She was dead tired. She had left her time at night and arrived in the past in mid-morning. She had probably been unconscious for a while after Daniele knocked her out, but she was still exhausted. For the most part, she had been running on adrenaline. But she knew that time was of the essence now. She had to keep pushing forward. The thing she needed would take time to make.

She took a cab to East Palo Alto, to the strip mall that housed Shen Photo.

It was a cramped little store, with a booth for passport photos and chairs lined up under the plate glass window and the far wall. Several families were waiting in the store, speaking Spanish and Chinese in hushed tones.

When the proprietor saw Adeline, he narrowed his eyes as if she was in the wrong place.

"Picking up?" he asked. It was the same sharp voice she had heard on the phone.

"No," she said, looking around, still confused.

He held his hand out. "Drop off?"

Adeline shook her head. "Drop off what?"

The man grimaced, clearly annoyed, and motioned to the bags lying in bins behind him. "Film."

"I don't have any film."

Adeline scanned the people sitting in the folding metal chairs then studied the man behind the counter, who was visibly nervous now.

"Okay," he said. "You go now."

Adeline did go, but she didn't go very far. She sat outside a Starbucks in the same strip mall, at a table with a clear view of Shen Photo, watching the patrons come and go, an idea forming in her head.

When she was sure the store was empty, she walked back inside and waited until the man emerged from the back room.

She held out the California driver's license for Daniele Danneros.

"I need this to be a real ID."

"No. Wrong place."

"I need it."

He shook his head. "Wrong place."

His eyes drifted from Adeline's face to the middle of her chest.

She knew what he was thinking. She glanced behind her, through the plate glass window, at the nearly empty parking lot.

She had thrown the ink-stained dress away. She now wore a sundress with flowers on it that she'd bought at Goodwill. She reached down and pulled it up, revealing her pasty skin, panties, and bra. "I'm not wearing a wire. I'm not a cop."

She let the dress fall back down. "I need help. I need a social. And IDs that will pass a background check."

The man inhaled and exhaled. Adeline felt her fate hanging in the balance.

"Four thousand."

She nodded, and he motioned to the picture booth.

FORTY-SEVEN

A deline slept in the next morning.

Upon waking, she made a list of all the things she remembered from her childhood and all the things Daniele had told her about her past.

For the future to exist, it all had to happen as it had before. That was up to Adeline now.

She wondered then about the nature of fate and the universe. She wondered if there was something even larger at work, if all these tiny slices of reality—these causal events—that stacked on top of each other led to something she couldn't imagine now.

She wanted to believe they did.

Yesterday she couldn't have conceived that she would be the person responsible for Absolom, for her father's exile from this timeline—and possibly Nora's death.

In a strange twist of fate, her father had confessed to the crime she had been framed for—a crime she might be destined to commit nineteen years from now. She was going to find a way to change that destiny. And get him back. Because she was in control now.

She was scared, alone, and strangely, also hopeful.

After making the list, Adeline wasn't quite sure what to do with herself. Her mother didn't have a class that day. She had no job, but she did need a new place to stay.

A half-hour spent on Craigslist turned up several good prospects. A few calls narrowed it down to a one-bedroom apartment sublet. It was located right off Sand Hill Road, close enough to walk to campus.

Adeline's best guess was that the guy on the other end of the line had partied too hard and flunked out of school and now needed cash.

When she met him at the apartment, his bloodshot eyes lent credence to her suspicion.

"Look," he said, holding his hands out, "I'm totally violating my lease here, so keep it on the down-low, okay?"

Adeline wanted to say, "No worries—I'm a time traveler from nineteen years in the future. I won't tell a soul."

Instead, she simply said, "Sure."

"If anyone asks, just tell them…" His red, watery eyes drifted to the ceiling. He wasn't a good liar. "Tell them… you're my cousin. From out of town. House-sitting."

"Totally."

"Hey, just so I know, what happened to your place?"

Adeline stared at the floor. "I'm getting out of a bad relationship."

It turned out she was a good liar. Or becoming one. She was becoming Daniele Danneros.

She spent the afternoon buying things for the apartment. The guy's bedroom featured a mattress and box spring—on the floor, of course—and a lamp box that served as a side table (the lamp sat on top of the box).

The living room wasn't much better: just a futon and two beanbags. At least the guy had cleaned up the place. Sort of.

When she finished buying the essentials for the apartment, Adeline splurged and bought a bike. Every dollar she spent was one less she had to invest, but the bike would cut down on her travel time around town (and save cab fares).

That night, she sat in the bedroom, scowling at the Netflix website. The user interface was atrocious. The selection was even worse. The vast majority of titles were only available via the mail. Who would want to wait for DVDs to come in the mail? And how could they even make a profit mailing stuff to your house—especially if you had to mail it back? It didn't make any sense.

She wondered how they had ever made it.

She biked to Blockbuster and rented the first season of a TV show that was a staff pick. It was called 24, and Adeline figured if they had the guts to name the show just one number, it had to be pretty good. And it was. In fact, it was about a guy racing against the clock to save his life and the country. Adeline definitely identified with that. She kept popping the DVDs into her laptop until it was late into the night. It was 8 a.m. for Jack Bauer, but it was bedtime for her.

Adeline arrived at the lecture hall early the next morning and waited at the front. When her mother arrived, she looked sick and haggard.

"What's wrong?" Adeline asked.

"Morning sickness." Her mother closed her eyes and took a deep breath, as if waiting for a wave of nausea to pass. "Sorry I'm late."

"Don't be." Adeline reached out and put a hand on her mother's shoulder. The feeling was indescribable. A moment she had imagined a million times since her mother had passed away.

Her mother seemed to read Adeline's reaction. "Are you all right?"

"I'm fine," Adeline said. She took her mother's bag. "Here, I'll get you set up for class."

Her mother exhaled, took a seat on the stool, and focused on her breathing. Adeline opened the laptop, plugged in the VGA cord, and began placing the handouts on the desks.

When she returned to the front of the room, she reached into the bag and brought out the last remaining item: a Hershey's chocolate bar.

Her mother held her hands out. "And I'm craving sweets. Busted. You know what that means?"

Adeline didn't. Her mother smiled again. She seemed to be feeling better.

"It's probably a girl. It's an old wives' tale: morning sickness and sweets means that you're having a daughter."

Her mother smiled then, gaze unfocused, as if thinking. Adeline wondered if she was imagining seeing her daughter go to prom. Or moving into her first college dorm. Or walking down the aisle on her wedding day.

That thought filled Adeline with sadness. She knew the future. Knew that her mother would never do any of those things.

But her mother didn't.

"Hey, what's wrong?"

Adeline looked up. Her mother had read the emotion on her face. She had always been good at that.

"Nothing. Just thinking."

"Well, be careful of your thoughts. They're more powerful than you think."

Her mother flipped open a notebook. "By the way, someone

dropped the class yesterday. Probably a good thing—he was failing. I don't know for sure, but I might be able to add you."

"That's okay. Really."

Her mother studied her. "Are you a student here, Adeline?"

"I am. Just not right now."

"That's all right. But are you all right?"

"I'm just trying to get back on my feet. Life has sort of thrown me for a loop."

Her mother formed that kind smile that had been the hallmark of her youth. "It happens. Life is about getting up. Not avoiding falling down."

FORTY-EIGHT

A week later, Adeline returned to Shen Photo in East Palo Alto.

Her new identity was waiting for her. As far as she could tell, everything checked out. It was a big piece in the puzzle that was the next nineteen years—until the moment she would place herself in that Absolom machine to travel back here to 2008.

Adeline set up an investment account at E*Trade. She remembered the broad strokes of the global financial crisis that was just starting to unfold—and even recalled some of the key dates.

She took bearish positions on firms she knew would collapse. She felt a bit guilty about betting against the companies, but she found absolution in the idea that this had already happened, and that the money she would make would ensure the future was possible. The profits from the E*Trade account would fund San Andreas Capital, which would fund various start-ups and eventually Absolom (and her trip to the past).

With her E*Trade account, she could short stocks and buy puts, but she wanted to go further. She needed more leveraged investments to increase her returns.

She found a small brokerage firm in San Francisco that was willing to allow her to buy credit default swaps for mortgage-backed securities issued by companies she knew were on the verge of collapse.

While she was buying up the troubled assets, she watched as officials from those companies appeared on TV, insisting that their portfolios of subprime mortgages were simply facing a stress test and were fine.

They were not fine.

And the credit default swaps backing their securities might not have been fine either if not for the Federal Reserve, which stepped in and essentially guaranteed them in order to restore confidence in the financial system.

Over the course of a year, Adeline turned a few thousand dollars into tens of millions. Not enough to draw too much attention, but enough to do what she needed to do. It was a nice nest egg to grow, and it would grow to be all the money she needed to create the future.

As the year progressed, it wasn't the growth in her brokerage account that interested her. It was a thing she hadn't expected: how close she became with her mother.

Three times a week, she joined her in class. She also began coming to her mother's office after class to help prepare for future lectures and grade papers.

In a sense, it was the thing Adeline had most wanted in life: a second chance to be with her mother, as a young adult, almost as peers, sharing an experience that was special to both of them.

Adeline knew it couldn't last. For that reason, she savored every second.

They were eating Chinese take-out in her mother's office, grading finals, when her mother said: "What are your plans for the summer?"

"I'm not sure. I know I have to move. My sublet is up."

"Are you staying in the area?"

"Planning on it. Why?"

"Well, I'm actually looking for some help around the house. I don't know if I mentioned it, but my husband is a postdoc in the physics department. He's gotten a job for the summer in Geneva, at CERN. It's a once-in-a-lifetime opportunity. They're building this massive machine called the Large Hadron Collider. Have you heard of it?"

Adeline smiled. "I have."

"Well, Sam is nuts over it. So is his friend, Elliott. He's been working on the project and has gotten Sam a job there this summer. It's supposed to start up on September tenth, and Elliott wants Sam to be there. This is like the Super Bowl of all Super Bowls for them. Sort of geeky, but it's also sort of adorable. Their entire community has been working on this machine for a decade. It's a big deal."

"I'm sure. So Sam will be gone all summer?"

"He will."

Adeline knew that her mother would die in approximately twelve years. She also knew she would have to leave her life at some point before she began to look like the girl she grew up to be—for her mother's sake, and especially her father's sake.

In fact, to be on the safe side, Adeline had decided not to come into contact with her father until she completed the other change she knew she had to make to be Daniele: cosmetic surgery.

She knew that her younger self would not meet Daniele Danneros until she was eleven—when Daniele was thirty years old. But it wasn't just the age difference that separated their appearances. She now knew that Daniele had slightly altered her face to ensure that no one recognized her. Adeline would have to go in for surgery at some point. She probably should've done it upon arriving in the past, but she didn't know then what she knew now. Such was the time traveler's burden.

Adeline returned her focus to the present and her mother's request. "Well, I'd be happy to help."

"Thank you. We'll be busy. I'm teaching summer school—I agreed to do it before I knew I was pregnant—and there's still a lot to do around the house."

"We'll get it done."

"Sam has promised to be back by the due date—September seventeenth. The LHC is slated to start up on September tenth, so that should be plenty of time."

Adeline simply smiled. She knew that the LHC would indeed start up on September 10. And her birthday was September 8.

She marveled that history was funny that way: what your parents tell you about the past is sometimes a heavily edited version. And there was still room for surprises.

FORTY-NINE

That summer, Adeline and her mother were virtually inseparable.

They painted the nursery, shopped for baby clothes at Goodwill, and stayed up late into the night assembling the crib.

"Really, you can go home," her mother said. "Once I start something, I get a little obsessed with finishing it."

Adeline knew the feeling. And now she knew where she had gotten it from. "I'm not going anywhere."

The floor was covered in pieces, as if a wooden treehouse had exploded in the room. The direction book lay flayed open, and her mother was following every step to the letter.

"Confession," her mother said. "I waited until Sam left to do this." She tilted her head. "I love him to death, but he's not very handy around the house."

Adeline laughed.

"He'd probably starve to death if left alone in the woods."

The smile faded from Adeline's face. "You never know. People are capable of a lot more than we might think—when life requires."

As Adeline said the words, she knew they were half for her own sake. Since she had seen him disappear in the Absolom machine, not a day had gone by when Adeline didn't think of her father and wonder how things had turned out for him in the Triassic.

Most of all, she dreaded the event she knew would come in nineteen years: she would have to stand in that room all over again and watch him slip into the past.

The events she was certain of, however, concerned her the least. Her focus now was the secrets in the past. The details that might help her save her father. Because she was going to get that chance. And she had nineteen years to prepare for it—assuming she could control the past. If things didn't happen as they had, there would be no future to save.

In June and July, the financial world slipped into chaos.

Federal regulators seized IndyMac Bank, making it one of the largest bank failures in US history.

The Fed extended credit lines to Fannie Mae and Freddie Mac and later took them over in September, around the time Lehman Brothers failed and the Troubled Asset Relief Program was announced.

Adeline rolled some of the proceeds from her credit default swaps into tech stocks with strong growth potential.

Closer to home, life assumed a routine. By day, Adeline helped her mother with summer school. In the afternoons and evenings, they worked on preparing the small bungalow in Menlo Park for the arrival of Sam and Sarah Anderson's first child. A child who, in a strange twist of fate, had returned home after nineteen years.

One afternoon, while grading papers in her office on campus, her mother said, "Are you going back to school in the fall?"

"No."

"Any particular reason?"

"I think the education I need is out in the world, not inside a classroom." Adeline looked up from the pages. "No offense."

"None taken. College isn't the right path for everyone. I'm

glad you have a sense of what's right for you—and are brave enough to go after it."

Adeline felt a pride rise inside of her she had never known. She had doubted before, but in that moment, she started to believe that maybe there was a larger force at work here, that this life gave and took and surprised, and that just maybe it all added up to something truly wonderful.

As the baby grew inside of her, Adeline's mother became more fatigued. Her projects around the house grew less ambitious.

In the second half of summer, they spent most of their time sewing. As a child, Adeline had thought her mother's hobby was the most boring thing ever invented. Here and now, at almost twenty years old, in the presence of the mother she had already lost once, she relished every minute of it.

In the corner of the small family room, they sewed baby clothes and toddler outfits that Adeline's younger self would soon wear. Finally, after all this time, Adeline saw what her mother loved about sewing, the joy of making something from scratch, the serenity of the motions, of creating something your child could enjoy, and doing something to help provide for your family. Like building a life, sewing was much more than knitting pieces together.

As summer came to an end and the first hint of fall descended on Palo Alto, their afternoon and early evening projects were cut shorter, and increasingly they found themselves sitting on the couch, watching TV, her mother grimacing as the child inside of her kicked relentlessly at night.

They watched the first three seasons of *LOST*, and Adeline and her mother both cursed the world when they learned the fourth season wouldn't be out on DVD until Christmas. They agreed that it was so, so unfair.

The idea of people being stranded on a strange time travel island made Adeline think of her father on Pangea. Except, of course, he wasn't battling a smoke monster and finding things buried on the island.

One night, during a game of Scrabble, her mother said, "Speaking of spelling things, I wanted to ask you something."

Adeline raised her eyebrows.

"Your name. It's so pretty. Sam and I have really struggled to find one we love. I wondered if you would mind if we named our daughter Adeline."

"Not at all. I'd love that."

Adeline's investment accounts continued to swell that summer, but she didn't spend much of the money. She did, however, buy a used Camry that had just gotten off a corporate lease. She needed reliable transportation for what was about to happen.

On Monday, September 8, 2008, around lunchtime, Adeline was sitting in the nursery, unboxing the baby monitor, when her mother called from the master bathroom, through the bedroom across the hall.

"Adeline!"

She ran in and found her mother clutching her bulging stomach. "I'm having contractions."

"Just breathe. They might pass. How close are they?"

An hour later, Adeline was behind the wheel of her car, driving her mother to the hospital.

The expectant mother had her eyes closed, whispering. "She's over a week early."

Her phone vibrated, and she answered it. "Sam. She's coming."

But he didn't get home in time. Adeline, however, was there to see her mother holding her infant form, the glow on her face, the twinkle in her eyes. It was the happiest thing she had ever seen.

Adeline knew it was about time to go. She made a deal with herself: she would stay one more night.

Her mother's eyes were still closed the next morning when she leaned over the hospital bed and kissed her on the head. She lingered a long moment over the bassinet, staring down at herself, thinking about what an unexpected life awaited that young child.

As she was walking out the front door of the hospital, her father was rushing in, gasping for breath, his clothes disheveled. Geneva was nine hours ahead. He must have caught the red-eye.

The LHC would go live later today. He had missed both births, but his life was about to change nevertheless.

In the used Camry, Adeline drove to Draeger's Market on University Drive, at the corner of Santa Cruz, and made her way to the bakery section. The woman behind the counter spotted her, set down a pastry bag, and wiped the excess icing on her hands on a white apron.

"What can I get you, dear?"

"I'd like a birthday cake."

The woman plopped an order pad on the metal counter and clicked a pen, ready to take notes. "Size?"

"The largest you have."

"Would you like a name on it?"

"Yes. I'd like my own name on it."

The woman looked up, surprised.

"It's my birthday today."

"All right. What's your name, dear?"

"Daniele. You spell it with one N and one L."

FIFTY

In the fall of 2008, Adeline moved to Santa Barbara. Her mother was taking maternity leave from teaching that semester, and she felt that it was best to leave the Bay Area. There was too much risk of running into her father or being photographed.

And besides, she knew from living with Daniele that San Andreas Capital had been based in Santa Barbara initially.

For a while, she lived the life of a loner. She learned all she could about quantum physics. She planned the events she knew had to happen. In the winter evenings, she read by the fire. When the weather allowed, she took long walks, listening to audiobooks and learning foreign languages, including German, Korean, and Chinese.

She kept in touch with her mother, who gave her updates on the infant that was now the center of her and her husband's lives.

In March of 2009, as the stock market was reaching the nadir of the bear market brought on by the financial crisis, her mother remarked on a lengthy call that "Sam wants to sell all of our stocks. He's convinced the bottom is going to fall out of everything. He wants to use the money to buy a bigger house. They're practically giving them away right now compared to prices a few years ago."

Adeline glanced at a real-time quote of the S&P 500 on the

monitor on her desk. The index was trading around 700. It had lost about half of its value from its recent peak. It didn't have much more to lose, but Adeline couldn't tell her mother that. And it answered some of how her parents would find themselves in such bad financial shape before Sam joined Absolom.

The correct answer to her mother's question was to stay the course and stay invested in low-cost index funds and high-quality companies with long-term growth potential. Instead, Adeline said, "I don't know. I'm not much of an investor."

Much as she wanted to, she couldn't change the past.

Her job was to ensure everything happened as it had.

If Adeline could use one word to describe her life in Santa Barbara, it would have been "quiet." She lived on a quiet street, in a small, quiet-looking house, and she herself was quiet (most of the time). She exercised, and she studied, and she went to art galleries and a few bookstore readings for her favorite authors—and not much else.

She was preparing for the future. She was also dreading it.

In the summer of 2014, she drove her new Toyota Camry for two hours down to Beverly Hills, to the office of a plastic surgeon whose work no one knew about but everyone saw on TV almost daily.

He sat on a round rolling stool, wearing a white coat, his hands pressed together as if he was about to pray.

"Tell me, Daniele: what would you like to change about your appearance?"

"My face."

"And why is that?"

"It's not quite right for my future."

★ ★ ★

After recuperating from the cosmetic surgery, Adeline drove up to Stanford for the first time since leaving.

It was her birthday, and she wanted to ride by her old house.

The streets were quiet in the Crescent Park neighborhood of Palo Alto, where her family lived. Her parents had bought the modest home shortly after she had arrived in the world. Adeline now knew they had used the money from stock sales to make a down payment. The timing was wrong on the stock dispositions, but the house was a good investment.

In front of the Spanish Revival home were letters in the yard that read HAPPY 6th BIRTHDAY.

People were streaming into the backyard, carrying presents and smiling. Adeline recognized the group entering through the wooden gate. It was Elliott, his wife, and their only child, a son named Charlie, who had just turned fourteen that summer. He was wearing a high school letter jacket and stood two inches taller than his father.

Adeline didn't dare go in. But she vividly remembered one scene from the party, the one that was about to occur. Beyond that gate, her younger self was standing with two of her new friends from kindergarten. She was wearing a floral dress her mother had made for her.

Approaching were three girls that lived nearby who also went to Adeline's school. For the past two weeks, the group of girls had heckled her mercilessly about her, in their words, "homemade hobo clothes." Looking back now, Adeline figured it was simply the stress of starting school that made the girls lash out. Adeline had been an easy target. Her clothes looked different. So they picked on her. But that ended on her birthday.

Charlie walked up, carrying her wrapped present. Within the hour, she would discover that it was a small speaker and microphone that could be tuned to different voice effects. Shortly after unwrapping it, she would overhear her father in the kitchen, opening a beer and handing it to Elliott as he said, "Seriously, dude, what did I ever do to you?" Adeline had loved that little singing machine. Her parents had likely popped champagne the night it broke (as she cried in her room).

But there was to be no crying at the party—or on the way home from school after that—because the teasing about her "homemade hobo clothes" came to an end when Charlie handed her the gift and looked her up and down.

"Adeline, love the dress. Where'd you get it?"

Young Adeline had turned her head to the mean girls as she proudly said, "My mom made it."

The memory made Adeline laugh, how large that event had seemed back then. Charlie was a football star, a high school heartthrob, and about the hottest thing on the block at the time. They hadn't been as close as siblings, more like cousins, and Adeline had never been more thankful than that moment.

The memory also brought a stab of remorse for what was going to happen to him.

Back in Santa Barbara, Adeline began the next phase of building the future. That began with San Andreas Capital.

She registered the domain name sanandreas.cc (she figured using the cc domain extension emphasized the firm's tagline: compassionate capital).

She put the word out that she was looking to make investments in early-stage private companies, but she didn't wait for pitches to arrive over the transom. She went after the companies she knew San Andreas had invested in. She also avoided start-ups that were too high profile, even though she knew they would succeed. She still needed to stay under the radar.

Her first meeting was with a Korean biotech company called Syntran. The CEO was perhaps ten years older than Adeline.

Her name was Hana Kim, and she had been born in Korea, educated in the US, and returned to her native land to earn an MD, PhD, and start a company with a lot of promise—and a huge need for capital.

The woman sat in the conference room of the small office in Santa Barbara, a slide with statistics displayed on the projection screen behind her.

"This year, in 2014, the number of people waiting for an organ transplant reached an all-time high at 124,000. But the number of people waiting isn't why Syntran is in business. We're in business because of the number of people who die in the US every day while waiting for a transplant. That number is seventeen. We're in business because we want it to be zero: here in the United States and around the world. We're going to make that a reality by providing synthetic, transplantable organs."

Adeline liked the CEO. She didn't much like the company's valuation or the terms attached to the preferred stock being offered, but she accepted it. As Warren Buffett had once said, it was better to get a piece of a great company at a good price than a good company at a great price. She sensed that Syntran was a great company.

The price she could live with.

Increasingly, what she couldn't live with was the loneliness of her existence. In a way, she felt like her father must have in the Triassic: alone, stranded in time.

That Christmas, as she stared at the fake tree in the bay window of her small home, she decided that she would remedy that in 2015. She couldn't stand being alone anymore. She knew Absolom would be founded in three years, but she didn't have three more years of solitude in her.

It was time to get out. Even if it broke the future.

FIFTY-ONE

In January of 2015, Adeline flew to San Francisco to attend a start-up pitch competition. A small contribution to the event had bought a sponsorship for San Andreas Capital and an invite to the finals and the happy hour networking session after.

The event took place on a Saturday night, in a hotel ballroom, with a large stage and a screen almost as large. The energy was electric, a mix of nerves and hopes and a feeling like futures could turn on the success or failure of these moments.

The audience included start-up founders and investors and students, and a smattering of bloggers. The geek factor was high in the crowd. Most in attendance would rather talk about the future and extremely obscure details of their work than themselves. Adeline felt strangely at home.

One presentation midway through the night impressed her more than the others. For its founder's style more than the company's substance—which she knew little about.

The company was called speedio, and the founder and CEO was standing on the stage, hands held out, his voice monotone.

"Hi, everyone. We're speedio."

On the projector screen, a picture appeared of a thin, toned man walking on a beach wearing nothing but a Speedo.

The presenter faked a pained expression. "No, not that kind of Speedo. Speed-i-o. As in speed.io—your website's only hope of survival."

The image changed to a picture of Keanu Reeves on a bus, leaning over Sandra Bullock, who was driving.

"Since I know you pack of animals have the attention span of a rabid squirrel on meth, I'm going to lead with this: if your website drops below a certain speed, your whole business blows up—like Sandra Bullock's bus in an amazing movie that we're going to pretend has no sequel."

On the screen, the image changed to a bar graph.

The presenter shrugged. "I hook you with memes. I close you with graphs. Here's what this one means: it's the bounce rate on the average home page on the web. For pages that take two seconds to load, on average, 9.6 percent of visitors bounce—or leave. If your page takes four seconds to load, you've lost 17.1 percent. Six seconds."

He inhaled sharply.

"I don't like to even think about this fact, but I will use it to get your money. At six seconds, 27.4 percent of visitors roll out. Gone. Poof. Probably for good. There's very likely an Angelina Jolie, Nicolas Cage, *Gone in Sixty Seconds* joke in there somewhere but I'm too lazy to dig for it, and I'm already seeing some glassy eyes, which means that, sadly—and ironically—the presentation for a company that speeds up information delivery isn't going fast enough."

That brought a bout of laughter from the crowd and sent the guy clicking forward a few slides. "If you've got technical questions, hit me up in the Q and A. I'm here for you. For now, let's just keep it simple: we speed up websites. Fast websites keep their audience and make money. Slow ones—well, no one knows what happens to slow web sites because no one knows about them. We have a free tier for small websites, and we charge for large sites. We're generating revenue, and we need money to scale 'cause it turns out making your website really fast takes a ton of servers and almost as many coders wearing very huge headphones and drinking very skinny Red Bulls."

The next slide showed headshots of the company's founders.

"Here's the requisite 'our team is awesome' slide with credentials that prove we're legit enough to date your rescue dog."

The image changed to bar graphs and years written under them. "And finally, our total addressable market is huge. As in, the whole internet needs to go faster, and we get paid to do that."

The final slide was a picture of a black man sitting at a very old computer terminal. Adeline didn't understand it. Apparently, some others didn't either.

"For those of you meme ignoramuses out there, this is Richard Pryor in the movie *Superman III*, which taught us everything we need to know about high finance: if you take fractions of a penny a bunch of times, you get a whole bunch of pennies and eventually dimes, dollars, and gold-pressed latinum, ladies and gentlemen. That's what we do—we make a very, very small amount of money every time we make a web page load faster. Thus, the *Superman III* business model. And with that, I cordially, unabashedly, while making eye contact, invite you to deposit your cash money into my Speedo."

The last line brought a wave of laughter and applause. As the questions began, Adeline decided that the CEO of speedio was smart and funny and probably a little overconfident and all the things she had been missing in her life. His name was Nathan Hill, and Adeline didn't know if he was part of Daniele's past, but she decided that he was going to be part of her future, even if it broke causality, because she couldn't take being alone anymore.

For that reason, she sat through the Q and A, unsure what some of the questions meant.

"So," a venture capitalist in the front row said, "I get how you speed up static assets—images, flash video, Java applets—but how are you handling dynamically generated pages? Say, an ASP.NET web form, for example. The ViewState is going to be different for potentially every visitor."

"Yes and no," Nathan said. "Even for a web form, the vast majority of the page is static—we can compress that. Same for the ViewState even. Have you ever seen some of the names on these .net controls? Like, what are the developers thinking? It's like a haiku poem or something. We take a name like txtLastNameGrandParent1 and change it to c18—assuming it's the eighteenth web control on the page. That's like twenty bytes saved right there. We change the name back when we post the form data to the originating server for server-side processing. Doesn't sound like a lot, but if you save twenty characters for every control on the page, those bytes add up, like fractions of a penny in *Superman III*."

After the event, Adeline approached him at the bar.

"Hi."

Nathan stooped to read her name tag. "Daniele Danneros. San Andreas Capital. Not familiar, but nice to meet you."

She gripped his hand. "Likewise." She stared into his eyes. "I'm interested."

"Okay. Wow. Nice. What size investments does your fund typically make?"

"I'm not interested in investing."

They had dinner the next night in a hole-in-the-wall Mexican restaurant that had excellent chips and even better margaritas. About halfway through, Nathan dropped some of his bravado—but not all—and Adeline got to know the real him, the one he hid from the people at work and the venture capitalists on the phone.

For the two of them, from then on, being together was effortless. Adeline thought one of the reasons their relationship worked was that it never got serious enough to interfere with either of their true passions. For Nathan, it was his company. For Adeline, it was the future. Those two things were, sadly, the main attractions in each of their lives.

But the relationship was enough to help Adeline hang on, until the fall of 2018, when an alert popped up on her computer. It was a notification for a video she had been waiting ten years to see—a video that would start it all.

She clicked the link and sat back as it played on YouTube.

In the clip, Elliott was standing on a stage with a picture of a spiderweb behind him.

"Thirty years ago, scientists at CERN invented a web that changed the world. That web we all know today. We surf it on our phones and tablets and computers. But there's another web waiting to be discovered, one far more important. It connects to you and me and every atom in this room. The web I'm talking about is, like the World Wide Web, unseen and extremely powerful. This web is a quantum mesh created by entanglement. And it's going to change the world. Even more than the last web."

Adeline waited two days before she sent her email.

Dear Dr. Lucas,

I saw your lecture on the quantum web at CERN. It's fascinating. In fact, I think your theories could be applied to create a technology with incredible potential.

I'm the founder and managing partner at an early-stage venture capital fund. We're small, but we have extensive capability—and capital to deploy.

At your earliest convenience, I'd like to discuss the possibilities.

Daniele Danneros

FIFTY-TWO

In their first phone call, Elliott was resistant to Adeline's suggestion that his ideas on quantum entanglement could be commercialized. But Adeline was persistent.

She sent an email the following day.

Dear Dr. Lucas,

Thank you for taking the time to talk with me. I know my ideas might seem far-fetched, but I assure you, we can make them a reality. You wouldn't be expected to toil on them alone. You can pick your team. And you are certainly not expected to take any risk. That's why firms like San Andreas exist. We know you have a comfortable teaching position and a well-respected lab at Stanford. If you decide to pursue Absolom, rest assured, there will be funding to compensate you for the risk and help you recruit the best and brightest to make this revolutionary technology a reality.

Imagine this: if we can make instantaneous transportation of parcels from one point to another, anywhere in the world, affordable and accessible, we will change human society. I assure you that it's possible. In time.

All I ask is that you keep an open mind and call me back if you reconsider.

- Daniele

Emailing Elliott made Adeline think of Charlie. She opened a window and did a search for him. She remembered the shape of what had happened, but not the details. An article on Palo Alto Online filled in those details.

Charlie had been a passenger in the car when it was wrecked late on a Saturday night. The driver died. Charlie's right leg was shattered in two places, and two of his vertebrae were fractured. He had been a rising senior that summer before the crash—with a full athletic scholarship to USC. The injury had instantly ended his football career. There were doubts about whether he would ever walk again unaided. The college had agreed to honor the scholarship, but Charlie never made it there.

Adeline remembered some of what happened next. She was too young then to have heard the full details—whether it was the pain medications he took for his injuries or the trauma of having his future changed in an instant—but it led him down a dark, spiraling path from which he never returned.

Adeline understood a little of that now—how a life could change in the blink of an eye. She knew there was even more pain ahead for Charlie. And for her.

When Nathan had texted and invited Adeline up to Mountain View, she knew something was up.

At their favorite Vietnamese restaurant, he slid a small velvet box across the table. Adeline swallowed and stared at it like it was a venomous snake.

"Relax," he said. "It's not what you think. Well, it sort of is, but—look, just open it."

Inside, Adeline found two very large diamond earrings. Diamond earrings she hadn't seen in ten years—since she had sold them at a jewelry store the first day she arrived in the past.

She stared at them, her mind reeling. Had he bought them from the store? Did he know she wasn't from this time? Was this his way of telling her? She had always held Nathan at arm's length, never letting him get close enough to discover the truth about her. Maybe she had gotten sloppy. If so, what did it mean? Was the present about to shatter as she held the two diamond earrings?

"You hate them," he said.

"I love them."

"We sold it."

Adeline looked up.

"Speed.io. We got the wire transfer yesterday. I couldn't tell you because of the NDA."

Adeline nodded. She was starting to breathe again.

"The sale has given me a lot to think about. I've spent way too much time on that company in the last few years. I want to change that. I want to spend more time with you. I want to see where things go. Maybe move in together—"

Adeline closed the box and pushed it back across the table. Daniele's words echoed in her mind: *Someone very special gave them to me. Someone who's no longer in my life.*

Since arriving in 2008, Adeline had assumed that the future version of herself had given the stones to her. But that wasn't the person she was referring to. Nathan was that person.

"I can't give you what you want."

He squinted. "What do you mean?"

"The thing is, I'm starting a company of my own now. And

like yours, it's going to take a lot of my time. I think it's what I'm meant to do at this point in my life."

Nathan shook his head. "Ships in the night. I get off as you get on."

Adeline motioned to the velvet box. "Should—"

But she knew what he was going to say: "Keep them. I want you to have them."

The next day, she took the earrings to a jeweler.

"I need to know, is there anything engraved on these stones? In small letters?"

The man put the stone under a microscope and said, without looking up, "No. They're completely clean. Not even a GIA inscription."

"I need something engraved on them." Adeline took a piece of paper and scribbled down the phone number for Shen Photo.

Adeline received an email from Elliott the following day.

Dear Daniele,

I actually discussed our meeting with a few colleagues of mine. We'd like to hear more about what you're proposing. No promises, but I'll say we're intrigued.

Elliott

Adeline smiled. She would soon see her father again. And then she would have almost ten years before she lost him again, and in those ten years, she hoped, was the answer to getting him back.

FIFTY-THREE

For reasons Adeline couldn't quite identify, she was nervous about the meeting with the scientists who would found Absolom Sciences.

Maybe it was because she hadn't seen her father in ten years. In his mind, in the case of Daniele Danneros, they were meeting for the first time. Would it be awkward? Would she be able to hide the emotions she knew would come during the meeting?

If living in the past had taught her anything, it was how to be a good liar. But even this would be a challenge.

She decided to have her associate partner sit in on the meeting and ask questions. His name was Greg, and he was a recent Stanford MBA. He was a ninja with a spreadsheet, golfed constantly, and loved grilling start-up founders. It was almost like a sport for him, as if he thought a certain amount of verbal pain had to be endured before an early-stage investment was allowable. Adeline told him to go easy on this group—they were scientists, not steel cage fighters.

A few months before the meeting, she had purchased a historic home on Cowper Street in Palo Alto. It was a Queen Anne-style house that had been used by a law firm, which had outgrown it. She had it furnished, but the seven-thousand square feet home wasn't staffed. She could have had some of her staff come up from Santa Barbara, but she didn't much see the point. Adeline and Greg would do the meeting alone.

They waited in the foyer for the scientists to arrive. Every few minutes, she wiped her hands on her dress and tried to focus on her breathing.

Why was she so nervous?

The door opened, and Elliott strode in. Dark bags hung under his eyes. He looked haggard, as if the weight of the world was crushing him.

He introduced Constance, who looked sick even then. To Adeline, she looked as fragile as the woman she had known in Absolom City.

Nora had the same haunted countenance as Elliott—and so did Adeline's father. She knew why. He had recently gotten bad news about his wife's cancer. Even at age ten, Adeline had seen how hard it had hit him.

Hiro was last through the door and the most aloof. He was one of the greatest minds of the group but easily the least social.

In the conference room, Elliott said, "Did you rent this place for the meeting?"

"No, in fact I recently purchased it, with the intent of making it an incubator for start-ups."

"It's a good location," Sam said. "It's actually a few blocks from our homes."

Adeline smiled. "Perhaps it's a sign."

The meeting lasted an hour, and at the end, Adeline asked the partner in her firm to leave. When he was gone, she addressed the scientists.

"There's one last item, I'd like to discuss."

Elliott leaned back in the room chair. "And what's that?"

"My role," Adeline said. "I want to be more than the person who funds this venture."

"What do you mean?"

"I want to be part of it."

"How?" Elliott asked. He seemed more nervous now.

Perhaps he sensed that something was amiss, that she knew that they had been faking their enthusiasm, that she was testing them.

Adeline pressed on before he could say any more. "What we're talking about here—Absolom—is monumental. It's a foundational technology, like few before it. Consider its predecessors. The printing press. Thanks to Gutenberg's machine, for the first time, information could be carried across long distances—granted at the speed of a horse or a ship. The telegram enabled text messages to be sent instantly. The telephone transported a voice, instantly, across vast distances. The web gave us instant access to pictures and text and video, from anywhere in the world. And now Absolom. Soon, matter itself will be able to travel anywhere, in the blink of an eye, just like text, and voice, and video."

Adeline paused, watching the group. They were nervous. Her enthusiasm was a sharp contrast to their own doubts, which they were hiding. But she needed to continue the ruse. Both sides did, if the future was to occur as it had. She pressed on.

"Imagine how Absolom will change the world. I want to be part of that. For the sake of history. You might think I'm not qualified. You're wrong. I don't have a college degree— in physics or anything else. In finance, I had a mentor, but everything else I've learned, I've taught myself, alone. And in my work, for the most part, I've been alone. I'm ready for that to change. I want to be part of a team. As I said, I don't have a formal education in this field, but I am a scientist in the strictest definition of the term: I'm an expert in the underlying science; I've studied it; and I've done my own research. That research has led me to Absolom, and I know I can contribute to the work that still needs to be done."

As the group was leaving, Adeline's father lingered in the doorway of the conference room. "I wanted to say that while this…"—he motioned to the projector mounted on the ceiling—"idea is promising, it's still risky."

Adeline thought, *if he only knew*.

What Adeline didn't realize was how seeing her father would change her.

She had always heard that you didn't appreciate something until you lost it. Well, she had lost her father once. She couldn't do it again.

She knew she would have to. In nine years, she would have to stand in that box in Absolom City and watch him travel to the past. The question was what she could do about it.

Her plan, all this time, had been to discover who truly killed Nora, prove her father's innocence after he left via Absolom, and bring him home.

But what if that wasn't possible? What would she do then?

She could hardly bear to think about it.

To Adeline, there seemed to be only one solution. If she couldn't prove her father's innocence—if she couldn't clear his name—she would still bring him home, and they would live in exile.

That night, a plan began to form in her mind.

A plan to build a place where she and her father and brother could go and no one would find them. They could build a new life and live in peace, without wondering if the authorities would find her father.

That place was an island in the Pacific. In the future, Elliott had told Adeline that Daniele had bought an island and was developing it, but until that moment, she had never understood what Daniele's plan had been. She saw it now. The island was a refuge of last resort if she couldn't clear her father's name.

The island became her secret project. She began researching

seasteading to expand it and hired contractors to draw up plans to create the ultimate self-sustaining escape. Off the grid. Off the map. A place to disappear to.

When the legal documents for Absolom Sciences were ready to be signed, Hiro requested a meeting with Adeline.

They met at the office on Cowper Street one morning, both sipping coffee in the conference room.

"I don't want to own my shares," Hiro said.

"Why?"

"Risk."

Adeline shook her head. "You'll be paid in addition to the equity—"

"Not that risk. The risk is... that I'll sell the shares and spend the money. I want you to control a trust that owns my shares and only allow me to sell a small percentage each year. The rest should go to these charities when I'm gone."

Hiro slid a page across the table.

"Why?"

"I have a sickness."

Adeline studied him. She knew what his sickness was. And she knew he would feel better once he told her. She waited as he spoke slowly, staring at the floor.

"It's the same reason I don't have a wife or a family." He looked up quickly. "It's not that kind of sickness. It's a compulsion I've never been able to control. I gamble."

The confession from Hiro wasn't the only one Adeline received that week. She woke the next morning to an email from Constance, requesting a meeting at her home.

Adeline arrived that afternoon, and she was reminded of

that day she had visited her in Absolom City, of how terrified she had been back then, of what she had seen.

This meeting started in the same way, with the two of them sipping tea in the living room, the doors to the backyard open.

"If we're going to be partners, I think it's only fair that I tell you something you should know about me. About my health." Constance set the mug down on the glass table with a clink. "I'm sick. I have been for a few years. And I'm getting worse." She opened her mouth to continue but seemed to reconsider. "Actually, I think I should show you."

She rose and made her way upstairs, to a room on the front of the home.

The hairs on Adeline's arms stood on end. It was as if she was reliving the scene from her past—and Constance's future.

The woman reached out a skinny hand and turned the handle to a bedroom with no bed, only pictures on the wall and notes. Adeline had seen these very pictures and notes before, in the bedroom in Absolom City. Only here, there were fewer pictures, as if Constance was only now beginning to build the tableau.

She walked close to the wall and studied a photo of a young man in his twenties, holding a large glass full of beer in a pub.

"After college, I took a year off before going to grad school. I was restless and wild back then. My father had just died. I was mad at the world. I had enough money saved up to travel, to not work, and simply indulge. And I did. I spent a hedonistic summer in Europe. A downright shameful fall in Hong Kong. A winter full of debauchery in Australia. I arrived home in California that spring out of money and ready to live a normal life again."

Constance turned and clasped her hands together. "But time and money aren't all that reckless interlude cost me. I didn't know it until years later, but somewhere along the way,

I contracted HIV. And I very surely passed it along to others during my romp around the world."

Constance inhaled. "I thought you should know. That's my interest in Absolom. The treatments for the disease have come a long way, and I want to get the best care possible—but it's more than that. I want to use the money to find whoever I might have infected. To notify them and offer to get them care as well."

Adeline stepped deeper into the room, scanning the pictures. It all made sense now.

"I hope that doesn't change anything," Constance said.

"It doesn't," Adeline whispered. "The past is the past."

But she wondered if it did, if Constance's secret was the piece she was looking for—if it somehow connected to Nora's murder in a way she didn't yet understand.

FIFTY-FOUR

With the founding of Absolom Sciences, Adeline moved to Palo Alto. She bought a small home a block away from her parents' house and Elliott's house.

For a while, her life was solely focused on work. At the Queen Anne-style mansion on Cowper, the small team refined the design for the Absolom prototype. They worked late most nights, kicking around ideas and running computer simulations.

Adeline got to see a side of her father and the Absolom founders she had never known—what they were like in those early days, at work, behind closed doors.

Hiro easily logged the most hours. He even slept in his office some nights. When he was in the midst of a technical problem, it dogged him like a ghost haunting his mind. And it was a brilliant mind.

When his work came to a logical stop, he would take two days off. Sometimes it was the weekend. Other times it was the middle of the week. He simply disappeared and returned, not exactly looking refreshed but ready to work again.

Adeline knew where he went. She had seen it in the future.

Sam and Elliott worked closely together, like two physics detectives working a case, sharing notes, and drawing on a whiteboard. Both men looked stressed, and Adeline knew it was not because of the load at work but because of the challenges at home, the problems they couldn't solve.

Nora and Constance worked together on the machine's hardware, trying to integrate Sam and Elliott's theoretical ideas with Hiro's software. They were the bridge between those two islands, and in a way, they were their own island, working away from the group most of the time.

That was fine with Adeline. Whether it was conscious or not, she had avoided Nora. She knew what would happen to her and that getting close would only make it tougher for Adeline to see that her murder occurred.

One night, at 2 a.m., Adeline's phone vibrated on her bedside table. She had always been a light sleeper. The stress of starting Absolom and ensuring things happened exactly as they had before had only made her more restless.

She answered the call and heard Hiro's voice on the line, sounding agitated. "I need an advance on my salary."

"How much?"

"Twenty thousand."

"Hiro..."

"I'm at the Bellagio. Ten to pay my marker, and ten so I can win everything back."

Adeline sat up in bed.

"You know I'm good for it," Hiro said. "I'll sell you some of my stock."

"You're not selling any stock. I'll send the money, but promise me: when it's gone, you'll come home."

"If it's gone."

"If. And when. Do we have a deal?"

That became a pattern, with Adeline serving as Hiro's financial firewall and Vegas giving him the release between long work sessions.

Constance periodically left for medical treatment and to visit someone from her past, to notify them of her medical condition and provide any assistance she could, including financial and moral support.

In the days leading up to those trips, Constance always looked stricken, as if the disease was overtaking her. Adeline soon learned that it wasn't that—it was the anticipation of what was to come, of delivering what might be a death sentence to someone from her past.

Many of the people she came into contact with had already presented with symptoms of the disease. A small number hadn't. And some tested negative.

Adeline could tell how the visits had gone—the person's outcome—just from Constance's demeanor upon her return. HIV was slowly destroying her immune system, leaving her vulnerable to a deadly infection. But it was what Constance had decided to do about her past that was killing her. And Adeline admired that—her courage and her honesty and her sacrifices. In fact, it made Adeline feel guilty for ever suspecting her of murder. Constance was perhaps the most selfless person she had ever met.

In the months that followed, Adeline caught glimpses of the other secrets the Absolom Six were keeping.

Outside the door to Elliott's office, she heard him pacing, talking on the phone, sounding exhausted.

"I don't care if he hates the counselors. You tell him we moved heaven and earth to get him in there. If he leaves, that's it—he's cut off."

A pause. Elliott sounded even more helpless when he spoke again. "Well, what choice do we have? If we don't draw the line, he will keep pushing our boundaries, Claire.

We talked about this. We've got to take a stand. For our sake and his."

One morning, at the team's weekly check-in, Sam was late.

"I'll go get him," Adeline had said, rising and leaving the conference room before anyone could object.

She found the door to his office cracked. Her father was sitting in a desk chair, swiveled toward the window, a phone held to his ear.

"I'm going with you, Sarah. I told you—"

Adeline pushed the door open slowly, but he didn't see her.

"I'm well aware that I've started a new job, and if I get fired, so be it—I'm going. I want to be there to advocate for you."

He turned suddenly, realizing Adeline was in the room.

She held her hands up, backed out, and closed the door.

He opened it a minute later.

"I'm sorry—"

"No," Adeline said, "I'm sorry. I shouldn't have barged in."

"The meeting slipped my mind."

"You've got a lot on your plate."

"I need to ask for some time off."

Adeline stepped into the office and closed the door behind her. "You don't have to ask for time off. I'm not your boss, Sam. I'm your partner. And partners take care of each other. You need time off. You take time off. I also have something that might help."

Adeline's father raised his eyebrows.

"A NetJets card. Traveling with a sick family member is tough enough. This will make it easier. And you can schedule the return flight when you're ready. Just in case you need to stay longer for more treatment or recovery."

Adeline realized another thing about time and families then: if you live long enough, the role of who takes care of whom gets reversed.

That wasn't the only role that had reversed. In Absolom City, after her father had been sent into the past, Adeline had been the one in the dark, racing to try to unravel everyone's secrets.

Now she was the one with the secrets. She had the power. She was pulling the strings. She was controlling the past. Which led her to a question she hadn't entertained before: how much the past had already been changed. By someone else. If she was an agent acting on the past, had there been others?

Finding out wouldn't be easy. But she had all the pieces she needed.

A week after he returned, Adeline's father leaned into her office and said, "Thanks again for the jet." He laughed and shook his head, as if still in disbelief. "It was amazing."

"You're welcome. Glad I could do it."

"Sarah would like to finally meet you—and say thanks. Are you free for dinner one night soon?"

"I am. Any time."

Adeline had been expecting the invitation at some point. She had been both looking forward to it and dreading it.

In so many ways, she was finally going home, to the place where she had grown up and where her mother had grown sicker. It was the place where they had become a family and where that family had been shattered.

On a Thursday in late November, Adeline stood on the stoop of her childhood home, watching the leaves of the maple trees rattle in the wind, the orange, red, gold, and brown tones mixing together as if the trees were on fire.

The door opened, and Sam ushered Adeline inside. Ryan was sitting on the floor of the living room, playing with magnetic blocks. The boy was about five years old, and at his father's behest he did a minimalist greeting and returned to building his castle.

As her mother approached, Adeline extended her hand, but the woman held out her arms and hugged her. Adeline thought her mother's arms felt frail, but her eyes still showed a strength that warmed Adeline's heart.

Her counterpart was nowhere to be found. Young Adeline was likely at a friend's house, supposedly doing homework while actually gossiping the night away.

It was an unusually warm night, so they had dinner on the porch, her mother wrapped in a shawl, her father in the V-neck sweater he had worn to work.

When the meal was done, Adeline's mother rose to clear the plates, but Adeline reached out and gently gripped her mother's wrist. "Please, let me."

When the dishes were collected, Adeline's mother showed her the sewing room. "It used to be a nursery for Ryan. I've been working in here since…"

Adeline thought she was going to say, *Since I got sick.* Instead, she said, "Since I stopped teaching."

Adeline picked up two pieces of cloth, consulted the pattern her mother had printed off the internet, and held them under the needle at the sewing machine. "Would you mind?"

Her mother smiled. "Not at all."

A minute later, when the sewing machine whined down to silence, her mother shook her head. "Didn't know you sewed."

"My mom taught me."

"Same here. I've been trying to get Adeline into it, but she has zero interest."

She studied the pieces of cloth. "It's been good therapy for me. Takes my mind off of everything. And makes me feel like I'm creating something to leave behind... that they'll remember me by."

Adeline nodded. She didn't trust her voice enough to speak. Someone her mother just met wouldn't be as emotional as she felt then.

"Lately," her mother said, "I've been too tired to make much progress. I mostly sit in here finding patterns for quilts that I will probably never make. But it feels good to have plans."

Adeline didn't know if she meant plans for the quilts or a plan to make them—a plan to live that long. She tried as hard as she could steady her own voice. "I could help you."

"I couldn't ask you..."

"I'd enjoy it. I lost my mother a long time ago. It would be kind of nice to sew again. It would remind me of her."

They began that night, and once again, Adeline sensed that it wasn't just pieces of cloth they were sewing together. For her, she was joining the pieces of the past, and it made her so happy.

FIFTY-FIVE

In the months that followed, Adeline spent several evenings a week at her childhood home, sewing and talking and enjoying those fleeting moments with her mother. She was doing what she wished she had done as a child. Back then, Adeline had always assumed her mother would get better. That it would all pass. Losing her had been unimaginable. That's part of why it had hit her so hard.

The pieces of fabric weren't the only things she was assembling.

In the Nevada desert, she was buying large tracts of land. The previous year, she had acquired a solar company, and they were already getting permits for the expansive solar field that would become known as the sea of glass.

The plans she filed with the state and federal regulatory agencies called for a massive power plant that could bring cheaper energy to the region. But she knew the power wouldn't be sold. It would be used to send people to the past. Including her father someday.

In the Absolom Sciences lab in Palo Alto, the machine was close to completion—or failure, depending on one's perspective.

Thousands of miles away, in the middle of the Pacific, Absolom Island was progressing nicely. The port was operational, and construction was well underway on the housing village, offices, and recreational facilities. She had told the construction companies that she was building a resort. Her checks had cleared, so they hadn't asked any other questions.

One Thursday morning, Elliott gathered everyone in the lab. He held up a small silver bar with an Absolom Sciences serial number.

"Ladies and gentlemen, behold one of the biggest, and possibly most expensive, scientific blunders in human history. And unfortunately, our blunder."

He placed the tuning bar in a small Absolom prototype, closed the door, and nodded to Sam, who typed on a keyboard.

A second later, the lights dimmed, and through the glass window on the door, the box flashed, and the bar was gone.

At the computer, Sam said, "Quantum entanglement tracking confirms that the bar should be three hundred miles away, in Death Valley."

He clicked the mouse and a live video stream appeared. Sam switched to the recorded footage, showing that there was nothing there.

"Elliott and I have repeated this exercise..." His head tilted back, gaze fixed on the ceiling. "Four million, two hundred and eighteen thousand times. Same thing every time. Entanglement tracking confirms the payload was delivered, yet it's not there."

Hiro spoke then. "Maybe the transmission process destroys the payload—or breaks it down. Maybe the atoms are shattered into subatomic particles and scattered at the delivery site—i.e. it's there, but it's in trillions of tiny pieces."

"Our tracking says the entangled particles are still intact."

"What this means," Nora said, "is that the many-worlds interpretation of quantum mechanics is true. Absolom works. It just doesn't work the way we expected."

"There's another problem," Hiro said. "I haven't been

able to solve the energy requirements. Frankly, even if these payloads were arriving in our universe, the power required to transport any meaningful amount of mass would be cost-prohibitive. Even if we solve the technical aspects, financially, based on the cost of energy, it will never be practical to ship things this way."

Adeline sensed that her moment had arrived. "This isn't a failure. It's what Bob Ross called a happy accident."

Elliott grimaced. "Bob Ross? The guy at University of Detroit Mercy?"

"Not that Bob Ross," Adeline said. "The landscape painter."

Sam held his hands out beside his head. "The guy with the big hair."

"That's the one," Adeline said. "What we have here is a Bob Ross-style happy accident. He said we never make mistakes on the canvas. Only happy accidents. And we need to figure out how to use this accident. We're certainly not the first in history to find ourselves in this position. Alexander Fleming found penicillin completely by accident. He went on vacation for two weeks and returned to find mold growing over his petri dishes, mold that prevented the growth of staphylococci. Even the discovery of plastic was an accident. So was the microwave. And gunpowder."

Adeline glanced around the room at the five scientists. "We've discovered something here. We just need to figure out why the world needs it."

Adeline knew the answer. But she wanted to give it some time—time was, after all, what it was all about.

Two seminal events in her past were drawing closer, and Adeline dreaded each one.

Absolom Sciences had moved into a larger building in Palo

Alto, but the individual offices of the Absolom Six were still close enough for her to hear signs of stress outside of work.

Increasingly, Elliott was growing desperate and frustrated with Charlie. The whispered calls had become shouting matches. In the mornings, he drank more coffee, and his eyes were more bloodshot—either from crying the previous night or drinking alcohol or both.

On her calendar, Adeline had circled the date that Charlie's suffering would come to an end. She dreaded that night. And she knew she had to be there.

The past couldn't be changed.

She would walk down that street and look at the convenience store's security camera and go into that apartment. She knew what she would find there.

Another date loomed large in her mind: her mother's death.

She had contemplated trying to stop it a million times. But that would break causality and the universe. And besides, there was no cure for her at this time. Maybe there never would be. Maybe time couldn't cure everything, despite what her father had said.

She visited her mother more frequently then. Adeline knew she was trying to hang on to something that she couldn't stop, as though time itself was sand slipping through her fingers.

At the door one evening, Adeline came face-to-face with her younger counterpart. The girl was twelve and cocked her head impatiently and yelled, "Mom! Your sewing buddy is here!"

She stormed out without another word, off into the evening, likely to a friend's house nearby to homework-gossip or indulge in social media feeds.

As an adult now, it was hard to even remember herself being that moody and self-absorbed as a teen. Yet there it was.

Adeline's mother appeared in the small foyer, a kind smile on her face. "You're more than a sewing buddy to me."

Adeline laughed. "Likewise."

The quilt they worked on that night was one they had been laboring on for weeks. It was a photomosaic made from hundreds of family photos of Adeline's youth—of her, her mother, her father, and Ryan. The individual photos combined to represent a picture of the whole family at home in front of the Christmas tree.

A stab had gone through Adeline's heart when her mother had shown her the pattern she'd created with a website called Mosaic Quilt—because she knew it was the last thing she had sewn. All this time, Adeline had wondered if her mother knew how it would end, if she had selected the mosaic quilt as a sort of swan song for her hobby and her life. If so, it was fitting. The tiles and pictures were little slivers of a shared existence together, hundreds of moments that, when knit together, formed the tapestry of a life. A family's journey together, one that would soon have no more pictures with the four of them.

Her mother was laying out the quilt's batting when she said, "I was just going to make one for the living room. But now I think I'll make three." She set out another layer. "So they'll all have one."

A part of Adeline wanted to ask, *Why not four—so you'll all have one?* But she didn't need to. She knew then that her mother knew, somehow.

Instead, she steadied her voice and said, "I think it's a great idea."

As she was walking home that night, under the maple trees and the streetlights, Adeline thought about that quilt, about the pictures that formed a larger image. There was a truth there somewhere, just out of her mind's reach.

For some reason, she thought about Constance's room with

the photos of the people from her past. And Elliott's room with the photos from the night Charlie died.

Once again, in her mind's eye, she saw herself on that street in Menlo Park, looking at the camera.

That was it. The world as a quilt of photos. All of history was a sort of photomosaic, waiting to be seen. And so was her life. More than ever, Adeline was sure there was a larger montage here. And she felt that there was a missing piece—a missing scene—that would join all the strips of film together, creating a loop with a beginning, middle, and end that all made sense once you had seen it all and zoomed out.

That's what she had been missing. That seminal scene. That piece of cloth that tied the others together.

She was going to find it.

The next day, Adeline was sitting in the office of another company in Palo Alto, one named after the seeing stones in *The Lord of the Rings*.

The man across the table was one she had known for years from her time as a venture capitalist in the Bay Area.

"What can we do for you, Adeline?"

"I need a piece of software, one I believe you specialize in."

"What kind is that?"

"One that can take a photo as input and find it in a supplied data source of images and videos."

He smiled. "Sure. We can do that. Most of our clients sign an annual operating contract. We can notify you in real time when we identify matches. Until you've found the person."

"That's not what I'm looking for. I'd like you to create the software, and I want to be able to operate it. I supply a photo, and it searches the data sources for matches. And speaking of sources, I want to license any that you're able to supply. I'd also like intros to government agencies and any other organizations you think might be willing to sell data."

That evening, Adeline was thinking about all the pieces in her life, of the past, the present, and the future, and the piece that was missing, the one that might tie it all together, when the doorbell rang.

She rose and opened the door, and on her stoop, under the glow of the porchlight, was Nora, standing in a three-quarter length black trench coat, a floral dress on underneath, smiling at her.

"Hi."

"Hi," Adeline said. "I wasn't expecting you."

An awkward pause passed as Nora stared at her, and Adeline finally swung the door open. "But come on in—of course. Good to see you."

She wondered if the tension was obvious to Nora.

As the door closed, Nora shrugged. "I figured it was time we talked."

Adeline swallowed. "About?"

"I thought we could start with all the things we haven't talked about."

FIFTY-SIX

A deline studied Nora's face. Slowly, terror was growing inside of her. Did Nora know her secret?

Had she finally figured it all out?

Nora must have seen the fear in Adeline's eyes. She held up her hands. "I just meant that it feels like maybe you and I got off on the wrong foot or something. All these years, the group has become so close, but it's just—it just feels to me like there's a gulf between us." Nora smiled, eyebrows rising. "Am I imagining that?"

"You're not imagining it," Adeline said quietly. She knew she was on precarious ground here. Where it led, she wasn't sure she wanted to go.

"Can we sit?" Nora asked.

In the living room, Adeline took Nora's coat, and they sat by the fire.

"Do you ever get this sense that everything around us is a slow-motion catastrophe?"

Adeline didn't trust her voice to speak. She nodded, still wondering if Nora knew more than she was admitting.

"It's not just this crazy pandemic. It's closer to home. For Sam and Elliott, the things they love are slipping away. Hiro and Connie are fighting their demons—different demons but both soul-consuming." Nora took a deep breath. "And then there's you and me. Two islands in the middle of the storm.

Both single women. Career-oriented. It seems like we have a lot in common, but I don't really know much about you, Dani. And I was sitting at home thinking, why is that? And why don't I do something about that?"

Adeline swallowed. This was dangerous. The more she revealed about herself, the more likely it was that Nora would figure out her secret. If she did, she might alter the past.

But that was only half the issue. Adeline knew that in seven years, Nora was going to die—possibly at Adeline's hands. Getting close might make the things she had to do harder. Adeline knew what it was like to lose someone close to her. Instinctively, she knew she was scared of getting close again.

Nora smiled. "Anyway, I was drinking wine—from a box— and I just thought, 'why don't I go over and take a chance?' With the lockdown, I know she's at home. Everyone's at home. We can't exactly go anywhere, but I thought maybe we could talk. Or binge-watch TV. Or just read in the same room. Or play a board game."

Nora's gaze shifted to the window. "I probably shouldn't say this, but I feel like Absolom is coming to an end. Frankly, I can't see what use our machine that beams matter to nowhere could be to anyone. I know you've invested a lot money—and your time—and I want you to get it all back. I really do. Maybe we can license it for research to universities or government labs, but it feels like that will end our involvement in it. And tonight, I thought, maybe this is our last chance to get to know each other. And I was a little sad about that, frankly. Like I had missed an opportunity to get to know someone great—wait, that sounds super weird. I think I mentioned the wine earlier. There was wine involved. If you kick me out, let's blame the wine tomorrow. Deal?"

Adeline laughed. "I'm not kicking you out."

"Good. That would be so awkward."

"We don't do awkward here."

Nora laughed, a heartfelt, belly laugh that she physically shook off, her head tossing from side to side. Adeline thought the woman indeed seemed a little drunk.

When the laugh subsided, Nora's tone was more reflective. "I've always been an introvert. But this lockdown has been too much solitude even for me."

"Same."

"It works on you," Nora said. "Being alone. Like every day is a replay of the one before. The isolation has also made me realize some things. It's like the music stopped on human civilization, and we were all marching around, going through life, mostly unaware of what we didn't have, and now that I have to sit at home and just think, I've finally recognized that I'm truly and utterly alone. But it's not just being alone. I feel like there's no one in my life who really understands me."

Nora swallowed and closed her eyes. "Anddddd... I think my wine-induced soul outpouring just violated the we-don't-do-awkward policy."

Adeline laughed. "Updated policy: we do awkward for the sake of soul outpouring."

Nora held a finger up theatrically. "*Wine-induced* soul outpouring. I'm blaming wine."

"Actually, I think wine-induced soul outpouring is exactly what this world needs right now. Even if it gets awkward. It's totally worth it."

"In that case, it feels like we're missing something."

Adeline smiled and rose and retreated to the butler's pantry and returned with an uncorked bottle of Chardonnay. "It's not from a box."

"I'll let it slide—this time."

Adeline poured two glasses nearly to the rim and both women took a long sip.

"What now?" Nora asked. "Do we drink wine and keep complaining and blaming said wine?"

Adeline let her head fall to the side. "Doesn't quite seem like our style."

"No. It doesn't."

"What does?"

"Board games," Nora said.

"Yes," Adeline agreed. "Board games—until we're too brain-dead to play."

"Or drunk," Nora added. "Not saying that will happen."

"That would never happen to us. We don't get drunk. We just get tired."

"Exactly. And when we get too *tired* to play board games, we—"

"Binge-watch TV," Adeline said, completing the sentence.

Nora took a long sip of wine. "I like this plan."

"There's just one problem."

Nora raised her eyebrows.

"The potential for a bad binge."

"A bad binge?"

Adeline nodded with mock seriousness. "It's a situation that arises when two or more people are binge-watching TV together, and one or more people aren't into the show—but they're too afraid to say anything because they perceive that other members of the party are into it. They endure hours of the show, suffering from extreme boredom under the watchful eye of an unknowing loved one, unable to call out for help. It's what's formally known as a bad binge."

Nora paused. "Wait. Is that..."

"A real thing? No. I just made it up."

Nora threw her head back and laughed. "But it is real—it happens."

"It totally happens. And needs to be planned for."

Nora held her wine glass up, saluting Adeline. "That's why you get paid the big bucks. You think of everything. Always imagining what could go wrong."

You have no idea, Adeline thought.

"So how do we avoid a bad binge?" Nora asked.

"Mandatory check-ins. At the fifteen-minute mark in episode one, we hold our fists out and do a thumbs-up or thumb-down. Same at the end of episode one and two. We need two thumbs up to continue."

"It's a little dorky, but it could work."

"It will work. And yes, it's extremely dorky."

Adeline refilled their wine glasses, and they started the board games phase of the evening, sitting at the table in the dining room, playing Scrabble, music on in the background.

Thirty minutes later, Adeline was laying down the tiles for the word *relativity*.

The next morning, in the lab, most of the Absolom Six were sitting around a raised metal table, looking haggard and tired.

Hiro had recently returned from a trip to Vegas. Adeline had last talked to him at 3 a.m. the previous night and knew he was returning a hundred thousand dollars poorer. She had cut him off, which was perhaps the only reason he was back at all.

Constance had been up late doing a video conference with someone from her past who lived in Australia. Adeline could tell from her countenance that the person had been sick, and that the experience was weighing on her.

Adeline looked up to find Nora staring at her across the metal table, a cup of coffee in her hand, a subtle grin on her lips. Adeline had to admit, last night had been the most fun she had had in a long, long time.

They weren't the only two who were slightly hungover. Elliott was guzzling coffee as if the dark liquid could vanquish the fatigue and stress that grew every day.

"Sam's late," he said.

Adeline rose. "I'll get him."

She once again found the door to his office cracked, but he wasn't sitting in the chair this time. He was standing at the window, staring out, in a daze, with no idea Adeline was there. In the reflection, she could see the tears creeping down his face.

"Sam."

He jumped at the word as if a needle had pricked him.

He ran his forearm across his face, the sweater soaking up the tears.

"Has it started? I lost track of time."

"You should go home."

"No. We need to figure this out. If we don't, we'll lose everything we've worked for. All the money you put in."

"Forget the work. And the money. Go home, Sam."

He inhaled and shook his head. "I'm not leaving you all to figure this out alone—"

"I lied before, Sam."

He squinted at her.

"I told you we were partners. We're not. I'm still the majority owner of this company. I control it. At the end of the day, I call the shots here, and I'm telling you to go home."

His chest heaved, but he didn't move.

"Besides," Adeline said, stepping out of the office, "I already figured out what we're going to do with Absolom. We don't need you right now. But somebody does."

He barreled past her then, his eyes full of emotion, hurt from what she had said or because of what was waiting for him at home—of what was happening in slow motion, the knowledge that these moments would be his last with the love of his life.

At the stairwell, he looked back, and Adeline thought he understood because his eyes said thanks, but his mouth didn't move.

When he was gone, she returned to the lab and the four waiting scientists, who sat silently at the table, all seeming to contemplate the things hanging heavy in their lives.

"Sam can't make it."

No one said a word. They knew why he couldn't make it. Like any real friends, they felt some part of his grief.

"I have an idea," Elliott said. "I've given it a lot of thought."

All eyes turned to him.

"Nuclear fuel rods."

No one said anything to his pronouncement.

"It's quite simple," Elliott said. "We offer a waste disposal service. Spent nuclear fuel rods are radioactively dangerous for about ten thousand years. We put the rods in Absolom, transport them to an alternate universe, and the world is rid of them."

"Yes, but not the world they arrive in," Constance said. "We can't just dump our poison on another world because it helps us."

"Of course we can," Elliott said. "The world is full of people dumping their poison on others for profit."

It didn't take a leap of imagination for Adeline to see where Elliott was coming from. The poison he was talking about wasn't nuclear. It was what Charlie was putting in his arm, the poison that had torn Elliott's family apart.

She also knew what Constance was really thinking. The root of her aversion was in her own past. She had spent half her life cleaning up the wreckage of one reckless year abroad.

"Technically speaking," Nora said, "we would be shipping them to a copy of our world—a world where humans are destined to evolve. That means, if the rods don't go back far enough in time, the radiation could alter the biology of species pre-dating humanity, which could impact the advent of the human race. We could be causing an extinction event in a universe we created at the moment we used Absolom to send the rods back."

Elliott shrugged. "Who cares? We created the split universe. It's ours to destroy."

"I don't see it that way," Constance said. "We should be mindful of our consequences. Even if it feels right now, we could regret it."

"There's another solution," Adeline said. "Prisoners." Adeline took a page from her pocket. "The latest stats I could find were from 2019, but that year, there were over two million Americans in either prison or jail. Including 2,570 people on death row. That's down from a peak of 3,601 in 2000."

Constance held a hand up. "Wait a second. What exactly are you proposing?"

Elliott set his coffee mug down. "She's saying we do the same thing I was proposing with nuclear fuel rods on murderers and terrorists."

Adeline held out her hands. "I'm simply saying that we license Absolom to justice departments to use as they see fit."

Constance closed her eyes. "We've created a death machine."

"On the contrary," Elliott said. "Today, killers are put to death. With Absolom, they will be given life—under the sun, in the past, where they can live out their lives in the only peace this universe has to offer them."

"We should get the licensing fee up front," Hiro said. "The Supreme Court will surely rule it cruel and unusual. I favor a no-return policy."

Constance still had her eyes closed. She was wavering on the stool. Adeline thought she was going to pass out. Instead, she pitched forward, opened her mouth, and emptied the contents of her stomach on the metal table.

FIFTY-SEVEN

That night, when Adeline went to visit her mother, Sam opened the door.

"How did it go today?" he asked.

"Some of the ideas didn't go over well."

"What ideas?"

She motioned him to the study, pulled the pocket door closed behind them, and told him the plan for Absolom.

He began chewing his thumbnail. "In a million years, I wouldn't have thought of that."

"Well, what do you think of it?"

"I'm not sure. I guess life in exile is preferable to death." He thought a moment. "Well, I guess that depends on the prisoner. But maybe that's part of justice: they don't get to choose their future."

Adeline moved to the door, but Sam spoke again. "What did the others think?"

"The reactions were... mixed."

In the living room, Adeline found her younger counterpart slouched on the sofa, earbuds in, staring at her phone. Adeline remembered those days. Her father had forbidden her from going out. He wanted the family to be together. She had thought it was ridiculous, that he was overreacting.

Ryan was building a LEGO robot on the dining table.

In the sewing room, Adeline found her mother sitting in a

large light-blue recliner with her eyes closed. The chair was stained in a dozen places where milk and spit-up and other baby fluids had leaked on it from her and her brother.

If Adeline hadn't been certain of the date, she might have thought her mother had already passed. Instead, she waited for her eyes to open, not daring to wake her.

"Hi," her mother said, exhaling slowly.

"Hi."

"Must have fallen asleep. I'm so tired all the time. In fact, I don't think I can sew tonight."

Adeline glanced over at the fabric printed with the photomosaic, the batting, and the backing. They had only finished one of the quilts.

"I'll sew," Adeline said. "You can read."

Her mother smiled. It was a sad, reflective expression. "Too tired to read."

That almost broke Adeline. But she held it together. "I'll play an audiobook from my phone. And we'll finish this together."

As the story unfolded, Adeline sat at the sewing machine and knit the photos of her family together, and her mother sat back in the chair, listening, drifting in and out of sleep.

At home, Adeline sat on the couch, feeling more alone than she ever had.

She felt as if the present was slipping away. And the future was rushing forward like an asteroid about to strike her world.

She opened her email and found a cryptic message there from the company she had hired to build the software that searched historical photos, trying to find evidence that Absolom Two had been used before to alter the past.

TESSERACT is done. When should we install?

Adeline typed a quick reply:

ASAP

She tapped the calendar app and stared at the countdowns she had programmed:

Charlie: 9 Days

Mom: 14 Days

Nora: 2,190 Days

Dad: 2,256 Days

The death dates were closing in.

The next day, a team came to Adeline's house to install the Tesseract array.

At the office, the Absolom Six met in the lab, which had been cleaned since Constance's accident.

"Where should we start?" Hiro said. "I'll just say that I don't have any new ideas."

"I think we should vote on the idea presented," Constance said. "I'll start. I vote no."

"This isn't a democracy," Elliott said. "It's a company. A company that has made a very large investment in a product that seems to have one use—and it isn't ours to use, only to offer to governments around the world. I think whether we make that offer should be Daniele's decision. Her decision alone. It was her money. Frankly, she's the only reason any of us are here. Or Absolom, for that matter. It was her idea in the first place."

"I've thought about it some," Sam said. "To be honest, I'm not really thinking clearly right now. I don't know what the right answer is. What I do know is that I don't want to vote. You can call that punting or whatever you like, but I just don't want to make a big decision right now."

"Then we should delay this," Constance said.

"Well," Elliott said, "that's nice in theory, but what do we tell the eighty-three people working here? You're laid off until we figure out what to do with our useless transporter box? We'll call you back when we get in the mood to decide."

Hiro spoke before the argument could escalate. "I don't want to vote either. I took this job to get out of debt and because I liked the science. What happens with Absolom is your call, Dani."

Adeline glanced at Nora, who was studying her hands, which were laid out flat on the table.

"Nora?" she prompted.

The woman spoke slowly, as if the words hurt coming out. "I think there are bad people in this world. People who can't be rehabilitated. People who only know how to take from others. I want to live in a world where those people don't exist, but we don't live in that world yet. Whether it's our place to do something about that, I don't know. What I do know is that I don't want to vote about this either."

That afternoon, Adeline sent the first emails that would begin the negotiations with governments around the world to license Absolom.

***

The next day, Adeline and Nora were the only two of the Absolom Six who came to work. She supposed it made sense: Sam and Elliott were dealing with their own troubles. Hiro was off gambling—at a private game operating outside the lockdowns. Adeline wondered if the stress of yesterday's discussion had set him off or if perhaps he simply didn't see the point in working on Absolom anymore—he probably sensed that the work was mostly over. Constance was at home, receiving a treatment.

Adeline looked up when Nora walked into her office.

"I know what you need."

"What?" Adeline asked.

"Distraction."

"You've got that right."

"My house. Tonight. Seven o'clock."

"What do you have in mind?"

"It's a surprise."

An hour after Nora left, Adeline got a text on her phone. It was from the Tesseract server in her home. It was nondescript, only two words:

NEW MATCH

Adeline hadn't expected a match so soon. She was still gathering data sources. Tesseract was currently only operating on publicly available images and videos.

She raced home, to the server room with its double-locked door, and sat at the terminal, where she launched the results viewer application.

She was unprepared for what she saw.

The image on the screen was Adeline's face, in black and white. She looked older than she did now, but not much older. She was standing on a sidewalk—what was left of it—wearing a thick black trench coat and a fur hat. Behind her was a crumbling ruin of a bombed-out building. Snow covered the street, and in the middle of it was a crashed Luftwaffe bomber plane.

The caption under the photo read:

Stalingrad

November 2nd, 1942

FIFTY-EIGHT

Adeline couldn't get the image of herself standing in the street in the midst of the Battle of Stalingrad out of her mind.

Nora must have seen the stress on her face when she opened the door that night.

"What's wrong?"

"Just... a lot on my mind."

Nora nodded, probably assuming the anguish was associated with the Absolom decision Adeline had made.

Nora's surprise, as it turned out, was an escape room—one that she had built in her garage from a plan she had found online (and items delivered to her home). It was a grand gesture, one that Adeline knew had taken a lot of time and effort. Nora had done it all for Adeline, to help take her mind off of the Absolom decision and the stress they were all going through.

It was such a Nora thing to do: kind and thoughtful and warm as a crackling fire on a fall night.

The escape room centered around a closed-door murder mystery with a ticking clock. The parallels to Adeline's own life couldn't have been more striking: the murder in her future was Nora's, and Adeline, despite her investigations in the future and the past, could only see one possible killer: herself.

Worst of all, she didn't know why in the world she would ever kill Nora Thomas. But no one else fit.

Unlike the escape room in Nora's garage, the clues weren't clear. Try as she might, Adeline couldn't see any of the others as the killer. And she knew her father would have to be framed for it—if the future was to be preserved. Breaking causality would end the universe.

When they had escaped back into Nora's home from the garage, Nora said, "You hated it."

"I didn't. It was a great idea. I'm just... distracted."

"Too distracted to be distracted?"

Adeline laughed. "I guess so. That's bad, isn't it?"

"It is. You need a vacation."

"Maybe."

"They're lifting the lockdowns. We'll be able to travel soon."

But Adeline couldn't take a vacation. She needed to be in Palo Alto for what was going to happen next. She had lived through it once. She dreading it happening again.

A week later, Adeline got the first responses to her requests for virtual meetings with government officials in the US, China, and India. They were interested in Absolom, as she knew they would be.

That night, Adeline sensed a change in the air at her childhood home. Her younger counterpart didn't look annoyed. She looked scared.

Her father moved through the house almost in a daze, as if in denial. Or maybe the stress of it had exhausted him that much.

Adeline reached out and pulled him into a hug. His arms felt lifeless hanging on her back.

In the sewing room, Adeline found her mother in the plush rocking chair, eyes half open.

In the weeks before, Adeline had clung to this time with her mother. What she saw now made her wish for the opposite: an end to her mother's suffering. That was an inflection point she couldn't appreciate in her younger years. But it hit her now like the force of a train.

Slowly, her arm shaking, her mother reached down and moved the rocker to a sitting position. Her voice came like a sheet of construction paper being crumpled up.

"What is it?"

"Nothing," Adeline whispered.

"Are you all right?"

Adeline's chest heaved, and she wasn't sure if she was going to laugh or cry. "No. I'm not."

With great effort, her mother rose from the chair, the motion making Adeline ache even more for her, and she put her arms around her, and Adeline hugged as hard as she dared and held on for what felt like an eternity. When she eased her mother back into the chair, she looked up at her, studying her eyes with an intensity Adeline didn't know was left in the woman.

"You know... you remind me of someone," she whispered.

A bolt of fear ran through Adeline. And then a thought—a risky thought: *I'll tell her, right now, while I still can.*

Before she could speak, her mother shook her head. "Probably just the meds playing with my mind."

When Adeline left, the second quilt was done, and her mother was sleeping in the chair under the first.

Try as she might, Adeline couldn't get to sleep that night. Her mind was filled with thoughts of her mother, and Charlie, and Nora.

She didn't go to work the next day. She paced in her living

room, teetering on the verge of doing something that would end the world: calling Elliott. Saving Charlie.

But there was no saving Charlie. The moment she changed the past, she threw it all away.

She tried to distract herself. First with books, then with TV; she reached for the wine bottle, but then put it back. She needed a clear head for what would happen tonight.

Finally, fatigue, and stress, and worry chased her down like a cheetah on the Serengeti, trampling her as she lay on the couch.

She closed her eyes, and when she opened them, it was dark.

A bolt of fear ran through her. Had she missed it?

She sat up, checked the time, and dashed out of the house. She drove the half-mile to Charlie's neighborhood but didn't park in front of the apartment building. She parked two blocks away and walked the dark streets with her head held high, knowing cameras were recording her journey, knowing those videos would one day play on the screens in the basement of Elliott's home in Absolom City.

Outside his building, she paused and looked directly at one of the cameras, creating the still image that would hang prominently in that room in Elliott's basement.

She climbed the wooden outdoor stairs to the second-floor apartment. She knocked on the door and waited, but no one came. She leaned closer and listened. The only sound was that of music playing inside.

She turned the handle, and the door swung in. It was a tiny apartment with a shared living and dining space that opened to a small kitchen.

Charlie was lying on the couch, unmoving, skin ashen.

Adeline closed the door.

The moment it clicked, the bedroom door opened.

Elliott stepped out.

He didn't look at his dead son lying on the couch. He stared directly at Adeline.

What he said, Adeline could have never expected.

And it changed everything.

PART IV

ENDINGS, BURIALS, AND BEGINNINGS

FIFTY-NINE

In the desert, a city called Absolom rose. In Palo Alto, two people who would change that city forever were laid to rest. And in the Pacific, an island was slowly transformed into a paradise, waiting for the future.

At her home in Palo Alto, Adeline woke to the sound of buzzing from her bedside table. She reached over and read the text message on her phone's lock screen. It was from her father:

Elliott may have told you, but Charlie passed away last night.

The three dots indicating that he was typing pulsed. Then:

I'm going over there.

Adeline typed a reply:

I'm so sorry to hear it. I'll stay at your house with Sarah.

The reply came a second later.

Thanks.

★ ★ ★

At her childhood home, Adeline didn't knock. She didn't want to disturb her mother in case she was sleeping (and she was likely to be sleeping).

The door was unlocked. For the second time in twenty-four hours, she let herself in to a home where tragedy was about to strike.

The living room was empty. Her younger counterpart and brother, Ryan, were both at school. She heard a whispered conversation from the hallway.

She waited in the foyer, knowing she should walk back outside. Or to the sewing room. Instead, curiosity compelled her like a strong wind to the cased opening outside the hall, just beyond the door to the master bedroom, where her mother was speaking in slow, labored breaths.

"Just listen, Sam. When I'm gone—"

"Sarah—"

He stopped talking. Adeline thought that her mother must have held a hand up.

"*When* I'm gone, when you're able, I want you to move on. Time heals all wounds. But it won't work if you don't give time a chance. Will you do that?"

Adeline heard his muffled voice but couldn't make out the words. He was crying, she thought.

But her mother's voice was clear. "It would make me so sad if I'm what keeps you from being happy."

They buried Charlie on an overcast Saturday morning. Afterward, the world seemed to stand still. Adeline knew that she was simply waiting for her mother to pass. She could hardly think about anything else. Life, in a strange twist of fate, had given her this gift, this chance to relive her time with her mother.

There wouldn't be a third time around. This was it, the last days and hours she would have with her mother. Adeline clung to them, but the force of nature that was time pried them away.

The day before her mother closed her eyes forever, Adeline finished the third and final photomosaic quilt. In the sewing room, she held it up for her mother to see.

She smiled and nodded, as if she was seeing something more than the quilt, as if she saw the missing piece in the photos or possibly the sum of them, a life complete. That thought gave Adeline some comfort.

She sat beside her mother for the rest of the evening, listening to classical music. When she left, she looked her in the eye and did what she always wished she could have back then: she said goodbye.

In her youth, her mother's memorial service had gone by like a dream, some surreal happening that didn't seem real. Now, Adeline drank in every detail. The way the funeral home smelled. The feeling of dampness on the grass in the cemetery. The birds calling out in the quiet afternoon. The weight of her father's arms around her. Of Nora hugging her, and Constance, and Hiro, and Elliott.

In a way, they were all broken now.

And strangely, they were about to heal the world.

In the weeks and months that followed, Elliott withdrew. His replies to personal texts and emails took days, sometimes weeks. He blamed himself for Charlie's death. There was nothing anyone could say or do to change that.

Sam wasn't much better.

With the ending of pandemic lockdowns and travel restrictions, Constance redoubled her efforts to find those in her past. Perhaps the loss of two people in her life had reminded her of how precious time was.

Hiro slipped deeper into his addiction. Adeline didn't know if it was because work had virtually ended or because of the loss of his immediate social circle, but he became borderline obsessed. His late-night calls were more frequent. The debts were larger.

Adeline tried to keep him solvent.

She soon found herself with a new challenge—in a different kind of environment: government bureaucracy. Adeline had never really had to sell anything before. She soon learned that the sales process wasn't something that came naturally to her. As a venture capitalist, she had been literally handing out millions of dollars. Even in competitive funding rounds, there was typically very little arm-twisting, assuming the fund had a good track record (and hers did). The closest she had come to selling anyone on something was negotiating valuations and deal terms, but she had to admit, she typically left money on the table (which didn't matter much in the long run if you were investing in a good company).

Selling a technology like Absolom to the United States government was a completely new challenge for her. It was complex and frustrating. She felt like a fish out of water. It total, she spent six months spinning her wheels. Perhaps the only thing that kept her going was the knowledge that this had already occurred, so it must be possible.

It turned out, there was an easy way to get the government to do what you wanted (within the bounds of reason): hiring a lobbying firm.

She did, and the first sale happened soon after.

Absolom was licensed by the United States, and the lobbying firm made sure the announcement was front-page news (and that they were mentioned as representing Absolom Sciences). There would need to be testing, but the promise of it shocked the world.

Adeline didn't need the lobbying firm for the next sales. Governments around the world came to her after the news broke. They wanted Absolom, and they were willing to pay for it.

The initial licensing payments and funding for animal testing brought billions into Absolom Sciences. They moved operations to Absolom City and began testing the machine.

That seemed to help Hiro, but Elliott and Sam remained detached, alive but not truly living. Sam had moved his wife's grave to Absolom City, and Elliott had done the same for his son, but even that didn't seem to help them. Adeline's heart ached every time she saw the two men.

While Constance had been vehemently against using Absolom on prisoners, she surprised Adeline by working night and day to make sure the machine was safe for humans.

Adeline's once close relationship with Nora faded for reasons she couldn't quite grasp. Nora was different. Maybe it had been the move from Palo Alto to Absolom City or perhaps she regretted the decision they had made about Absolom, or maybe it was simply the way it was, that the friendship had run its course, that time and distance had taken its toll on their bond.

Adeline had to admit: she was different too. She was now the chair and CEO of a multi-billion-dollar enterprise, one that was written about endlessly in the press. She was in the public eye, relentlessly scrutinized.

She had never felt so alone. Even in the past, when she had landed on that grassy patch in the middle of Lomita Mall, she hadn't felt this isolated. It was a strange kind of isolation. With her wealth and access to power, she could have almost anything she wanted. Yet nothing made her happy.

She was, in a sense, trapped in time, waiting for the seminal event that would turn her world upside down again: Nora's death.

She was determined to right the wrong of that night—to discover who had killed Nora and clear her father's name. As such, she began making preparations. She placed cameras throughout Absolom City. And in Nora's home and in the homes of the other Absolom scientists. Those cameras would reveal for certain what happened that night. After nineteen long years, she would soon know the truth. Before that, she might even glimpse a clue as to who would commit the act that had ripped her life apart, setting her on a course to her past.

Watching the video feeds became almost an obsession for Adeline, much like gambling was for Hiro, and sorrow was for Sam and Elliott.

At the back of her mind was the unrelenting fear that none of the Absolom scientists would turn out to be the killer, that the person she was looking for was the person she saw in the mirror—that she was destined to kill Nora for some reason she didn't yet understand.

One morning, Elliott and Hiro came to Adeline's office at the Absolom Sciences building.

They weren't on the schedule, but she knew what they were there for. She had been watching the cameras hidden in their offices and homes.

"Our part of the Absolom trials is done," Elliott said.

"I'm aware," Adeline replied, leaning back in her chair.

"We'd like to work on a passion project."

"What kind of passion project?" Adeline needed to sound

convincing—as if she truly didn't know what they were destined to work on.

"The kind that requires some resources."

"Such as?"

"Two of the Absolom prototypes. Some capital. Probably a lot. Some privacy. We'll also need a few excavation drones and a permit to do some digging in Death Valley to verify our experiments."

"Experiments on what? Absolom?"

"Correct."

"Have you told the others?"

"No."

"Why not?"

"I know it's been a while, but I feel that Sam is still grieving. He needs space."

"I feel like the same could be said for you, Elliott."

"True. But I've decided to stop grieving. I'm going to start working again."

Adeline stared at him. "I take it you're not going to include Nora and Constance in these experiments?"

"Constance..." Elliott began and stopped, seeming to consider his words a moment. "Constance is unlikely to be interested in our particular project. Same for Nora."

"And what about me?"

"We just assumed you have your hands full with running the company."

Adeline stared at the two men. Elliott cleared his throat. "Look, we both—Hiro and I—need to work on something, and this is important to us. It would mean a lot. The project isn't commercial. But, as I said, it's important. To us."

Adeline smiled. He had no idea how important it was. To everyone. To the past. The present. And the future.

She nodded, and with that, work on Absolom Two began.

SIXTY

As a child, Adeline's vision of the world was that of something that changed gradually.

Like so many things in her life, her perspective was quite a bit different in adulthood. To her, the world seemed to change slowly for long stretches, then very rapidly, in great shocks that happened almost instantly. Nine-eleven. The global financial crisis. The COVID pandemic.

And then the shock she helped give the world: Absolom.

It wasn't the announcement of Absolom that changed the world. It was when they saw its power.

That day was a Saturday in November. Adeline thought the government had selected a weekend for the first departure for several reasons. The most important was so that the world could watch. They told the press it was so the victims' families could be present to witness the sentence carried out.

That morning, those families stood in the viewing booth, mothers and fathers and their children—at least, the children the man in the Absolom chamber hadn't taken from them.

He stared at his victims' families with hate-filled eyes. That fire vanished as the machine began to vibrate. Fear took its place. He opened his mouth and screamed, but no one could hear it. A flash filled the chamber, and he was gone.

So was the world before.

Overnight, crime rates plummeted.

Adeline had always heard the saying that the devil you know is better than the one you don't. That's what Absolom was to the world: a new devil.

Prison was a known. So was the death penalty. They were the devils the world knew.

Conceptually, the world knew what Absolom was: a box that sent a person to the past, in an alternate universe. What they didn't know was what truly happened there. Exile was certain. A lonely death was certain. But how? An exotic disease? Starvation? Being torn apart by an animal?

In the absence of certainty, a mind tends to imagine the worst. That's what Absolom became to the world. The phrase "A fate worse than Absolom" quickly supplanted its predecessor: "A fate worse than death."

Before the first departure, the Absolom machine had been an idea. In those small moments as it hummed to life, the world saw something else: a person who was pure evil, with hate in his heart, instantly hollowed out, gutted, cowering with fear, and then, gone. In an instant, they saw evil wiped from existence.

As Hiro predicted, Absolom was challenged all the way to the Supreme Court, where the plaintiffs argued that it was cruel and unusual. It was certainly unusual. Perhaps cruel. Most importantly, it was a machine that removed evil from the universe. That was something the world needed, and the Supreme Court found in favor of the United States government.

The following week, after the lower court's injunction was lifted, the lights in Absolom City dimmed again, and an African dictator guilty of genocide and crimes against humanity left the universe forever.

In the desert, Elliott and Hiro dug holes and filled them back in. Adeline knew what they were looking for, knew they weren't finding it, and knew that one day they would. And Nora would die soon after.

That thought haunted her. In a way, it dug her deeper into a hole of her own, and like the ones Hiro and Elliott were digging in Death Valley, she wasn't finding what she needed. And like them, she kept digging.

In a fateful twist, it was Nora who gave Elliott and Hiro the insight they needed to make progress on Absolom Two.

That revelation was given casually at a lunch Elliott had requested. His email to the Absolom Six had simply asked that they all meet up for a meal, in private, to catch up.

Adeline had arranged for food to be delivered to the conference room in her office suite. About halfway through lunch, Elliott had cleared his throat and said, "Do any of you ever think about why Absolom failed?"

It was clear to Adeline what he was after—a clue as to why he and Hiro weren't finding the tuning bars they kept departing with Absolom Two.

Nora didn't seem to follow. "Well, I guess that's a matter of opinion. Some would say it's a raging success. A force for peace and crime reduction."

"No, not that," Elliott said. "I mean, as a shipping technology. Why didn't it work?"

Nora finished chewing a bite of her salad. "Isn't it obvious? Causality. Absolom always transmits to the past. It's the nature of transmission. Sure, with enough power, maybe you could get it down to a month or two or maybe even a week, but that would require a massive amount of energy. And obviously, you could only send something to the past that you knew was already there."

Elliott leaned back in the rolling chair, considering that.

"So... wait, tell me what you mean by that."

"Well, it's fairly obvious. If you ask me, the one thing we learned from Absolom is that you can't move matter in space without moving it in time. Displacing an object in the present—with no effect on time—is not possible based on the laws of physics in this universe. You can send something to the past, but only if it already happened. In fact, if it happened, then it will happen. It has to happen for us to continue to exist. That's why you can't just decide to ship something and do it. You'd be sending it to a past that has already happened. If you really could ship anything you wanted to the past then what happened—the series of events that got us here—would no longer have occurred in the way it did before. You'd be changing the past, which isn't possible. Obviously we don't know what would happen, but my guess is that our universe would probably just wink out of existence in some causality collapse."

"But," Elliott said slowly, "if you knew something had been sent to the past... then you could send it."

"Yes. In fact, you—or someone—would have to send it to ensure the universe continued." Nora studied his serious expression and laughed. "Why, Elliott, do you know of something that was sent to the past?"

"Not exactly."

SIXTY-ONE

The world wasn't the only thing Absolom had changed. As the months and years slipped by and the machine in the Nevada desert hummed with departures, the Absolom Six changed. Adeline didn't know if it was simply growing older or the death of Charlie and her mother, but the six scientists who had aided world peace seemed to find only war within.

Adeline felt it inside of her too. She saw it on the video feeds inside the homes of the other six.

She had this unrelenting sense of time slipping away, and she still had no idea who Nora's killer was.

But she began preparing for the event.

She ordered furniture for the guest bedroom and arranged it just like her room had been at the home she shared with her father and brother. She stood in the room, studying the placement. Yes, it was just as it had been when she had come here.

She was sitting at the kitchen island, pouring a glass of wine, when a text message arrived from Nora:

Busy?

Adeline activated the video feed of the inside of Nora's home. She felt a twinge of guilt for invading her privacy, but she rationalized it as a simple safety precaution. Nora was going

354

to be murdered, and she needed to know who did it. For her father's sake. She couldn't prevent him from going to Absolom, but she could clear his name before she got him back.

On the video feed, Nora was sitting at her kitchen island, a glass of wine towering by the phone.

Now they were ships in the night.

No. Everything ok?

Yes and no. Can I come over?

Sure.

Adeline watched on the video feed as Nora downed the glass of wine, grabbed a sweater she draped over her shoulders, and walked out. Ten minutes later, they were sitting in Adeline's living room with full wine glasses.

"You ever wish," Nora began, "that we could go back to Palo Alto? Before it all started?"

"I do."

"I mean, Absolom has been good for the world, but everything has changed. I miss us."

"Me too."

"Life was so much more simple then."

Adeline said nothing, only took a sip of wine, thinking about how much more complicated it was about to become.

Nora downed half her glass. "I have a secret."

Adeline's heart beat faster. "You do?"

"Sam and I have been seeing each other."

Adeline swallowed, relieved that the secret was one she was well aware of.

Nora squinted at her. "You knew."

"I knew."

"I guess I should've figured that. You don't miss anything. And I should have informed you. As my employer, you should know about workplace relationships."

Adeline held up a hand. "First of all, I'm not your employer—"

"You are, Dani. It was different in Palo Alto. Before. When the company was small. Now, with..."—Nora motioned with her hands, all around—"with all this, the city, the machine, what it's become..."

"It's different," Adeline said. "I'll give you that. But within these walls, at home, what do you say we go back to Palo Alto, to the way things were?"

Nora drank the rest of the wine. "That sounds good to me."

Adeline refilled the glass, and Nora seemed to relax a bit.

"We've been going slow, Sam and me. Like, middle school speed." Nora laughed and shook her head. "We're both scared. We're both still hurt. And lonely. We're like two porcupines trying to mate."

Adeline laughed then, but she was crying inside because she knew how it ended. At least, she thought she did.

SIXTY-TWO

In the days leading up to Nora's death, Adeline grasped for clues as to who would kill her. Try as she might, she couldn't find any.

Elliott and Hiro spent day and night in the lab. When Hiro wasn't there, he was in Las Vegas.

Constance was almost always away for medical treatment or to search for people from her past. She had a sense of her own time drawing to a close. She was racing against the clock too.

Nora and Sam were nursing a nascent romance that would soon die with her.

And Adeline couldn't sleep. She kept thinking about all the clues, all the pieces that never seemed to add up. She sensed that there was still a missing piece here, but try as she might, she couldn't see it.

It wasn't just the mystery of Nora's murder that loomed ahead. It was the loss of her father. As with her mother in Palo Alto, Adeline felt her time with him slipping away, and she couldn't help but try to hold on.

At a lunch with him the week before Nora's death, Adeline said, "You should start working out again."

Sam glanced down at his shirt, feigning insult. "Is the dad bod really that bad?"

"It's not that—it's for your health. You never know."

"What I do know is that at my age, I seem to be almost

supernaturally cursed to wear these love handles and flab. I've tried dieting. And exercise. The curse of the dad bod resists all earthly countermeasures."

"Have you tried cutting out alcohol?"

Sam snorted. "I'm a widower with a teen and a pre-teen at home. By the known laws of physics and human biology, I cannot survive without alcohol."

Adeline shook her head, feeling slightly guilty about her adolescent behavior. "Are they that bad?"

"No. In fact, there have been times when those two kids were the only thing that kept me going. They're my life. And they've given my life meaning that I couldn't have imagined before. Especially after Sarah passed."

Those words healed a wound so deep inside of Adeline she hadn't known it was there.

The following night, Nora and Adeline were sitting in her living room, sipping wine and chatting, almost the way they had so many years ago, in another place, in another time. If they were indeed ships in the night, every moment they spent together brought them closer, back to the place they were before.

"Do you know what Hiro and Elliott are doing out in the valley?" Nora asked.

"Not specifically," Adeline lied.

"Do you know generally?"

"Generally, they're working on their passion project."

Nora raised her eyebrows. "Seems like the only passion projects going on in this strange oasis in the desert are obsessing over dead people."

And Adeline thought: *truer words were never spoken.*

★ ★ ★

Adeline waited and watched the calendar until Nora's murder was three days away. Then two.

Knowing it was coming—and that she still didn't know who the killer was—left her with a sense of impending doom. She searched, and still there were no clues.

Hiro and Elliott had locked themselves in the lab. They were close to their discovery.

Adeline felt the two events racing toward her now, two unstoppable trains powered by the force of time, about to collide.

Constance returned from China. She was so exhausted from her trip that she stayed in bed the entire next day. She was getting sicker. For years, she had been slowly losing her battle with the disease. Now she was losing it quickly.

A black cloud hung over Sam. The anniversary of his wife's death loomed two days away.

Adeline realized then that Nora was going to die within hours of the anniversary of Adeline's mother's passing. She wondered if that was significant.

The night before Nora's death, Adeline barely slept. It was the same as the night Charlie passed away.

But this time, Adeline didn't just toss and turn in bed. She stared at her phone, at the video feed of Nora's bedroom, where she slept peacefully, not a care in the world, completely unaware that it was her last night on Earth.

She flipped to the other feeds.

Hiro and Elliott were talking in the lab, empty coffee mugs on the table, a stack of metal tuning bars scattered like an overturned box of toothpicks.

Sam was up late, reading a book by the fire, two empty beer bottles sitting on the raised hearth.

No matter how hard she looked, Adeline couldn't find the missing piece that would solve this mystery of past, present, and future. And it was driving her crazy.

Sometime just before morning, she drifted off to sleep.

Adeline's buzzing phone woke her.

Groggy, half awake, she fumbled through the covers and found it and raised it and squinted against the bright Nevada sun blazing in through the windows.

Nora was calling.

This had to be it.

Adrenaline shot through Adeline's veins as she answered, her voice scratchy.

"Hi."

"Hey. Can you come over?"

"Everything all right?"

"I don't know."

Nora sounded scared.

Adeline jumped out of bed. "I'll be there in a minute."

When the call ended, she checked the time.

4:38 p.m.

She had slept almost the entire day.

She opened the app for the camera feeds and clicked on the group for inside Nora's home. She saw only black boxes. They were offline.

Why?

Fear rose inside of her. She checked the wireless access point they were connected to near Nora's home. It was online.

They should be working.

She pulled the feeds from the cameras outside. Nora had gone for a run that morning with a friend. She followed the two women around the city, to the little café where they ordered smoothies after the run, watched them chatting and sipping as they strode home. Nora was inside almost an hour, then took a car to work, and left at lunch.

Adeline pulled up the history of the cameras inside her home. Nora fixed a sandwich, read a paperback book at the kitchen island, and went upstairs and napped. When she got up, she went to the bathroom, and when she came out, she marched directly to the camera in the bedroom, peered into the lens, pulled it free, and jerked the wire out. She repeated that throughout the house, depositing the cameras on the dining room table.

They were waiting there when Adeline arrived.

"I found these cameras hidden all over my house!" Nora yelled, pacing in the hall outside the dining room.

"How?"

Adeline knew she had said the wrong thing as soon as it left her mouth.

Nora cocked her head. "Did you know? Did you do this? Please don't lie to me, Dani."

"Yes."

"You knew, or you did it?"

"They're my cameras."

Adeline expected Nora's anger to explode. Instead, she deflated. Hurt replaced her fury.

Nora's voice was a whisper.

"Why?"

"It's complicated."

"Is it because of Sam?"

"No." But that wasn't entirely true. It was because of her father. And Nora.

"Please tell me the truth. It's all I ask."

"The truth is complicated."

"We built a time machine to an alternate universe together.

I think I can handle complicated. Tell me. You owe me that."

"I can't."

"Then get out. And don't come back until you can."

Adeline walked out and stood on the front stoop, trying to find the words that would heal the rift between them. She knew that if she didn't, she wasn't coming back—not before Nora died. Unless, she was, in fact, the one who had killed her.

But she couldn't find those words. She stared at the door, feeling her last chance being washed away by time.

Her phone buzzed in her pocket. Adeline pulled it out and read the message from Elliott. It had been sent to the group: Nora, Sam, Constance, and her.

Hiro and I need to see you in the lab. It's urgent.

It had begun.

Again.

SIXTY-THREE

When all of the Absolom Six were present in the lab, Sam said, "Why all the cloak and dagger?"

Elliott pointed to a prototype for Absolom Two, which was sitting in the center of the room.

"You'll see, Sam."

Elliott reached in his pocket, took out a small tuning bar, and walked past the group, letting everyone see the Absolom Sciences serial number.

He placed the metal bar inside the Absolom machine, closed the door, and moved to a computer terminal nearby. He typed the departure sequence. The machine hummed and flashed, and the bar disappeared.

The room was utterly quiet as Elliott walked to a metal table, picked up a hard plastic box, and opened it so the group could see the contents.

It was a tuning bar that was discolored and pitted with age. But the serial number was still readable. It was the same number as the bar that had just been sent to the past.

It was clear to everyone present what the bar meant: Hiro and Elliott, during their time in the lab and digging in the desert, had figured out how to make Absolom Two send payloads to our universe.

Sam stared at the box. "Impossible."

"It's real, Sam. After all these years, we've finally done it. What we always meant to. But it's more than that—"

Nora cut him off. "It's Pandora's box, is what it is."

Elliott shook his head. "What do you mean? This is the future. The biggest discovery in human history."

"No, Elliott, this could be the end of human history."

Elliott exhaled. "That's absurd."

Nora pointed at the box. "Think about it. What if this is the reason for the Fermi Paradox? Why are we alone in the universe? What if this is the reason?"

Sam glanced between the two of them. "I don't follow."

"What if," Nora said, hands held out, "every sufficiently advanced civilization ends shortly after this discovery? That's what's going to happen if we use this machine to send something to the past that doesn't belong there. A causality failure. In an instant, our universe ceases to exist. Is the risk worth it? Of course not. We should destroy it. And never tell anyone it's even possible."

"We're not going to destroy it," Elliott said. "And besides, we still have work to do."

"What work?" Adeline asked.

"We have two issues," Elliott replied. "Location and time. We've been working on it, but we can't get the payloads to arrive exactly where and when we want."

"And power," Hiro added. "Transmissions still require a massive amount of power. It's not financially feasible for shipping."

To Adeline, Elliott said, "I take it you're in favor of continuing development?"

"I am."

"This is insane," Sam said. "I agree with Nora—this is too dangerous to mess around with."

The dissent from a close friend seemed to put Elliott on the defense. He spoke slowly now, as if fighting to maintain his composure. "This is the key to the past—"

"The past cannot be changed," Nora said.

"I accept that," Elliott shot back. "The question is: have we already done it?"

"How would we know?" Nora asked.

"We could search historical photos," Sam said. "For ourselves. And maybe other Absolom staff."

Adeline turned to him, and a thought occurred to her: she had only used Tesseract to search for herself. And she had found herself. What if the others had also traveled to the past?

Nora locked eyes with Constance. "What do you think?"

Constance glanced around at the others. "I share Sam and Nora's reservations. This *is* dangerous. It's already gone too far. We should end it here and now. Let's destroy it before we leave tonight."

Elliott held his hands out and took a deep breath.

"I know you're all concerned. And perhaps a little in shock. Let's take some time to consider—"

Nora laughed. "Of the things we have, Elliott, time is clearly not one."

Adeline drove straight home. Because that's what she knew she had done. What she didn't know was what to do next.

Nora was going to die in a few hours. The moment she had waited almost twenty years for was here—and Adeline still didn't know who was going to kill her.

A text message appeared on her phone. It was from Nora:

Did you know?

What?

What E and H were working on?

Yes.

You've been keeping a lot of secrets lately.

Adeline sensed that she had one chance to understand what was about to happen. She had to seize it.

Can I come over?

No. Don't even try. I'll call the police if you do.

Adeline paced, trying to figure out what was happening.

She had to figure out who had killed Nora in order to clear her father's name. But it was more than that. A killer was about to go free, a killer who might kill again—her or someone else.

On her phone, Adeline pulled up the Absolom City camera feeds. Her father and her younger self were trudging along the sidewalk, on their way to Nora's house. On the porch, they rang the doorbell and waited until the front door swung open, and they disappeared inside for approximately thirty-seven minutes.

She opened the feed for the cameras in the crawl space and attic of Nora's home. In the green tint of night vision, she saw that there was no one there.

Adeline remembered what was happening inside. Her father and Nora were telling her that they had been seeing each other. Adeline had felt betrayed that night—for herself and her mother. Rage had overtaken her. They had argued, voices rising until Adeline had shouted, "How could you tell me on the anniversary of Mom's death?! What's wrong with you?! Both of you!"

On the phone, in the video feed, the front door flew open, and young Adeline stormed out into the night, tears streaming down her face.

Adeline switched to the feed of the crawl space and the attic. There was still no one there.

From her memory, Adeline knew she hadn't killed Nora. Her father hadn't either.

As she stared at the feeds, she knew that left only one possibility.

Absolom Two.

A way to travel to the past.

There was one issue: that technology had yet to be perfected. As Elliott had said that night, he and Hiro hadn't figured out how to send something to an exact time and place.

But they would. Adeline was living proof of that. In a few short months, her younger self would be sent through Absolom Two back to 2008.

And then what? The obvious conclusion now was that at some point in the future, the machine would be used to go back in time to murder Nora. But by whom? And why?

Conceivably, the reason was to ensure that Absolom Two was completed.

Which left the question: if Adeline could control Absolom Two, and Absolom Two was the only way to kill Nora, did that mean that she had killed her? That she was going to kill Nora in two months?

The only other possibility was that she would lose control of Absolom Two after she had used it on her younger self. Which probably meant she was going to die in two months.

She had that much time to figure out what was going to happen that night.

On the video feed, Sam gave chase, and Adeline watched her younger self get into an autocar. After the car disappeared into the night, her father walked home, tapping a text message on his phone.

Adeline wanted to leave, to go to Nora's house. But she couldn't. Not without breaking the universe. Because the night Nora had died, Daniele Danneros had been at home the entire time.

Thus, Adeline stayed home. She paced the first floor, trying to see the piece she was missing. But it wasn't there.

She opened the feeds for Elliott, Constance, and Hiro's homes. Elliott was sitting in his study, deep in thought. Constance was gone. From the past, Adeline knew she had gone to San Francisco for medical treatment.

Hiro's home was empty. He was in the lab, working through the night.

It was all happening as it had.

The sun rose on the front of Adeline's house, and it seemed to be laughing at her, as if it had known all along that she couldn't figure it out. She knew it was the sleep deprivation and the extreme stress affecting her, but she just wanted to curl up on the floor, pull her hair out, and scream until she exploded.

Instead, her phone rang. She knew who it was before she answered: the Absolom City Police.

They informed her, as Nora Thomas's employer, that the woman had been found murdered that morning. They had some questions. Two detectives would be visiting her soon to ask those questions.

By standing agreement with Absolom Sciences, the police had access to view the cameras throughout the city. That would soon lead them to Sam and Adeline.

For now, they wanted her consent to access the deceased's email, phone, and work computer.

Adeline gave her consent and said she would send an email to legal providing formal authorization. She knew what they would find in those records—specifically, her text chain with Nora last night. Adeline would have some explaining to do.

But at that moment, those files weren't the ones that concerned her most. It was the historical records in the Tesseract—and an idea Sam had given her last night: what if she wasn't the only one who had used Absolom Two to travel to the past?

In the server room in the basement, Adeline logged in and did something she wished she had thought to do years ago: she uploaded photos of Elliott, her father, Constance, Hiro, and Nora.

SIXTY-FOUR

Adeline was sitting in her living room when the doorbell rang.

She opened the door and welcomed the two detectives and offered them coffee (which they declined).

Their names were Billings and Holloway. Two people she hadn't seen in nearly twenty years.

They recounted the broad outline of the crime with clinical efficiency. When they were done, they let a silence settle in the air. Apparently, awkward silence was the detectives' signature move. Did they thrive on awkwardness? Was it taught at the academy? Was the slide that introduced it labeled *Silence: Your Secret Weapon*?

Adeline stared at them, waiting for the question she knew was coming.

It was Billings who asked it. "In reviewing Dr. Thomas's phone and email records, we came across a rather contentious text exchange between the two of you last night."

She didn't ask a question. She just stared at Adeline, using the oppressive silence again.

"We had an argument. Yes."

"About?"

"I placed cameras inside Nora's home."

"Can we ask why?"

Adeline had mentally rehearsed the lie, and it came easily

now. "Since Absolom was used on the first prisoner, all of us—the six founders—have received death threats. It was just a precaution."

"A precaution for all of the Absolom Six? Or just Nora?" Billings asked.

"Everyone. Yesterday, however, Nora found the ones inside, in the main living areas. We fought about it."

"When's the last time you saw Dr. Thomas?"

"Early yesterday evening."

"Where?"

"At the main Absolom Sciences building, at a meeting in the lab."

"Where'd you go after?"

"Home. For the entire night."

Holloway took out a pad. "And can we—"

"Verify that? Yes. You can."

The videos of the crawl space and attic of Nora's home would verify that either Sam or Adeline had committed the crime. The police were likely collecting the forensic evidence from the crime scene now.

When the detectives left, Adeline sat in the living room, almost in a catatonic state.

Right now, her younger self was standing in the cemetery, hating her father, listening to his words, feeling lost, reeling from her belief that Nora was taking her last parent from her, not knowing that he really would be gone soon. That moment in the cemetery, when he spoke those words, *Time heals all wounds. But it won't work if you don't give time a chance*, had been the anchor that kept her from drifting away, the gravity that had pulled her to him for that hug—the hug right before the drone had pierced the gentle morning with its commands to step away. It would shoot him and bring him to the ground seconds later.

There was nothing to do but wait. While Adeline waited, sitting in the chair, thinking, sleep overtook her.

When she woke, Adeline felt like a bus had run over her.

She tried to push up from the chair. Her arms were weak. Her mind wouldn't focus, the thoughts slow, like she had been drugged.

It was the stress of it all. It was consuming her, pulling her down like a boat anchor tied to her feet. She wasn't ready to sink. She was going to fight. And it had to be right now. She was running out of time.

What happened next?

Elliott—he would be the first to go to the police station. And she had to tell him.

She called him, and he answered on the first ring.

"I was about to call you," he said.

"About?"

"Last night was all wrong. I shouldn't have even showed it to the others. We should just go forward with Absolom Two. Who cares if they approve or not? It would be easier with Nora and Sam's help, but we can figure out—"

"Nora is dead."

Silence stretched out on the line. When he spoke, Elliott's voice carried the tone of true surprise.

"I... Are you serious? When? How—how do you know?"

"The police were here."

"Is she missing or—"

"She's dead, Elliott. And the police have arrested Sam for her murder. You should go down to the station to help him. Take Tom Morris with you. And we need to hire an actual criminal attorney. A good one. Someone with experience in complex celebrity trials."

Adeline showered and got dressed and checked her email. As usual, her inbox was overflowing. There was an email from Hana Kim, the CEO of Syntran, requesting a meeting. Adeline had been putting her off for months. It still wasn't the right time. Adeline wrote a short note saying that she was attending to an important issue and couldn't return emails, set it as an autoresponder, and sent it to all of her unread messages.

Next, she called a private security firm and hired them to interface with the police, to use any resources necessary to learn the details of the investigation. She needed every advantage she could get. Maybe there was some small detail in the evidence that had been gathered that would give her an edge. Or some clue about who was going to use Absolom Two.

She drank coffee on her covered porch, watching the sun on the horizon, feeling the weight of time bearing down on her. Right now, in an interview room, the two detectives were asking her younger self what happened last night. That young woman's concern was turning to fear. Standing there, the sun warming her face, sipping the hot coffee, the fear was starting to grip Adeline too.

Shortly before eleven, a text message arrived from Elliott. It was addressed to Adeline, Constance, and Hiro.

I'm sure you have all heard about Nora. We need to talk. Sam's still at the police station. Let's meet there for lunch. He thinks we might be in danger.

A second passed, an icon indicating that he was still typing. Another message appeared.

And he wants to figure out who killed Nora.

Hiro texted back, saying he would be there. Constance said she would too, but she'd be late.

Adeline typed out the message she knew she had to send:

I'll bring sushi.

In her home office, she typed out a short note:

LOOK UNDER THE TABLE

She cut the page into a small rectangle, the size of the slip inside a fortune cookie, and placed it in her pocket.

She wanted to cry as she wrote the second note. It was longer, and she knew the words in it would cut her father open like a knife. She had never seen this note. She knew only that it informed her father that if he didn't confess, more evidence of his daughter's guilt would be given to the police.

As it turned out, she didn't need to know the exact words. She only needed to write what came to her—because that's what had already happened.

She placed the note in a small envelope and sealed it. She didn't worry about DNA or fingerprints because she knew her father wouldn't turn it over to the police. He loved his daughter too much.

SIXTY-FIVE

In the police holding cell, Adeline had lunch with her father, Elliott, Hiro, and Constance.

In her pocket, she kept the short note instructing her father to look under the table. She would deposit that under one of the plates, in the center of the table, just before leaving.

Halfway through lunch, she reached beneath the table and taped the small envelope to the underside. It was a tiny action that would have a huge impact, a gavel slamming on the judge's bench, the sentence as much as certain.

What hurt her the most was the hope she saw in him. Here, during lunch, he was a wrongfully accused man searching for the truth that would set him and his daughter free and identify the person who had killed the woman he loved.

By the end of the day, he would be a confessed murderer, disgraced and destined to be separated from his family forever.

After lunch, Adeline waited for the call she knew was coming.

It was mid-afternoon when her phone rang. It was Elliott, and he was drunk and hysterical.

His long-time friend's confession had rattled him. He cursed, threw accusations, and finally, descended into crying.

To Adeline, it seemed as if the world was breaking. The

people around her were breaking. Nora was gone. Her father was in prison. Elliott was shattered. Hiro was battling his demons. Constance was clinging to life.

Adeline knew it was up to her now.

A few hours later, she was back in the police holding room with her father. His demeanor was different now. He was a man defeated. Confused. Scared.

And in that room, she was to him what he had been to her back then: a lighthouse in the darkness, a beacon of hope and steadfast support.

"Are you going to ask me if I actually did it?"

"I don't need to. I already know the answer."

Adeline made her way to the other holding room, where she had spent the day nineteen years ago. Her younger counterpart was waiting there, and as she opened the door, she saw the young woman she had once been, a person who was about to have a huge hole blown in her life.

At home, Adeline showed her to the guest bedroom, which her counterpart eyed wearily before turning to her.

"I want answers."

"You should sit down, Adeline."

"I don't want to sit down."

Adeline placed a hand on her counterpart's shoulder, guided her to the bed, and sat beside her.

"What I'm about to say is going to be hard to hear."

"What is?"

"It's going to hurt, but I promise you, it's going to get better. You just have to give it some time."

Her eyes filled with tears. Adeline saw the hurt she had once felt in her younger self. And she knew that fear was giving way to rage.

"Everyone keeps telling me everything is going to get better. But things just keep getting worse."

"They always do," Daniele said. "Before they get better."

In her home office, Adeline entered her father's weight in the Absolom destination algorithm and stared at the predicted arrival date.

The Late Triassic.

It was very nearly the worst possible outcome. Just the thought of him trying to survive there made her nervous.

To distract herself, she spent the rest of the night researching the epoch. There were pictures of dinosaurs and large reptiles—which were at the top of the food chain at that time. There were jungles and volcanic explosions burying those jungles in lava and simulations of the giant continent of Pangea separating and the world never being whole again. In a way, it was a strange symbol of her life. Two halves breaking apart. Now she was trying to bring them back together. Upstairs, her younger self was trying to pull away. And like the Triassic, she knew how it ended.

Adeline woke to an app notification on her phone. Tesseract had found more matches.

She bounded out of the bedroom and down the stairs. In the basement, she closed the door to the server room and logged in to the terminal.

She wasn't prepared for what she saw. Dozens of matches. She didn't understand it. It was wrong somehow. It had to be.

But it was all right there. In black-and-white photos. And

color photos. And videos. A tapestry that laid a mystery written across time.

Adeline felt as if she was looking at a photomosaic, one that formed a bigger picture. An answer. But it was still missing a piece.

What was happening here was stranger than she ever imagined. And much larger than one woman's murder.

SIXTY-SIX

Before she left the next morning, Adeline cracked the door to the guest room and peered in at her younger self. The girl had slept in her clothes, with only a quilt drawn over her. Adeline recognized the quilt. It was one of the three photomosaics her mother had made. Her mother and Adeline had made.

In the Absolom holding cell, Adeline showed her father his predicted arrival date. He barely reacted, as if she had told him the weather tomorrow.

"Get your head in the game, Sam. This is a survival exercise now. Don't just blindly march through this. You need to be studying survival techniques while you're waiting for departure—and those strategies will vary based on the destination environment."

It was so strange for her, almost being the parent now. Adeline couldn't help wondering if that was the way of life: things coming full circle. They certainly were for her.

At home, Adeline found her counterpart in the bedroom writing in a notebook. She knew what she was writing. And that her younger self was hurting more than she ever had in her whole life at that moment. She knew what she needed: a firm hand to guide her.

"Don't you knock?"

"I did knock," Adeline said.

"But apparently you didn't wait to barge in here."

She nodded to the notebook. "Working on something?"

"It's none of your business."

"On the contrary. What you're working on is my only business now."

Adeline took a step closer and spoke again, her voice steady and calm.

"You're making a list of the people who might have killed Nora and framed your father."

"You can't stop me."

"True. Nor do I want to. I'm going to help you, Adeline. We're going to figure it out. Together. And we're going to get him back."

Adeline turned and strode out, pausing at the doorway. "But right now, we're going to have dinner. And we're going to be civil."

When Adeline's counterpart left to visit Sam, she texted Elliott, Hiro, and Constance, requesting that they come over.

They met in her basement.

"Let's start with who killed Nora," Elliott said. He seemed to be in a perpetual state of being either hungover or slightly inebriated.

"We don't have time for that right now," Adeline said.

Elliott stared at her. "I'd say there's always time to figure out who killed your friend and colleague."

"We need to focus all of our energy on saving the one friend we can. His name is Sam Anderson, and very shortly, he will be sent back to the Triassic. The only question that matters is how do we get him back?"

Constance squinted. "Well, frankly, forgive me if I'm missing something, but what will we do when we get him back? I mean, he'll be a wanted fugitive."

Adeline had never told the group about Absolom Island. She wasn't about to now. If one of them was the killer, it might be the only place in the world she and her father could escape to.

"I'll take care of what happens after. How do we get him back?"

"To put it bluntly," Elliott said, "we can't."

"A-2," Hiro said.

"What does that mean?" Constance asked.

Elliott shifted his head from side to side. "If we transmit him with Absolom Two, we can tag him with entangled particles and use a recall ring—but that's all theoretical. *And* A-2 has never been used on humans. *And* we don't even have the date and location targeting worked out. Our payloads are all over the map—and timeline."

"But," Adeline said, "with A-2, you would know what universe he's in."

"Yes," Elliott said. "We would."

"What is a recall ring?" Constance asked.

"It's a prototype we've been developing," Hiro said. "A device that could make the promise of Absolom shipping a reality. You tag a recall ring with entangled particles at an originating Absolom Two machine. Then that machine can use the entangled particles to find the ring—and the mass it's attached to—in space and time, across the multiverse, and bring it home. You would still have to use drones or human drivers for last-mile delivery, but you could ship something to any Absolom port in the world."

"Or," Adeline said, "pull something from the Triassic to the present."

Elliott exhaled. "In theory. But it's a long shot—and we won't be able to send a recall ring with Sam. They'll search him before departure. It's far too large."

"Let's solve the Absolom Two issue first," Adeline said. "How?"

Hiro shrugged. "Easy. We tell the government that Absolom needs maintenance. We swap out the control modules with the A-2 modules. No one will know."

Adeline was sitting at the kitchen island when her younger counterpart returned from her visit with her father. She remembered what had been said, how suspicious she had been of Daniele back then.

"How was the visit?"

"Informative."

Adeline cocked her head. "Do you know the biggest mistake people make?"

"Asking rhetorical questions?"

She smiled. "Making up their minds before they have all the facts. I hope you won't make that mistake, Adeline."

As her younger self walked up to her room, Adeline realized why she had done what she did all those years ago. She needed her counterpart to investigate Constance, Hiro, and Elliott to get close to them. Elliott would come to trust her, and for that reason, he would text her when Absolom Two was ready, urging her to keep Daniele away. She would take control of the machine at that moment and send her younger self to the past, to 2008, to start the cycle.

But what would she do after? Would she go back to that night at Nora's house and kill her? The past had to occur as it had. Or else the universe would break. Someone had to go back and do it. Adeline's greatest fear of all was that she was that person.

The next morning, Adeline visited the print shop inside the Absolom Sciences headquarters.

In the corner, a large-format printer was rolling off a banner for a retirement party for someone named Steven.

The plotter/cutter beside it was slicing up a roll of vinyl for truck decals.

The print shop manager, a man named Roger, who was in his sixties, was sitting on a stool at a raised table with a rubberized top, using an X-ACTO knife to touch up a directional sign that read *Café*.

At the sight of Adeline, he hopped off the stool and took his thick glasses off, letting them dangle from a cord.

"Miss Danneros. Wasn't expecting you."

"Hi, Roger."

"What can I do for you?"

"I'm wondering if you're able to print something on a small plastic surface."

"Sure. Well, how small?"

"Say the size of a driver's license?"

"Oh yeah. That's no problem. Do you have a file?"

"I was wondering if you could show me how to do it. It's for a personal project."

He shrugged. "Of course."

"And I know this might sound a little crazy, but I need an ink that washes off in water."

"Believe me, we've seen crazier. I don't have any of the disappearing ink right now, but I can order it. We've used it before."

He must have read Adeline's surprise. "Some guys down in IT wanted some a few years ago. For an April Fool's prank, I think." Roger smiled. "Planning something similar?"

"This is no prank. I guess you could say it's for a birthday party."

A week later, Adeline was placing the ID under the printer. She reviewed the layout of the Absolom Sciences intern badge, clicked print, and watched as the California driver's license for Daniele Danneros was covered in the disappearing ink.

As she watched the present cover the past—and future—she couldn't help but wonder about the nature of time itself, and causality, and specifically where the driver's license had come from in the first place. She could ask the same question about the diamond earrings that would also travel to the past with her younger counterpart. The license and the earrings were like the universe itself: its past before it existed was a mystery. When and how had the two items been created? What form had they existed in before they came into the universe? In that answer was the true nature of time, and it was stranger than Adeline had ever imagined as a child.

SIXTY-SEVEN

Adeline put all of her efforts into preparing for the future. Her years of work on Absolom Island were coming to fruition. The roads were done. The automated bungalows and offices and facilities were ready. Yet, aside from the construction company staff, it stood empty, waiting for the moment when it was needed.

Adeline spent as much time as she could visiting her father, drilling him on survival techniques.

His own island loomed in the past. Pangea. There would be no automated paradise waiting for him there.

She watched the bitterness and suspicion grow inside her younger self.

Elliott and Hiro worked day and night on testing Absolom Two, ensuring it was safe for her father. It was hard to think either one of them had killed Nora and framed her father, given the effort they were seemingly putting into making it possible to bring him back.

That's what bothered Adeline the most: in the puzzle that was her life, the pieces didn't quite fit.

A text lit up her phone. It was from the CEO of Syntran, again requesting a meeting. She apparently had ignored the email autoresponder. Adeline had to respect her persistence. She sent a message back telling her to proceed with whatever she thought best for the company. Adeline had bigger issues at the moment.

Hiro managed to update the Absolom machine two days before Sam departed.

When Adeline had asked Elliott how sure he was that it would work—that Absolom Two would indeed deliver Sam alive, and in one piece, to the Triassic, the older scientist had simply shrugged. "Pretty sure."

"Pretty sure?"

"Look, it worked for the mice we tested it on."

"How do you know?"

"The mice fossils we recovered indicate that they were alive at the time of arrival."

That didn't make Adeline feel much better, but there was nothing she could do about it. Time and life had taught her one thing: you do all you can, and at some point, it's either enough or it's not. The tides of a life and your efforts either carry you in. Or sink you.

Adeline barely slept the night before her father's departure. She had lived it once, and she had never truly gotten over seeing him disappear in that box.

But she knew she had to watch it one last time.

As she stood in the viewing booth, waiting for the glass to change from black to transparent, she reflected that time had another magical quality: steeling the soul. She looked down at her younger self, in the row in front of her, knowing a wave of agony was about to hit her.

Adeline knew that she herself could tolerate seeing her father ripped out of the universe. That was the advantage of time. It conditioned the heart to the worst assaults. Or maybe it was natural to feel less as one grew older. Maybe a mind could develop scar tissue too. Emotional scar tissue. Adeline had her share.

The glass turned transparent, revealing the Absolom machine in the center of the room.

Her father was lying on the floor, wearing the thick white departure ensemble.

He pushed up and glanced around at the machine, seeming surprised, then through the glass door, up to the viewing booth.

His eyes met his daughter's stare, and Adeline remembered exactly how that felt—as if a hot poker had been run through her.

She watched her counterpart break then. She stood, practically jumped to the glass window, and slammed her fist into it. A gong sound echoed through the room, loud and borderline disorienting, as if the waves were rattling Adeline's brain.

Adeline remembered the pain from that blow, remembered ignoring it as she pounded the glass. The scream that accompanied the beating was even worse, the word "Dad!" drawn out like a battle cry.

She rose, stepped outside the two rows of chairs, and put her hands on her younger counterpart's shoulders. Gently, she guided her back to her seat and stood watching as her father got to his feet and tried to smile. His lips were shaking, preventing a smile from forming. He managed to draw it across his lips on the second attempt.

The machine vibrated.

Adeline's counterpart reached over and put an arm around her brother.

One memory that had always stuck with Adeline was the

moment the first Absolom prisoner had disappeared in the box. In that split second, she had seen total fear in the man's eyes.

She didn't see that in her father. He was scared, but in his eyes, she saw resolve. She saw hope. She saw a man who believed he had a future. A man who was alone but believed that he wouldn't always be alone.

What she realized in that moment was the difference between the two men in the box. The first Absolom prisoner had no hope. Her father did. Hope was his anchor to this world.

In that instant, Adeline saw how powerful hope was. It was the true lever of Absolom. It was how the machine had transformed the world. Because it took the last shred of hope from even the most hopeless.

She blinked, and her father was gone.

She was still standing there, and like the man in the box, she held on to hope. She would get him back. Soon.

SIXTY-EIGHT

Adeline knew that everyone lied to themselves at some point in their lives. It was part of preserving one's ego. Maybe it was more than that, but the task for Adeline was somewhat different. She actually had to lie to her younger self. If she didn't, the past wouldn't occur as it had. The universe would cease to exist.

So she did.

Adeline watched as her younger counterpart spun her wheels, searching Constance's home for clues about whether she was the killer. Then Elliott's residence. And finally, the empty home Hiro owned in Las Vegas, with the tunnel that led to the high-roller room beneath the strip.

All the while, that nineteen-year-old girl Adeline had once been grew more suspicious of the woman she knew as Daniele Danneros—the woman she would become.

Adeline prepped the two items her younger self would need. The first was the California driver's license. It was buried beneath the Absolom Sciences intern ID, in plain sight, but unrecognizable, just like Adeline herself, thanks to the cosmetic surgery.

The other was the diamond earrings Nathan had given her. They were a link to a life she had left behind. They would be her younger counterpart's only hope of survival in the world after Absolom.

★ ★ ★

During that period, when her younger self was searching for answers she would never find, Adeline had challenges of her own. The biggest was how to transmit the recall ring to her father in the past.

There were two problems.

The first was size.

By government agreement, Absolom Sciences could transmit up to twenty-five grams without approval. The recall ring was significantly more massive than that.

In Adeline's basement, she, Elliott, Hiro, and Constance discussed whether they could make it smaller. Hiro insisted that they couldn't. But they could separate it into pieces.

Adeline remembered this moment from nineteen years ago. She walked to the stairwell, saw her younger self standing there listening, and stared until the young woman retreated up the stairs.

In the privacy of the basement, the Absolom scientists settled on a solution: they would break the recall ring into parts and transmit them back. To do that, they arrived at the only path Adeline could see: they embedded the parts of the recall ring in Absolom prisoners and sent them to Sam's timeline.

Constance was against operating on the prisoners. She felt it was morally wrong to do something to someone without their full knowledge. Adeline knew that she was right. But there was nothing she could do about it. She either sent the recall ring back embedded in the Absolom prisoners, or she lost her father forever. The prisoners would be exiled to the past one way or another. Being operated on gave them the chance to save an innocent man, one Adeline cared about a great deal.

The second problem was ensuring the prisoners—and the

pieces they sent to the past—arrived at the right time and near enough to her father for him to find them.

They spent months in Death Valley running tests, trying to ensure that the payloads arrived at the right location and time. With each tuning bar they found, they edged closer to perfecting Absolom Two.

Adeline lobbied the government for permission to operate on the prisoners—and received it after some cajoling.

She couldn't help but wonder what would happen if one of the prisoners arrived at the same time as her father. They were the worst of humanity. And time in the Triassic, alone, probably wouldn't be good for their mental health.

But there was nothing she could do about that.

The final worry the team had was simply about causality. Would sending the prisoners to Sam's timeline cause it to cease to exist? They were, after all, disrupting a timeline that had been created from their own, technically changing the past before he arrived. That discussion led them to the conclusion they had arrived at before: the past could not be changed. If they had already sent the prisoners, then his timeline would be preserved. They were simply doing what they had to do, what time and space required to exist. If they were right, when Sam arrived, the prisoners they were sending after he departed would have already been there a long time.

One night, Adeline set her alarm for 3 a.m.

When it went off, she rose and walked down the hall to her counterpart's bedroom. The door was closed, but she was gone. The photomosaic blanket was spread across the bed, a reminder of the past.

Adeline knew where she was. At that moment, she was in the basement of Hiro's home in Las Vegas, talking with Elliott and

Hiro, slowly becoming convinced that Daniele Danneros was planning to use Absolom Two to get rid of her and kill Nora.

Once again, she wondered if it was true.

She knew it was half true—she would indeed use Absolom to send her younger counterpart nineteen years into the past. But what would happen after that? That was the real question, the true challenge ahead.

She knew by the time her younger self got back home, she would have decided to trust Elliott and Hiro and spy on the woman she knew as Daniele.

It was all happening as it had, the way it had to happen.

The next morning, at breakfast, there was a change in the air, a tension between Adeline and her younger self. Even Ryan sensed it.

But it was necessary.

Adeline went upstairs to prepare for the day, knowing her counterpart was hiding a burner phone with a listening app in her study.

After the shower, she found a text message waiting on her phone, a short note from Hana Kim, the CEO of Syntran, again requesting a meeting. She was even in town and willing to come to Adeline's home. The woman was extremely persistent. It was the reason she had gotten to where she was.

Adeline sent a quick note back, letting her know that she could meet for a few minutes but had meetings all afternoon. She was meeting Hiro and Elliott out in the desert then, to search for more tuning bars.

She also knew that they would be sitting in Elliott's office that morning, listening to the conversations in her study via the app on the burner phone Adeline's younger self had hidden under a chair.

* * *

Constance came by shortly before lunch and informed Adeline that she was going to Germany to meet with a man from her past whom she believed might be infected.

Hana Kim arrived about an hour later, and Adeline could tell she was excited about something.

They sat in the study, speaking Korean, the CEO giving a wide-ranging update about the company. When she was done, she opened her laptop and pulled up a picture of a dead body.

"Did I ever tell you how my father died?"

"Yes. While waiting for a transplant."

Hana nodded. "That's true. He was waiting for a transplant. He was very sick at the time. He had gone to America, to New York City, for an experimental treatment. But he actually died in a plane crash. I was a year old at the time—on September first, 1983. His plane was en route from New York to Seoul, but it had stopped in Anchorage, Alaska, to refuel before continuing on the Pacific leg of the flight. At some point, the plane got off course and drifted into Soviet airspace. It was shot down by a Soviet Su-15 interceptor. About ten years later, we learned that the wreckage crashed into the Sea of Japan, but the details were kept secret back then. The downing of the Korean Airlines aircraft was one of the tensest moments of the Cold War. We knew my father was sick, but I thought I would see him again. His death was hard, but it was compounded by the fact that there was an empty casket at his funeral."

Hana motioned to the laptop screen, at the body. "At Syntran, I believe we have an opportunity to right that wrong as well. And we can do it with our existing technology. In fact, we've already created several successful—"

Adeline held up a hand, stopping the woman from saying another word.

She stared at the screen, feeling her body go numb.

This was the answer. The piece she had been missing. If her theory was correct, it would solve everything. But not if the woman continued describing what she was working on.

"I'm afraid I need to cut our meeting short," Adeline said.

Hana bunched her eyebrows. "This is a significant expansion in our product offering. It's a small market size, but we think it's a valuable market. We're envisioning selling this to governments around the world. In instances where a government employee was lost in the line of duty—and a body can't be recovered—this would allow that nation to provide the family with some closure. Same for large multinationals. I can also see a use case for Absolom. This would give the families a body to bury. That's the other reason I wanted to meet with you, to see if you could facilitate an intro for me. The publicity would put it on the radar of—"

Adeline took a pad from the table and wrote the address of a roadside diner outside of town and a short message:

Meet me here in 30 minutes

Hana scrunched her face at the note.

"Well, I'll see what I can do," Adeline said. "But I'm afraid that's all the time I have for now."

Thirty minutes later, she was sitting in a booth at the back of the small restaurant, Hana across from her.

"What was that about?" Hana asked.

"The venture capital industry is getting very cut-throat. I'm concerned someone might have bugged my home."

"Really?"

"It's a crazy world out there. Now, about this new service,

what would you need to create a body? And does Syntran place any identifying marks on the replicas? Like a serial number or something?"

That evening, Adeline sat on the back patio, an empty wine glass on the table, staring at the sun hovering over the mountains beyond the sea of glass.

She heard the door open, and her counterpart marched in.

"Tough day?" the younger woman asked, motioning to the wine glass.

"No. I'm celebrating."

"Celebrating what?"

"A discovery. One that could change everything. A very unexpected discovery."

"In the desert?"

"No. I knew what we would find in the desert. This... this I didn't see coming."

The next morning, Adeline started the process to exhume Nora's body. There was some red tape. She needed approval from the cemetery as well as Nora's next of kin—a cousin in Pennsylvania. Getting consent was easier than she had expected.

"As you know," she said on a call to the cousin, "Nora worked for my company, on Absolom. We believe she may have been exposed to subatomic particles during a recent experiment. We need to test her body to see if others she worked with might be at risk."

Two days later, she was standing in the morgue, staring at the body. She knew the private investigator Elliott had hired to follow her was on the other side of the glass, watching, making a video he would later send to Elliott, who would share it with the younger Adeline.

It didn't matter. They weren't seeing what she was seeing. She bent down and confirmed her suspicions.

Finally, it all made sense.

The missing piece was on that table.

The future wasn't what Adeline had imagined.

SIXTY-NINE

Adeline dreaded what she had to do next. Well, she dreaded half of it. The part where she betrayed her younger self and sent her to the past.

The other part was a moment she had waited nineteen years for: what happened after. The future was waiting, and she had to take control of it if she was going to get her father back.

On that fateful day, the private security contractors arrived at her home in black SUVs with tinted windows, dressed in tailored suits that somewhat hid the sidearms in shoulder holsters.

A few hours later, the delivery from Syntran arrived.

Adeline's younger counterpart got home about the time the box was being placed in the garage.

"What's that?" she asked.

"It's for a trip I'll be taking."

"Trip where?"

"It's none of your concern."

The teenager glanced at the two black SUVs.

"I've hired some additional security," Adeline said. "For the house. And the office."

"Private security."

"Yes. I needed people who only answer to me."

★ ★ ★

At dinner that night, Adeline's younger counterpart was on edge as she waited for Elliott's message.

Adeline knew what that message would say—knew that it marked the point at which Absolom Two was finally precise enough to use.

Adeline felt her own nerves growing. The moment she had waited so long for was finally here. Everything had to happen precisely. There was no room for error—now in the present or in the past.

Adeline took the box of earrings from her pocket and slid them across the table. The glittering diamonds were the last reminder she had of Nathan. Soon, they would be this young woman's lifeline in the past.

"I got you a small gift," Adeline said.

Her counterpart took the box and quickly began removing the wrapper.

"What's the occasion?"

"New beginnings. I feel like we got off on the wrong foot."

When she opened the box, young Adeline glanced at the stones. "They're beautiful."

"Someone very special gave them to me. Someone who's no longer in my life."

Adeline's counterpart set the box down beside her plate. "Sorry, I need to—"

Adeline rose. "Please try them on."

Hastily, she attached them to her ears and forced a smile.

Adeline leaned forward, fingers interlocked. "They're perfect."

That's how she would remember her younger self, in that moment, wearing the earrings that were the bridge between her past and this person's future.

What came next was less pleasant.

Her counterpart excused herself, retreated to the half bath in the hall, where Adeline knew she was exchanging text messages with Elliott.

Adeline sent a message of her own—to the private security team.

Proceed with phase 1.

A reply came a few seconds later:

Commencing

Adeline didn't like this part. But it was the path of least resistance.

Right now, the second security team was breaking into Elliott's home. The city's security cameras would capture it all, but it wouldn't matter. The vans had old license plates taken from a junkyard. The team members were wearing balaclavas.

Adeline had verified that Elliott's wife wouldn't be home (she was in Europe). There was no chance she'd be harmed. But the police would respond. They would call Elliott, and he would have to leave the lab.

Adeline knew he would return. But not in time. At least, not in time to stop her from sending her younger self to the past. She knew because it had already happened.

Hiro was a tougher challenge. She needed him. But she would cross that bridge when she arrived at it.

Adeline moved to the hall off the foyer and stood by the door to the half bath. She drew the injector pen from her pocket and waited until the door opened. The younger woman turned when she realized someone was standing there, but it was too late. Adeline held the injector to her neck, pressed the button, and reached out as her body went limp.

★ ★ ★

From the security cameras, Adeline knew Hiro was still in the lab with the door locked, as Elliott had instructed. What the two men didn't know was that Adeline had updated the software on those door locks. It had an override code only she knew.

At the Absolom Sciences building, the private security contractors unloaded the box at the loading dock.

The security guard merely said hello to Adeline. He was used to the scientists bringing items into the labs at all hours. Asking questions of the person who owned the company—and ran the experiments that kept it going—would only get him fired. As such, he didn't ask any questions.

Adeline had the security team bring the box down to the lab level and set it outside the door to the Absolom Two lab. She didn't want them to see what was inside—or what was going to happen beyond the door. She instructed them to wait outside the building and alert her when Elliott returned.

With her phone, she unlocked the door.

Hiro was standing at a rolling cart beside the Absolom Two prototype, studying a computer screen. He spun when the door lock clicked open and reached down to his pocket, Adeline assumed for his mobile phone, to call Elliott.

"Don't do it, Hiro."

"How'd you get in here?"

"I had the software updated." Adeline threw a letter-size envelope at his feet. "Look at those pictures, Hiro."

He reached down, opened it, and began rifling through the historical photos Tesseract had found. The photos that showed Adeline in the past. And the others.

"What is this? A trick? Photo manipulation?"

"It's real, Hiro. It's the past. And our future. It's the answer we've been looking for." Adeline turned and pointed at the box outside the door. "And here is the other one."

Hiro shook his head. "This is a ruse. You're going to kill Nora."

"Look at what's in the box, Hiro. Please."

"No."

"I know you're going to walk over here and look inside this box because you're the only one who can operate Absolom Two. Besides Elliott. And he's too suspicious of me. This has to happen. Because you have to send me back."

Hiro swallowed hard and shook his head. "No."

Adeline walked over and opened the top of the box. Two body bags were lying inside. One was breathable. The other wasn't. She unzipped them enough to expose the faces, then stepped away, giving Hiro plenty of room.

Hiro had said no, but he walked closer and looked down at Adeline's younger counterpart, breathing in and out, still knocked out from the drug Adeline had injected her with, but alive and well.

"Nineteen years ago, I woke up in that Absolom machine. It transported me back to March of 2008. My birth name is Adeline Anderson."

Hiro's voice was a whisper. "You're lying."

"I had cosmetic surgery a few years after I arrived in the past." She studied him, mentally searching for the key that would unlock his trust.

"In that home in Las Vegas, in the basement, you saw me when you exited the tunnel."

Hiro studied Adeline's face as she continued recounting the memory. "You grabbed me and pulled me inside and locked the door and turned and walked down the tunnel, to the room with all the doors and the muscular bouncer sitting on a stool. He was reading a hardback book that was wrapped in thin plastic like you might find on a library book."

Hiro's eyes went wide.

"Look at the other body, Hiro."

He stared down. "What is this?"

"The other answer. All this time, we made an assumption. A very big assumption. And we never even thought to question it. That assumption was wrong. We can fix all of this, Hiro. But I can't do it without you. And we need to hurry. You know I can't operate the machine. And soon, I'll need to go through it myself."

Still staring at the bodies, he swallowed. His chest rose and fell in labored breaths.

"Okay."

Hiro helped Adeline drag the two bodies into the lab and place young Adeline in the Absolom machine. He set about programming two recall rings for Adeline—for the next phase of the plan—and then began prepping the machine for the first departure.

"Date, time, and location?" he asked.

"Monday, March 17, 2008. Around 10 a.m. Stanford. Lomita Mall, right next to the machine shop."

Hiro typed on the keyboard. "Okay. Ready."

Adeline peered inside the machine. Her younger self was waking up, looking around, confused.

A fist pounded on the door, and Elliott's muffled voice called into the room. "Daniele! I'm calling the police."

"Sorry," Adeline whispered as she swung the door to the Absolom chamber closed.

She stepped closer to Hiro. "Send her."

Adeline watched as Absolom hummed to life and transmitted her younger self to the past.

One down. Two to go.

"What now?" Hiro asked.

"Now we get Dad back."

SEVENTY

Elliott pounded harder on the door, screaming.

Hiro stood at the computer terminal next to the Absolom prototype. "We should tell him."

"It's too risky," Adeline said. "He could try to stop us. We tell him after. Help me get the body in the machine."

When the black bag was inside Absolom, Adeline closed the door, and Hiro keyed in the departure sequence.

As the machine hummed and the bag disappeared, Elliott stopped pounding on the door. He was leaving. Adeline didn't like that—he could be going to the police. But she couldn't let him in. She couldn't take the chance that he had a gun—and could stop her. The past had to happen as it had.

She would deal with him after it was over.

Adeline felt nervousness growing in her stomach. The next thirty minutes would determine everything: her future, her father's future, and the fate of the universe itself.

No pressure.

She walked over to the metal table and put the large envelope of photos Tesseract had found back in her pocket and then slipped the recall ring on her wrist. She put the other ring in her pocket. She would need it soon.

Hiro stared at her. He was nervous too. This would be the first time a recall ring was ever used. What they were about to activate would reach across universes—time and space—back to Pangea, to a place where her father had either lived or died.

"Activate it, Hiro."

He typed on the keyboard and turned to her. "Ping was successful. Ring is active."

"Pull it through."

The next few seconds were the longest of Adeline's life. Would her father arrive as a mangled mess? In pieces? In a haze of particles and dust?

The Absolom machine hummed and flashed. In the middle of the chamber, her father appeared.

He looked like death.

He was skinny, his hair grungy, his face streaked with blood and dirt. But it was his eyes that shook Adeline. They were hard and hollowed out, like an animal. Someone who had been fighting for his life—and had the life driven out of him.

But he was alive.

When his eyes came into focus, and he saw Adeline through the machine's glass door, his gaze softened. A smile formed.

Seeing her and the lab and the world he knew seemed to bring him back. Almost instantly, his eyes morphed back to the man Adeline had known in the two eras of her life: as a child, when she was Adeline; and as an adult, when she was Daniele.

She knew that he was seeing Daniele—his business partner and friend and the woman who had been so kind to his dying wife, and then the guardian who had taken in his children when he had been banished from this world. Adeline wanted to tell him who she really was. And if things went right, she would have that chance. If not, leaving that unsaid would be the greatest regret of her life. The next few minutes would determine whether that opportunity came.

To Hiro, Adeline said, "Have you rekeyed his recall ring?"

"Yes. It's entangled with this universe now."

Adeline opened the door. "Welcome back."

Sam's eyes welled with tears.

"How?" he asked, his voice breaking with emotion.

"We'll get to that. But we need to do something else first."

Sam nodded, and didn't say any more.

Adeline closed the door, motioned to Hiro, and the machine hummed again.

The government would launch a full investigation into the power and Absolom usage tonight, but that was a problem for the future. Right now, Adeline had to ensure there was a future.

For the third time in her life, she watched Absolom send her father to the past.

Then, for the second time in her life, she stepped into the machine and felt it hum and vibrate and she joined him in the past.

SEVENTY-ONE

Adeline arrived in the foyer of Nora's home.
Hiro's targeting was good but not perfect. She was about two feet off the floor when she snapped into existence. She landed awkwardly, feet thudding on the floor as she reached out to brace herself on a wall with her hand.

"Hello?" Nora called from the kitchen.

She stepped out into the hall and stared at Adeline. "I told you not to come over."

Nora's gaze drifted to the front door. The locked door. "Wait. How did you get in here?"

Before Adeline could answer, the air next to her crackled and began to hiss.

She stepped aside and watched as her father appeared, also a few feet off the floor.

He landed with more grace, in a crouch.

Nora's mouth fell open. Adeline could only imagine what was going through the woman's mind. She had just seen this man leave her home—dressed in normal clothes, at a normal weight and well-groomed. Now he was wearing what Nora would instantly recognize as an Absolom departure ensemble, and he was slightly emaciated and completely dirty. He smelled terrible.

"What is this?" Nora asked.

"It's Absolom Two," Adeline said.

"I got that far. Why are you here?"

Adeline could see that Nora was scared now. It was the sight of her father that had done it. The fact that he had been sent via Absolom for some crime in the future. She could almost see Nora putting it together.

Nora took a step back, as if she was going to run. Her foot crunched on the broken glass on the floor.

Adeline glanced around. The package should arrive any second.

"Nora, it's not what you think."

The air between them in the hall crackled again. Adeline expected to see the black bag emerge.

Instead, Elliott appeared.

His foot slipped on the rug as he landed, crashing to the floor, but he scrambled to his feet, raising his right arm, a gun held out, trained on Adeline.

"Don't move!"

Adeline's heart hammered in her chest. This wasn't part of the plan. She expected the universe around her to shatter, to dissolve like an oil painting exposed to heat: the view bubbling into blisters that peeled and flaked away. But reality held. For now. So far, this had already occurred.

Elliott didn't look back at Nora. He took a step toward Adeline. "She's here to kill you, Nora."

Adeline's father cocked his head. "Is that true, Dani?"

"No."

"Activate your recall ring," Elliott said. "Leave this time, right now."

Adeline ignored his command. "How did you get here?"

"I broke down the lab door and tied Hiro up. He told me the lies you used on him."

"They're not lies, Elliott. I can prove it."

As if on cue, a crackle emanated from the edge of the foyer, just inside the dining room.

The black bag snapped into existence and dropped to the floor with a thud.

Elliott's eyes went wide.

"Open the bag," Adeline said.

"What is it?"

Adeline turned to her father. "Unzip it."

He stared at her and then at Elliott and finally Nora. He stepped toward the bag.

Elliott held out his other hand. "Stop, Sam. It's probably a weapon."

He was too late.

Adeline's father reached down and unzipped the bag, revealing the body that looked exactly like Nora. He reeled back at the sight. Elliott froze, gun still held on Adeline.

"How?" Sam asked.

"A long time ago, I funded a company called Syntran. It grows organs for transplant. Along the way, they figured out how to grow human bodies from a DNA sample—even how to use telomere trimming and epigenetic manipulation to age the specimens. They grow the replica, age the organs so that they're the right size, harvest them, then provide the remaining body to families for burial in cases where their loved one couldn't be recovered."

"The morgue," Elliott whispered.

"Yes," Adeline said. "That's why I had Nora's body exhumed—to verify that it had the Syntran serial number. To verify that a Syntran replica had been buried."

Adeline pointed to the body on the floor. "This is the corpse the police will find. It will be buried. Not Nora."

For a long moment, it was utterly quiet. "We made an assumption," Adeline said. "We assumed that Nora was murdered tonight. That assumption was wrong. She wasn't. She was replaced—and made to look like she was murdered so that we would complete Absolom Two. So the future would take place. There's a far larger process at work here."

SEVENTY-TWO

Nora looked from Adeline to the body on the floor. "Hold on. Did you just say *murdered*?"

Adeline nodded. "It's a long story. The happy ending is that you're not going to be murdered."

Her gaze drifted over to Elliott, who was still holding the gun, staring down at Nora's replica. Adeline wondered what he was thinking. What had his plan been? Had he imagined himself stopping Adeline from killing Nora, and then traveling back to the future until he could take the time to develop his own replica for Nora? It was the only real solution that Adeline could see. If that was Elliott's plan, what then? Saving Charlie was his real objective. For him, Absolom Two had always been about the son he had lost.

"It's not over, Elliott."

"What do you mean?"

"The night Charlie died, in his apartment, you walked out into the living room and told me never to speak of that night until we met at Nora's house—and that I would know when. And that when the time came, to tell you that everything was going to be all right."

Elliott cocked his head. "I didn't see you that night."

As soon as he said it, comprehension dawned on him.

"Not yet," Adeline said. "Not yet."

Elliott let the gun fall to his side. A tear rolled down his face. "Not yet," he whispered.

To Sam, he said, "It's good to see you again."

His old friend nodded.

Elliott turned back to Nora. "You too. It's been longer for us than for you."

"I want to hear about that."

"You will," Elliott said. He reached down to the recall ring on his wrist. "But I need to get back to the lab before I contaminate this crime scene with my DNA. And I need to apologize to Hiro."

He pressed the button and the air crackled and he was gone.

"What happens now?" Nora asked.

"Now," Adeline said, moving to the black body bag, "we recreate your murder."

Sam helped Adeline lift Nora's replica and move her to the kitchen. They placed the body with the head protruding out into the hallway so that it would be seen from the front door the next morning.

"We need to make the incision," Adeline said. "Syntran left the organs in and simulated a time of death, but the body still needs to bleed."

Adeline watched her father walk to the kitchen and take the knife from the butcher block. She swallowed, heart beating faster, waiting for the moment that had been nearly two decades in the making, a moment that would change everything for them.

He paused, looking at the knife, his back to her. "We have a problem."

He turned to the two women. "The knife was hidden in the toilet compartment, and Adeline's DNA was found on it, but she never touched it."

Adeline walked over and took the knife from him. "Her DNA is on it now."

Her father stared at her, confused. Slowly, comprehension seemed to dawn on him.

"Hi, Dad."

He reached back and put a hand on the counter, bracing himself. "How?"

"Absolom Two."

His chest rose and fell faster as his breathing accelerated.

"How far back?"

"All the way to 2008. I was there when Mom gave birth."

"You... you were *that* Adeline? The TA she told me about?"

"I was."

He reached out and touched Adeline's cheek. His hand was still dirty, but Adeline didn't care. She pressed her face into his fingers. "I had surgery," she whispered. "A few years before I met you as Daniele."

Her father studied her face and shook his head. "I thought I was the hero. But it was you, all along. The price you paid. All those years you gave to this. Half your life. Most would have given up."

"It was a small price to pay to get you back." Adeline turned to look at Nora. "And to save you. That's why I hid the cameras. I was trying to figure out what was going to happen."

"I understand," Nora said.

"What happens now?" Sam asked.

"Now," Adeline replied, "we start living the part we've all been avoiding. The future. A wise person once said that time heals all wounds. But it won't work if you don't give time a chance. I think we've given the past enough time. Our wounds are healed. It's time to do what we were always meant to do, the real reason Absolom Two exists. It's time to give the future a chance. And to start helping others."

PART V

ABSOLOM ISLAND

SEVENTY-THREE

In the lab, Adeline stepped out of the Absolom machine and joined Elliott and Hiro at the computer station.

"Ready for us to bring them home?" Hiro asked.

Elliott had clearly filled him in on what had transpired at Nora's house in the past.

"Not yet," Adeline said.

Using her phone, she disabled the cameras in the lab and told the two men her plan.

Elliott just shook his head. "You've been two steps ahead the whole time."

"Yes, but I didn't know how all the pieces fit until now."

To Hiro, she said, "Go ahead. Bring them home."

The Absolom machine hummed, and Adeline's father appeared in the chamber.

Adeline opened the door and held up a hand. "We need to transmit you again."

"Why?"

"There will be an investigation into this prototype's usage tonight. They'll know from the power consumption. We can't have your DNA here. And you can't stay here."

He nodded. "Where exactly am I going then?"

"It's a place called Absolom Island. And it's the future. Nora will be joining you there. So will I. All of us will. Eventually."

Adeline closed the door and watched her father disappear. When Nora arrived, Adeline told her about Absolom Island and watched her depart.

Elliott pointed to the computer screen. "We're already getting a ton of emails about the power usage. What are we going to tell them?"

"The truth. We had to use the prototype to avoid a temporal disaster. And that it won't happen again. We're shutting down all further development of Absolom here. We're moving everything to the island."

Elliott bunched his eyebrows. "What exactly are we going to be doing on the island?"

Adeline drew the envelope from her pocket—the same one she had shown Hiro. She handed it to Elliott and watched as he flipped through the photos the Tesseract program had found. He paused on one that showed Adeline standing in Nanking in late 1937. The next photo was of her and her father in a village in northern Sumatra, Indonesia in 2004. The next page showed Elliott and Charlie in Cambodia in 1975.

"How long have you had these?" he asked.

"I found some photos that had me in them years ago. I only thought to look for the rest of you after Dad mentioned it the night you showed us Absolom Two."

"Charlie's in these pictures. How?"

"I couldn't exhume his body—not without your permission— so I couldn't confirm that he was replaced with a Syntran replica. But I knew we'd get him back when I saw these photos."

"You could have told me."

"I could have. But I didn't know what you would do. I couldn't risk you disrupting the past until I knew how it all fit together."

"And how does it fit together?"

"Absolom Island, Elliott. It's the key. It's a place to do what we did here tonight, with Nora: rescue people who are lost in time. People who are going to die but deserve a second chance. People like Charlie."

She reached out and gripped his shoulder. "In fact, he's the second one we're going to save."

SEVENTY-FOUR

A top a high dune, on an island in the Pacific, Sam stood and watched the waves crash into the beach as the sun set in the distance.

He reached out and intertwined his fingers with Nora's.

Neither said a word. They simply watched the sun slip over the horizon and the dark curtain of night spread across the sky, the stars shining brighter than he had ever seen them—at least in this world. The night sky reminded him of Pangea, an island much like this one—uninhabited and full of wonder. But he was safe here. And he wasn't alone. This was a home. A place for a second chance.

He and Nora walked along a crushed stone path back to a small cottage overlooking the sea. An empty, newly made village spread out around it, waiting for its residents to arrive. To Sam, it almost felt like he and Nora were the only people in the world. And that was sort of perfect. It was what he needed. He sensed that she did too. They had been here for a week, and in that time, without all the pressures and worries of the outside world, they had both decompressed. And gotten to know each other, in a way he thought they never would have before, in the normal world.

As much as he loved the little bubble he now inhabited with Nora, Sam wondered what the date was. He knew Absolom could only send matter to the past. How far back had the machine sent them when it transported them to the island? A week? A month?

There had been no contact with the outside world. If it had been a week, then Adeline, Elliott, and Hiro were just now getting to the point where they were fighting to control the Absolom Two prototype in the lab. He wasn't sure how long it would take them to wind down their affairs in the US and make their way to the island, but he hoped they didn't hurry. More time with Nora on the island was just fine with him.

For now, they had everything they needed here. The pantries in the cottages were full of meals ready to eat, or MREs. Clean water flowed from the taps. There were even new clothes hanging in the closet.

Sam was especially thankful for that. Upon arriving, the first thing he had done was strip off the Absolom prison uniform and take a hot shower. He had soaked in the tub after that, and Nora had joined him, using a washcloth to clean the wound on his back.

"How did you get this?" she had asked.

"It's... a long story."

"Dinosaur attack?"

"Prison fight."

Nora laughed. Then stopped. "Wait, you're serious?"

"I am. Like I said: it's a long story. But it's in the past. All I care about now is the future." He turned in the tub. "Back there, in Pangea, I thought about what I would do if I ever got home. I thought about all my regrets. One was you. Not committing. Not taking the next step with us. I want that. I want to start over—to focus on the future. If you want to."

"I do. But Sam, what kind of life can we have here? I'm technically dead. So are you."

"If you think about it, it's perfect. Remember what you said in London?"

Nora squinted. "About feeling like a fraud."

"Yes. You felt like confessing. You hated the way the world saw you."

"I did."

"Well, nobody here is going to look at you like that. This is a new beginning. For all of us. And you were right about what you said in that hotel in London. There is a larger process at work here. This is what it was all about: the work we're going to do here."

Sam took her hands in his. "From here, we can go anywhere in the world. Anywhere in time. Our future is written in the past, and it's the adventure of a lifetime."

SEVENTY-FIVE

In the lab, Hiro programmed the Absolom Two prototype for the day Nora died.

"I need to arrive in the early afternoon," Adeline said. "In the toilet compartment of the master bathroom. And by the way, your targeting is still off by a few feet—vertically. I almost broke my ankle when I arrived at Nora's."

"My parents always told me to aim high."

"Hiro, was that an Absolom dad joke?"

He shrugged. "I'm at that age."

Adeline laughed and stepped into the machine.

When she arrived inside Nora's home, her feet were indeed closer to the floor this time. She landed with barely a sound.

She set the note on the floor, knowing Nora would find it and go searching for the cameras. She marveled at the revelation that she was actually the person who had sabotaged her own grand plan to see what had happened inside Nora's home that night.

She activated her recall ring, musing to herself at how strange time and causality was.

The next morning, Adeline stood in the kitchen of her home, staring down at a tablet, where a livestream of a news reporter was playing.

In a surprise move today, Absolom Sciences announced it would no longer operate its namesake technology and that it would cease all future development of related quantum technology at its Nevada headquarters. Its government clients have entered into a perpetual license and will now operate the Nevada facilities through an international consortium.

In what looks like related news, the UN and nations around the world have formally recognized the newly created Pacific Island republic of Absolom...

The doorbell rang, and Adeline turned the tablet off and walked to the front door, where Hana Kim was waiting. Once again, they met in the study, and this time there was no hidden listening device. Adeline had instructed her security team to sweep the entire house. She didn't want anyone to hear what was about to be said.

"Thank you for providing the replica of Dr. Thomas."

"Of course," Hana said. "Out of curiosity, what was it for? A second memorial service?"

"No," Adeline said slowly, "it was for the first service, a few months ago."

Hana squinted at her, clearly confused.

Adeline walked to the window and gazed out at the street. "I'm going to tell you something that only five people in the entire world know: what really happened to Nora Thomas."

When Adeline had finished the story, Hana was silent for almost a minute. "Can I ask why you told me?"

"Do you know why I invested in Syntran all those years ago?"

"Because of the potential of what we're doing."

"Half right," Adeline said. "The other half is that I saw myself in you—someone who had lost their father tragically, someone who was working to make sure that never happened to anyone else like you. There's something very special about people who truly want to leave the world better than they found it. A lot of people talk about it. Far fewer actually do it. What I didn't know then is that what you were building was the key to saving someone I cared deeply about: Nora. And that what I was creating was the key to giving you what you've always wanted: a way to save your father. A second chance to actually get to know him."

"I don't understand."

"I want to tell you about a place called Absolom Island. It's a place where we're going to rescue people who are lost in time. People who died tragic deaths, who deserve a chance at a full life. There's just one thing we need: bodies to replace the people we take from the past. We need a Syntran lab we can operate. When it's operational, I promise you that your father will be the second person we rescue from the island. And once we have him back, thanks to Syntran, you can give him that life-saving transplant."

SEVENTY-SIX

Working methodically, Adeline, Elliott, and Hiro shut down the Absolom labs in Nevada. The employees were given generous severances. Ceasing development on the Absolom technology made the government inquest about the unauthorized Absolom departures easier to get rid of.

At home, Adeline faced a far greater challenge.

After school on Tuesday afternoon, she led Ryan into the family room, where he sat on the couch and Adeline perched on the edge of a club chair.

"I told you that Adeline went back to college."

Ryan nodded, eying her, concern deepening by the second.

"I know she hasn't responded to your texts or emails."

"How did you—"

"There's something I need to tell you."

He swallowed but didn't look away.

"It's something I said to you a few months ago. And twenty years ago."

Ryan bunched his eyebrows.

"It's over and we're going home and Dad is waiting there for us."

"He is? Wait. What?"

Adeline pressed on. She knew the words that would convince him, knew she had to get through them—the quicker the better.

"When you were eight, I was volunteering at Noah's

House, a non-profit shelter for kids who had been removed from their homes by social services. There was this big box of LEGOs in the garage. They were yours. I thought you didn't want them anymore. You hadn't played with them in years. I donated them to Noah's House. When you found out I got rid of them, you lost it. You were so angry with me. Screaming and balling up your fists. And then when I told you who I had donated them to, you didn't say another word. You were really conflicted. Still so angry, but you knew you weren't playing with them anymore. And that they were doing more good at the shelter. You got a truck load of LEGOs that Christmas. They were stacked around the tree so high you could barely see the other presents."

Ryan opened his mouth to speak. Adeline kept going.

"When you were six, you broke your leg and sprained your other ankle really badly. You were in a wheelchair for a month—until your ankle healed enough for crutches. I was pushing you in the street, but I didn't realize how much speed we were gathering. Finally, I couldn't even run fast enough to keep up. The wheelchair was pulling away, and I was losing control. I've never been that scared in my entire life."

Even recounting the memory of it shot a bolt of fear through Adeline.

Ryan's voice was just above a whisper. "What is this? What are you doing?"

"I knew I had to stop you before you got hit by a car. I lunged and pulled on the right handle of the wheelchair to steer it toward the ditch. I stood there in the street, panting, doubled over with my hands on my knees, watching as you crashed into that shallow ravine. Those seconds were probably the scariest of my entire life. Even scarier than watching Dad disappear in Absolom."

The color drained from Ryan's face.

"The yell that came out of you shattered me. I was terrified and winded, but I turned and ran back to the house. I thought my heart was going to explode inside my chest. I threw the door open and screamed for Dad, telling him you were hurt—and hurt badly and maybe dying—and I ran to my room and slammed the door and locked it and buried my head in a pillow and cried and cried until I had a headache and felt sick."

Ryan swallowed hard. "Impossible."

"I heard you crying when Dad carried you back into the house. I stayed in my room. Even through dinner. That night, Dad had to break open my door—it ripped out part of the frame. He made me come out and showed me that you were okay and that everything was fine. I felt terrible. But you forgave me—just like the LEGOs."

"How—"

"Two days after Mom died, I skipped school and went over to Caroline Marshal's house and got the drunkest I've ever been in my life. I think it all finally caught up with me, and I was regretting not spending more time with her. I stumbled home. I don't remember it all, but I remember throwing up all over the living room. And in the hall going to my bedroom. I passed out. When I woke up, I was still drunk. I threw up again in the toilet, and when I left my room, someone had cleaned up the mess in the living room. It was you. It had to be. Dad was somewhere—I can't remember where—but you never said a word. To him. Or to me."

"How is this possible?"

"Ryan, I know this is going to be hard to hear—"

"Just tell me."

"I'm your sister."

"What happened to Daniele?"

"I'm also Daniele. I always have been. I sent myself back in time using Absolom."

Ryan sat back against the couch cushion and breathed out. "No way."

"It's true."

"To when?"

"2008."

"Why then?"

"I don't know exactly. There's something about that time—about the loop. It sort of all started then, right before my birth."

"And you... you became Daniele? How did you know to do that?"

"Some of the things I said to myself—that Daniele had found herself alone, with very little money, and had made good investments to support herself. And then there was the obvious clue: I sent myself back in time with an Absolom intern ID around my neck. But under that ink was a California driver's license for Daniele Danneros. When I saw it, I realized the truth—what was going on and what I had to do. I knew history couldn't be changed. When I saw the ID, I knew I had sent myself to the past to ensure things occurred the way they had to happen."

"But where did the ID come from in the first place?"

"It's a mystery of space and time—the same kind of mystery as the universe itself. Where did it come from? What was it before? No one knows the answer to that."

Ryan shook his head. "This is going to take some getting used to."

"I know."

"Wait. You said Dad's at home?"

"He is. But not the home you know. We're moving, little brother."

★ ★ ★

A month later, Adeline was standing on the deck of the ship she had chartered to Absolom Island. It was another calm day on the sea, and she knew that around sunset, they'd sight land.

At lunch, Ryan said, "Will there be other kids?"

"Not initially," Adeline said. "But soon there will be. Kids and teachers, and people from all walks of life, from all around the world and across time. The island will be the ultimate melting pot."

When she was finished eating, Adeline prepared a lunch tray for Constance and made her way belowdecks, to her friend's stateroom. She found Constance lying on the bed, reading a book. Her eyelids were heavy, and her skin was ashen.

When they had set sail, Adeline hadn't been sure the woman would live long enough to see them arrive at Absolom Island. For that reason, Adeline had been coming down to check on her several times a day.

Constance smiled. "Are we there yet?"

Adeline set the tray on the side table and sat on the bed. "Almost."

"Did I tell you? I found the last one."

Constance had told her—a few days ago—but Adeline knew her memory was slipping. And she didn't want Constance to focus on that. She used one of the skills her very strange life had bestowed upon her, one that would likely come in handy when rescuing people in the past.

"No," she lied.

"When I found him, I thought, that's the last thread." Constance took a few deep breaths. "Maybe that's what the end of a life is: tying together those last few threads."

Adeline thought about her mother, and the photomosaic

quilts they had sewn together, and she thought Constance was right.

When she left, Constance was sleeping.

In her own stateroom, Adeline slipped beneath one of the mosaic quilts. She couldn't remember her life ever feeling so complete. But as full as it was, she was still missing one piece. A very important one.

SEVENTY-SEVEN

The sound and motion of the waves on the ship's hull slowly rocked Adeline to sleep. A knock on her stateroom door woke her from the nap.

When she opened it, she found Ryan standing in the narrow passage. "We're here."

On the deck, Adeline stood beside Hana, Ryan, Hiro, and Elliott and his wife, Claire. The shoreline of Absolom Island was barely visible on the horizon.

Adeline raised a pair of binoculars to her eyes and quickly found the dock where her father and Nora were standing, waiting as the sun set behind them. His arm was around her, and they were both smiling, staring at the ship coming in. They looked happy, happier than she had ever seen her father.

A container ship arrived a few days later. Onboard was the Absolom Two device, the Syntran components for a lab, and the Tesseract server array.

When the containers had been offloaded and moved to the Absolom Rescue Center, the ship left, and the team began setting up the equipment. The facility had everything else they would need, including a sewing room where they could make time-period specific outfits (and 3D-print the other items they needed), a hospital, and a reorientation center for those rescued from the past.

While the pieces were coming together to rescue people from the past, there was still one challenge: identifying who to rescue. After all, the past couldn't be changed. Like the tuning bars in Death Valley, Adeline and her team could only go back in time if they were certain that they already had. She needed proof to be sure.

Before she left Absolom City, Adeline had made a deal to identify those people. In the Absolom agreement with nations around the world, she had received two very important things. The first was formal diplomatic recognition of Absolom Island. The second was a data-sharing agreement that granted her access to vast government archives of photos and videos—records never seen by the public.

As soon as Tesseract was set up in the Rescue Center, the government data would begin streaming in. From here on, the program would search the photos and videos of disasters, wars, famines, and other devastating events for evidence that Adeline and her team had been there. Those photos were the outline of their future missions.

The night they finished setting up the Absolom Rescue Center, Adeline walked along one of the island's gravel paths to the bungalows overlooking the sea, warm wind blowing through her hair, a carton with dinner in her hands.

At the house on the end, she knocked on the door, but didn't wait to go inside. Constance was often too tired to answer.

Inside, the home was decorated with all the things Constance had brought from Palo Alto and Absolom City—everything except the room with all the photos of her past. Her secret. That was gone now.

That was perhaps what Adeline liked most about the island: there were no more secrets here. The bedroom Constance hid from the world was gone. So was Elliott's room in the basement where he searched for clues that he had rescued Charlie. And Hiro's tunnel in Las Vegas where he hid his addiction from the world.

They had left their secrets behind.

As Adeline walked through the home, calling Constance's name, she realized that Absolom Island had lost its first resident.

They buried Constance the next day. It was a simple grave by the sea, on the south side of the island, where the sun would always shine on it.

The island's entire population was there: Adeline, Ryan, Sam, Nora, Elliott, Claire, Hiro, and Hana.

The final line of Elliott's eulogy was: "Absolom has lost its first citizen today. And tonight, we'll add our first."

SEVENTY-EIGHT

In the Absolom Rescue Center, Adeline studied the machine. It was almost exactly like the Absolom Two prototype from the lab in Nevada, with one exception: the chamber was larger.

The original Absolom machine was built for one-way trips. For one person. This machine was built for more. More people. And trips both ways.

One of the biggest challenges in operating an Absolom device on the island was the power required. There simply wasn't enough room for a solar field large enough to gather what Absolom needed. Luckily, the island's electrical infrastructure had been built with future growth in mind. Thanks to a combination of tidal turbines, a geothermal plant, and a small solar array, they could generate the power the machine needed.

Or so they thought. Tonight's departure would be the first test.

Adeline stepped into the chamber. Elliott joined her. The body bag with the Syntran replica was there waiting, ready to go back.

At the command station, Adeline's father and Hiro checked the departure sequence one last time. Sam looked up at them, smiled, and Absolom Island disappeared.

Adeline and Elliott arrived in a small bedroom. Dirty clothes lay in heaps on the floor. Rock-and-roll posters covered the walls. An unmade bed filled most of the room. On a bedside table, a lava lamp belched lumps of red wax that floated free and tangled together.

Through the closed door to the living room, music was playing, "Undone – The Sweater Song" by Weezer.

The body bag was lying on the floor to the right of the door.

Elliott began breathing faster. Adeline sensed that being here again was triggering for him. The pain of what he remembered happening in the next room was still real for him, even with the prospect of saving his son. The next few minutes would decide his fate. It had happened this way once—and must happen again.

"What now?" Elliott whispered.

"You go out there."

Elliott shrugged, fear in his eyes. "And?"

Adeline put a hand on his shoulder. "And say what you wish you had said when he was alive—the words you've held inside all these years."

Elliott swallowed and nodded.

Adeline knew that what came next would be a sort of surgical operation—performed with words. Elliott knew his son was sick. In the next room, he was lying on the table, waiting for the conversation that would save him and set him on a new path.

When Elliott opened the bedroom door, the Weezer song was winding down, and Charlie's voice rang out. "Hey!"

"Charlie—"

"How'd you get in here? You broke into my apartment!"

"I just want to talk—"

"Get out! Get. Out."

"Son, listen to me. Please."

"I'm calling the cops."

"We both know you're not going to do that. And I know

something else. I know that if you stick that needle in your arm, it will be the last thing you ever do. You won't get high, Charlie. What's in there will take everything from you. I know you've already had a lot tonight. You can't take any more."

"How... What—"

"I'm asking you to trust me. If you don't, it'll be the last thing you ever do. I promise you, Charlie. I know it seems like you can never get away from your troubles, that they're always in your mind. You've self-medicated, and you've tried to get clean, and what you're holding now is the only thing that's ever made you feel any better. But only for a short time. There's a better way, son. I'm asking you to give me five minutes to show you. That's all."

Another song started up, "18 and Life" by Skid Row. The opening chords partially blotted out the voices, but through the din, Elliott's voice broke through, filled with emotion, cracking.

"I can't imagine."

A second later, he said, "Put it down, Charlie. Please."

As she waited, Adeline's heart pounded in her chest. Every second felt like an eternity. She felt tears well in her eyes as the door opened.

Elliott came into view. He was crying too, the tears flowing down his face.

The door swung wider, and Charlie was standing there. His black hair was greasy and stringy. He was rail-thin, cheeks gaunt, eyes sunken. But he was alive.

"Who are you?"

"Charlie," Elliott said slowly, "this is Adeline Anderson."

He shook his head. "No way. Adeline Anderson is like thirteen years old."

"Not anymore," Elliott said, staring at her. "She's all grown up now. And she's the reason I'm here."

Adeline held out her hands as Charlie had done so many

years ago at one of her birthday parties and repeated the words he had said to her: "Want to fly?"

He squinted, and Adeline was surprised when he recited the line she had said back. "Will it make me dizzy?"

"Yes. But you'll like it."

Charlie held out his pale, bone-thin hands, and Adeline put a recall ring around his wrist.

"We're going to take a trip," Adeline said. "Your dad will join us soon."

"Remind me again," Elliott said, "what should I tell her?"

"That she can never speak of seeing you here—until we all meet at Nora's house. She'll know when. And when that time comes, to tell you that everything is going to be all right."

Adeline gripped Charlie's hands and reached a finger over to press the button on the recall ring. Elliott was already unzipping the body bag as the room disappeared.

SEVENTY-NINE

Charlie was given his own bungalow by the sea. In those first few weeks, he kept to himself, but Adeline knew from her conversations with Elliott that the time had been difficult. Hana went to see him daily and did everything she could—medically—to help with the withdrawal symptoms. But the true fight was in his own mind.

He got worse for a time, and then, slowly, he got better.

In a way, that was the island's ultimate power: it used time to heal.

Elliott and his wife, Claire, lived next door to Charlie, and while they gave him his space, they were also there for him, waiting, hoping that they would become a family again.

Adeline watched as her father and Nora grew closer than they ever had been in Palo Alto or Absolom City. They shared a bungalow with a small garden behind it. They home-schooled Ryan for now, until a proper school could be established.

Adeline's brother had taken up surfing and spent most days exploring the island.

It was the transformation in Hiro that surprised her the most. For the first time since Adeline had known him, Hiro was happy. Like Charlie, it seemed that time on the island was chasing his demons away. It seemed that his addiction had finally released him.

One morning, Adeline was sitting in Hiro's office, sipping

coffee, when she said, "How accurate are your Absolom arrival calculations?"

The physicist snorted. "Can't believe you'd even ask me that."

"Can you hit a moving target?"

Hiro squinted. "Of course. The Earth is a moving target."

Adeline cocked her head, confused.

"Our planet is constantly moving through space," Hiro said. "If you go back in time even a fraction of a second, Earth is not where it was when you left."

Adeline had never even considered that. She pressed on. "What about if we're trying to arrive on an airplane—in mid-flight?"

"Are you serious? You want to do an Absolom rescue on a moving airplane?"

"I'm serious."

"Cool."

"Is it doable?"

"Sure. We'd have to get the flight plan."

"It won't help much. We know this flight got off course before it was shot down. We don't know exactly where it happened—only that the Soviets downed it somewhere around the Strait of Tartary, between the Sea of Japan and the Sea of Okhotsk." Adeline held up a finger. "Complicating matters is that we don't know the exact time it went down either."

Hiro stood and paced. "What we need is a probe. An Absolom probe. A small device loaded with cameras in all directions. We send it to the past, somewhere in the sky, it takes pictures, and it automatically recalls itself after a fraction of a second. We can use the photos to pinpoint the exact location of the plane."

Adeline could tell he was excited about the idea. "You love this, don't you?"

Hiro nodded. "I do. I love the math of it. Building things.

And the risk of departures and recall." He looked up. "Not that there is any risk. I work it all out before you depart. But..."

"I know what you mean. It's a little like gambling in that way."

"It is," Hiro said slowly. "But I don't miss gambling. Maybe I traded one obsession for another."

"Maybe you traded an unhealthy obsession for a healthy one. I think that's how it goes sometimes."

Two months later, thanks to Hiro's Absolom probe, Hana and Adeline went back to 1983 and rescued Hana's father.

EIGHTY

In the Tesseract review room, Adeline sat at one of the stations, scrolling through photos. The one on the screen was from the Imperial War Museums in the UK. It was dated September 14, 1940—a week after the Nazi bombing campaign known as the Blitz began.

The photo was from London, of a town house where a family was standing on the front stoop with two visitors in front of them: Elliott and Charlie.

Adeline used the aging algorithm to estimate Elliott's and Charlie's age in the photo. The software predicted that they were approximately six months older than they were now. It would probably be their first mission to the past. That made sense to Adeline. Charlie would likely be ready then.

She added the picture and departure date to the schedule of upcoming missions.

The next photo Tesseract had tagged was from an archive in the United States. As Adeline studied it, she realized it wasn't a photo but a black-and-white drawing that wasn't dated.

It was, however, beautifully done, clearly by a talented artist. It depicted a frontier family sitting around a fire in front of a covered wagon. The family's three children were holding what looked like marbles in their hands. Adeline sat to the left of the children, her father on the right, both smiling. The father of the family was whittling a stick of wood with a small knife.

Adeline opened the accompanying files and found a picture of a journal entry that was apparently below the drawing (she could see the lines and shadings of it at the top of the writing).

Fellow travelers came to call today, a man and his daughter, bearing fresh-baked bread and a cured ham. By some miracle, they also gave the children marbles to play with. I wish they had conveyed them privately to Oliver and myself, for we would have saved them as gifts for Christmas.

At dinner, they recounted that, like us, they were in search of a better life for their family and had come out here to seek it. Try as I might, I couldn't place their accents, and they were a tad circumspect about divulging their roots. But I suppose that's fine. Smart even. You never know what grudges strangers might be carrying around and what scores they're looking to settle. Out here, holding your tongue about yourself might help you live longer.

Adeline studied the drawing and journal entry. There was no date. Or location. That was a problem.

There were two more files associated with the group. One was a map with a line drawn across present-day Colorado, southern Idaho, northern Nevada, and ending in northern California. Adeline recognized it as the California Trail from the nineteenth century, the dirt road traveled by hundreds of thousands of settlers going west to the gold rush in California.

The trail had a series of numbers along it, and the second file was a scan of a notebook with the corresponding numbers. Adeline quickly read them, focusing on number 49:

Nov 14, 1852: Came across what we thought was a wrecked wagon. Suspected it was an Indian trap at first. Would have kept moving along if not for the smell of the bodies. Oxen dead too. Too long dead to butcher. Unfortunate.

The wagon was cracked like a ship on the rocks. Best guess is a windstorm got them. I didn't think that was real common in these parts, but there it was. Maggie yelled at me to pass them by, insisting they likely got the cholera. But I buried them. Kept the mother's journal in case any of their kin come asking about them. The kids had marbles. I know I should've buried the toys with them, but I slipped them in my pocket to give to Mary and Luke at Christmas. Ain't proud of it. Guess that's why I confessed it here. Likely all the kids will get this year unless we make a strike early.

And with that, Adeline had what she needed: location and date. In her mind, she began putting the mission together. They would approach the family—with gifts—share a meal and invite them back to their camp. At a safe distance, perhaps on a nearby ridge, they'd watch the windstorm destroy the wagon, then give the family recall rings and bring them back to Absolom Island, where they would find exactly what they were going west for: a better life for their family in an unsettled frontier.

Adeline spent the afternoon sewing the outfits she and her father would wear. The hum of the sewing machine always made her think of her mother and her teaching her the craft. Sarah Anderson would forever stay in the past, but in so many ways, she was here with them too.

Two weeks later, Adeline and her father were walking along the California Trail in northern Nevada in November of 1852.

It was cold, but there was no snow on the ground, only a rocky, dusty path worn with ruts from wagon wheels and the trudging of oxen and mules.

Mountains rose to the right and left like rock giants silently watching the procession.

"Dad?"

"Yeah?"

"When we were arrested in the cemetery in Absolom City, did you ever think it would end this way?"

He shook his head and laughed. "In a million years, I didn't see this coming—rescuing people in the past."

"It's wild, isn't it?"

"It is, but the future is always stranger than you imagine. In my experience, things rarely turn out the way you expect them to. And in a strange way, it makes sense."

"How?"

"Time and causality."

"What do you mean?"

"Well, consider the tuning bars—the breakthrough that made Absolom Two possible. You think about the outcome, you go search for that result, and if you find it in the past, you conduct the experiment."

"Right, but how does that apply to Absolom One?"

"Same principle. When we created Absolom, we weren't trying to build a time machine. We were trying to build a machine that saved our families. Sure, we wanted to help others, but our intention was to create a better life for our families."

He paused a moment. The wind blew through the passage, whipping dirt against the clothes Adeline had sewn.

"Did you know your mom used to teach a psychology class about beliefs and reality?"

Adeline smiled. "I did. In fact, I helped her teach it once upon a time. The class was PSYCH 20N: How Beliefs Create Reality."

"That's the one."

"It was all about how our perception of the world around us is shaped by our convictions, mental health, physical health, and environment."

"Well, I think our beliefs are more powerful than that," her father said. "I think they—along with time—are the unseen engine of the universe."

"The missing piece," Adeline said.

"That's right. I think beliefs and time determine our future. All those years, when you were thinking about creating a machine to get your lost family member back—and when Elliott was thinking about it—I think it shaped our future."

"That's where the missions come from."

"Yes. Like the universe itself, you can't say what happened before they existed, only that they do."

With that breakthrough, Adeline saw it all.

Absolom Island was like the United States of America. A new version. Where America had been a melting pot of people from different places, attracting the best and the hungry and the outcasts from around the world, Absolom Island was a melting pot of people from different times, offering a refuge for people from across the past to build a better future.

Absolom—the machine itself—was a physical manifestation of the march of humanity. It was a device that removed the worst members of human society and rescued the innocent. Adeline wondered if that was the true nature of civilization, if that was humanity's great work.

"Do you think the world will ever figure out what we're doing on the island?" Adeline asked.

"Yes. It's inevitable."

"What do you think will happen then?"

"I don't know. But that's one thing I've learned about time: sometimes life gives you problems you can't solve today. That's what tomorrow is for. And that's why you keep going."

The trail rounded a rock outcropping, and ahead, Adeline spotted the covered wagon off to the side. Rocks formed a ring around a crackling fire, and three very dirty kids sat around it, holding their hands out to warm them. Their mother was writing in a journal—or perhaps drawing—and the father was lying down, hat over his eyes.

He wasn't asleep, though, because as Adeline and her father approached, he rose and pushed the hat back. "How do you do?"

Sam nodded. "Hello."

"Y'all on your way to California?"

"No," Sam said slowly. "We're going a little farther than that."

The man studied him. "I see. Well, you looking to trade then?"

"We don't have anything to trade. We actually just came to help."

EPILOGUE

A deline set the coffee mug down on the desk and searched her personal files for a picture of Nathan. She held her breath as she uploaded it to the Tesseract program.

On the screen, a message blinked with a single word: *Searching...*

Thanks to the last mission with her father, and that conversation on the California Trail, she felt like she had found the missing piece in the grand scheme of things. She understood it all now, the strange force at work, the unseen hand of time.

But she was still missing a very important piece in her own life.

On the screen, that piece appeared in the form of dozens of photos—pictures of her and Nathan, together, performing Absolom rescues in the hours and minutes before earthquakes, tsunamis, volcanic eruptions, and other disasters.

The photos told the story of a life together, one spent in service of people only they could save.

Three days later, Adeline was standing in a hotel ballroom in San Francisco, watching start-ups pitch investors. It was the same place where she had met Nathan for the first time.

He saw her before she found him. He walked up behind her and mumbled, faking a cough, "San Andreas Capital sucks."

Adeline chuckled and turned to find Nathan smiling, a badge hanging from his neck that read 2525 Ventures. Its logo featured a large bus with the numbers written across it.

He shrugged. "See, the joke is that San Andreas Capital never loses money so—"

"I got the joke." She pointed to his name tag. "2525 Ventures?"

"It's the bus number from the movie *Speed*."

"You are *obsessed* with that movie."

"It's a great movie. And it works: we make sure our portfolio companies never slow down and blow up."

"How long did it take you to come up with that?"

He exhaled, letting his head fall back. "Days. Literally days. It was so difficult."

"And how's it going?"

He lowered his voice. "I'm sort of over it, to be honest. I'm starting to look for something else. How about you? I saw where you sold your company to the government. Or did that forever license deal or whatever."

"I've started something new."

"Oh, really?"

"And this time, I want you to be part of it."

"What would we be working on?"

"It's sort of like bus 2525. It's about saving innocent people. And every second counts."

He stared into her eyes, a smile forming on his lips. "I'm interested."

AUTHOR'S NOTE

Thank you for reading this novel.

As you might have guessed, this book has a lot of my life story in it. Many of the details have been covered in my previous author notes—the loss of my mother, the birth of my daughter and son and trying to raise them, and my career in internet start-ups.

I do hope that you enjoyed the novel and that it's given you some escape from the hectic world around us.

I owe thanks to so many who contributed to this work: my wife, Anna; my publisher, Head of Zeus; my agent, Danny Baror; and the many booksellers, librarians, and readers who spread the word about *Lost in Time*.

Thank you again.

—Gerry

PS: to see a listing of my other books, please visit agriddle.com

ABOUT THE AUTHOR

A.G. RIDDLE spent ten years starting and running internet companies before retiring to focus on his true passion: writing fiction. He is now an Amazon and *Wall Street Journal* bestselling author with nearly five million copies sold worldwide in twenty languages. He lives in North Carolina.

Visit agriddle.com